Katz Pajamas

Bob Henneberger

www. temptpress. Com

Books by Bob Henneberger

Crackstone Chronicles – Extinction

Crackstone Chronicles – Connections

Crackstone Chronicles – Extraordinary Solution

Katz Box

Katz Cradle

Hunting Paradise

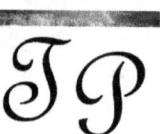

Tempt Press
PO Box 77
Colchester, VT 05446

Published by **Tempt Press**
P.O. Box 77, Colchester, VT 05446

First Print Edition, 2010

Copyright © 2010 Bob Henneberger

ISBN: 978-0-9830118-4-2
Library of Congress Control Number: 2010936745

3

To Sandy

The attempt and not the deed confounds us.

CONTENTS

23. Lost and found
24. Only the lonely
25. Somewhere to run, nowhere to hide
26. What goes up, must come down
27. Turn over a rock and you have a rolling stone
28. Now, where was I?
29. Good night, sweet prince
30. The Katz' Pajamas
31. No rest for the weary
32. Watch your mouth
33. Who comes around, goes around
34. Home sweet home
35. He was a dark and stormy knight
36. Who's that knocking at my door?
37. Reach out and slap someone
38. Will you have fries with that?
39. By any other name
40. I can see clearly now
41. Are we there yet?
42. All's well that just ends
43. I do?

1

Hell of a way to start the day

I'd been on this case for less than three days and up to this point I'd been shot at, propositioned, and sent on a six thousand mile goose chase.   I felt like Captain Ahab, with only a suburban clapboard wall to wail on.   Excuse the bad metaphor, but I was about to drop this whole deal as fast as a gnat on a frying pan and tell the woman who hired me that I wouldn't be working for her much longer.   Not to toot my own horn, but I'm a damn good private investigator and I can make a decent living without cases like this one.

The drive to my soon to be ex-client, Marcia Satterwhite, felt somewhat relaxing after a difficult week.   The temperature was in the low eighties, a good breeze blowing in off the Pacific Ocean.   In this part of the civilized world, a stiff breeze off the ocean means clean air to breathe.   Plus the skies were as clear in LA as they had been for months.

Along the route to Marcia's address in Maywood I noticed neighborhoods change; at first middle class, then run down tract houses as I got closer to her street.   In daylight, her small dumpy ranch didn't look like it fit a woman who drove an expensive car and could push hundred dollar bills at me as fast as she had.   But that had been a nighttime visit, only dim outlines of the place were visible.   I expected a home in Malibu on the ocean from her, not this hole.

I rang the bell for a solid minute with no answer. Stepping back, I walked to the driveway and peered in through a narrow grimy window in the garage door; window and siding hadn't been cleaned since the Eisenhower administration.   But I could make out Marcia's late model silver Mercedes parked between unopened moving boxes.

Maybe she's out with a friend. That bitch has friends? Well, ace detective, where's your client now?   Maybe the person who kidnapped her daughter also made off with the mother.

Wondering who would pay my final bill, I moved back to the front of the house, peeked into another window. Nothing there. The living room looked the same as it had when I was last in it; that same stale atmosphere forced its way into my nose. All was quiet, but the hair on the back of my neck began to stand at attention.   I always pay attention to my subconscious; so far it has kept me alive.

Slowly I placed my left hand on the door knob and turned it.

Why am I even thinking of going in there?

The front door slipped open as I drew my revolver and walked in.

Oh shit, what now?   Go in you dummy, this feels just like a patrol back in my insane Marine days, except now I don't feel quite so invincible since I now realize I can get killed doing this type of crap, and I do want to live past 100, you know.

Pulling back the hammer of my Smith and Wesson Model 58 revolver, I walked into the living room.

So, I forgot to get her to sign a contract when she first met with me.   So, I need to have her sign one before I can tell her I quit. My partner, Cassandra, has been the business minded one ever since she started at Cheshire Katz Agency.   I can recall all kinds of minutia, but my mind sometimes just ignores business details; it's not my thing.

If I die trying to get this woman to sign a lousy contract I'll come back and haunt someone for sure!

8

I stepped through the living room to the closed swinging door between the dining room and the kitchen. With the barrel of my revolver on the white enameled door, I inched it open.

Oh no! Mama!

A woman was laying face down, her legs half bent, her arms close to her hips and her head turned to one side. Lying there just as my mother had. I felt cold, as if I was wading through a silent, deep snowy landscape. An atavistic part of me dreaded seeing her better. Meanwhile I found that I had automatically moved around the body; finally I glanced at what I could see of her face. At first it didn't register. Another slow motion wave of cold dread washed over me as my thoughts chattered along. I clung to logic. No, this face was Marcia. This was not my mother lying on the linoleum floor. That had happened so many years ago.

I started breathing normally again. Traffic sounds from outside registered. Marcia Satterwhite lay lifeless near an overturned chair while thick dark red blood pooled beside her head, spreading towards the back door demonstrating that even after death, blood tries to clot in an open wound, a detail that also told me that she had been dead for a while.

Just late yesterday, Cassandra had phoned her, so my client had to have been shot less than eighteen hours ago.

I stared, dropped my revolver to my side and slowly released the hammer, barely able breathe around the tight knot forming high in my throat.

"Damn it! Damn it!" I said in a hoarse whisper.

Things like this just don't happen by themselves. Somebody does it, then leaves the mess for everybody else. It was hard for me to switch gears. Scenes from distant childhood kept intruding. Long ago, I had discovered my own mother like this, in our kitchen, in another pool of blood.

Snap out of it, get out of the past. I had to think straight. Stop thinking altogether, even better. Call the cops and don't touch a damn thing.

But, for a murder scene, nothing seemed out of place. I didn't feel good thinking that, but it looked normal. It didn't appear as if she had tried to flee the kitchen, and I could see no defensive wounds on her, save the single bullet hole in her head. She had been surprised, either by someone she knew, or by someone who had managed to sneak up on her. The entry wound was against the floor, so I couldn't see any gunpowder residue, but I did notice a small torn corner of paper still clutched in her right hand.

How do I get myself into these situations? It has to be a flaw in my personality. Just what happened here, leading up to this moment?

It started with this woman, Marcia Satterwhite, calmly walking into my office two afternoons ago, hiring me to find her missing daughter, Becky. No, it started several months ago just as I was finishing another case; that's when I first met Fred Lepus. But, before I ever met Fred, he had complicated my life in so many ways. No, he screwed up my case before I ever got it.

2

The old hat trick

It was a warm, inviting Southern California morning in late May of 1977, the suburbs smelled of blooms. Early Summer flowers in pastel and bright colors, splashed against trellises hung on clapboard walls, pleased the eyes. For what is essentially a desert, Los Angeles and its suburbs sprouted gardens as if it were a Hawaiian Island, a lush green paradise that lived on borrowed water.

A short, thin thirteen year old girl walked towards the front door of the compact, three bedroom ranch house where she and her mother lived. A solemn pause. She looped a strand of her dark blonde hair around one finger, considering her options. Her mother had told her never to answer the front door bell, like now, while she was alone at home. She must always obey her mother; to do anything else was dangerous. In situations like this, she would always walk to the front bathroom window and peek out at the person ringing the bell. If it was her only and best friend from down the street, she would open the door and talk through the screen. That would still be living up to her mother's orders of not going out of the house, or not letting anybody in.

So she stood on top of the closed toilet seat, letting her blue eyes settle on the man who was still ringing the front bell, loud, impatient jerks.

"I know you're in there, so listen up!" He raised his voice while looking at his watch. "Your father sent me here, and I'm not leaving until you read this note he wrote you."

The man was going bald in the middle of his scalp. She could see where the leftover fringe of hair turned white around the edges. More whitish hair, longer, formed tufts between the top of his head and his ears. He leaned on the button again and continued to talk to the door.

"It's getting late. I have lots to do in my life besides wait around, so at least talk to me through the damned door, kid!"

The girl slowly walked to the front door, looking at the floor.

"Daddy sent you?"

"Yeah! Somebody's there!" The man paused. "He sure did, and he sent you this note."

The man pulled a small piece of yellow paper from his coat pocket, bent over, and stuffed it under the front door. He looked again at his wristwatch, then loosened his tie before he unbuttoned his top shirt button.

The girl took just the edge of yellow paper, pulled the entire note to her side of the door, then opened it as if it were dangerous. In a near whisper, she read it out loud.

"Honey, I thought about what you asked me last week, and I've decided that it would be better for you to come live with me. I hired this man to take care of you for a short while so I can arrange everything. His name is Mr. Lepus and he will keep you safe and bring you here, so go with him as quickly as you can. Love, daddy."

She looked at the dark, stained texture of the closed door, and began to cry.

"Daddy sent you? Where is he now?" she asked, her voice still quiet.

"What! I can't hear you!"

"I said why can't he come here himself?"

"It's getting late, kid," Lepus reached into his rear pocket and produced a white cloth handkerchief. He patted his sweating brow with the cloth. "Well, he has to fix things legally so you can live with him. He's at his home, and I'll take you there, so open up the door now, kid."

"This is Daddy's writing," The girl paused. "But how do I know he sent you here?"

"Here, look at my driver's license. It's got my picture and everything," He pulled it out of his wallet and shoved it under the door.

The girl looked at the plastic encased card two times over, and smiled. "That picture makes him look like an old Bugs Bunny," she said to herself as she bent over and shoved the small card back out under the front door.

"But, how do I know Daddy sent you here?"

"Gees!" The man leaned against the door. "What ya want for proof?" His voice grew more exasperated with each breath.

"I don't know," The last syllable stretched into a question. "What about his address?"

"That's easy! 148 Lakefront for his office, and 2744 Garden Lane for his home," The man stood up straight. "He said you'd be tough to convince, so he told me that he used to call you kitten, like the girl on the TV show, but you asked him to call you honey, after your cat, Pokey, got run over."

"Daddy sent you! He's the only one who knows that."

The girl opened the door with a growing smile on her young face. She felt happier than she had in several months, even though this was a stranger.

As the door opened, the man rushed in. About five feet seven inches tall and a slight build, he looked shorter than she expected. Collapsing on the couch, he glanced at his watch. His breathing was still labored, panicked.

"God it's hot out there! Listen, we're running out of time; you've got to get some clothes and come with me."

"What about my Mommy?" The girl hesitated for a second.

"What about her?" The man stared at the girl. "What would she do if you waited here to tell her?"

The blonde girl looked at the floor. "She would hit me again."

"That's why I'm here. That's why your old man paid me to get you, so hurry up."

"I want to bring some of my toys. If I'm leaving, I want to bring my dolls and my books," she insisted.

"Look, we have to go now," The man looked at his watch. "We're late and it's getting nothing but later. We have a plane to catch, and we won't be alone for much longer, so get a change of clothes and get back here."

"I have to bring my small box of jewelry," Becky insisted.

"How small?" Fred asked.

"Very small."

"Fine, stuff it in a backpack or something," Fred acquiesced.

"All right, I'll be back in a minute."

She turned and walked to her room as she mulled over the reasons she should leave, and if she should stay.

"Kids! Why do I take jobs like this?" Fred muttered to himself.

He looked again at his wrist watch. His left eyelid began to twitch. He rubbed his nose rapidly several times, then got up from the sofa and began to pace in front of it.

"Look at the time! He'll have my head served up on a platter because of this, and it's all that kid's fault!"

The girl walked back into the living room with some clothes and her small jewelry box stuffed into a small backpack slung over her right shoulder.

"I'm ready, let's go."

"Great! You'll see your dad in a week or so," The man opened the front door for her and continued to talk. "I hope you like to fly, I'm not ready for airsick kids!"

"Don't worry," The girl looked straight at the man as they left the house. "I love to fly."

3

Dumb Bunny

And, here I was, about to meet Lepus, the bane of my existence from that point on. My life was complicated enough.

"Did you ever wonder about the difference between fiction and reality? I can tell you there isn't much. I mean for the most part people fantasize about what they can't do, while other people write about it. Outside of fiction, all possibilities are out there in reality, somebody's reality."

"And what does that have to do with how we send you your payment?"

"Nothing, it has more to do with the job I just did," I replied.

What did he expect, call me fishmeal?

"That's what I thought. So, we can move the four thousand nine hundred and sixty five dollars directly into your account?" The bank manager remained expressionless. "That's your daily fee, plus expenses, plus our bonus for this job."

"I guess so, if it's easier to do it by computer."

Somehow I guessed it was easier for him than for me.

"This is 1977, after all. From one bank to another, it's easier since we all use much the same computer systems."

"I suppose there'll be a charge."

"Just ten dollars at each end."

"Now I know to over charge twenty dollars next time," I commented.

"Just sign these bank forms, and we'll be through."

The balding bureaucrat shoved three sheets of paper at me with several places to sign and initial with my bank routing and account numbers already neatly typed. It seemed simple, although I never did like humorless bankers, the bane of my financial existence since I became an adult. Well, since my

15

girlfriend often tells me I have yet to assume adult status, perhaps guys like him will be my foe forever; such windmills I shall forever charge.

At least his institution was depositing a tidy sum in my Los Angeles bank for a two week job that could have been much worse. I guessed this would make the next quarterly payment to my bank loan and to the government. What an existence, the exciting life of a private investigator; covering expenses and meeting payroll.

Sighing, I opened the door to the hallway. This particular bank, in Silver Springs, Maryland, had just moved into their new office building sided with that reflective glass which made it look like a four sided mirror. I suppose the reflective siding helped keep the inside cool on those hot humid summer days, but I didn't like the architecture; it looked like a Rubik's Cube I had seen in Germany just three days earlier, yet something else new to confound the masses. On the fourth floor, the manager's inner office led to a much larger room with a dozen smaller cubicles made from neck high, subdued orange partitions. Many of the small cubicles had personal pictures tacked to their inner walls and other small things to show individuality; good luck to the galley slaves with that concept. Near the elevator, I saw a friend waiting for me.

"Benjamin," Billy Sullivan motioned for me to hurry.

"What are you doing here, I thought we were through with business?"

"Just one more thing before you head back to Los Angeles," Billy walked towards me.

"My flight leaves this afternoon," I stabbed my finger at the down button.

"I know, I took the liberty of changing it," Billy's face fell into a sheepish expression as the elevator door opened and we both walked on. "You're leaving in two days."

"No, really, I'm though for this time," I insisted.

"Not quite," Billy patted my back. "Something has come up, it's connected to the job you just did."

"For the bank?"

16

"Sure," Billy sounded sarcastic for just a second. "That gentleman you handed over to the German police not three days ago for stealing all that money has an acquaintance right here in Washington who thinks he knows you."

"I have a fan club, that's nice," I gave Billy my best business expression. "I have a very beautiful girlfriend back in Los Angeles who I haven't seen in two weeks and I don't want her to forget what I look like."

"Absence makes the heart grow fonder," Billy said, with serious expression.

"For you, I'm willing to make myself absent," I patted my chest.

"When do I get to meet her?" Billy asked, something else sneaking into his tone. "She sounds interesting."

"Oh, I don't think you need to meet her right now, mostly because you might be bad luck for whatever the two of us decide our relationship is," I paused. "Besides, I get the feeling lately you don't even remember who I am."

"You're Benjamin Katz," Billy grinned for the first time. "You own Cheshire Katz Detective Agency, you're six foot one, one hundred seventy pounds, light brown hair, brown eyes, twenty six years old and you've worked with me since you were an eighteen year old corporal in the Marines."

"You know what they say, smart asses make wise cracks."

Losing my smile, I wondered what the subtext to all this was.

"Maybe the next time you come out to Los Angeles we can all go to dinner, I suppose," I paused, more for effect than anything else. "I haven't told her a thing, and I won't."

"Anyway," Billy said as the elevator door opened on the lobby of the building, wanting to change the subject again. "I need to fill you in on a problem that's come up while I give you a ride to the hotel that I've checked you back into."

"Thanks," I shook my head slowly as we walked to his car. "There had better be another fee for this tacked on addition to the job."

17

"There always is," Billy unlocked the car doors. "You don't have to play the starving small businessman with me, you know."

"I know," I slid into the passenger seat. "It's just that the business now has two mouths to feed. Besides, if I relied on what you paid me for these part-time gigs, I'd starve."

"Right," Billy didn't look at me. "That's not the real reason you're sent on these missions, just remember that."

"Well, what is it this time?"

I was annoyed. Although money isn't a big motivation, I do like to have enough to pay the rent and eat.

"The fee, or the problem?" Billy looked at me.

"How about both?"

"One hundred fifty dollars a day plus expenses, and Fred Lepus," Billy looked through the front windshield.

"The first item I know and love," I said sarcastically. "Somebody with a name like Fred Lepus, however, will need some explanation."

"Lepus is a low rent detective here in DC and he's on a case to find a missing person."

"Let me guess, the person should remain missing?"

"I should say so," Billy glanced at me, then looked back out to the heavy traffic in front of the car. "The missing gentleman in question is an informant, the one who gave us the location of the person arrested in Germany."

"So, why not just have the local cops tell this Lepus fellow to take a hike?"

"This informant wants to deal only with the person we sent to Germany, for some reason we have yet to ascertain. And then, well, there's the person Lepus is working for. Third, the boss does not want any other agency to work with this informant."

"Why?" I asked. "Lepus is working for someone who wants to rat out our informant, right?"

"Something like that."

"Okay," I paused. "Who's the informant?"

"I can't say."

18

"Can't or won't?"

"Does it matter?" Billy looked at me.

"The only thing that matters to me is who this informant guy is and why he's singled me out to save his ass," I mused.

"Like I said," Billy kept looking at the traffic in front of the car. "I can't say."

"And that's worth a few hundred bucks, I suppose."

"Probably more than that, but that's all you're getting," Billy chuckled.

"Okay, who is Lepus working for?"

This would be easy, or at least it should be, and the money could go for fun stuff instead of taxes or bank loans.

"Paul Robertson," Billy paused. "Robertson works for the Chinese embassy here in Washington as a public relations consultant."

"Oh, this sounds like a bunch of fun."

"Keep your shirt on," Billy smiled, still looking into traffic ahead. "No double ought stuff, just get this dumb ass Lepus fellow out of the way if you can, or least help the informant get lost again. We can't take the chance of him becoming known, he can't be compromised.   You offer the most expedient way we could think of right now to make sure he isn't."

"Okay if I shoot this Lepus fellow?"

"After you meet him, you may want to."

"If Lepus is that stupid, why bother? Why not just hide the informant again after dumping Lepus?"

"Because he isn't quite that stupid. Lepus has already found our informant and stashed him somewhere nearby. Didn't I just say we're paying you good money to do all that?"

"So, you want your corporate muscle to stop Lepus and to hide the informant again."

"Right."

"I suppose I'm still working for the bank?"   I asked.

"Yes."

"My going rate, just to be clear?" I asked.

"Right."

19

"Give me the address where I can find Lepus."

Billy reached into his inside coat pocket and handed me a medium sized envelope.

"His addresses, his photograph, and some other useful items."

Billy pulled into the parking lot to the hotel I had just checked out of several hours before.

"Your rental car is still here, rented for another two days. The keys are in the envelope," He added.

"Thanks," I scrambled out of his car.

"You're paid well, and this last job you did wasn't that bad."

"I guess so."

Billy drove away as I looked for the dark blue Ford I had left in the parking lot. Ah, there it was.

. . . .

Lepus' office was shabby and hard to find, but find it I did, on twenty second street, not far from the Lee Highway in Arlington, Virginia. His office had begun its life as a working class one story brick structure, topped with shaggy shingles. On a brick house the only painting required is the wooden trim so how hard can it be to paint the trim? I wondered how badly the roof leaked in a downpour as I scanned the jungle of trees and overgrown, small thickets which wound around the sides of the structure; I assumed it was the same or worse in the back yard. The bushes out front didn't look like they had been trimmed anytime in the last decade.

Continuing to scan the area, I parked on the opposite side of the street and walked, casual walk, to the front door. I don't think families inhabited many of the houses anymore since most bore signs proclaiming that a chiropractor, or travel agent, or whatever, resided inside. Standing on Lepus' postage stamp porch, I looked up looked up at a ceiling composed of half rotting four inch bead board. Never repaired. The storm door's return spring was missing and I had to pull the damned thing after me as I walked into Lepus' office.

Before I could focus anywhere else, the pungent odor of forty years of mold growth hit my sinuses like a sledge hammer. Then I saw the actual secretary, perched behind an old metal office desk. There was no sign of anyone else in this front room. Leaning on the desk with her elbows, wearing a low cut blouse with a big scoop in the front of it, her ample cleavage greeted me as my eyes got used to the dark. A ratty couch and coffee table stretched just to my left. Three rickety wooden chairs clustered in front of her desk. The room was covered with old wall to wall carpet; that had to be the source of much of the moldy odor, at least I hoped it was.

"And, your name is?" she asked. She seemed to be somewhere around thirty, made up to look like a blonde teenager.

"My name is Benjamin Katz."

"Why did you want to see Mr. Lepus?"

"Is he here?"

"No," She smiled at me. A vacuous smile. Well, maybe that's not how she intended her expression to be, but it was. "Will I do?"

"No," My smile was a friendly, non-committal smile. "Well, maybe."

"What sort of work are you looking for?"

"Actually, I'm a private investigator from Los Angeles, and I have some information about a case he's working on right now."

"Really," Her voice took on a southern drawl. "What agency did you say you're with?"

"Cheshire Katz."

"Now, that's in Los Angeles?"

"Like I said before."

I heard a soft noise in the back room, maybe the kitchen. It was a shoe shuffling on the floor. The game's afoot.

"What's your name?" I asked.

"Cathy Rumson," She still hadn't lost the fake cheery disposition. "I must say, you're a real cutie."

"Thanks, I think," I kept looking at her. "Can we continue talking about the case your boss is working on right now?"

"Which one would that be?" She fluttered coy eyelashes at me.

"Kidnapping a mysterious man for someone named Paul Robertson."

"If I did know what you're talking about, what's in it for us?"

"Unless you're Fred Lepus, nothing." I listened harder. "Where is he?"

"Who?"

"Your boss."

"I'll tell him you came," Cathy finally dropped her smile. "Are you doing anything for dinner?

"Will I be having dinner with your boss?"

"No, he's not as much fun as I am."

"Maybe not, but I do need to talk to him, soon."

Another muffled noise from the back.

"Well," I tore off a message note from the pad on her desk. "Here's the phone number at my hotel, please make sure your boss calls me very soon; there might be a lot of money at stake."

She also tore off a piece of paper and wrote her phone number on it. "Call me anytime."

Taking the note, I left. I quick stepped it back to my blue Ford. drove off, then circled the block, backing into a driveway five doors down from Lepus' office. I didn't have to wait long until an old Chevrolet Impala with faded green paint, accented with rust spots, shot from Lepus' driveway and turned left, away from me. I followed it. He didn't seem to pay attention to anyone behind him as he rushed towards the DC Beltway. A few minutes later, he sped south, turning off on US One, then he headed south again towards Mount Vernon, never once noticing my car. Right after a large shopping center, he turned into a tightly packed subdivision, then parked his old car in front of a another house in need of repairs, although not as many as his own office.

As he rushed to the front door, I drove by at slow speed, looking at everything, then parked my car on the street three doors down. Lepus stormed through the front door. I cautiously approached the house. I looked up and down the deserted street. No faces staring out any windows that I could see. At two in the afternoon, most people were probably still away at work. The door was ajar.

Revolver drawn, I pushed the door open. There Fred Lepus stood, staring at a man crumpled on the floor. A bright red pool of blood spread from around his head onto the parquet floor. a series of handcuffs and manacles lay in a stuffed chair pushed to the center of the room. Perhaps he had been trapped there before someone had let him loose, then shot him in the head.

"At least I know you didn't shoot him since there was no gunshot after you came in here," I said, using a booming voice.

Lepus jumped straight up in the air, maybe several inches, grabbing his chest, then fumbling for a holster tucked in his waist at the small of his back.

"Don't move your hands anywhere near that gun," I leveled my revolver.

"Who the hell are you?" Fred stuttered. "What you got to do with this!"

"Nothing," I paused. "My employer hired me to stop you from turning this man over to the person who hired you."

"Who the hell sent you!" Fred yelled.

"Why not stop shouting," I motioned with my free hand for him to lower his voice. "Do you want the cops to come here right now?"

"Hell no!" Fred shouted, this time in a loud whisper. "How did you find me here?"

"Do you mean to say you never saw me behind you?"

"Damned, you must be really good," Fred hissed the rest of his breath out between aborted gasps. "Will you put that oversized gun away, for Christ sake."

23

"Don't think so," I had some reservations about this man's abilities. "I was tracking you no more than two cars back the whole way here, and you never saw me?"

"Impossible!" Fred stammered again. "I'm a professional and I know when I'm being tailed, and you sir, did not follow me."

"Then," I shook my head, "how did I get here?"

"You already knew he was here, you must have killed him."

"You were going eighty to ninety miles an hour on the Beltway, how could I beat you here?" I didn't know why I was explaining this to him, but I did it anyway. "You waited in the back room while I was talking to your secretary, and we both drove here at the same time, you idiot."

"I don't know how you did it, but you've got to be the one who shot this guy," Lepus pointed to the body and shuddered.

I continued to aim my revolver at his head. "You can't tell when you're being tailed, so my guess is that the last time you came here, the person who hired you also followed you here, and killed this man after you left."

"No way!"

"Keep it down," I motioned again with my free hand. "I want to get the hell out of here before the cops get here."

"I guess you might be right," Fred seemed to calm down. "You really think that Robertson guy killed him?"

"That would be my guess," I pointed to the corpse. "Did you even do a short background on Robertson?"

"No," Fred pointed to the front door. "Can we get outta here?"

"You might want to wipe your fingerprints off the door," I didn't want the cops getting to me through this idiot, at least not right away. "I can only hope that whoever shot this poor man wiped down the place before they left."

"Oh," Fred pulled a handkerchief out of his rear pocket and wiped the doorknob. He looked around the room quickly. "Can we leave now?"

"Just a minute," I snapped.

I moved closer so I could see the dead man's face. I didn't recognize him at all. Why would he ask for me to help him? Oh well, I may never know.

Lepus was agitated, garbled sounds. I motioned for him to go first. As he passed me through the door, I holstered my revolver and followed him.

"Why should I have investigated Robertson, the guy who was paying me two thousand bucks, to snatch that stiff back there?" Lepus' voice had taken on a slight whine.

"You kidnapped that man?" I pointed back at the house and deliberately leaned into Fred Lepus' personal space.

"Hell no!" Lepus backed up a bit. "That guy, the stiff over there, called me and asked if I could come up with a place to hide out for a while."

"Did he know you before he hired you?"

"No," Fred paused, thinking. "He said he got my name out of the yellow pages."

"And how did Robertson come into all this?" I asked, amazed.

"He called me right after and said he was a friend and he would be paying me well." Fred looked worried.

I didn't think he was bright enough to see that he had made a huge mistake.

"You could have done a ten minute investigation into who these people were," I shook my head.

"Why?"

"If you had, you would have found out that Robertson worked for the Chinese embassy."

"He don't look Chinese," Fred said, surprised.

"You really are a moron."

"I'm a professional. I've been an investigator a long time in this town," Fred turned and glared at me. "Who the hell do you work for?"

"Right now, the Chase Manhattan Bank."

"What the hell do they have to do with this?"

"That was my case, but now it belongs to the cops," I stared back at him. "Are you going to call the cops to report this?"

"Hell no!" Lepus insisted. "I just finished up a hot case out West and I got some serious follow up work on that case I gotta get to right away. Can't afford to waste time here on this mess. My other job pays a lot more than this thing anyway."

"I'll call them."

Apparently it didn't occur to him that there was more to this murder than he had so far figured out.

Lepus raced to his car and roared away; forever, I hoped. I drove to a safe location, called Billy and explained everything to him. He said that he would handle all the details with the local cops and he promised my name would not show up in the police investigation. At least I didn't have to get involved any further, plus I got one more day's pay, again minus the twenty dollar transfer fee. When will I learn.

4
Home sweet home

I admit that my apartment isn't the envy of the upwardly mobile, nor the model of California living, but the rent's one fifty a month. Close to my office building, lots of museums, government buildings, restaurants and Chinatown. I've been there for a few years living near some great neighbors. Now, having just finished a more than dull assignment in Germany, I needed a break before tackling another job. My girlfriend and partner in my detective agency, Cassandra, was out of town for a few days investigating a missing teenager. The girl's parents thought she ran away with her boyfriend and they just wanted her back with no police involvement. They were good friends with the boy's folks. I had a divorce case I had to return to tomorrow, but for the day, I was puttering around in the basement, relaxing.

"Benjamin," Paul Green walked down the basement steps. "I thought you were still in Germany?"

"I finished yesterday and flew back last night," I nodded at him since standing up and shaking hands is way too formal.

Paul worked for the IRS as a field investigator who worked with the FBI, tracking down mob types who never pay taxes on their real incomes.

"Loading for that cannon you carry?" He pulled out a stool to sit on.

"Is that why you're down here?"

I looked across the workbench and nodded toward a large container of empty nine millimeter brass.

"Right," Paul nodded, then looked at his bucket of empty brass. "It's time to reload some."

"Some?" I smiled at him. "There's a lot more than some in that bucket."

"It's been longer than usual," Paul replied.

He pulled the nine millimeter die set off a shelf above the bench.

"Anything interesting going on?" I asked.

I finished loading the three hundred empty cases I had brought down an hour earlier.

"Not much," Paul looked over to me. "Do you have a case coming up?"

"I've got one I have to get back to tomorrow."

"Interesting?" Paul asked.

"Just another divorce case."

"Who is it this time?" He was always interested in the spicier cases of mine. "The wife?"

"This time it is," I put the last loaded cartridge into a plastic shell box. "She thinks her cheating husband is about to liquidate his assets in order to hide cash. Also, she thinks he's figured out that she'll file for divorce soon."

"You seem to be getting a lot of those cases lately," Paul shook his head.   "If it were me, I wouldn't ever consider getting married myself."

"I can separate myself from it," I thought out loud. "Besides, I'm particular about which divorce cases I take."

"What do you mean?"

"I only work for the aggrieved party, if you're the cheater, I'm on your ass like a teacher's paddle."

I was quite comfortable with my moral parameters.

"You get the damndest cases, Benjamin," Paul laughed. "All I ever get to do is audit books and occasionally go with the FBI on a bust."

"It has its downside," I unscrewed the crimping die from the single stage press I was using and placed it in the box. "Sometimes the aggrieved spouse shoots at me."

"I guess that's why you carry such a big gun."

"Yeah," I laughed. "If I miss, the concussion will knock them down."

. . . .

28

Kate Folger told me her husband would probably be somewhere north of San Bernardino and that if I headed towards Snow Valley, I should see the turn off to a ranch.   Her directions were confusing since a lot of houses with ranch sized lots were tucked away in the hills around here.

It was a bright day in the country; most of the smog from Los Angeles didn't reach this place. There wasn't a cloud in the sky and the temperature was in the mid seventies. Even the mountains here rise out of a semi-arid desert, but all the trees keep their beautiful green leaves all summer. Something was always blooming it seemed, so the scents and sights weren't all that bad as I pulled to the side of the road and took the top panels off my Porsche. Some scent almost like honeysuckle rose up from the roadside, but not quite.   Someday I should learn more about plants, but not today.   Pleasing non-polluted air rushed over my face and head peaceful scenery rolled by, left me feeling, right there and then, that life could be good to me.

About five miles after I left the interstate and started up state road 330 I saw a sign, it wasn't one of life's little signs, but a small handmade sign for a yard sale. But this was the middle of the week , not a weekend; this had to be Kate Folger's soon to be ex-husband's yard sale.

Andrew Folger was a real estate developer, specializing in small shopping centers, strip malls, as well as inheriting vast sums of money, although he made even more money than he inherited; that's what his wife wanted half of. Her lawyer knew about all the bank accounts in Los Angeles and Mexico as well as the three homes that were on the public record. Since the property was in both their names, he couldn't get mortgages without her signature.

Before I left for Germany for two weeks on a pressing case, I had been investigating Andrew's love of women; Andrew liked women a lot, or he liked a lot of women. At last count, I had taken pictures of him loving six women, four of them half his age. His wife and her lawyer, were very happy with my work so far on the case. Kate felt that her husband was becoming suspicious of her behavior, maybe because at home she couldn't hide her increasing anger , as I delivered each set of pictures to her lawyer, who then passed them on to her. By the third set of pictures, the lawyer ceased telling Kate about them.

The house I was headed for belonged to Andrew's best friend and college fraternity brother. I drove for several minutes on a long driveway before I saw the house, a three story giant draped over a small hill. Three sides of the massive structure were made of glass and steel, with an immense redwood deck extending from the rear of the house to the right. I could faintly smell the chlorinated water from the huge swimming pool and hot tubs. All this wealth reminded me of my middle class upbringing. No private pools, no fox hunts to miss, just cows to milk and fields to plow. In every society, there's the elite upper class, and, way under them are us schmuck detectives who investigate them and make their lives miserable; I kind of liked that natural balance of life.

A magnificent green lawn with manicured hedges swept from the brick drive-through and porch and outlined a formal garden. If I wasn't mistaken, there was a small grove of walnut trees growing to the right of the house. Their shade covered that side of the redwood deck and behind the small grove of trees there appeared to be yet another house; perhaps it was a guest house. I'm always amazed at the people in this area and how they spend their money.

In addition to making money, Andrew also liked to collect things, especially old cars. Kate's lawyer told me she thought Andrew had over a million dollars tied up in old cars. Besides the BMW he drove and his wife's Mercedes, Andrew had only two cars registered with Motor Vehicles in California. One was a 1936 Bentley, the other was a 1929 Rolls Royce. What wonders would await me?

About five hundred yards from the main house was a horse barn and there they were, a collection of immaculately kept cars spread over a lush green pasture. I guessed that this large pasture was for the horses, but I wasn't sure. Amongst the surrounding hills of brown at least four acres of lush green grass showed that he must have quite an irrigation system. Water is like gold in Southern California, and this guy looked like he had plenty of both.

As I parked my car, I saw a small crowd gathered around what looked like an auction taking place right in front of the colossal home. The cars in the pasture kept catching my eye. I recognized a Cord Duesenberg, an old boat-tailed Bugatti, I saw six Rolls Royces and several Bentleys parked together then there were five Packards next to the Bentleys. I couldn't figure out his groupings; there was a 1949 MG-TC all by itself, all the Mercedes Benz were bunched together, in addition to a 1954 300SL and two mint 1954 190SLs, he had a brand new 69 Gullwing, the rest were in random order.

As I made my way to the auction, all I saw up for sale at the actual auction was office equipment; well, maybe I could use something. Bidding on something would make a good excuse for my being there so I bid on an intercom set, including enough wire to hook up the four stations. I bid only twenty five bucks, but I got it. The next item up was a small wooden two drawer file cabinet. I liked the look of it and it might fit in the back of my Porsche. There were only two bidders, and the other guy stopped after five bucks so I got it for five fifty. What a deal, but ethics stopped me from bidding on a box of office supplies.

"Excuse me," I said.

I approached the three men in suits behind the folding table situated on the brick drive-through directly in front of the entrance door to the mansion. They seemed to be the ones taking money.

"Did you win a bid on something?" The man on the left asked.

"Yes," I quickly looked to my right and spotted my stuff. "I got the wooden file cabinet and the intercom."

"Right," He looked at a sheet of paper. "Pay the man in the middle thirty dollars and fifty cents and you can pick up your stuff over there," He pointed to his left.

"Say, are those cars over there going to be auctioned off?"

31

I looked at the man in front of me who seemed to be in charge. I recognized Andrew Folger from the photographs I had taken, although this time he had his clothes on.

"Sorry." His reply was like a quick bark. "They're already sold."

"Darn," I looked sad. "I love old cars. Could I just go over and look at them?"

"Sure," Andrew threw me a level glance. "Don't get in them or touch them, but you can look to your heart's content."

"Thanks."

It didn't take me long to shove the stuff I bought into my own car; Andrew watched me as I did it, seeming to like me better once he saw I drove a Porsche. While he and his friends were busy taking in money from the auction, I made my way around the expensive cars and took down descriptions, and vehicle numbers of all of them. I'd bet that there was more than two million dollars worth of cars on that field. I should have taken my camera so I could shoot pictures of all of them, but I guessed that would have gotten me thrown out right away. I wondered how much he sold them all for.

"Just what the hell are you doing?" I looked up as two large men approached me from the direction of the auction.

"I'm just admiring the fancy cars," I answered.

I recognized the two men who were with Andrew while he was taking in the money from the auction. My eyes focused on the auction. The small crowd was dispersing. Andrew was alone at the folding table, looking at me.

"I think you'd better leave right now," The larger man on the left said in a menacing tone.

"Why?"

"Because this is my property and I said it's time to leave," the other guy said.

"Did you guys buy these cars?"

I might as well find out some useful things.

"We might have." The larger man looked at his friend and smiled.

"I bet you paid a lot for them, like maybe five dollars apiece?" I cleared my throat. Maybe less?"

"You've got a smart mouth, kid," The smaller man said.

I looked carefully at them. Kid? They didn't look much more than mid forties.

"I've heard that before." I nodded like a good youngster should. "I guess I'll be going now."

"I don't think so," The big guy moved a little towards me. "I think you and I need to talk a bit."

"Okay," I put my notebook in my outer coat pocket. "Don't get your panties in a bunch about it."

"What was that you just put in your pocket?" The larger man asked. Both of them walked to within two feet of me and stopped.

"A notebook," I shrugged my shoulders.

"Let me see it."

"No," I replied.

It looked like they were going to try to block me from leaving.

"I said, let me see it," The bigger guy insisted.

"No."

The smaller man lunged at me, trying to grab my right hand. I suppose they could tell I was carrying a pistol. I caught his hand as he grabbed for me. Pulling him down, I thrust my knee into his face; he was out cold before he hit the grass. At least the soft turf kept him from being scraped, although he wasn't awake to appreciate that.

The larger man paused for a second as his friend fell to the ground. That gave me enough time to regain my balance and kick him in the stomach. He let out more air than he had just gulped in as he crumpled to his knees.

"I'm leaving now," I said. "All I wanted to do was take some notes on the cars here. I love old cars. I would like to collect them myself sometime when I have more money."

All he could say sounded like a gasp for air. Well, it was a gasp for air.

"I would have left like a nice boy if you and your friend would have let me."

I walked back to my car. There, waiting for me, was Andrew Folger. He was holding a thirty eight colt revolver. The pistol was at his side, and his hand was shaking noticeably. I took quick note that the hammer wasn't cocked, nor did he have his finger near the trigger.

"What do you want?" By now I felt annoyed. "I paid for this stuff."

"Why did you hit my friends?" His voice was unsteady.

"They tried to hit me first," I shook my head. "That was a big mistake, just like the one you're about to make."

"Who are you?" He asked. He didn't seem aggressive, just scared.

"Are you sure that thing is loaded?" I nodded towards the Colt with the four inch barrel shaking in his right hand.

"I'm sure," He looked down at the pistol. When his eyes came back up to look at me, I had my Smith and Wesson pointed at his head.

"Well, I think you should drop it, don't you?" I pried a smirk onto my face.

"Who the hell are you?" He threw revolver in the dirt.

"Nobody important," I kicked his pistol away, got in my car and sped out.

Cheshire Katz would be receiving a five hundred dollar bonus in a week. Yes, the wife and her lawyer liked me a lot. Sometimes I do feel as if I lead a charmed life.

5

Life goes on

Benjamin, you'd better take this call yourself, on line two," Cassandra's voice crackled over the used but functional intercom.

It had been only a week since I bought it. Although she agreed to use it, Cassandra still didn't know if it was ethical to keep it, even though Kate Folger had served her husband with the divorce papers and she said I could keep all the stuff I bought. Oh well, time will tell if the intercom will stay.

When I picked up the phone, I heard a frightened woman talking on the other end of the line. Although not tearful, her voice broke frequently in halting, almost explosive bursts of words. Low, hoarse words came in over the bad connection.

"Oh, Mr. Katz. Can you find my baby, my daughter? She's been gone for a week and the police are no help at all!"

"I can try, but I need more information. First of all, who are you? And what's your daughter's name?"

"My name's Marcia Satterwhite, my daughter's name is Becky. She's thirteen years old, and she's about five feet tall. She has blonde hair, and dark blue eyes. There's a small butterfly shaped birth mark on her cheek."

"Right or left cheek? How close to her nose, or ear is it?"

"Wrong cheeks," The voice on the phone paused. " It's on her left," Marcia answered as her voice trailed off.

"Can you come down here tomorrow, with a picture of your daughter? Did Miss Pales give you my daily rate?"

"Yes, yes, she did! Can I come there tonight? I don't want to wait until tomorrow! I want you to start tonight!"

I considered my mood and the time of the day, "It's three thirty now, can you get here by five?"

"Yes, I'll be there," Marcia hung up.

I leaned back, sinking into the leather chair. I swiveled around and looked out the window of my fifth story office into the afternoon sun. Compared to a city such as Chicago or New York, this metropolis seemed more expansive; its streets wider, its buildings lower. Like any West coast city, space was the coin of this realm. As the sun pierced through the haze in the western sky, the buildings of downtown Los Angeles had a dirty, gritty golden look to them. Although the filtered air in my building held little of the foul smells of the street, I could almost taste the pollution in my mouth as I stared into the thick outside air.

Even though I had met some of my best friends here, and I fell in love here, I never did like this city that much. I grew up in rural Pennsylvania. The city of angels seemed to me more and more like an overpopulated farm in the middle of a desert, although I have to admit it did have the best restaurants I'd ever found.

The first detective agency I first worked for grew to four branch offices, all owned by George Sterling, who was sort of a friend, but as time went by, he seemed to fit too well into the Los Angeles mind set for my taste. Periodically, while I worked for him, George had offered me the branch manager's position at each and every new office that opened. Although I refused every proposal, I stayed friendly with George, and took occasional assignments from him. I discovered that I liked to work freelance.

Then two and a half years ago, I won a large sum from a lawsuit, much to my amazement. Even now I'm perplexed, because I have to be the first person still alive to successfully sue a Las Vegas mobster. I spent it all, fast, on opening my own agency, Cheshire Katz Investigators which had begun to earn enough money to support both me and my partner, Cassandra Pales.

I met Cassandra just after I opened my agency and just after she finished her master's degree from UCLA. George

Sterling's secretary and Cassandra's mother, Betsy, are good friends and they set the two of us up on a blind date.

I enjoy the memory of when we first set eyes on each other. Cassandra's parents lived in a large house in Huntington Beach with a great view of the ocean. Looking me up and down carefully after answering the doorbell, Betsy paused as if remembering that she and her friend set me up with her daughter in the first place. She called her daughter to the living room. Cassandra looked beautiful in her light blue dress, it clung seductively to her firm body and the blue harmonized so well with the soft hazel color of her eyes. Her auburn hair was long then, almost to her waist.

"I always expect the worst from blind dates," I blurted, before I could stop myself. "But your daughter is one of the most beautiful women I've ever seen."

"Thank you," Cassandra replied, nervous. "You're not a disappointment either. Where are we going?"

"Cassandra! Be more gracious," Her mother scolded.

"I had a choice. Should it be the Bob Dylan concert, or a symphony," I replied.

"So which one are we going to?" Cassandra asked.

"It took a long while to decide, but I was able to get two tickets to the Dylan concert. Hope that'll be all right?"

"That sounds Okay," Cassandra shrugged her shoulders.

"All right?" Betsy interjected. "She's been trying to get tickets for that concert for two weeks!"

"Mother!" Cassandra protested.

. . . .

"Benjamin," Cassandra stepped through the open door to my office. "Benjamin, are you awake?"

"Yes?" I spun my chair around and brought my thoughts back to the immediate problem.

"Do you want me to stay until she gets here?"

"Were you listening to the phone call earlier?"

"Yes. I thought of taping it, but decided it was too normal. Missing children are, unfortunately, all too normal."

37

I sighed, "But, when we can find them safe and sound, it's worth the effort. Sort of like that teenage girl you returned to her parents."

"You're right." A happy look passed over her face. "But this one could be her father, most of the kidnappers are."

"Yeah, and those cases are easy to solve."

"And they pay well," Cassandra added. "And we still need another two thousand dollars to scrape up by the end of this month or that damned bank will start to send us hate mail."

"I know, I know. I'll talk to this woman, you can go on home."

"Okay. It's been a long day. I need to take a break anyway," Cassandra turned to walk out of my office. "See you tomorrow afternoon."

"Afternoon?"

"Yeah," She didn't turn to face me, as she walked to the front door. "You always forget I have a morning seminar on Thursday."

I watched her as she walked to the front office door, opened it, then walked down the hall. The outer door closed slowly with a click.

"She always did look great walking away," I observed.

I shook my head and leaned back in my chair. Putting my feet up on the edge of the desk, I closed my eyes and smiled.

6

Hindsight is better than no sight

The door opened with a sharp clank, causing me to catapult from my desk chair, shake my head, and stand firm on my size thirteen feet. Instinctively I reached for my forty one magnum Smith and Wesson under my left shoulder, but before my right hand made it to the butt of my pistol, a slender woman wearing dark glasses and a paisley print scarf over her hair walked through the outer office.

Dressed in a mid-calf length black skirt and a light green, almost white blouse and wearing only small gold earrings with no other jewelry, the woman paused as she looked into the open office. She had put on practically no makeup, which made her slight acne scars more visible. I guessed her to be thirty five to forty years old. She was followed by a strong scent, which I later learned was a variation of jasmine, but I'm not that good with women's perfumes; I can only tell when they're too much, and this practically made me sneeze.

Her sunken cheeks and jaw were set in such firm control to make her appear more of a statue than a real person. Quickly taking off her designer sun glasses, she looked around my office with probing red, swollen eyes.

"Are you Mr. Katz?"

"Yes, I am most of the time. Please come in," I walked around my desk as I smoothed out my coat. "Are you Mrs. Satterwhite?"

"Yes," Her voice quavered, which she changed into a cough.

"Before we get started, could you please tell me who recommended me to you? I always like to know, even if you picked me out at random from the phone book," I asked.

She remained silent and stared at me with an expression that could kill.

"I use the information to judge what kind of advertisement works best," I added.

39

"Oh, if you insist, it was my sister. She said she met you some time ago, and you're the only private investigator she knew in Los Angeles."

"What's her name, if I can ask?"

"Who's investigating whom!" Marcia stared defiance at me. Her voice grew stern. "Her name's Nancy Satterwhite."

Nancy Satterwhite? I thought, puzzled. Who the hell's that? The same last name?

"Do you have a recent picture of her?" I asked.

"Who, my daughter? Yes, here it is," Marcia nervously thrust a color snapshot at me. "You met her in Atlanta," she added.

"Who?" I asked, studying the picture which was too far out of focus to distinguish anything but blurred facial features.

"My sister, Nancy. Her name was Fowler then. She was married to that rat, Brian, at the time; he worked at Georgia Tech, do you remember any of that?" Marcia asked with an edge to her voice.

"I remember now," I acknowledged. "I did a background check for a company, a chemical company I believe. He was up for a job as a team leader in a chemical weapons development lab. What happened to Brian? I never followed up on that case after I sent in my final report."

I remembered, all right. That was a stupid little three day investigation in which I met some of the strangest people ever. But, Nancy I will never forget, she was gorgeous.

"Nancy caught him with his thing stuck up some bimbo in his office and she dumped him then and there. He didn't get the job, her money, or anything else!"

Marcia flashed a an abbreviated, wicked smile. Then, an abrupt switch, her face went back to pissed off, shut down.

I grinned as I remembered listening through his office door at Georgia Tech, not that long ago. I had thought at the time that a conference between a coed and a professor should not include her panting 'faster, faster' and his responding 'oh, god! oh, god!'. Coeds at Tech were almost non-existent, but I noticed a quite a few non engineering type women passing

40

through his office.   It had been almost as if he was showing off for me.

"I'm not surprised at all," I slowly shook my head. "Where's your sister now?"

"I would rather pay you to find my daughter. I already know where my damned sister is."

"All right."

Time to back off a bit, I'd rather not get too much verbal abuse before I went home for the day.

"Are you presently married?" I continued, keeping a controlled expression.

"I've never been married," She was almost shouting again.

"Where's the father of the child?"   I was almost afraid to ask.

"I don't know, I don't even know who the goddamned father is," Marcia folded her arms across her chest and glared at me.

"Excuse me?"

"I was artificially inseminated!   I don't know who the sperm donor was, and I don't care if anybody finds that amusing or not; this isn't a joke, it's real! All I want is for you to find my girl!"

Marcia shifted from one side of the chair to the other. Underneath the harsh stare, I sensed displaced anger. More than one thing eating at this woman. That was okay, so long as she didn't continue snapping at me like a shark in a feeding frenzy.

"The reason I asked is, that most kidnappings are done by relatives. Estranged fathers, or mothers steal their children rather than accept court orders," I kept my voice professional.

"I don't have that problem, the biological father doesn't know how many, or who the hell his damned children are, and I don't give a rat's ass either. The police went through all this with me," Her eyes said she was tired of answering useless questions.

"I'm sorry. Where was your daughter when she was kidnapped?"

41

"She was," The woman paused, started to choke, looked at the ceiling. With an effort she switched focus back to me. "In front of our house, riding her bicycle. The neighbors said they didn't see anything, but someone must have. She was only out of my sight for ten minutes while I fixed dinner. When I got back, she was gone, and that was three days ago!" Marcia halted. Again, another glance at the ceiling as if she was counting the holes in the tiles. "My baby's gone and I didn't do anything wrong! It's not my fault! I did my part as a mother and all, and this is what happens. You've got to find her for me."

I watched her sliding in and out of control as she spoke to me, and boy was I leery of her. Tears began to form in the bottom of Marcia's already red eyes.

"What have the police done?"

"Nothing! Not a God damned thing!" She leaned over the desk. "I just can't take one more thing now! Not one more thing!"

Ah, she had been drinking. Breath mints couldn't hide that much booze, especially when she tried to inflate my nostrils with her turpentine breath

"Have the police talked to your neighbors?"

"I suppose they did talk to a few neighbors, then they left! I don't want to talk to those people again! They don't care about me, or about my daughter! I want you to find her. They aren't motivated to do a damn thing but I'll motivate you. I'll give you plenty of money to find my baby."

I needed a few more thousand to keep the bank off my ass that month, only a few thousand more. I ain't cheap, but I sure am easy.

"Did you drive up here?" I asked in a reassuring voice.

"No, my car's in the shop. I called you from the dealer, then I walked here"Marcia sat up straighter in her chair. She smoothed out the fabric over her lap and sniffed a little.

"Can I take you home? You can tell me more about your little girl, and I can see where your neighborhood is. I'll canvass your neighborhood myself tomorrow."

42

"Sure, that would be okay," She wiped her cheeks with the back of her hand.

Neither one of us spoke during the car trip to her subdivision. The trek was a short hop from my office in central Los Angeles to Marcia's home in Maywood, somewhere off Atlantic Boulevard.

As I drove through streets in the dark, I thought back to my encounter with Marcia's sister. Nancy Fowler was the exact opposite of her sister, Marcia. Soft and graceful, Nancy also had a hidden edge. Brian, Nancy's husband, had played a game of cat and mouse with me as I tried to investigate him at his job on the Georgia Tech campus. He knew I was there to investigate him for a high paying position. He had ended the game with an invitation to his home for dinner.

At that time, the Fowler's house was a gem in the rough; I kept thinking that the level of renovation was much too high for someone on an assistant professor's salary.

The furnishings in that house reflected a low level battle between the couple. Heavy furniture from some Sears collection competed in each room with lighter, fine antique pieces. Even the wallpaper in the dining room was an unlikely combination of styles.

I ate a well cooked and politely served dinner, but I felt as if I were sparing with two heavyweights the whole evening. I remembered Nancy's beautiful face, and one of the greatest bodies on ten continents. As she smiled and flirted with me a bit too much she cast some pretty sharp barbs at her husband. That behavior had lasted through the evening. Sitting next to me now in the car, Nancy's sister, Marcia, shifted and sighed continuously, tears sporadically washing down her cheeks.

Just before we arrived at her house, she cleared her throat and spoke, "Nancy still lives in Atlanta."

"What?" I turned quickly to look at her for a second.

"You asked. My sister still lives in Atlanta. Last I heard from her oversexed ex husband, he was living in San Francisco, or somewhere around there."

43

"What about your daughter? Who were her friends in the neighborhood? Have they any ideas about what happened?"

"I haven't asked them. There aren't many young children on my block. The only girl her age lives three doors down on our side of the street, I think."

"Why don't you ask her mother tomorrow, then talk to the child yourself. It would be better for you to call her before me."

"I guess. What else can I do?" She still sounded determined, but her shoulders slumped.

"Tell me more about yourself. How long have you lived here?"

"Not long, about a year and a few months. I work for a radio station, I work in sales," Her voice was flat, mechanical.

"Where did you live before?" I turned my car into her driveway.

"We moved here from Chicago. The radio market is much bigger here, and, well, I get a lot more money on the coast."

"Where was your daughter born?"

"You mean, where did I get the insemination?" Marcia said, indignation rising in her voice.

Lady, that's a hell of a sore spot you've got, I thought as I looked at her, although I kept my voice quiet. After a moment, I added,

"Yes, it might have a bearing on the disappearance."

"Oh, Atlanta," Marcia said. "Come in with me," She pointed out the front windshield.

"Okay. Did your brother-in-law do the procedure?" I asked.

"What? No, his friend did it, he was a medical doctor. Brian was only a PhD."

"Was it that guy named Snibly, or Snidly?"

"Snively, Richard Snively was his name. I had everything done over a few months while I stayed with my sister," She paused. "If you met Richard while you were investigating Brian,

44

he must have been visiting friends in Atlanta. Richard moved to Miami quite a while ago."

I remembered Snively. I hardly knew him at all, but his name was in my mental files none the less. I had met him only once while I was in Atlanta. I bet he was the one who told Fowler that I would be investigating him on the Tech campus, and what I looked like. Snively had a high pitched, whiny voice and a limp handshake.

"Where is this guy Snively now?" I asked.

"Like I said, he moved to Miami, Florida. Why are you persisting in this, anyway?"

"I dwell on anything and everything until we find Becky."

"You're right. Do you want to come in for some coffee?" Marcia asked.

"Thanks, I'd like to see her room."

"Becky's room is at the end of the hallway, the room to the right," When Marcia turned on the hallway light, I noticed several groups of photographs, most of them of Becky at various ages. One photograph at the end of the hall showed Becky, as an infant, being held by Nancy Fowler. Brian Fowler and a short stocky man with dark medium length hair stood next to Nancy and Becky. That's Snively; I forgot he was that ugly.

Becky's room looked like that of a quintessential thirteen year old girl, populated with stuffed animals and dolls placed on dressers, tables, and the floor. Posters of characters from children stories and movies filled the walls.

I explored several drawers of the dressers and found nothing save unsorted clothes, and unmatched socks. A small jewelry box housed only predictable costume jewelry and a few coins. Several porcelain figures stood on the table next to her bed, but they held nothing in or on them of interest. I then looked under her bed, and unearthed several books, and a few more dolls, but nothing else. I collected a small pile of children's books from under the bed, <u>Dr.   Doolittle</u>, <u>Where the Wild Things Are</u>, <u>Alice in Wonderland</u>. At the time, I speculated that she had run away from her mother. If I were Marcia's kid, I would have been tempted to run. I opened one of the books

45

and noticed the date due slip in the back.   She was as bad as I am, it was a month overdue. As I was looking in her closet, Marcia came into the room.

"I'm afraid to come in here much, I think it's spooky. At first all I did was cry when I looked in her room, now all I do is get goose bumps. I hope she's not dead, or worse, but I'm afraid," Marcia sat down on Becky's bed.

"If she's alive, she's alive and that's the best thing we can both hope for, next to finding her."

I tried to sound as comforting as possible as I continued to look under the toys in the closet.   What a dippy remark that was.   I've never been able to deal with distraught women, even today I really need to work more on that.

"I'm sorry it's not clean, but I didn't have the heart to move anything in it.   I want it to stay just the way it was when she disappeared. It's so much like she was, everything is," Marcia began to cry again. "I just can't do any goddamned thing right!"

Not wanting to concur, I changed the subject.

"I don't see anything out of place here.   Let's go out to the kitchen and get some coffee," I held up the overdue library book. "I like your daughter's choice of books, but this one's overdue. Maybe you'd better return it so Becky won't be cut off from the library before she comes home."

"Yeah, sure, sure," Marcia's face had reverted to listlessness.

As we passed the pictures at the end of the hall, I asked. "Could I have this for a few days? The other picture you gave me wasn't as clear, this one would be better in making any identification, if someone has seen her.   If you have the negative, I could make a copy," I shrugged my shoulders, still not comfortable standing close to her.

"I could never find the negative; go ahead and borrow the picture."

Taking the photo off the wall, I noticed that the paint behind the picture was a slight but noticeable shade lighter than

46

the rest of the wall. A heavy smoker in a house can pump a lot of crap on every surface.

"But I do want it back when you're finished," Marcia added.

I walked to the kitchen after her with the picture in my left hand. Marcia reached into her purse and pulled out a wad of hundred dollar bills.

"Here, here's five thousand dollars. Your secretary said you charged a hundred fifty dollars a day plus expenses. Take this on account and find Becky. I want you to talk to me every day and give me receipts for everything you spend over daily charge. If it takes more money, let me know. All I want is my daughter back. I'll give you five thousand above expenses if you find her for me, please."

My thoughts, as always, led me into scenarios of best possible earnings, but money can be the root of all evil, and this might have been the test for me. Marcia seemed to be quite at home with dispensing large sums of cash. She drank her coffee in a few quick gulps, then poured another cup. There was a strong smell of many pots of coffee and many packs of smokes in that kitchen, along with the faint smell of burnt toast. Maybe that was this morning's breakfast.

"Do you want to spend the night?" She asked, looking at the table.

Oh, shit, I knew it. I thought I attracted a better class of women.

"I'm not propositioning you, so don't get any ideas; I just don't feel right about staying alone tonight, not without Becky," Marcia paused, looking into my eyes. "I'm afraid something might happen."

I too was afraid something might happen. I took in a deep breath.

"You should stop drinking coffee and try to get to sleep. Just lock all your doors and windows and you'll be all right."

And, I knew I'd be all right as long as I left there real soon.

7

And blow your house down

"I apologize for it bein' so hot, but the fuckin' air conditioner's broke in the whole stinkin' building," Irving snorted.

Irving Lopez was a squat man of unknown origins and uncertain end. His hair was cut in the classic used car salesman down on his luck style and his suit proved that polyester can rumple.

"Oh, I didn't notice," Fred replied.

Fred Lepus stood, almost at attention, in front of the Lopez's very large, very oak desk. Sweat beaded on the bald portions of Fred's head, wetting the white tufts of hair.

"Shit! You're sweatin' like a stuck pig! Ha ha!" Irving laughed, shifting his plump body.

"Oh," Fred swallowed hard and rocked slightly on his feet.

"You was wondering why I asked you here in such a hurry?" Irving squirted a smile at Fred.

"Those men who deliver messages for you almost don't take yes for an answer," Fred's return smile looked as if a crowbar had delivered it.

"Yeah," Irving leveled his eyelids into slits and glared at Fred. "You're working for a hump named Peterson, ain't you?"

"Well, maybe," Fred's voice searched for new highs. "Why?"

"I want that you should work for me; I want that you should be my eyes and ears, and nothing else."

"Just what would that entail?" Fred began to calm down as his pulse rate fell below one fifty. "What am I supposed to look for?"

"I done business with Peterson, and am still doin' business with him and all that's left of the educated assholes in his gang, but I don't trust him as far as I could throw him, so I want you to keep an eye on the bastard and all his friends for me."

"If I'm working for him, should I quit?"

"God! They said you was stupid, and I told them you couldn't be that stupid," Irving stepped out from behind his desk and put a stubby arm around Fred's shoulders. "I went to bat for you, and look where it gets me! Of course you keep working for the bum, how else can you keep a close eye on him," Irving's gaze remained fixed on Fred as he took his arm down and stepped one pace away.

"Sorry," Fred's voice rose again.

"That's all I want from you," Irving waved Fred away. "My boys'll be in touch if you don't send me word every other day or so, you get my drift?"

"Yeah," Fred's voice was almost a squeak.

. . . .

"Mr. Lepus," Becky looked at Fred as he sat in the heavy Naugahyde chair in the corner of the hotel room.

Fred drew in one breath after another as if each one would be his last and he needed to savor them all.

"Mr. Lepus," The small, slight girl again tried to catch his attention.

"Yeah, I'm here," Fred cast his gray-green eyes on the small girl. "But not for long. We've got to get the hell out of here, right now!"

"I wondered why we've come to New York instead of Chicago. That's where Daddy is, not here," Becky cocked her head and looked puzzled. "Do we go to Chicago now?"

"No, kid," Fred took a deep breath. "I came here to New York to be somewhere safe, but safe it ain't, so we go now."

"When do we go to Daddy?"

"He told me to keep you on ice for a while, at least until the heat's off and you can go live with him."

49

"Oh."

"Look, we'll take a plane to Charlotte now."

"Who's she?" Becky asked.

"Charlotte is a town in North Carolina, that's where the only man I know who's meaner than the one I just talked to lives, plus, he's a relative of yours."

"Grandpa." Becky sighed.

A frown grew over her forehead as she slumped back down on the edge of the bed and folded her arms across her chest.

"I've never had the pleasure of meeting him, but I see you have."

"Once and it wasn't fun," Becky mumbled. "I learned the word bastard from him."

"But he's rich and he could save your life and mine," Fred insisted. "I don't think that pig I just left knows you're with me, and we need to get going before he figures it out."

"What about Grandma?"

"I've never met her, but from what I've heard, your Grandpa is safer," Fred replied.

"Danger, are we in danger? I'm used to danger," Becky brightened up as quickly as she had soured. "I like adventures, I read about them all the time. Can we go on an adventure, Mr. Lepus?"

"I think we're in the middle of one, kid," Fred glanced at his watch and bounced to his feet like a jack rabbit. "We gotta get packed and into a cab right now. Our plane leaves in just two hours; I made the reservations before I came back up here to the room."

8
Boys will be boys

It was eight o'clock in the evening when I arrived at my apartment in the Civic Center/ Little Tokyo section of central Los Angeles on Fourth Street. I know it's not a very safe neighborhood after dark, but it's close to so many things, including my office. The structure itself is substantial, and I have the best neighbors in the building anyone could ask for. All of us are single men, most of whom work for law enforcement in one way or another; all of us are armed to the teeth and most of us can arrest people. The local gangs know it, so our building is sort of a no-man's land in the ongoing turf wars. It's kind of noisy during the day, but at night there's not much din except the occasional siren or gunshot. There hasn't been a burglary attempt here for over two years. That last attempt was by a junkie, but she didn't make it past the outer door to the building before the cops got there and dumped her into the local holding tank.

Mulling over the conversation with Marcia in my head, I decided that I needed input from a woman. So, I admit I need help appraising women under stress; the stress could be mine, or theirs.

The phone rang nine times before Cassandra answered, her acquired Southern California accent sounded annoyed.

"Hello, who is this?"

"Me, Benjamin. Did I disturb you? I hope you weren't in the middle of something?" I asked in a soft, teasing tone.

"What I was in the middle of is none of your business, but your timing is still lousy. What is it?"

"That music, don't tell me, let me guess," I paused for a second to listen. "Mozart, symphony number twenty nine, I love that piece."

"Yup, this is not name that tune, so why did you call me?"

51

"All right, that woman with the missing daughter came in and I need to talk with you about it. I got a funny feeling about her, and I need your feedback."

Cassandra sees into people very differently than I do. Maybe she could catch more about this woman than me, at least that was my reasoning at the time.

"Did she pay you yet?" Cassandra asked.

"Always the mercenary. Yes, she gave me five thousand in cash tonight, on account, and I'm going to pay off our creditors tomorrow."

"I'll meet you in the office," Her voice took on her accountant tone.

Since she was far better than I with money, Cassandra handled the books for our business.

"Give me two hours," I said. "I need to look at the yellow pages for a while."

"Are you that bored?"

"No, just looking at car dealerships within walking distance from our office."

"There's a Mercedes dealership eight blocks up from us," Cassandra said.

"I know, but I want to see if there are any others."

Marcia didn't seem to live in a Mercedes neighborhood, at least a neighborhood where people take their cars to a dealer for service.

. . . .

As I have said many times, my apartment building is not in the most upscale location of Los Angeles, but I still get disappointed when I'm attacked just blocks from my home.

I was turning a corner to head down Hill Street, minding my own business, when a long green Buick pulled up beside me. The side window was treated with such a thick sheet of dark Mylar that, like the police might be, I was suspicious. The mirror like window slowly lowered, and a sawed off twelve gauge leveled at the side of my Porsche.

Thinking of the possible repair bill, I bolted through the red light sending one small half-ton truck and three cars into spins as they tried to avoid me. Hell, my Porsche 911 can beat any '72 Buick ever thought of, and it did so for six blocks.

The Buick dropped from my rear view mirror, and reappeared in front of me, green and nasty as I sped through the sixth red light. The son of a bitch knew the side streets better than I did! He spun his car sideways, knocking two other cars out of their lanes. The way in front was blocked. I pulled my Porsche slowly into a driveway and onto the sidewalk. I leapt from my car with my revolver in hand.

Although it was late in the evening, the sidewalks were crowded. The pedestrians did not seem in the mood to participate in a gun battle. Some of them scattered, others stood, frozen and gawking, as the Buick backed up with its rear wheels screeching and smoking. It crashed into three cars, shoving a parked car onto the sidewalk. A tall muscular man stepped from the driver's side, aiming his shotgun at me. Everybody between me and the gunman, and I mean everybody, fell in unison to the sidewalk, leaving my assailant a clear shot at me.

Not to be someone who stands out in a crowd, I too fell to the cement as I fired twice at the man with the shotgun.

Just behind my two loud shots, the shotgun roared with both barrels. All the buckshot scattered into parked cars and store fronts. One of my forty one slugs splattered parts of his left arm over the side of the green Buick. The other projectile went through the Buick's door, was deflected downward and lodged in the asphalt of the street. The gunman threw his sawed off into the back of his car. As he grabbed his left arm, he shouted, "Shit!" Erratically, he crashed his way out of the scene and down a side street. I considered shooting at his car, but there were too many people around. That man had no finesse at all, crashing into more cars than the king of a demolition derby.

A few semi-wrecked cars hobbled from the scene while other drivers stepped from their vehicles and stared in disbelief. Most of the pedestrians ran from the block, but a few stalked up to me and demanded to know what was going on, like I knew;

some moron wanted me dead! The police didn't show up for ten more minutes. After taking statements from the few remaining witnesses, they released me after I promised to make a full statement the next day. It was obvious that the other gentleman initiated this gun battle, and I wasn't at fault. They let me go on my own recognizance, as if I don't recognize myself and the situations in which I find myself all too often.

. . . .

"Where the hell have you been?"

Cassandra was in the office when I opened the door.

"Give the cash to me, before you blow all of it tonight," She held out her right hand and smiled. "I'll put everything in the night deposit so we'll have it for the bank payments."

"I don't like you carrying around this much money at night. Besides, I don't trust the banks enough to shove five thousand dollars into a night deposit slot."

I guess she was upset that I was late and hadn't called her.

"You won't believe how dangerous it can be out there in the dark street sometimes."

Her angry expression melted into a concerned frown.

"I don't like you carrying that much money around anytime, night or day; we have to pay the bank two thousand or risk the business."

"Don't take it out on me," I felt defensive. "It's not always my fault that I interrupt your night life, such as it is."

She gave me a long, slow glance before she snapped, "You got me out of a long hot shower; I was trying to escape a real bad day," She paused only long enough to grab a fresh breath. "That idiot who hired me to tail his wife spent two hours trying to convince me that his wife is Raquel Welch. He wants me to follow a movie star around to find out who she's sleeping with. If he hadn't paid two hundred dollars in advance, I would have shot him right there in the office"

"Do you think you could get some pictures of her for me?"

54

She glowered, not deigning to reply.

"Okay, don't get so huffy," I held my hands up. "I won't tell you about someone trying to blow my head off tonight, if you're not nice to me."

"What?"

"Someone tried to kill me tonight, with a twelve gauge shotgun."

"Again?"

"Ah, you're concerned."

"You're alive, right? And I don't have to bail you out like the last time."

"Just a little sympathy?"

Cassandra hugged me.

"I'm sorry, I know how you like to plunge into things before thinking about the consequences."

I left that straight line alone and stuck to the gun battle.

"Not this time, the son of a bitch just pulled up beside me and stuck the damned shotgun out his window."

She stepped back to look at me. "Did you kill him?"

"No," I paused. "And he didn't even put a scratch on my Porsche."

She smiled and slapped my shoulder, but not hard.

"Did this have anything to do with that woman who came here this evening?" She asked.

"I don't know, but I sure as hell want to find out who this guy was, and better yet, who hired him. I don't think he had anything to do with the Satterwhite woman, though; maybe, but I don't think so."

Cassandra slumped back against the desk. "So what couldn't wait till tomorrow?"

"I'm sorry it's so late, but as I said I was unavoidably detained. I need you to meet the Satterwhite woman tomorrow, and talk to her about her daughter. Something doesn't feel right about our new client. She says she never married, and that she had the child from artificial insemination."

"She probably does get a lot of grief about it, never marrying and having a child. That's not exactly a common thing to do outside of soap operas or the news."

Sitting up on the edge of the desk in the center of the outer office, Cassandra relaxed a bit. She cocked her face slightly to the left and looked at me.

"Maybe, but I get the feeling she isn't telling the whole truth. Just talk to her about where she thinks the kid is, about her boyfriends, about her love life; anything she wouldn't mention to a man," I paused, knowing she wanted to hear more of a reason. "You know, I always wished I'd had a mother, or a sister while I was growing up, I might understand more of what's going on in these situations."

"You do as well as any other man I know." Cassandra placed her right hand on my arm as the right corner of her lips rose in the beginning of a smile.

"I don't know," I took her hand and slid it down my arm and placed it between my palms. "I should feel a lot more sympathy for this woman, but this funny feeling of dread stops me."

"Is that the only funny feeling you have?" She asked.

"No," I paused.

I wrinkled my brow with wicked thoughts, but I had to stick to business.

"I met her sister and brother-in-law several years ago in Atlanta, and there's something strange about them then, too."

"Like what?" Cassandra sat up a little straighter, and moved her hand back to the desk top.

"It's hard to pin down, but something is weird about them."

"Why were you there?"

"I had to investigate her brother in law, Brian Fowler, for a company which was considering him for a high clearance job."

"You worked for George then, didn't you?"

"Yes, I did, it was my first year as a detective and I was younger and more foolish then. It was routine work, I don't remember finding anything totally off the wall about him, but he just didn't seem to be the research type. I mean, he didn't publish a lot, and nobody seemed to know exactly what he did."

"What was his specialty?"

"The company wanted him for chemical and biological warfare research, but what little lab experience he had was in genetics."

"That's a little weird," Cassandra shook her head. "But there might be reasonable explanations for everything."

"I remember more. The sister, Nancy Fowler, had a case full of trophies."

"What's so strange about that?"

"I can recall that house they lived in, it was very large, and quite old for the area. The two of them were spending a lot of money fixing it up. The family room had two curio cabinets, full of pictures and fancy glassware, and Nancy Fowler's trophies for high power rifle marksmanship."

"So, why can't a woman like those kinds of rifles?"

"No reason, but not many do, you don't."

"Don't start that again."

"Okay, I'll save it for later, but you will have to practice using your pistol before your life depends on it; like me tonight."

"Yeah, yeah, I remember, but for now let's stick to the subject."

"All right. Mostly men compete in high powered rifle events; women compete in skeet, and trap shooting, as well as some pistol events," I thought for a second about Nancy. "For a woman as concerned with being and looking like a lady as she was, I just thought it was an unusual sport for her."

"That's a bit unexpected, I'll have to admit."

"The man who was visiting in Atlanta, and who I ran into several times on campus, was the same one who did the artificial insemination for Marcia."

Cassandra leaned her body towards me. "That's interesting just by itself."

"I thought so."

"Okay, anything else?"

"Yeah, I'm going to Miami tonight."

"What! Do you know how much that'll cost!"

"Round trip is four hundred and eleven dollars. I bought the ticket before I came here; I thought it was a very good deal considering it was on such short notice," I handed her an envelope. "Here's the other four thousand, please put it in our account tomorrow, not tonight, and don't get so damned possessive about my company's money."

"Somebody has to, or our company will go broke and I'll have to start all over somewhere else. So you spent one thousand dollars already'" She folded her arms across her chest. "One of us has to keep an eye on expenses around here, and for whatever reason that person has been me for as long as I've worked for you."

"You know why expenses are high lately." I didn't want to get into this again. "I've been buying a lot of equipment, like the cameras, lenses and all that video stuff."

"I guess you're right," Cassandra exhaled noisily.

I could tell she didn't want to get into that discussion again either.

"It's just been a lot of cash going out and not that much coming in lately."

"We've bought all the equipment, and we had to take out a loan for just half of it," I started my defensible position yet again. "As soon as the loan is paid off, all the income will be ours."

"I know that," She sighed. "It's just that if the client cuts off the money, I don't want us to be stuck paying for expensive trips on our own dime."

"The doctor who inseminated Marcia lives in Miami. Atlanta is close, that's where her sister lives. Maybe the daughter's there, and even if she's not there, I think those two people could be of some help," I said. "As far as I know, that's her whole family; you know me, I work on intuition. This girl is very young and I think some member of her family has taken her, probably for the girl's own protection. Whatever happened, I think the answer's back East."

What about her parents?" Cassandra asked.

"Her father's in North Carolina, and her mother's in Naples Florida," I replied.

"What if she was kidnapped for money, or because she's a good looking young girl?"

"But, the case doesn't fit a kiddy porn profile. If it was for money, you'll hear about it shortly and can tell me. I'll call you as soon as I get a hotel room in Miami. Besides, don't worry, the client is paying for it, anyway."

"Well, okay. What if the kid just ran away from home and is still in her neighborhood somewhere?" She asked.

"That's a possibility I thought of, but, where would she go?" I paused for a second. "Her mother says she has no real friends, so my guess is that if she didn't just head for Sunset Boulevard, she'd head for one of her relatives back East."

"So, you think this is a domestic kidnapping?"

"I think she was taken, but I'm pretty sure it wasn't a stranger doing the kidnapping."

"But what makes you think her relatives have anything to do with the disappearance?" Cassandra asked.

"I don't trust the girl's mother," I paused. "Maybe she abuses her daughter; I definitely feel she's a bit crazy."

"Maybe she didn't trust you."

"What's not to trust about me?" I asked in a hurt tone. "She just gave me a weird feeling, you've met people like that before."

Cassandra nodded.

"That friend of her brother-in-law, the doctor in Miami, specialized in fertility and genetics, that's not a common field. No one ever knew exactly what either one of them was up to. Marcia Satterwhite's father is a soldier of fortune type, he runs a school for would be John Waynes somewhere in North Carolina. Her sister, Nancy seems like a nice stable woman, someone the girl might trust. I never met her mother, but maybe I should. There's too many possibilities in that direction to pass up looking into them."

"All right, but don't spent the whole five hundred you're taking with you," She relaxed and unfolded her arms.

"With you as a watch dog, the company will never go broke," I patted her shoulder. "I'll check in with the Miami police department as soon as I can, maybe they'll help since it's a missing child case."

"What was that about the car dealership you were looking up in the yellow pages," Cassandra paused, then looked at me.

"Marcia said she walked from a dealership to our office so I wondered what kind of car she drove."

"And," Cassandra asked. "How many dealers are near us?"

"I found only one Ford dealer, besides the Mercedes dealer."

"Is her neighborhood a Ford or Mercedes neighborhood?"

"Most definitely a Ford neighborhood; a used Ford neighborhood," I replied. "But, could you call the Mercedes dealer and pretend you're Marcia asking about your car."

"Sure, as soon as I'm out of class, I'll get started. Call me when you get there, and have a good trip," Cassandra got up and walked to the door. "What about our local cops?"

A puzzled look grew over my face, as I drawled. "Naw, not yet. If I get into this with them now, they'll be on my ass every step, maybe later," I remembered the gun battle that night. "Could you do me another favor?"

"What?"

"I'm staying here tonight long enough to write a report about what happened for the police, could you notarize it and deliver it to them?"

"Okay, I'll deliver the report and talk to the woman tomorrow, just leave me her name and address," Cassandra said.

"I'll try to call earlier next time," I replied with a smile.

"Jealous?" She asked softly, as she shut the door behind her.

Unfortunately I am.

9

Who's the fairest in all the land?

Reading Katz' hastily drawn map with one eye, Cassandra negotiated the last few streets in Marcia's neighborhood, parking in front of a line of dried up, spindly orange trees which grew in a narrow strip of soil between the sidewalk and the street. She straightened her coat, adjusting the holster hanging off her left shoulder as she started to walk.

"So why am I doing this?"

She had ignored the obvious rhetorical question for blocks. It pestered her as she walked up the sidewalk and pushed the doorbell.

No response. She tried again, with the growing sensation that a bloodshot eye examined her through the peep hole.

"Hello," Cassandra used her most professional voice. "Hello, Ms. Satterwhite? My name is Cassandra Pales, I'm Benjamin Katz' partner."

No response.

"He asked me to come by today to ask you a few more questions."

No response.

"May I come in?"

Cassandra stood a bit further back from the front door, to give the person on the other side of the door a wider view; the better to scrutinize you, my dear.

"Where the fuck is that bastard!" A voice hissed through the door.

"Which bastard do you mean?" Cassandra kept a straight face.

"Your dip shit boss."

Marcia opened the door in one dramatic yank, her expensive clothes looked slept in. Unkempt hair hung about her face.

"He's in Miami by now; he's there to talk to Dr. Snively, and then he's going to Atlanta to speak to your sister."

"I don't have a sister."

Marcia's rage was enough to lay waste to the whole front yard, including Cassandra. Her breath alone could kill, leftovers of late night binging.

"May I come in, Ms. Satterwhite?" Cassandra didn't want to enter without a confirmed verbal pass.

"Yeah, yeah, get your ass in here."

Marcia gestured that they move into the dark living room, and pointed to a sofa against the back wall. After looking around for a minute, Cassandra settled into the identified sofa.

"I came here to get some more background information on your daughter," Cassandra ventured.

No response. Cassandra got out a pad and pen.

"Well, Let's just begin," Cassandra cleared her throat. "How long have you lived here?"

"I told that man you work for yesterday, I just moved here from Chicago," Disdain dripped from her words. "I want my daughter back," Marcia's eyes had narrowed to rock hard slits. "She's worth everything to me now."

"I know, but how many months have you lived in this neighborhood?"

With an abrupt switch, Marcia appeared to deflate. She slumped as she spoke. "What the fuck difference does it make to you?" Cassandra could just make out the words.

"Excuse me, I can't hear you," Cassandra phrased it as politely as she could, sensing an impending explosion.

"About five months, you Barbie doll bitch," Marcia snapped.

"All right," Cassandra made a note.

"This place sucks big time, you know."

"Oh." Cassandra followed the change of subject. "What does Becky think of Los Angeles?"

"Who gives a shit!" Marcia exploded, then again cut herself off as Cassandra made another note. "What I mean is I move where I can find work. You know I don't have, or ever want a husband, and, well, Becky and me have to live on what I earn; we move for financial reasons, that's what I meant."

"So, does Becky like it here? Has she made any friends?"

Yeah," Marcia pointed to her left. "The spick girl down the street likes to hang out with Becky. She's okay and all, but I don't trust the mother, if you know what I mean."

Cassandra wrote 'bigot bitch' in her notebook.

"Exactly when did you notice your daughter missing?"

Marcia rose to her feet and walked forward, unsteadily. Placing both fists on her hips, she screamed into Cassandra's face, "Don't you ever call me a rotten mother, you whore!"

Cassandra wiped the spray off as much of herself as she could. In one smooth motion, she stood, still within Marcia's personal space.

Marcia stepped back . Her legs were shaky enough to make her stumble but she caught herself on the arm of a winged back chair.

"I'm sorry," she stammered. "I'm upset as hell, and I guess I'm a little too intense."

"I'd say you're a bit more than a little upset," Cassandra continued her glare at Marcia.

"Don't call me upset, you skinny perfect face shit head whore," Marcia held on to the arm of the chair. "If you want upset, I can damned well give you upset! Who the hell do you think you are, the cops or something! Asking me all these insulting questions! I pay you to do what I want, and you had better remember that, miss perfect ass shit head!"

"Perhaps we should continue this discussion when you're a bit more under control," Cassandra remarked.

The two women locked glances again, but it couldn't last. The situation felt comical all of a sudden, though Cassandra kept a neutral expression. Marcia half fell, sideways, into the chair. She gulped for a large breath of air.

"Wait." She exhaled, slowly. "I'm better now, let's get this over with."

"All right," Cassandra sat back down. "How do you feel about your daughter's disappearance?"

"What are you talking about?" Marcia's face began to turn mottled red.

"I only wanted to know how you felt about Becky vanishing?"

"Why!"

"Because, to be quite honest with you, you don't seem to care at all that your daughter is missing. It appears to me that you're just shouting, going through the motions of wanting her back because you think you should, on a logical level of some kind."

Cassandra braced herself for the next onslaught. Perhaps in a rage, Marcia might tell her something useful. A nervous twitch rolled across the drunken woman's face; no more anger.

"All I would like to do for the money you're paying us, is to find Becky," Cassandra added.

Marcia sighed, "I guess that's all I want too. I'm sorry about yelling at you and all."

"All right."

Cassandra settled back into the sofa, wondering what it was, in addition to mood swings from all the booze, that made Marcia act so erratic.

"Really, I'm sorry," Marcia's eyes seemed to focus on Cassandra for an instant.

Cassandra jumped at the chance to get the interview back on track, "It must be awful to lose someone so close to you, even if it's for only a few days."

"What have you found out?" Marcia leaned forward. "Do you know where she is?"

"I apologize," Cassandra shook her head. "I was only assuming that Becky would be missing for a short time. Let's always hope for the best possible outcome."

"Yeah," Marcia sat in the chair she had been leaning against, folding her arms across her chest. "That's what I thought! You dip shit dicks don't know enough to fill a gnat's ass."

"Okay"Cassandra paused again to be sure Marcia was still focused. "Benjamin told me you work for a radio station here in town, which one is that?"

"So what! What do they have to do with anything?"

"Well, They could announce something on the air, maybe offer a reward or something."

"Uh, not those cheap bastards," Marcia shifted in her seat. "I'd rather not talk about my job, it has nothing to do with what I'm paying you for!"

"Then, what about your relatives? Your father, mother, and your sister?"

"I told you I don't have a sister. My father's, uh, my father's nothing," Marcia became agitated again. "My whole family's dead!"

Feeling enough was enough, Cassandra tossed her notebook and pen back into her purse.

"I think I have enough information for now," She stood, then headed out the door.

A few steps behind her, Marcia purposefully pushed the door shut.

Back in her car, Cassandra paused for a full sixty seconds, her hands gripping the steering wheel like a miser grips an almost empty tube of toothpaste.

"THAT was the meanest bitch I've ever met!"

Driving back to the office, she plotted how to uncover each and every lie she knew in her heart that Marcia had uttered. If they found that child, they could never give her back to that raging drunk, never.

10

It's always darkest

The nagging reminder to save money rang in my head as I directed the cab driver to find a cheap motel close to the Miami airport. Well, it wasn't that cheap and it wasn't that close to the airport. It was a nice business class place on Biscayne Boulevard with a fifth floor view of the ocean. I love expense accounts almost as much as I love clients who pay in advance.

A hot shower late that morning felt good, so did the large breakfast in the cafe at the end of the block. As I lingered over a steaming cup of coffee, the aroma of eggs, bacon, pancakes and toast, images of enjoying a Sunday breakfast with my father and brother kept recurring to me. We often went to a small diner in my hometown in Pennsylvania,. It was one of the few good memories I had from that time in my life.

Up in my room, I paused over my revolver packed into my suitcase. That's the only way I could fly with a weapon, no one had stolen it yet. Should I wear it? Not while visiting the cops, that might be a bad idea.

This trip back East was bringing more recent memories back, of my contract with the Fowlers. When I had gone to their home for dinner, Brian Fowler had directed me into the den to wait until dinner was on the table. The den was all his, with heavy mahogany shelving and dark, vinyl upholstered furniture. An oversized brass tool set guarded the oak and beam framed fireplace. The only concession to Nancy in that room were two fine glass display cases, with darkly stained wood shelves, and glass on three sides. Inside one case were numerous trophies belonging to Nancy, plus pictures of her and her family spanning several decades, but my mental images of them were blurred.

Try as I might, I could not bring any of those images in porcelain and metal frames back into focus.

I hauled out the phone book but could find no Richard Snively listed. A call to information confirmed that he must have an unlisted number. By noon, I was asking a sergeant for the officer in charge of missing persons, at the Miami police station. The policeman directed me to Lieutenant Parker.

At Parker's office, two plain clothed officers sat working at two of the five desks. The large room was silent except for occasional bursts of typing. Each officer wore the same uniform, a long sleeved white shirt, rolled up, and a plain tie, loosened at the collar.

"Which one of you is Lieutenant Parker?" I asked towards the middle of the room.

One of the men looked up, annoyed at me for disturbing him, but didn't answer.

"I am" A small stocky man, came through a doorway to my left, his voice tinged with a distinct Southern accent. "What can I do for you?"

"Is there somewhere we can talk? I'm from Los Angeles, and I think there might be some information here about a missing child back in California."

"Who are you? The parent? A policeman?"

"Can we talk somewhere?"

Edwin Parker seemed to notice suddenly how I loomed over him. "Come on back here," he answered, motioning to an adjacent room.

We each sat at opposite ends of a tiny, Formica topped table. Parker leaned over and pulled the door shut. "Okay, what do you want?"

"I'm a private investigator, working for the mother."

"I thought so, you didn't look like anybody important."

I should charge clients more for the abuse I take in this job.

"Look, I came here to help find a missing child, are you going to help, or what?" I stared straight into his eyes.

67

"Keep talking, I'll tell you what I'll do and when I'll do it."

"The child was conceived through artificial insemination, and the doctor who did the procedure lives here now. His name is Richard Snively, and all I need is some help in locating him as soon as possible, he may know something," I looked at the policeman who shifted a bit in his chair.

"I'll find out, but why haven't the cops from Los Angeles called us? What made you come here to look the doctor up?"

"I don't know what the cops in Los Angeles are doing, or not doing. The mother thinks they're not doing anything," I answered.

His neutral expression threatened to turn severe. . "But, why are you here to find Snively?"

"I told you, he's the one who artificially inseminated the mother of the missing child, and I have a hunch he may know something about where the child might be."

I began to notice that look in his eyes, a look like I was the Hell's Angels meanest biker here to take his daughter to the prom.

"You wait here, I'll be back with someone who can answer your question. Are you carrying a gun?" Edwin demanded.

"No, wanna check?" I asked, raising my arms.

"I don't see one but I'll look anyway," Parker patted me down, then walked out of the room.

My life is never simple, never. Almost as soon as the door closed, it opened again. Parker walked, more slowly, followed by man, taller than me, with a medium build. They sat down facing me.

"This is Captain Osborne, from Homicide"

"Snively's dead, isn't he?" I shook my head. It was obvious; I just knew I had landed in a world of crap.

"Good guess," Carl Osborne answered as he pulled a pair of handcuffs from his coat pocket. "Now, stand up, spread your legs, grab that table and tell me why I shouldn't drop you in jail right now for murder."

68

"Well, for one thing, what about my rights, and for another I just got here and haven't had time to do anything, let alone murder someone."

But I was already standing, following his directions. Osborn searched me for a weapon. This was the second cop to feel me up in five minutes and I didn't even get a dinner invitation out of it. Not finding a weapon, Captain Osborne shoved me back into the plastic chair.

"You have the right to remain silent. You have the right to an attorney before you are questioned. Anything you say can and will be used again against you in a court of law. Do you have any questions, because I sure have one hell of a lot of them for you," Osborn paused to draw in a large breath.

His voice sounded smaller than his physical size. It didn't have the Southern twang that Parker's did, but he still swallowed half of the vowels coming out of his mouth.

"Yeah, do you have any idea who killed him?" I asked.

"We were hoping you might have some light to shed on the case. It's not often we have someone walk into our headquarters and ask for information on someone who was murdered the night before." Carl Osborn didn't wait for a response, he just gulped in another breath and continued. "When did you get into town, and where did you come from?"

Osborn got up, stepped closer so that he loomed over me,

"I got into town late last night and I stayed in a good hotel with a view of the beach. My father tried to convince me I came from a drunken stork, but I think you want to know that my business is based in Los Angeles."

"I hate a wise ass private dick, especially from California," He glared at me. "You got your plane ticket?"

I slowly reached into my coat pocket and handed my ticket to Osborn. I'll bet he thought Miami was a real special place. The home of the pink plastic flamingo and Bebe Reboso.

"I'm not a wise ass, I'm only trying to lighten you guys up some," I looked from face to face in the small room, determined not to be intimidated. "Call the Los Angeles Police Department and ask for a Lieutenant Hatton, he'll vouch for me." I hoped.

Osborn nodded towards lieutenant Parker, who walked out the door.

"Why was he killed? What was he mixed up in? Drugs?"

"Why don't you tell us?"

"I've told you all I know about the guy. I'm looking for the biological father, and possible funny business with the donor sperm; it's just a hunch, but I thought it might be worth looking into."

"Just what makes you think Snively is capable of doing anything like that?" Osborn asked.

"You'd have to meet the man to understand," I paused to collect my thoughts. "I ran across him in a case I worked on a few years ago. When I did that investigation, he tried his best to avoid giving any straight answers. Almost all his published research was in genetics, do you want more details?"

"No, I get the picture. What's the crap about who the kid's father is, do you think Snively might be the father?"

"Maybe he wanted the kid back, who knows?"

"Artificial insemination would be the only way he'd have any children," Osborn shook his head.

I knew he was gay when I shook his limp wristed hand several years ago in Atlanta.

"The man spent nothing but three dollar bills the whole time he was in Miami." Osborn added.

So the captain was stuck in his stereotypes.

"How long did he live here?" I asked, changing the subject.

"He moved here from Atlanta seven or eight years ago," Osborn paused. He pressed his lips together. "I think he was fired from his last job in Atlanta a few years before he came down here."

"That's long before I met him in Atlanta." I thought about the time frame, trying to recall more detail; there wasn't any.

"And, did you meet him since then?"

"Not at all," I slowly shook my head. "He was one of Brian Satterwhite's friends and Brian was the person I was doing a background check on."

"Nothing more?" Osborn still looked suspicious.

"Like I said, that was a little more than two years ago and now I'm looking for a missing child. The child's mother has a connection to Snively."

Parker walked back into the room. "Katz checks out. The police in Los Angeles say he's a good guy, we shouldn't hassle him too much; some, but not too much." The two men exchanged a look.

"It seems like he doesn't know anything," Osborn said.

"How about sharing something with me, like who put out his lights? I flew a long way to talk to a dead man," I had to ask, there might be some information here for me after all.

"We really don't know," Osborn replied. "Snively wasn't into drugs. All we have to go on is his sex life. He made it with some big names here in Miami, some of whom would not like their sexual preference known."

"Well, you haven't helped me locate the missing girl, and I haven't helped you, unless he was practicing black magic on the unborn here," I remarked, and kept my eyes on their faces.

"That we didn't know, but we can check it out," The captain showed some reluctant surprise.

"I don't suppose you'll share the answer to that with me when you find out, will you?" I asked.

"I don't suppose we will," Osborn agreed.

"You want to book this guy?" Parker asked, wistfully.

"No, I don't think he did anything, this time."

"Gee, thanks."

I stood up as quick as possible and left the police station with what I felt was another piece to the puzzle, although I thought it might be a piece to a completely different puzzle.

After encounters like the shotgun guy and the cops in Miami, I often wonder why I stick with this job, but, usually I like it since there's always something new and exciting every day. Even if some people shoot at me, I still get to meet interesting

71

folks.   Finding missing kids, nailing cheating husbands, tripping up thieves, in the long run is fun.   It must say something about my psyche, but if I look too deep into that, it won't be fun anymore.

I spent the rest of the morning looking around Miami, as well as asking about the good doctor. Whether he had no friends, or he had tight lipped friends I don't know, but no one was willing to tell me anything about Snively.   It was a little after three in the afternoon when I got back to the motel room and called my office.

"Cheshire Katz Agency, may I help you?" A soft voice asked.

"You always find a way, my love." I smiled to myself.

"Oh, Benjamin. Did you find anything?"

"I found out that Snively was killed last night."

"What? Why?" Cassandra demanded, interested.

"I can't tell yet; the cops don't know or won't say. All they confirmed was that he was gay, and covering that up, along with who his partners were, that might be a motive," I answered.

"Didn't you notice that when you met him before?"

"Of course I did, but it didn't matter to the case I was working on at the time. He didn't ask me out for a date or anything," I didn't need any sarcasm from her. "How was your day?"

"Sorry," Cassandra paused. "I talked to Marcia this morning, and I told her where you were."

"What did you think of her?"

"She says she loves her daughter very much, and wants her back more than anything in the world."

"What else?" I asked.

"I don't believe anything she says," Cassandra said. "And most of the time I don't believe she even wants her kid back.

"Why?"

"She said she works for a radio station, and she doesn't. She said she just moved to Los Angeles five months ago, but she's been here for almost two years. She said she's never been married, and she was," Cassandra took in a deep breath and

72

continued. "She definitely does not drive a Ford, she owns a Mercedes five hundred class sedan which is only one year old. She also owns a four bedroom house in Malibu, on the goddamned beach! It's taxed at over four hundred thousand, probably worth a whole lot more."

"Busy morning," I shook my head at all that information. "Why did she bring us to that rundown ranch house?"

"The neighbor lady in the working class neighborhood said the kid lived there full time, but the mother was gone a lot, sometimes for a week or more," Cassandra said. "I haven't gone to the Malibu house yet."

"She sounds stranger and stranger."

"She sounded like a first class bitch this morning," Cassandra added.

"Lots of money she doesn't want us to know about; drugs, perhaps?"

"I don't know yet," Cassandra said.

"So long as she pays us for finding her daughter."

"Marcia sent me the money you spent on your trip to Miami this morning. The cash was in an envelope stuffed under our office door when I got back to the office. She was too drunk to deliver it herself, so my question is, who did it for her?"

"Or, why; I don't know," I paused. "Maybe she has an entourage in addition to the house on the beach. You've been busy today."

"That drunken bitch was acting so far from reality that I started checking into her past right away."

"You don't trust a client who pays in advance for expenses, with cash I presume?" I asked.

"In cash all right and, no, I don't trust her; only crooks deal in cash," Exasperation tinged Cassandra's voice. "If you do find the daughter, I don't think we should give her back."

"I tend to agree with that conclusion," I said. "If I do locate the kid, I'll have you contact the child protection services first, and we can give them the girl."

"So we need to consider what to do very carefully," Cassandra said, slowly. "I don't care if that woman is rich as hell."

"You did deposit her money, didn't you?"

"You bet."

"Where does she work? You don't own a big Benz and a house on the beach with a radio station job, even if you're the on air talent," I observed.

"She works for the U. S. Emigration service, she's an assistant district supervisor." Cassandra paused. "She hasn't worked for them long, and she might not be working there much longer since they haven't seen her for five days. They also seemed surprised she even had a child, let alone that the kid is missing."

"Why did Marcia lie to us? Didn't she know we'd find out? Why work a middle management government job if you're rich? Is she using that job as a cover for something?"

"Don't ask me, ask her when you get back. I think we should get out of this one, I've got a bad feeling about it," Cassandra said. "She could be working for the mob, or a drug runner using her new job for cover."

"I've got that same bad feeling, but I'd better do some fine ass covering before we do get out."

"Good idea; where are you going next?"

"I'm going to try to locate her mother in Naples first, then try to see her sister, Nancy, in Atlanta, I already rented a car and bought the ticket. Could you find out if the brother-in-law is in San Francisco?" I asked. "Just make a few phone calls, his name is Brian Fowler. He's a PhD in Biology so check the universities first. If you do get in touch with him, ask him about Becky."

"I'll do it, but call me when you get to Atlanta," Cassandra said. "I'll wire you more of her money if you need it. Bye, and be careful."

"You too; I'll try to get to Atlanta tonight and I'll call you from there. One more thing, who was she married to?"

74

"I don't know for sure but her married name was Peterson. She lived in Chicago, and it was real easy to check on her there. She didn't seem to have a job in Chicago, but I haven't had enough time to really find out. Do you want me to get more?"

"Yeah, check with the cops, see if she filed a missing persons report. Also, ask around to make sure she really does have a child. I think it's time the cops were let in on this, in case Marcia didn't file a report. I think you should run all this by Mark Hatton just in case, besides, Hatton already knows what I'm up to because the Miami police called him today to check on me."

"Okay; one more thing," Cassandra's voice hesitated.

"What?"

"The police didn't like your report on the shooting. What they definitely didn't like is that you didn't deliver it in person."

"I can't help that," I paused. "What did they say?"

"They told me that the other car was a stolen vehicle, and that it was wiped clean when they found it early this morning."

"Where did they find the car?" I asked.

"Somewhere near El Segundo," Cassandra answered. "Near the airport."

"And, they have no idea who it was?"

"None," She paused. "First you get shot at, then this Snively person is killed; I'd watch my back if I were you."

"Damn it!" I muttered into the phone. "That creep with the shotgun might well have worked for someone involved in this kidnapping after all."

. . . .

To save money, I rented a compact car for the drive to Naples. The drive across the state on US 41 was, to say the least, interesting; I had never seen the Everglades up close and personal.

Although I called Marcia's mother, Florence Satterwhite, several times, before I left Miami and twice along the one hundred and twenty mile trip, I had yet to speak to her on the

75

phone.   All I got was an answering service; they had no clue as to why Ms. Satterwhite was not home, nor where she was now.

Temperatures in the mid eighties, high humidity and hardly any breeze made me glad I had insisted on air conditioning in the rental car.   Why would they offer a car without air in this state? Lots of Spanish moss, hanging in gray clumps off dead tree branches.   Maybe when I made it to the Gulf coast, the atmosphere would become livable again.   By the end of the trek across the Everglades, I was hopeful that the child would be with her grandmother, and I could collect my fee without further discomfort.

The address I had for Florence Satterwhite was on Gordon Drive; wherever that was.   With a gas station state map that had a crappy little map of Naples, at least I knew the general direction.   With the help of a second friendly gas station attendant, I was able to find Gordon Drive.

It was right on the Gulf of Mexico and it didn't look at all like the neighborhood Marcia Satterwhite lived in.   The section of Gordon Drive that Marcia's mother lived on was a late forties, early fifties collection of huge mansions, most of them on well landscaped large lots.   Florence's house appeared to be a five thousand square foot two story mansion with commanding views of the Gulf.

I rang the bell three times before anyone answered the door.

"May I help you?"   A middle aged Hispanic woman asked.

"I'm looking for Florence Satterwhite,"   I politely replied.

"Madam is not here now,"   She curtly reported.

"May I speak to her later in the day?"   I inquired.

"She is gone for the rest of the week,"   The woman paused, assessing my intentions.

"I'm an employee of her daughter's, and I have family business to discuss with her,"   I interrupted.

"Madam is visiting relatives for the rest of the week, you can come back next week."

As her accented voice faded, she closed the door in my face. This was curious. Why did I get an answering service when there was a servant at home. Was Florence actually gone, or was she there and not in the mood for visitors? Was she visiting her granddaughter somewhere, or was she there with the granddaughter in the house not wanting to see strangers?

Canvassing the exclusive neighborhood, posing as a private detective working on a missing child case, how about that for a cover, I ascertained that none of her neighbors who would speak to me knew much about Florence, nor her comings or goings. One maid across the street thought she saw Florence leaving in a cab yesterday, but she wasn't sure.

I had a three thirty flight to Atlanta, so I had to cut my inquiries short.

11

Through the mist of time

I had gotten a late afternoon flight to Atlanta from Naples. It cost twice what it should, but last minute tickets are never cheap, plus all I could get was a first class seat; I should always get that kind of bad luck. I hoped the mild weather was a good omen as I checked into the same hotel I had stayed in several years before. Tonight, the spring evening was light, warm and inviting, unlike the gray November when I had last visited Atlanta. The hotel was on Peachtree, but a bit north of the main downtown area. The Hyatt Regency called to me, as did the new Westin, but the fear of no more advances from our client led me to this place again. The lobby had a new decor, but my room looked very similar, except for a new color TV set. By the number of lumps on the bed, I surmised that the mattress had to be the same.

While it was still light, I asked my cab driver to take me to the address on Morningside Drive, where I had dined several years before. The neighborhood seemed completely transformed; what had been a transition neighborhood several years before was now all upper class. Older houses had almost all been brought back to their former glory. Built from the turn of the century through the fifties, large two story brick, the homes sat far back from the street with manicured lawns, formal gardens. Nancy Satterwhite's house stood out as the jewel of the block, a massive brick structure, at least five thousand square feet with columns and wide front and side porches.   Her home must have been built just after the turn of the century. It had a very Southern Victorian feel to it.   The landscaping was flawless, and the exterior was a sight to behold.

"Stop the car here.   Wait for me, I'll be back," I told the cab driver.

"It's your money, take as long as you want." The cab driver cut the motor, leaned back in the seat and began reading an Arabic language newspaper.

A young black woman answered the front door.

"May I help you sir?" She asked.

"I'm looking for the person who lived in this house a few years ago. Her name was Ms. Fowler then but I believe her name is Satterwhite now."

Nancy had to be still living here. The smell of that unusual perfume gave off a faint but perceptible reminder. During my previous visit, she had told me that her father was friends with a perfumer in France, who had made a special scent for her, a blend of several distinct scents.   She had refused to tell me the exact combinations.   I wasn't that good at identifying them, but I recognized a combination of rose and cinnamon drifting towards me.

"Miss Satterwhite has been very busy since early yesterday morning, around town and out, she's not receiving visitors now. May I leave your name and telephone number for her?"

"My name is Benjamin Katz, and I'm here at the request of her sister, Marcia.   If she doesn't want to see me, come back and tell me, and then I'll leave."

"I'll tell her," The young woman paused to visually evaluate me again, "Wait here."

In two minutes the door opened again. Nancy stood there, clothed in a full length red dressing gown, cut very deeply down the front, revealing a large portion of bare cleavage.

She stood a few inches taller than her sister and her complexion and composure was cleaner, crisper than Marcia's. Her light brown hair fell over her shoulder, part way down her back. She seemed to radiate the knowledge that she knew who she was and what she wanted from her life and from others in it. Her beauty struck a chord in me.   Regrettable The same notes plucked several years before.

"Benjamin, it is you. What is this about my sister? How is she, and why are you here?" Nancy asked as she motioned me to come inside.

Her voice range was soprano and quiet, inviting and dangerous.

I had been staring at her for the past several seconds, not wanting to take my eyes off the beautiful image she displayed. Why would she show such interest in someone she had met once? I did, however, excuse myself to pay the taxi driver.

"How have you been these past years?" Nancy was asking as I walked back up the front steps.

"Just fine. I hope I haven't come at a bad time."

"Not at all, I was just getting dressed for an evening engagement. What brings you to the neighborhood?"

"Your niece is missing, at least that's why your sister hired me."

"Becky?" Nancy abruptly sat down in a solid oak corner chair in the hallway. "Marcia didn't tell me that."

My eyes wandered, all innocence, down at Nancy and couldn't help but notice the unobstructed view of her ample bare white breasts in the loose gown. I took in a shallow breath before I spoke.

"Do you know what might be going on? Is there some reason the child should disappear? Is there someone who might take her?"

Nancy stared at the floor.

"No." Her voice was soft.

"Your sister claims to have been artificially inseminated. Was she?"

"Yes, she was, but why should that matter?"

"Who was the biological father?" I asked.

Nancy paused for a second while she looked up at me, "I don't know; the sperm was from a sperm bank and that sort of information is sealed," Nancy hesitated a while longer. "Even if she were to know, what could it matter?"

"It might mean the real father found out, and he wanted to take the child back."

"Oh, no, that could never happen; she never knew," Nancy insisted.

But did you know? I thought as I asked my next question, "Was your sister ever married?"

"Yes, but she was single when she gave birth to Becky. She's so up tight about telling people how she had Becky. Deep down I think she's a little ashamed about it. She loves her daughter as much as any mother should love a child, but, well, you know what I mean. Dad raised us, and he's so conservative." Nancy rose and walked towards the den. "Could you wait here while I finish dressing? Paula will get something to drink for you while I'm gone."

Nancy aimed a gentle smile at me. She passed close enough to brush her hair lightly against me as she walked out of the den. In a few minutes Paula came into the den.

"Can I get you something to drink? Perhaps a light snack to go with it?"

Paula was about twenty five years old. She had an unassuming honesty to her face.

"A cold beer and a small sandwich, ham if you've got it," I asked.

"We do," Paula paused. "I'll be right back."

I glanced around the den, again thinking back to what this house had looked like several years before. The sense of a man living in the house was gone, even the curtains in the room seemed less substantial. Antique, almost unusable chairs had replaced his Naugahyde recliners. The fireplace in the den, minus the heavy brass tool set, seemed functional. Two display cases still stood on either side of the fireplace, along with the wall of books. There were more trophies for rifle matches, the more recent ones bore the inscription, Nancy Satterwhite. I remembered that she told me that she had been the first girl in her high school ROTC to win in rifle competition; I thought a

81

female in a high school ROTC was unusual enough. There was no sight of anything in the display cases belonging to Brian Fowler.

In the second case, figurines of glass and porcelain partially hid a small gold picture frame outlining a photograph of Nancy, Brian, Becky, and an older man. I vaguely recognized the gold frame from my visit several years ago, but I didn't remember that picture in it.

Paula brought my sandwich and beer as Nancy entered the den, dressed in a satin, scarlet evening gown with a deep V cut in the back. Nancy stood about five feet nine inches tall in her high heels.

"That dress makes you look quite beautiful." I couldn't help but notice as I scanned Nancy from her head to her feet.

"For a woman my age?" Nancy teased.

"For a woman of any age, you are very beautiful" I answered, and God, she was beautiful.

"Paula, take his food into the dining room. Let's talk there while you eat," Nancy glanced at me speculatively. "I like what you say."

A Queen Anne table greeted me as I walked in; I don't know if it was a reproduction, but I do know it looked expensive. Along both sides of the expansive dining room stood old sideboards, one of which had an ornate Victorian silver service on top of it. This room felt several hundred thousand dollars better than it had when I was here before.

"Aren't you going to have anything?" I asked.

"No, I'm going out to dinner. I have some time before I have to leave, and you can stay here as long as you like. You could spend the night in the guest room if you haven't checked into a hotel yet."

Nancy sat next to me, perched on the edge of one of the chairs.

"Thank you, but I already have. When's the last time you saw your sister?"

Nancy paused, staring at the fireplace, then she looked at me and said, "Months ago, I guess. I visited Marcia and several friends at the same time; it was less than a year ago."

"How was she then? Was Becky all right?" I asked.

"Marcia seemed tired but Becky was fine. As a matter of fact, she was supposed to come out here and visit me this Summer; we were going to spend a week at Panama Beach. I own a summer place on the beach there. The kid was so looking forward to that. Marcia didn't act like her usual self, but her work life has gotten worse since she took that job in immigration," Nancy answered.

"What about her job bothered her?"

"She didn't like dealing with the mass of Mexican immigrants, she was especially bothered by the children, the thousands of poor children she had to order back to abject poverty in Mexico. She said she felt like the Queen of Hearts, randomly sentencing innocents to death," Nancy said.

"Do you think Becky's disappearance had anything to do with Marcia's work?" I wondered out loud.

"No, I don't think so. She kept her two worlds far apart. She would tell strangers that she still worked at a radio station, and most of the people at work didn't know she had a child," Nancy answered.

"Don't you think that's a little unusual?"

"You have to remember that my sister and I were raised by a man who considers himself a soldier of fortune and who's paranoid as hell. Daddy still trains would be mercenaries for a living. I took the whole thing with a grain of salt, but Marcia took it as gospel. She's not all that bad, she just takes everything very seriously, and when it comes to protecting Becky, she's even more serious than usual."

"I just have to ask another question," I hesitated, but I had to know.

"What," Nancy seemed willing to talk.

"Is your sister rich?" I paused. "I know it seems strange, but she owns a house on the beach at Malibu and an expensive Mercedes which doesn't correlate to a mid level government job."

"I know," Nancy laughed. "Our dad is a multi-millionaire and gives both of us expensive things like houses and cars. Marcia resents it and pretends not to accept them even though she takes everything. She has always had a job."

"I guess I understand," I replied, but didn't quite believe her.

"I, on the other hand, like being rich." Nancy threw me a playful glance.

"If you hear from Becky at all, please give me a call." I handed her one of my business card.

Nancy looked at her watch. "Well, I have to go now, but don't rush your food. Paula will get you more if you like," Nancy said. "Will you be staying here long?"

"No, I'm leaving in the morning."

"I remember, the last time you were here, you ate dinner and ran away; I didn't even get to know anything about you," Nancy said.

"You've got to leave in a few minutes, so I guess there's not enough time now either." I kept my eyes on Nancy's face.

"You've got time to tell me about yourself, I've been curious since we first met," Nancy insisted. "You've been asking me questions ever since you came in here, and that's all you did the first time we met, and I've got questions about you."

"All right," I replied, not imagining what they would be.

"Where are you from, where, and how did you grow up?" Nancy asked, smiling.

"A bland way to start," I said, with some irony.

"I know, but that's the kind of question I really like to ask. It tells me about a person." Nancy lowered her head then looked up at me. "I just want to know."

"Well, all right. I grew up on my family's farm in Pennsylvania, it's a little north and west of Gettysburg; the farm has been in my family since 1797."

"That's a long time, who's on it now?"

"Not me, I couldn't stand the isolation, but my brother and his family are running it now; they're raising twelve kids on it." I really didn't want to go back there, that's not the quiet place for pleasant dreams for me.

"Twelve?"

"My sister-in-law didn't have all of them, they adopted ten children."

"Why did you leave?"

Leave? The image slid back into my waking life. I was six years old. The blood stained sheet over that lump on the floor; that lump was my mother. I saw my father cry for the first and last time in his life. I looked at my brother's face; the horror and shock was the same as I had on mine, but I couldn't see it in myself, nor could I feel it. I didn't feel anything at first. Leave. Nothing would ever be the same again. Leave. I was six years old, and all I wanted to do was leave, then and there.

"Earth to Benjamin."

"Sorry," I began again. "Memories have a way of stepping in and taking over."

"Well?" Nancy asked again. "Why did you leave the family farm?"

"The first reason was that I didn't like farm life, but the main reason is that I decided to be an all American hero and duck bullets in Vietnam."

And I never felt safe at home again; I had to leave. I enlisted in the Marines when I was seventeen.

"Why don't you plan to come back to my place tonight, and stay longer than an hour this time; plan to spend at least the whole evening. Atlanta has a lot to offer, and I want you to tell me more."

Nancy rose, leaned over me then lightly, slowly, touched my cheek with her left hand; she softly kissed my other cheek.

"I may just do that. I won't keep you, Nancy, except to thank you for your hospitality," I managed an embarrassed smile for her benefit.

Paula came into the dining room after Nancy left. "Can I get you anything else, sir?" Paula asked.

"You can stop calling me sir, and call me Benjamin." I gulped down the sandwich. "Did you know Brian Fowler?"

"I came here while they were getting their divorce, it was not a friendly divorce."

"I understand that Mr. Fowler was fooling around, and that's why she divorced him." I finished my sandwich and stood up.

"That's what the reason was all right. Do you know that he made more than one pass at me, one of them right in front of Miss Satterwhite," Paula held her hand over her mouth.

"Was that Marcia, or Nancy Satterwhite?" I asked.

"Oh, it was in front of Nancy. Mr. Fowler wouldn't even come into the same room with Marcia Satterwhite," Paula said.

"Why?"

"I don't know, but those two avoided each other like they each had the plague." Paula hesitated, looking troubled. "I don't mean to pry, but what's happening about Becky?"

"Marcia says she's missing, kidnapped. I don't know where she is, although I feel good about finding her. Since I never met Becky, could you please give me a little idea as to what she's like?" I asked.

"She's a lovely child. She's so bright, she acts almost like an adult." Paula smiled. "She's God's gift to this family, I can tell you that; she isn't like the rest of them."

"When's the last time you saw her?"

"Thanksgiving week, she and her mother came here for a visit; Becky was so happy and beautiful. Please find her! I pray that she's all right."

"Me too, and I'll do my best to find her. Do you know where Mr. Fowler is now?" I asked, as I put down my empty beer glass.

"Yes, he's in San Francisco," Paula said. "I can give you his address if you like, it's in Miss Satterwhite's address book; I type a lot of letters, and mail them for her."

"That would be a help."

When fate sometimes smiles at me, my policy is to cooperate with it as long as it lasts.   Paula returned with the address written on a small piece of stationery.

"Just between you and me, I think someone who knew Becky took her; I think some relative took her to get her away from her mother," I told her in a confidential voice. "Do you think I could have a look at Miss Satterwhite's address book, to copy down a few addresses?"

Paula thought for a few seconds, then said. "Do you really think some one of Miss Satterwhite's relatives took Becky? I don't know. . ."

"I don't know for sure myself, but I have my suspicions, and a list of names, but no addresses." As I relaxed my shoulders, I consciously avoided holding my breath.

"I guess it would be all right, if I stand over you while you do it. Becky is such a sweet girl, I don't want anything bad to happen to her."

"Great. Neither do I, and this will definitely help a lot."

Feeling that I wouldn't have enough time to copy the whole book, I leafed through it quickly, writing an occasional address down in the notebook I always carry in my coat pocket.

There was Brian's address in San Francisco. There were a lot of Fowlers in Boston. There were also two names under 'Investigators. 'George Sterling, with a note. 'West coast', and Fred Lepus with the note, 'East coast'.

Lepus!   I thought I would scream right then.

Marcia's married name was Peterson, so I turned to that page; there it was, Marcia and Phil Peterson. Those names and the address had been crossed out, and Phil Peterson with a Chicago address was written underneath; I quickly copied the address down. There was another Chicago address for an M. and P.   Peterson. That must have been Marcia's in-laws.

Underneath 'S. 'was the North Carolina address of their father, Z.   Satterwhite. Florence Satterwhite had the Gordon Drive address in Naples, but the phone number was different than the one I had; I wrote that down.   Also there was Richard Snively, with a Miami address crossed out.   How the hell did she know to cross him out?   Maybe she had just dropped him from her Christmas list.

Behind me, Paula was acting nervous, having second thoughts about letting me read her boss' private address book. I closed the book and handed it back.

"You've been more help than I can say." I stood up.

"You're welcome, I just want to help Becky," Paula said, staring at the floor, and looking somewhat flustered.

"I think you have," I smiled at her.   "I need to call a cab to take me back to my hotel."

"No." Paula smiled back at me.   "Ms. Satterwhite took the Jaguar, so the Mercedes and driver are still here."

"Thank you."

A Mercedes and driver?   She wasn't kidding about being rich; how much money did their father have and how much did Marcia have?

12

A rolling stone

Within thirty minutes I was back in my hotel room trying to reach Cassandra on the phone. It was too late to call Florence Satterwhite; I would try the next day.

"Benjamin, no one but you manages to interrupt me like this," she declared.

"You interrupt my thoughts at the oddest moments yourself."

"I'm sorry, I was taking a cat nap. Oh," she said in a mischievous, bright tone. "This is Benjamin, isn't it?"

"Not a Katz nap? It's me, you catty girl, you. What did you find out about Marcia's husband?"

"He's a lawyer in Chicago; I think they were married for about three years, and got a divorce not long ago. Marcia already had Becky when they got married, and, I don't think Marcia ever had a job in Chicago."

"What about Brian Fowler? Did Marcia report the missing child to the police?"

"Wait a minute, why the big hurry?" Cassandra asked. "What was that about me interrupting you? You didn't expect me to let that one slide by, did you?"

"I want to get it all together and get home."

"Get what together, and get to whose home?"

"When I'm tired, my mouth works on automatic too much; bad jokes and worse innuendos. I didn't mean anything special," I sighed. "The longer I'm stuck in this case, the more nervous I get. Already the Miami cops have me down as a possible in an active murder case and someone in Los Angeles wants me dead. The bank owns everything but my shorts, and you give me a hard time about having the hots for you, which you know I do."

"Okay, already, no more sad stories. Brian Fowler is in San Francisco, but the university he works for hasn't seen him in a week, they don't know where he is. If they don't see him in a few days, they'll fire him since he's only an adjunct instructor and no one likes him anyway. The cops don't have any report of Becky as a missing child either."

"Shit, I knew this was beginning to sound fishy," I scanned over all that had happened in the last two days. "I want out now!"

"Me too, write it all up, come back here, and let's drop this client fast."

"That means we give the money back to her," I pointed out. Genuine disappointment.

"To every silver lining, there's a black cloud, but let's get out from under it while we're still dry," Cassandra said.

"Well said; I'll see you tomorrow afternoon, Bye."

I used the plane trip back to Los Angeles to write a lengthy report of everything I had done and had discovered in the past several days. The funny feeling that had begun to bother me in the pit of my stomach grew.

I always made it a practice to cooperate with the police, and I didn't plan to make an exception in this case. If they asked me about the murder in Miami, or the disappearance of the child, I could produce a complete file, with all the information I knew and all the people involved. The one thing I was missing was a signed agreement between my agency and Marcia Satterwhite. I had to see Marcia to get her to sign one, then I'd drop her faster than a bird drops a plastic worm.

My only real problem was sweet Cassandra. She had a bad habit of telling me, 'I told you so, I told you always to get the client to sign a contract first!' I hated to hear her nag like that, it always digs at me, especially when she's right.

13

Lost in my work

I arrived in Los Angeles at noon. The first thing I did
was call Florence Satterwhite's real phone number.

"Hello, Satterwhite residence," I recognized the
Hispanic servant's voice.

"Hi. I'm the gentleman who came to visit the house
yesterday, the one who works for her daughter," I paused. "Is
Ms. Satterwhite at home?"

"She was due in late last night, but she hasn't come here
yet," The voice on the other end of the phone sounded worried.
"I do not know where she is now; maybe you can call later
today?"

"I will, thank you."

That was strange. But, this whole affair was getting
strange.

Trundling to my Porsche in long term parking, I had
visions of dents but the car appeared okay when I got to it. It
seemed to take as long to get from the airport to my office as it
had taken to fly from one coast to the other. It wasn't that far a
drive over 105 and up 110 to get downtown and near my office,
but it took almost ninety minutes. The wide expanses of
pavement might as well have been a mall parking lot. My
Porsche can accelerate from zero to ten miles an hour in the
blink of an eye, which it did countless times until I passed the
accidents near the race track and then near the coliseum. At
times like this I wish I had an automatic transmission.

The office was locked. Cassandra had left a note on my
desk, saying that she was out at the target range, like I asked her
to do with annoying regularity; she hated to practice because it

91

made too much noise. I grabbed a contract from the file, typed Marcia's name on it, then headed out.

She had just acquired a position on the firing line when I joined her. Ah, the distinctive smell of smokeless powder and the loud booms of an indoor shooting range, nothing quite like it.

"Are you going to see her today?" Cassandra asked.

She lifted one muff of her ear protectors to hear my answer. She wore foam inserts in addition to the ear muffs, a habit she acquired from me.

"I'm seeing Marcia, yes."

I already had foam plugs in my ears as I reached for the second pair of protectors which she had hung next to the shooting bench. I guess she hoped I would meet her there.

"Did you get a contract signed while I was away?"

I knew a frontal attack might work. No, I truly didn't, but I tried it anyway.

"You mean you didn't get her to sign anything! You idiot, what if she accuses us of something?"

No surprise, Cassandra is very consistent; that's one of the many reasons I love her. She took aim and fired five shots at the combat target positioned twelve yards away. She put the pistol down on the bench, then pressed the return button to bring the target back to her.

"I am impressed," I looked at the closely spaced holes in the center of her target.

"You should be; after lots of practice, I'm not so bad anymore."

"You were never bad," I could tell she wanted to show off a little bit. "You just need to be consistent in difficult situations."

That wasn't quite the praise she was looking for, but her criticism wasn't the response I was looking for either.

Cassandra glared back at me, "Anything involving you can turn into several difficult situations," She paused. "Whether or not the cases require firearms, they're still difficult."

She fired two more clips, with the same results.

Looking closely at the targets, I said, "Well, you're damned good. How often have you been coming out here to practice?"

"Not that often," Turning to me, she asked, "Do you want to try it before we go?"

Sending the target out to its maximum of twenty five yards, I placed five large holes within a two inch radius in the center of the target's head.

"Even with plugs and earmuffs, that gun of yours could kill anybody's hearing," She complained.

"Wait till you hear me shoot a forty four magnum with three hundred grain hunting loads," I teased her. "This is a whisper compared to that."

"No thanks," She took off her eye protectors and checked the target as I pulled it from the carrier. "That's really good shooting, though."

"I spend a lot of time here."

"I guess it's better than time spent in other nefarious places." She gave me one of her looks that made me wish we were intimate again. She could try to be flip with me, but her looks always gave her away. Cassandra's been my best friend ever since the first week we met.

"Now, if I could only talk you into joining me at the gym," I said.

I emptied my revolver into my left palm and stuffed the empty shells into my coat pocket.

"You mean that marshal arts place you go to three times a week?"

"That's the place," I nodded. "You'd like it."

"Maybe later. "I still don't see why you take so much time out of your week for this stuff."

"It keeps me in shape, the gym as well as the time here at the range," I paused, considering saying more; hell, why not. "You know, there are two female instructors at the gym I go to; learning some close quarter combat moves couldn't hurt in our line of work."

"I suppose you're right, it sounds logical, and it might even be fun," Cassandra paused to think. "Maybe I'll join you there if I take fewer classes next quarter."

"How much longer do you have?"

I always wondered how she could be a full-time student plus work for the agency.

"At the rate I'm going, it'll be at least two more years." She shrugged her shoulders. "If I had opted to stop at the Masters, I'd be done, but like an idiot I chose to plod on."

"You might as well do it right."

I didn't know what else to say. She was really good at academia and I did want her to finish.

"Is Marcia at work or at home today?" I asked as we made our way out to the lot.

"She said yesterday that she's taken a week off from work. She was too upset to do her job, at least that's what she told me," Cassandra shook her head. "Although her boss didn't know about any vacation."

"According to her sister, their father gives both of them a lot of money so she doesn't have to work at all," I said. "Judging by her sister, Marcia should have a ton of money."

"I suppose that explains the car and the house on the beach," Cassandra said. "But, that still doesn't explain all of it."

"All of what?"

"Something else is going on with that woman," Cassandra insisted. "I still think she's dealing drugs."

"You may be right; I guess I'll go talk to her. I'll get her to sign the contract, then dump her."

"Good luck, you'll need it; she's unstable," Cassandra shook her head.

"She didn't seem that bad to me, a little whacked out, but not so bad I can't reason with her," I paused to think back, to double check.

"Maybe not," Cassandra sounded doubtful. "When she talked to you, she might have been semi-rational, but when I saw her she alternated between crying and shouting, or kept her lips squeezed shut so tightly that I thought she would gag any minute.

Her arms were tightly crossed on her chest almost the whole time. That woman has some serious problems, more than just losing her child."

I stopped walking and looked back at Cassandra. "Do you think she knows who kidnapped her daughter?"

"Hell yes, don't you?"

"Well said," I agreed.

"There's more than one thing we're not getting out of her, I think she knew about that murder in Miami, maybe more."

"Murders? In the plural?"

That should have rung bells in my head at the time.

"Ah, you've been reading too may cheap detective novels again." I continued. "She's afraid of something, and she lost her daughter but I don't think she'll cause lot of trouble for us, just enough trouble to get us to walk away from her."

"Well, be careful." Cassandra folded her bare arms across her chest and stared at me. "Besides, I've never read any of those dumb detective novels in my life, they're stupid."

"If they're so dumb, why are you a detective?" I didn't wait for the answer.

14

This is where I left off

So, all that brings me to the body in the kitchen.   I guess it's not all my fault, at least the dead woman in front of me isn't my fault.

"Well, as I live and breathe, Mr. Katz, what brings you here?" As he spoke, Lieutenant Mark Hatton pushed open the kitchen door and stood in the doorway; he grinned, but the smile didn't reach the rest of his face.

Not having any time to think, I reacted. I spun around and pointed my revolver at his head.

"Drop that gun, now! Just a damn minute, Benjamin! That's one dead body in front of you; how would you explain a dead cop on the floor?" Mark blanked out his grin and held up both hands toward me.   I lowered the pistol.

"Mark, how long have you been here?"

"About ten minutes; we parked at the end of the block and were waiting for the coroner and the lab boys to arrive." Mark's partner came in at that moment

"Yeah, you'll have to move your car from out front to make room for all of them." the partner said to me as he glanced around the kitchen.

Like a good cop, he was taking note of where everything was, and why it might be there, everything is a clue.

Mark had been waiting there long enough to know damn well I didn't do it. The son of a bitch was playing one of his jokes on me. I ought to have socked his jaw off, but he's a cop and there was a corpse on the kitchen floor, so I just played real friendly and counted to ten. I sighed a bit when I remembered that I hadn't cleaned my pistol since the shooting range, and now I stood over a dead woman, with a recently fired gun.

"I'm working for Marcia Satterwhite; she said her daughter, Becky, was missing. She hired my firm to find her," I said, waiting, willing myself not to flinch.

"You used to work for her, as you see. She was shot maybe eighteen to twenty four hours ago. I was half expecting to see you," Mark Hatton paused, staring into my grim visage with a bland, half smile. "Your name was prominently displayed on her refrigerator door and Cassandra called me and told me most of the story yesterday;that's why we came out here today when she didn't answer her phone."

My eyes snapped to the left, and saw my business card on the dingy tan refrigerator door, held on by a butterfly shaped magnet.

"I have a complete report of everything I've found out so far. Before you ask, when we go downtown, you can copy it and have your own; some of it might be interesting reading."

"I'll bet it is, most of what you get involved in turns out to be interesting reading to us," Mark grinned wickedly. "I enjoyed that little report you gave us about the shooting a few nights ago, although I do wish you'd come to some conclusion about it."

"Forget the damned shooting, how was Marcia shot?" I asked.

"With a pistol, about a thirty eight caliber.   She was shot four times in the head from a moderate distance."

"No powder burns?"

"Nope, but we'll have to wait for the report. Whoever did it knew what he was doing."

"Any ideas who that might be?" I asked.

"Your second sketchy short story might tell us something, Benjamin," Mark watched me. "I think the man who shot at you, and this murder might have something in common."

"It might, although a man with a shotgun was after me, and this was a pistol shooting as far as I can see. What about the kid, Becky? My partner tells me Marsha never reported her child missing to the cops, why not? And why did she hire me instead?"

"I don't know the answer to any of that, but I'll find out as soon as I can," Mark answered.

"You did notice that torn corner of a page gripped in her hand."

"Yes, we both saw it right away," Mark replied. "The lab boys will take care of it."

"I don't suppose you'll share any answers with me, will you?" I already knew his reply, but I always ask my cop friends anyway.

"I don't suppose I have to. This is now an official murder investigation and you're out of it." Mark's smile faded again.

"Well, if I'm out of it, at least you can throw me a few tidbits to satisfy my curiosity," I probed. "Like, where did you pick up that awful cologne?"

"I suppose I could tell you something, maybe some time in the future, that is," Mark relaxed a little. "Oh, the cologne is from my new girlfriend, you'll have to meet her; this woman may be the one."

"I'd like to have dinner with both of you soon, but please don't use that stuff when we go out together," I made a sour expression. "Normal people don't smell like that."

I followed Mark to police headquarters where he read my report carefully, but asked no more that three or four questions.

"Do you have any idea where the child is?" I asked when it was my turn. "In her pictures she carries an innocence that I'll bet her mother never had, I'd like to know she's all right."

"If somebody reports her missing, we'll find her. If I need her for our investigation, we'll find her," Mark answered.

"I feel some obligation to find her, though."

"Benjamin," Mark was friendly but frank. "It sounds to me like the girl's with some of her relatives. It looks to me like this Satterwhite woman was into drugs, maybe dealing; the murder has the feel of a drug deal gone bad. Maybe the girl's relatives knew what her mother was doing and took her away for the girl's own good; she's probably better off now anyway. There's been no kidnapping demands, nor have there been any reports of her running around this city in the past few days. Just let it go for now, okay."

"Look," I objected. "If the family refuses to file a missing person's report on the kid, why don't I?"

"No, you can't but we might do that, anyway. I just want you to let it go."

I paused for a few seconds, looking at my friend. Somehow, I felt that the girl still needed someone to see after her best interests, but maybe my pal was right.

"Listen, " I added. "Marcia's mother lives in Naples, Florida. She was supposed to get back home last night, but she's missing. I have a funny feeling about that, could you check on that? I have the address and phone number."

"I will."

"Mark, I have a stupid question."

"I'm used to them, go on," Mark smiled.

"When you find out who's the official next of kin, let me know. Marcia Satterwhite left me with at least five thousand in cash as a retainer."

"You and all of her creditors will find out as soon as I know, I'll be in touch as soon as I find out."

"And," I thought of one last item, trivial, but I had to ask. "Could you turn in all the books to the library. I noticed a number of them under the kid's bed."

. . . .

When I arrived back at my office to pick up my luggage, Cassandra was still there, waiting.

"Guess what happened?" I asked innocently.

"Marcia was killed, and I was the last one to see her alive," Cassandra said, with a dazed look on her face.

Mark Hatton was at the murder scene before I got there," I sighed. "He played one of his little jokes on me by letting me find the body."

"Sounds like you had a harder time than I did," Cassandra relaxed a little.

"That just scratched the surface," I replied.

"What's going on?" She pulled up a chair next to me. "You seem to be taking this worse than you usually do."

"It's just that that whole scene reminded me of my mother," I sighed. "I don't like being reminded."

"Your mother?" She asked.

"I never told you."

"What?"

"She was killed."

"Murdered?" Cassandra touched my arm.

"That's what the police said," I kept staring at her.

How much do I tell, how much do I want to relive?

"I looked at all the police files, and it wasn't much to go on. I even tried to go over some of the details, later, with my father, and some of the people who were around at the time and knew about it. Her death never did make any sense. Not much was stolen, and no one saw anything strange. I know we were isolated, out on a farm, but no one saw anything."

"When did it happen?"

"I was six."

"I'm so sorry," Cassandra put her hand on my face and began to gently stroke me.

"Most of the time, I keep it hidden, even from myself. But, seeing that woman lying dead in her own blood on her kitchen floor just sort of all brought it all back," I couldn't believe I was telling her, I must love her.

"Who found your mother?" Cassandra asked.

"Me," I couldn't say anything else.

"Benjamin," Cassandra kissed me. "Why didn't you tell me before."

"I guess I still haven't sorted it all out myself," I sighed again. "I can't believe I'm telling you."

"I'm glad you are," She was now holding me with both her arms. "I love you, if you haven't noticed by now."

"I've noticed," I kissed her back.

"Any time you need to talk something like this through with me, please just do it."

"Okay," I fell into silence.

I was torn three ways, between wanting to tell the woman I loved everything, my strong sense of emotional isolation, and my sworn obligation not to tell civilians about my secret life as a spy.

15

Family ties

The week before Marcia hired me, Fred Lupus took Becky away from her mother.   Becky went willingly.   Although she felt some obligation to her mother, she was afraid of her as well.

"It's all really green here," Becky looked at Fred who was busy negotiating the narrow gravel road. "Not like Maywood at all."

"Yeah, yeah," Fred slowed the rental car down as he approached an almost one hundred and eighty degree switchback in the road as it negotiated a steep grade.   "Are you sure we're on the right road?"

"74 to 226 to Polkville, then take the fifth right turn on a gravel road," Becky glanced at a map and some written directions. "This must be the right road. How far since we left the paved road?"

"Six miles."

"Then, we'll get there in another eight miles."

"Why does he live so dammed far away from anything?"

"I don't know," Becky looked back down at the map.

"Shouldn't be too much longer," Fred paused. "It's real pretty out there."

The higher elevation took the edge off the warm and humid early summer day. The temperature had fallen at least five degrees since they began driving up the gravel road. Firs and hemlocks lined the road. Deep and lighter green leaves enveloped the seldom used road more and more as they climbed to what Fred Lepus knew would be certain trouble.

....

"Why in holy hell did you bring that bastard here!" The older man snapped, outrage in his voice. Just under six feet tall, he looked to be in exceptional physical shape for a man of his age. He brushed the short white peppered hairs of his crew cut with the palm of his right hand.

"Don't shout so loud," Fred insisted in a loud whisper. "She can hear every word you say."

"I don't give a shit if she can read my mind, it's the same message, get the hell out of my life."

"But, she's your granddaughter and you have the resources to take care of her."

Zeb shrugged his broad shoulders, then walked to the blonde wooden desk in the back of the room.

"I still want to know what you're up to, bringing that kid here," Zeb sat down in a wooden desk chair, which rocked as he moved his frame in it.

Fred Lepus' eyes darted around the Spartan office, nervousness increasing every second.   He glanced at Zeb, then at Becky. The thirteen year old girl's fine features appeared pinched, her wide eyes seemed to understand more than Zeb had said so far. Becky stood staring at the two adults with her hands folded behind her back.

"Look, kid, why don't you wait in the car," Fred was adamant.

"I don't want to be alone," Becky kept a careful focus on Fred. "I want to stay here with you and my grandpa."

"You ain't no kin of mine," Zeb tilted his body in the wooden chair so he could see Becky clearly. "Just get the hell off my place with this two bit detective, and stay away from me, now!"

"Please try to contain yourself for a minute," Fred looked back at Becky and insisted with his expression that she leave.

"No, he hates me just like Mama does. I can sit down here and wait 'til you're through."

Becky sat in a metal folding chair next to the front door and slowly crossed her legs, her eyes moved from Fred to settle on the older man.

"You have nothing to say to me, slime ball." Zeb glared at Fred. "Get back down the road and out of here before I have some of my boys use the two of you for target practice."

"The two of us are not through with you, not by a long shot," Fred retorted.

With a burst of speed, the detective gathered Becky up, and carried her out the door. He shoved her into his rental car and slammed into it himself. Gunning the car more than necessary, he blasted down the road away from Zeb.

"Where are we going now?" Becky asked.

"To Florida," Fred replied, the complete, solemn, private investigator.

"Who? " Becky asked. Dr. Snively or my grandma?"

"Much to my dismay, your grandmother," Fred answered.

"She hates me too," Becky observed, "Why not go to my Aunt Nancy?"

"Your Aunt's part of the problem."

. . . .

"Is Ms. Satterwhite at home?" Fred asked in his most formal tone.

"Who may I say is calling?" The maid responded from behind a half open front door.

"My name is Fred Lupus, and I'm accompanying her granddaughter, Becky, here for a visit with her grandmother."

"You are Madam's granddaughter?" The maid opened the door a bit more and smiled at Becky.

"Yes, I am," Becky quietly replied.

"Come in and wait in the parlor." They were ushered into the foyer.

"So, that's what the abomination looks like after thirteen years!" Florence stormed in from the side room.

"Please," Fred insisted. "She's right here and that's not a nice thing to say to your own granddaughter."

"Just because she dropped out of my daughter, doesn't mean she has to be related to me."

"Well, I think that's the definition of related to you," Fred interjected.

"Shut the fuck up, you sniveling weasel!" Florence shouted.

"At least take into consideration there's a kid here, will ya?"

"Who put you up to this?" Florence demanded. "That whore daughter of mine?"

"Just what is your problem?" Fred asked. "I came here for some help, but I can see this trip was a bust."

"I live by God's plan, and this abomination is not part of that plan!"

"Not very Christian of you, is it?" Fred observed.

"Get the fuck out of here right now, or I'll have you both shot within the hour!"

. . . .

"Where are we going?" Becky asked after a long silence in the car.

"To Washington, you'll be all right there," Fred paused. "I'm really sorry I put you through all this; I didn't know they were both that bad."

"Why can't I go to daddy's house now? He wants me there."

"Like I said before, your step-father asked me to keep you on ice for a while. While the heat's still up, you need to be nowhere until it's safe."

"What are you talking about, Mr. Lepus?"

"Your old man thinks it ain't safe for you to be in Chicago with him right now, so he's paying me to keep you under wraps for a while."

"So," Becky paused. "Daddy wants me to live with him after everybody calms down."

"You got it, kid."

"Who lives in Washington?"

"Me."

"Will I live with you?"

"No way, kid," Fred shook his head. "I was hoping your grandfather or grandmother would look after you, but, well, you were there."

"I'm used to it, don't feel bad, they all treat me like that."

"A kid ain't supposed to be treated like that," Fred looked at Becky in the front seat next to him. "I'm gonna find someone you can live with who'll treat you right."

"Why can't I live with you?"

"That ain't right, besides I lead a very dangerous life and I can't have a kid tripping me up all the time, and maybe getting hurt."

Becky swallowed, "Who do I go with then?"

"I think I know a broad who's just the right one to look after you."

"What's a broad?"

16

The tie that binds

A little over a year went by, but in all that time, Marcia Satterwhite's murder remained unsolved. Cassandra and I calculated the final refund of money for the heirs of Marcia's estate to be twenty five hundred dollars. I said I would feel guilty padding our expenses more than that, and Cassandra said she refused to return any more than that.

Legal heirs were as hard to pin down as suspects in Marcia's murder. She left no will, or so everyone thought for months. The Probate court was dividing her estate among her daughter and all her close relatives when Phil Peterson, her ex-husband, produced a will which seemed to be written in Marcia's handwriting. This will left everything to her daughter, Becky. In the event that Becky were also to die, all the money would be left to her sister, Nancy.

Marcia's estate turned out to be more substantial than Cassandra or I ever could have guessed. She owned three houses and two apartment complexes in Los Angeles, six houses and eight buildings in Atlanta, twelve huge bank accounts as well as a large stock portfolio. Her exact net worth at the time of her death was six million three hundred thousand dollars, give or take a few ten thousand; quite a bundle of money for just a working stiff, bad pun.

I informed each member of the Satterwhite family that I wanted to wait until the court decided who would get the money before I paid what I owed Marcia. That was a transparent ploy to stay involved in the Satterwhite family's business long enough to satisfy my curiosity about Becky's whereabouts and to perhaps discover who killed Marcia.

As it turned out, I received a year of interest from the money before I had to write a check to the estate at the final reading of the will. No one objected to the wait, since it was such a small sum of money compared to the millions at stake.

107

Between Phil Peterson, Nancy, and Zeb, there were three legal claims and one lawsuit for Marcia's millions. The probate judge assigned to the case appointed an attorney to try to settle this matter out of court if possible.

For a few weeks, the police considered Nancy, her mother and Zeb Satterwhite suspects in Marcia's murder. Money seemed like a good motive for murder to them and to me. It seemed adequate until the police uncovered the fact that Nancy was worth more than her sister, her mother was worth more than either daughter, and her father was worth more than all of them put together. Marcia, it turned out, was the poorest member of the Satterwhite family. The relatives by marriage were all out of the running for the money except for Marcia's ex-husband, Phil Peterson. The will did not directly mention him but he forced his way in by lawsuit.

No one ever located Brian Fowler. He lost his teaching job in San Francisco, as well as any chance for obtaining another one.

Mark Hatton felt Brian was still alive, but had gone underground for some reason. After searching for him for six months, Mark gave up because he no longer considered Brian Fowler a suspect.

Neither Mark nor the Miami police could make any solid connection between the murder of Richard Snively and Marcia, other than that they knew each other and had mutual friends, and, one assumed, mutual enemies. Mark also abandoned the idea of a tie-in between Marcia's murder and the stranger who had tried to dismember me with a twelve gauge.

The Miami police finally attributed Snively's murder to his sexual preference, mainly because of the target of one of the shotgun blasts. He had been shot twice from point blank range, while Marcia was shot six times from a distance of about thirty feet. A shotgun killed Snively, and a nine millimeter handgun killed Marcia Satterwhite. Both murders remained unsolved.

Florence Satterwhite did fly first class to Los Angles and back to Naples. The airline confirmed her arrival at Naples, but no one had seen her since then. Her mansion was empty and her personal banker was left to take care of all her financial obligations. The police in Naples handled the missing person's case, but it was now a cold case.

My agency grew in the intervening months. I was dubious about expanding operations, but my partner convinced me it was the obvious thing to do. Our debt was gone and the number and quality of cases was way up. We took on two part-time investigators to handle more of the paperwork cases such as skip tracing, background checks and asset chasing. They were nice enough guys, though we hardly ever saw them.

Although Cassandra was now an official half owner and partner, she still had the outer office, and I had the private office, but we took turns answering the telephone.

. . . .

Years ago, I had met Mark Hatton as I left the Marines after my tours were up. We were both Lieutenants, but he outranked me as a first lieutenant. He was an MP, and I was, well, I was something else; we both mustered out in Long Beach. He was from Los Angeles, a city I had never visited. He tried for six months to get me to join the Los Angeles police force, but for several reasons, some beyond my control, I could not. I found a job as a private investigator with George Stirling's agency about three months after I left the Marines in 1973. The government insisted I stay in the reserves, but that's another story for another time; neither Cassandra nor any of my friends in Los Angeles knew I was still in the reserves. Mark and I have stayed friends for a little over five years now. Since he was married about six months ago, he, his wife Mary, Cassandra and I have been good friends.

It could be called serendipity that the four of us were at dinner together at Mark and Mary Hatton's home the night before the Satterwhite family crashed back into my life.

"Do either of you want more coffee?" Mary Hatton asked.

She poked her head around the corner of the kitchen as she leaned towards the rest of us in the dining room; all three of us shook our heads. Mary cooks a great spaghetti dinner, though I wish she'd use less cilantro. I like the smell of the sauce and the garlic bread. That aroma remains long after the meal, and I find it agreeable.

"I don't think I could hold even one more ounce," Cassandra smiled as she stood. "Do you need some help?"

"No, thanks," Mary replied, walking back into the dining room. "We'll do all the dishes later."

"Something to make him feel useful, I suppose," I teased.

"Speaking of useless," Mark looked at me. "I heard today that those strange Satterwhites are back in town, have you heard why?"

"You have better sources that I do," I replied, thinking he just wanted to pump me for information. "What do you think they're here for?"

"Something about the murdered woman's will," Mark said, glancing at Cassandra with a grin.

"Something about it," Cassandra grinned at me; I knew what she was up to. "It all boils down to Benjamin never getting that woman to sign a contract with our agency."

"Not that again," I sighed.

"Now, who's useless," Mark laughed out loud. "I love bringing that up again and seeing your expression."

"Very funny," I nodded. "Is that all this was about?"

"Pretty much," Mark continued to smile. "I don't have that much to tease you about, other than your continually being shot at around town."

"That's not very funny," Cassandra shot me a loving glance. "I never know when he won't duck."

"Did you guys ever decide who shot the Satterwhite woman?" I was changing the subject, for obvious reasons.

"No," Mark answered. "But, I still think it had to do with a drug deal gone bad."

"Her blood work showed nothing other than booze, right?" Cassandra asked.

"No, nothing," Mark agreed.

"And, as I remember her, there had to be lots of booze in her," Cassandra said.

"You were looking for her daughter, right?" Mary asked.

"Yeah, but we never found her," I answered.

"I feel sorry for that little girl," Mary shook her head. "A low life drunk for a mother and no father, I hope she's all right."

"We assume that some of her more stable relatives have been taking care of her," Mark said reassuringly.

"So, you know where the daughter is?" I asked.

"I can't say," Mark answered quickly.

"Is it still an open case?" Cassandra asked.

"Yes."

"I just hope the girl shows up to collect her mother's millions," Cassandra added.

"Are you guys still interested in a long weekend in Maui this August?" Mark stood up and motioned for us to follow him to the living room.

"It's January," I said. "That's the best time to speak of Maui."

We stood up and trundled to the comfy reclining chairs in the living room.

"I can speak for only myself, but I think the four of us in Hawaii for four or five days in August would be a blast," Cassandra said.

"Me too," Mary chimed in as she snuggled by Mark on the two seat sofa.

. . . .

The next morning I received a call from Nancy Satterwhite's lawyer.

The week before, I had called him. I meant just to inquire about the complex drama unfolding; I have to admit I still had some morbid curiosity about this strange case. The lawyer informed me that the final decision on the heirs to Marcia's fortune would be announced that morning in the court appointed attorney's office. I could have mailed the refund check that morning and been done with it, but I felt a little haunted by some unfathomable desire to see that family again. As the internal debate raged, I just sat, looking at Cassandra who had arrived at work and was busy putting her things away in her desk. Her auburn hair formed a wispy curtain behind her crisp profile as she leaned over to open a lower desk drawer. The short scene brought back the mental picture of the night, about three months before, when I had moved out of her apartment again, and we became just friends. At least that's what we told each other, but I never thought we could cool off to that level again. In the almost three years I had known her, our lives have always been entangled. We have always been close friends and most of the time close lovers.

"Benjamin," She had said that night. "This isn't working as I'd like it to, I can't go through another night without any sleep. Why screw up a good working friendship with a relationship?"

We had been discussing whether she should stay with the detective agency once she finally graduated from school. I wanted her to continue to work with me, and she wasn't sure. I didn't want us to drift apart because I'd be traveling a great deal and she might be working for some university somewhere, maybe not where I lived. That bothered me a lot, but I had trouble putting it into a simple declarative sentence, like, 'I would miss you so much I might explode'. When it comes to this level of emotional relationship, I get flustered. And inarticulate.

"I don't know," I answered her. "Sometimes I love you so much, and other times I could jump out a window. I guess I feel about our relationship the way I feel about Caster Oil."

"Just what the hell does THAT mean?"

"Medicine is only good for you if it makes you feel miserable while you're taking it. Don't get started again, intellectually I know that's stupid, but I can't help the way I feel. I keep thinking that we should be great lovers and never fight again, but it never works out that way, does it."

"No, and I guess it's no one's faul," She sighed. "Maybe we just need to arrange a way to have disagreements without so

112

much dramatics.   I've noticed that we're both the same, stubborn as hell; I'll never stop loving you, though."

As Cassandra walked into my office, my attention came back to the present. I shook my head a little and looked into her eyes. Only a small favor, I thought; small my ass, but I asked her anyway.

"Could you run this refund check by the lawyer's office for me?"

That was a rhetorical question; I knew I had to do it myself.

"No way José! That one was your screw up, not mine!" Her response was emphatic from her eyeballs to her feet. "I still remember how we got stuck with all that because you forgot to get her to sign a contract. I know Mark believed us, but he still teases you about it, like last night."

"All right, I could mail it, but I'll go down there."

"A glutton for punishment?"

"Yeah, yeah," I conceded.

She was right.   I just had to go down there in person. It must be intuition or masochism, perhaps both.

"Are you coming back?"

"I don't know when I'll be back, maybe later this afternoon. Are you going to be here for the rest of the day?"   I asked.

"I have to meet a dishonored bridegroom and tell him that his new bride was, and still is, a hooker," Cassandra looked disgusted.   "I know it's just a job, but sometimes we need to think about to drawing the line with some of these cases."

"You get all the fun cases.   All I get to do lately is catch the white collar criminal, stealing the office pens," I groused.

"Oh, you get all the high profile industrial cases, especially overseas investigations like that trip to Italy just recently."

"You mean looking for that embezzler?"

"Yeah." She sighed.   "I could have helped you find that guy, I even speak Italian."

"He stole over a million bucks from Chase Bank and tried to hide out in Italy," I shook my head. "I don't know what he was thinking because he was so easy to find, besides, that job wasn't that much fun."

If she only knew; on that trip I sat around a third class hotel for a week or so listening in on a Greek national talk about his deal with a Saudi arms merchant. The food was bad, and the accommodations made my apartment look like the Ritz. All that dweeb did was brag about how many women he slept with. He never did say anything I could believe the whole time I was there, what a bust.

"Ten days in Italy not fun?" Her expression was halfway between anger and disbelief. "Like hell."

"Back to the case at hand."

"I'll be here around two this afternoon. Bernie said he'd drop off the background checks for Boeing along with the billing sheets," She said. "He'll be here somewhere around eleven."

"Well, say hi to him for me," I sighed. "I'll probably be at the Satterwhite party then."

"Maybe you'll get to meet some of Marcia's rich relatives, there might even be a rich pretty one there, just for you," A sly grin slipped over her face.

"Thanks a lot, see you sometime this afternoon." I walked out the door.

17

Fit to be tied

The lawyer's office was decorated in the style necessary for the dispensing of millions of dollars. The wallpaper was a light seventeenth century French design on a strong blue background. Two chairs were heavy, wooden, and upholstered with leather. The rest of the chairs were less substantial, but all from the same period as the wallpaper. The waiting room floor was dark oak parquet; from the receptionist's desk back, a thick, lush carpet covered the floor.

To my left, I recognized Nancy, nobody else. She was seated next to a man in his mid sixties. On the opposite side of the room a younger man sat, dressed in a pin striped business suit, holding a briefcase. He was in his mid to late thirties, average height with short dark hair. With his lean muscular build, he looked like a ballet dancer dressed as a mobster.

I was about to speak to Nancy about the check for twenty five hundred dollars, when a second older man appeared in the waiting room and spoke, "Will you all please come into the conference room."

On him, expensive clothes seemed natural.

As I started to speak, he held my elbow, and directed me to the conference room adjacent to the waiting room. I gave up trying to say anything and went with the others into the large room and took a seat around a large highly polished oak conference table as he introduced himself.

"Good morning, my name is Mr. William Waters, the court appointed attorney. Besides the several motions and suits, there have been many other problems with this estate, and there continues to be more. The bulk of the Satterwhite estate was to go to Miss Satterwhite's young daughter, but she seemed to have disappeared. No one in her immediate family knew where she was. Miss Satterwhite's sister was then to receive the estate, but

115

this morning the court received a message from an investigator named Lepus in Washington DC, stating that the daughter, Becky, is alive and well. We all hate to postpone again, but the court felt that there was no choice but to examine the possibility that Becky is alive to claim the estate. Are there any questions?"

"Yes," Nancy asked. "Why haven't the police been able to find her before now? They've been looking for her for two years."

"I cannot answer that question, nor can I assume that the child Lepus claims to be Becky is in fact Becky, until we meet the child and check her finger prints. Nor do I know for a fact that the police have been looking for the child past the initial six months of their investigation into her mother's murder," William replied.

There was a moment of silence, then Nancy asked another question. "Will she be brought here?"

"Yes, that is my information at this time. The child should arrive here in a few days," William said.

After a few more moments of silence, William continued, "My secretary will be glad to assist you in any problems you might be having. Please feel free to contact this office at any time during normal business hours. We hope to be at a point where serious negotiation can begin in a few days, so I hope this small delay will not inconvenience any of you."

His secretary entered from the waiting room, while William disappeared through another door, at the same time. The act seemed to have been rehearsed and perfected over many such meetings so that now it was a polished military drill.

The other people seated around the table with me looked at each other as the secretary said, "You may wait and talk in here for a few minutes if you like; I'll be out at my desk."

The older man, still next to Nancy, spoke to her in a gravely, authoritative voice, "I know that twit over there is Marcia's jackass ex-husband, but who the hell's that one?" He asked, pointing to me.

Before Nancy could answer, I piped up, "I'm the one Marcia hired to find Becky. The only reason I came here is to give a refund to the lucky winner of the estate, remember me, Benjamin Katz?"

"My name's Zeb Satterwhite, and I think you must be the world's worst investigator. You didn't find squat but you charged a bloody fortune to do it," he retorted.

And I'd rather be back in the Marines ducking bullets than to be there with that old fart, but I made the best of it anyway.

"You can either take the refund, or sign a paper giving it back to me, I don't care," I used my cultured, annoyed voice.

"You wimp private dicks couldn't find your ass to wipe it. I could never figure why my daughter paid for that!" Zeb said, raising his voice.

If he wanted tough, I could give him tough. I have one hell of an act that's hard to follow, let alone put up with.

"Look, old man, if you don't shut up, I'll stuff this check up your nose then pound it back down your throat." I rose to my feet, towering over Zeb Satterwhite.

Zeb stood up, and being three inches shorter, had to be content with glowering up at me.

"Daddy, sit down and cool off. Benjamin was a helpful man, he did a lot in the two days before Marcia died," Nancy tugged at her father's shirt sleeve.

"When your daughter died, I dropped the missing child case," I added. "I never took it up again, and as far as I know, neither did the police."

I could see the resemblance between this old coot and Marcia.

"Well, I don't want you to drop the case," Zeb remained standing.

"You want me to look for your granddaughter? The lawyer said she was already on her way here," I replied.

"I don't have a granddaughter. The only thing I want you to find is who killed my daughter." Zeb sat back down.

"Daddy, we've been over and over this," Nancy insisted.

"To hell with it! That girl's a bastard, and not part of me, or my family," Zeb said in a loud voice. "Marcia might as well have been raped!"

"Have you talked to the police out here about Marcia's murder?" I asked Zeb.

"Yeah, and those dip shits didn't tell me anything. All they said is that they're still looking into it," Zeb answered.

"They don't feel too good about a private investigator poking into an active case," I almost sounded like my friend, Lieutenant Hatton.

"I asked that smug ass lieutenant if I could hire a private dick, and he said I was welcome to waste my money if I wanted to," Zeb said.

"You asked him about me, didn't you?" I already knew the answer.

"Why would you think I asked about you?"

"That's the way that smug ass lieutenant talks about me to all my clients," I forced a social smile.

"You'll work for me," Zeb grumbled in a statement of fact, not a question.

"Only if you'll come by my office and sign a contract, then leave me alone to do my job," I stared down into Zeb's eyes.

"Deal!" Zeb answered. "How much?"

"I keep the twenty five hundred, plus one fifty a day, plus expenses."

"You draw the daily and expenses against the twenty five hundred, and I'll give you ten thousand if you find her murderer," Zeb glared at me.

"I'll draw against the twenty five hundred, only until it runs out, then you start to pay me each week," I returned his glower.

"Deal. You write it up and I'll sign it."

"Daddy, what in the hell are you doing? You're throwing your money away; the police couldn't find anything, neither can he."

"It's my money, and I think he knows damn well who killed my daughter. Besides, I can fire the son of a bitch any time I think he's screwing up."

"Wait just a minute," The man, who up to now had been silent, entered the conversation. "I know it's not much, but that twenty five hundred belongs to Marcia's estate."

"Shut the fuck up, you piece of shit." Zeb glared at his end of the table. "I'll put my own twenty five hundred in the pot, you ain't going to get it anyway."

"We'll see about that." The younger man snapped back.

He had to be Marcia's ex-husband, Peterson. He seemed mighty concerned about the money.

"If you don't watch your step, you'll be worrying about more than Marcia's money," Zeb turned his back to Peterson.

"You don't scare me, old man," Peterson glowered, then seemed to collect himself, then went stone faced again.

"He should." Nancy looked briefly at him, then she turned to her father.

What was it about this family? I knew they were rich, but I also knew I had better leave before I killed the golden son of a gander.

I rose from my seat to leave. Nancy rose a second later and followed me to the door.

"In spite of everything, it has been good to see you again."

I turned to Nancy, who was approaching me with her hand extended.

"It's been good to see you again, too," I said, confused, but I also extended my hand.

As we shook hands, she passed me a small note. I put my right hand swiftly in my pocket and kept walking towards the door.

As I left I turned to Zeb, "My address is in the phone book, come by late this afternoon and sign the contracts."

18
Dèjá pew

"Well, what happened, did you give the money back?"
Cassandra eagerly asked.

She was in the office looking at the clock when I
returned.

"Why didn't you come with me for the tryouts?"

I opened the filing cabinet, pulled out a contract form
and walked to the typewriter.

"What the hell are you doing? What happened?"

"I need to type up some special provisions on one of our
contracts."

"All right, but who did you make a deal with? Not that
family again?"

"Yes, I did. How does a ten thousand dollar bonus
sound?"

"It sounds like trouble," Cassandra sounded worried.

"I think it sounds like a lot of money. If you're not
interested, I can keep it all for myself." I began typing.

"I see that look in your eyes," She studied me carefully.
"It's not the money."

"No, it's not," I kept typing.

"What?"

"I'm pissed off."

"Not that either," She put her hand on my shoulder.
"Maybe because Marcia stretched out on the kitchen floor
reminded you too much of your own mother."

"Maybe."

Cassandra looked over my shoulder as I filled in the
conditions and name on the contract. "Who's Zeb Satterwhite,
the father?"

"You're on your way to winning the jackpot," I murmured.

"So we find his daughter?"

"No, Zeb is Marcia's father and Becky's grandfather. We have to find the murderer of Marcia," I replied.

Cassandra backed away from me. "No way, I don't like this at all."

"Well," I finished typing. "I want to finish this case once and for all. This thing has harassed me for over a year."

"It does have to do with you finding Marcia's body in the kitchen, doesn't it?" Cassandra softened.

"I guess so."

"I can understand that," She put her hand on my shoulder.

"Do you realize that I've known Nancy Satterwhite for almost three years?" I said. "Marcia's murder has always bothered me because I have this nagging feeling that I should know who murdered her. It's not just the link to my past, it's this nagging feeling that I could have done something to end this long ago. I want to find out who did it and I might as well get paid for it."

"Well, if you put it that way, I might as well help you and split the money," The concern in her voice was making a liar out of her.

"Oh," I remembered Nancy. "Nancy Satterwhite passed me a note as I was leaving the meeting."

"Like high school all over again; what did it say?" The gleam in her eye spoke volumes.

I pulled it from my pocket and unfolded it, "Promise you won't laugh."

"No promises," She grinned at me. "What does it say?"

"It says," I read, "I have what you want, and I can give you more than you'll ever need."

Cassandra's face contorted into a smothered grin.

"Here's her hotel, and room number," I added.

She snorted, and put her head face down into her hands. "What do you plan to do?"

121

"So what are you implying?" I asked.

"Just what is that note implying?"

"It could mean that she has some information for me," I replied.

"And the fork really did run away with the spoon," She began to laugh out loud.

"Oh, fork you, you promised," I cracked a smile.

"Well, stud, what's next?" She tried unsuccessfully to remove the smirk from her face.

"If you're going to be jealous, I may just visit her tonight," I paused. "She still looks beautiful."

"It's your life, do what you want," She shrugged her shoulders with her smirk still in place.

"To change the subject, do you remember that idiot I met from D. C, Fred Lepus?" I asked, walking back to my office.

"Yeah, you met him just before we took on Marcia Satterwhite as a client. Who would ever hire him? You said he'd have trouble finding his way to the bathroom," Cassandra followed me to the interior office.

"His name was in Nancy's address book a year ago, and his name came up in the lawyer's office today," I said.

"At the reading of the will?"

"That's been held up again, because of a message sent by Lepus to the court," I replied in a disgusted tone. "Lepus claims to have found Becky alive and well, and ready to inherit her mother's millions."

"He can't be trying to pawn off a phony to collect the money," Cassandra sat in the chair beside my desk. "He's not that dumb."

"No, if he has the child, he has the real Becky because Lieutenant Hatton has Becky's fingerprints, I'm sure Lepus knows it." I pulled my Smith and Wesson, still in a shoulder holster, from the drawer; I pulled off my coat and strapped the pistol on.

"Expecting trouble?"

"Yes, I'm expecting Zeb Satterwhite. Once you meet him, you too might want to be armed."

122

"Oh, great! I wish you'd stick to little old ladies looking for the crooked palm reader who skipped town," Cassandra said resignedly.

"I have two phone calls to make before Zeb comes here. One to our favorite Lieutenant, and the other to George Sterling," I said.

"Why George?"

"He knows Zeb, and I think he knows a lot more about the Satterwhite family than he'll say," I replied. "When I was investigating Brian Fowler, I asked George if he knew Nancy or her father."

"What did he say?"

"At first he wouldn't admit it, but he finally said he knew them, a long time ago, but then lost touch," I paused remembering the scene. "And what's strange, once he admitted it, he talked as if he liked them."

"He's your friend, I know that, but I never did trust George Sterling too much. I'll call the lieutenant if you like, to tell him we're on the case." Cassandra stood up.

"Thanks, he'll take it better coming from you, I think he had a crush on you."

"He's married," Cassandra paused as she walked to the outer office. "We were in his wedding, remember?"

After dialing the number and exchanging pleasantries with his secretary, I spoke to George.

"Hello, George, this is Benjamin."

"Hi, what can I do for you? You usually call only when you want something, Benjamin."

"You sound hostile, George."

"No, but Zeb Satterwhite came to see me yesterday and wanted me to find the murderer of his daughter. I refuse to work for that son of a bitch, so I gave him your name."

"Well, I'm working for him; thanks for the money, and the words of encouragement. I hate to be nosy and abrupt, but, why do you hate him so much?"

"I don't hate him, he's just trouble. He still runs a school for commandos where he teaches them to kill people and who

123

knows what else. He has a lot of even stranger friends who'll kill you without a second thought."

"What about his daughter?"

"Which one, Nancy, or the dead one?"

"The dead one, why did she die?"

"I wouldn't put it past her father to kill her, but who knows," George said.

"How well do you know this family?" I asked.

"I served under the old man in the army; he was nuts then, and he's worse now," George answered.

"What about his daughters?"

"Nancy's tough. Ever since Zeb's son died in a car accident a long time ago, he's hated his daughters for not being a replacement. Nancy and her sister had to be tough to put up with him. I actually didn't know Marcia that much, but I've known Nancy off and on for a long time, she tried to hire me a few times."

"What for?"

"To find Becky," George answered.

"Then Nancy didn't know where the girl was?" I asked.

"You thought she had the kid?"

"Yeah, I don't care if she did have more dough than Marcia, six million bucks is still a good reason to kill," I said.

"I think she wanted the kid back worse than anyone. Nancy loved Becky more than Marcia ever did," George said.

"So who kidnapped the kid?"

"I've got no idea, if I did I'd have gone and brought her back long ago," George said.

"And then you send Zeb to me?"

"This has turned into one case that needs to be solved. I refuse to deal with Zeb anymore, but I think you can. If you need my help, call and you've got it, but don't bring Zeb anywhere near me or I'll blow his fucking head off," George said in a quiet voice.

"You sound like you would. Thanks, and I'll call you again, bye."

As I hung up the phone, Cassandra was standing by the door to my office.

"Well, what did Mark say?" I looked up at her.

"It's okay with him if we look down all the blind alleys, but, to use his words, if we find anything, give it to him and get the hell out of his way," Cassandra said.

"Why don't you like George?" I asked out of curiosity; she had told me before that she didn't like him, but never why.

"He gives me the creeps when he talks, I never believe him when he tells me something. There's either something he's not telling me, or what he has just said is an out and out lie," She shrugged. "I know my mom's best friend works for him, but I still don't like him."

I was silent, as usual she was honest with me about her feelings.

"What's our client list like now?" I asked.

"I have two," Cassandra replied. "But they're mostly paperwork cases, simple background checks, which aren't due for another three weeks, how about you?"

"I just finished the last of the paperwork on that stalking case, so this case is it; this case should be enough."

"Was that stalking case the one for the actress?" Cassandra looked sideways at me. "I didn't have to wonder too hard why you wanted to do that one by yourself."

"She's not that famous an actress," I pasted a semi-guilty grin on my face. "I guess that's why the cops didn't try too hard to find the zealous fan."

"Wasn't she a actually a porno star?" Cassandra still didn't seem too happy about that.

"I suppose you could say that," I shrugged. "I've never seen any of her works, so I wouldn't know."

"That's a good thing, I suppose." She smiled at me for the first time while talking about that case.

"Her agent hired me, and I dealt mostly with him," I shrugged again.

Maybe I should have let her do this case, but I hadn't liked the agent too much and was afraid of letting him loose on the woman I loved.

"I guess I'm still more peeved about all those overseas assignments you never take me on," Cassandra complained, again.

Every time we get into a discussion about who gets what client, she always gets around to that.

"Most of those overseas jobs are for companies I've worked with for years before you started here, and they trust me."

"Take me with you, at least."

"Next time, sure."

Not likely, I thought to myself.

The outer office door opened and a loud voice shouted, "Where the hell's everybody!"

"Our client," I said in a low voice as we walked to the outer office to see Zeb standing in the doorway, glaring at the two of us.

"Just sign this then give me an address where I can send the bills." I handed Zeb the contract.

"Shut your trap and let me read it." Zeb snatched the contract and sat at the desk. "I don't sign jack shit until I read it."

"What type of pen writes on jack shit?" I quizzed.

Cassandra pulled me aside and whispered in my ear, "Let me try talking to him, he has to be holding back some important information."

"He'll bite your head off," I whispered back. "I don't think a pretty face means anything to him."

"What the hell're you two planning over there, do you want me to sign, or walk?" Zeb snapped at us.

"Oh, don't pay any attention to him. My name's Cassandra Pales and I'm his partner. I'd like to ask you a few questions about your daughter, Marcia."

"Do you let this broad run things around here?" Zeb asked me.

126

"Sometimes," I answered as Cassandra moved to her desk and opened the upper right drawer.

"Pussy whipped, why should I hire a pussy whipped wimp," Zeb shook his head. "And I sure as hell ain't going to deal with a bimbo detective."

Cassandra pulled a pistol out of the drawer, a three eighty automatic. Zeb didn't see her get her pistol because he was staring intently at me.

"You shouldn't have made her mad," I told him. "She was going to be pleasant to you and everything."

Zeb shot up out of his chair, lunged towards me and reached for my revolver, visible in my shoulder holster. I blocked Zeb's hand just as he grabbed me in a headlock; for an old man, he was nimble. I managed to slam my fist into his left kidney. He let out a loud groan and loosened his grip on my head so I easily pulled my head back out of his grip. While Zeb and I struggled, Cassandra stalked over and jammed the pistol into Zeb's back.

"Leave my partner alone. Sit back down or I'll blow a hole in your back," she said in a loud, steady voice.

He walked slowly away from me as Cassandra took the pistol out of his back, staying just out of reach.

Zeb started to speak, but she shouted, "Shut up until I tell you to talk!"

"Told you not to get her mad," I whispered to Zeb, as he straightened up his collar.

She walked around to face him, resuming her normal voice,"Why do you think your daughter was murdered?"

Zeb scowled, "I don't know why, I think it had to do with some sort of a scheme she and Nancy's ex-husband cooked up. Don't know what any of them were up to, but I do know that a lot of people wanted Marcia and Brian dead."

"How do you know that?" I asked.

"Because some of my friends were approached by certain people and offered a contract to kill both of them," Zeb reluctantly answered.

"How do you know they didn't kill Marcia," Cassandra asked.

"I told them not to and they didn't."

"Write their names on this piece of paper." I threw a pad of paper in front of Zeb.

"I told you my friends don't kill my family, and they don't!"

"I don't give a zip what you think, let us check them out," Cassandra insisted.

"I'll give you the name of the man who wanted to give the contract, he's no friend of mine."

"That'll be a start," I said.

"Where does this guy live?" Cassandra asked.

"He doesn't," Zeb said.

"What do you mean?" Cassandra asked.

"The man in question is dead," I said. "Most likely our friend here killed him."

"How do you expect us to find anything out if you kill the best source of information?" Cassandra asked in a cold voice, looking at Zeb.

"That's why I'm paying you, find out!"

He signed the contract and backed off. I tore off his copy and stuffed it into Zeb's hand as he stormed through the door.

"Well, I'll be damned," I smiled as I glanced at the name on the pad.

"What name did he write?" Cassandra asked.

"The name of Richard Snively, and Zeb's hotel room and phone number."

"Snively? Isn't that the guy who was killed in Miami just before Marcia was shot?" she asked.

"One and the same. I wonder if Zeb shot him, or had one of his trained monkeys do it."

"What's more important is why Snively wanted Marcia killed, what deal did those two have going on and where is their other partner?" Cassandra asked.

"But were there only three partners? If Brian Fowler is dead, then there might not be anyone alive who knows what they had going," I thought for a moment. "What we need to do is to locate Brian Fowler, if he's still alive, to find out what Marcia was up to, and why Snively would want her killed."

"Mark Hatton doesn't think Fowler had anything to do with it."

"Mark Hatton didn't know what Zeb just told us, at least I don't think he did."

"Do you think I should go to Miami?" Cassandra asked.

"No, I met the cops there when Snively was killed, and I should go back there myself. I need to find out why Snively was fired from the medical college. I'll bet it has something to do with the killings. You should go to San Francisco to try to locate Fowler. "

"All right, I'll let you go to Miami, but on the next job, I get the longer trip," Cassandra stared at me.

I thought I saw the beginning of a smile, but I wasn't sure.

"Thanks for helping when Zeb grabbed me; I wasn't expecting an old man like him to be that fast."

It was good she was fast, or I might have really hurt that son of a bitch before he had gotten around to agreeing to pay us for this case.

Cassandra patted me on the back. "I see why you spend so much time in a marshal arts gym, you could have finished him yourself but I just got mad."

"Well, I'm going home to pack. I'll call you as soon as I get some information. Where will you be?" I asked.

"I'll leave a number with our answering service," she answered. I'll probably be in San Francisco for a while, unless I find out Fowler's gone somewhere else, or is dead."

19

As you were, so shall you be

The flight to San Francisco was smooth and much easier than driving there and back. Cassandra liked these small commuter flights since there at least seemed to be more personal space. She could usually grab a seat by herself so she could sleep, or catch up on reading for whatever class she was taking that quarter.

By now, all she needed to take were graduate seminars which met only once a week. Sometimes she could arrange an independent study course which met only when the professor chose. That gave her more time to work on cases, but the downside was finding the free time to actually do the research, reading and writing. So, she took advantage of a clerical service three blocks from the office, which also typed up final reports for Cheshire Katz. Research for her dissertation started and soon dissertation hours were all she would have to sign up for; the end was in sight.

．．．．．．．．．．．．．．．．．．．．．．

"I still cannot believe that this loser Brian person got a job at Berkeley." She tapped the gearshift knob of the dull green pinto from the local rent-a-wreck, planning where to start.

The personnel office seemed the obvious answer; eventually they directed her to Faculty Records, where a slender young guy, outfitted in blacks and grays that seemed to match the office interior, looked her up and down. His stare hesitated at her chest, then rose back to her eyes; a dim bulb, she thought.

"I think we found what you asked for, " He said. "You know that most of these records are confidential, even though he only worked here for six months and it was over a year ago."

"Okay, you've already told me two facts," Cassandra tilted her head slightly. "Let's try for a few more, what address did he give?"

"The Ramada Inn."

"You're kidding."

He turned the paperwork towards her. "Not at all, look for yourself."

She had long taken for granted her speed reading skills; they served her well here. Brian had listed the Ramada Inn near the airport as his temporary residence. He listed Snively as a reference. Professional organizations included the expected, and one unexpected; he had a private pilot's license .

"Not much help," Cassandra sighed loudly at the young clerk. "Thanks anyway," She said goodbye before he could get out his request for a date.

The city didn't hold that many small airports, so, back at her car, Cassandra dragged the yellow pages open to 'airport' listings. There's a small set of airports, besides the main airport, and he wouldn't be there anyway.

Better to drive to each landing field rather than to call since a call might send Fowler running for the hills. She didn't want the trip to be a bust, so she set out in her fiery Pinto chariot to each small airport listed in the bay area.

At the third airfield, Cassandra noticed a familiar name; not Brian Fowler, Brian Satterwhite. Like the others, the ambiance of this very small airport was dirt. An inch of greasy dirt covered the counter while a herd of dust elephants roamed the dull expanse of floor towards a stack of oily engine parts lining the East wall.

"This is too easy," she said out loud.

She rang the small silver bell at the empty counter, paused for a full minute, then rang again.

"All right, all right." From behind a tattered curtain hung from a door frame behind the counter, a slightly overweight woman strutted, in a very tight pair of stretch pants and a puffy white blouse tumbled out.

"Yes. I'm looking for Brian Satterwhite."

131

"Why?"

"I need a pilot," Cassandra saw 'no deal' written across the woman's face. "I'm an old friend from back East."

"You got the wrong Satterwhite."

"Not if his name's really Brian Fowler."

"Just who the hell are you, anyway?"

"My name is Cassandra Pales," She paused to read the large woman's face," I really don't want any money from him, and I'm not a cop."

The woman stared stoically at her. "You a rent-a-cop?"

Cassandra sighed, "You watch too many movies. Sorry, it's been a long week."

"Week's over," The other woman growled. "Get the hell out of here."

"Wait a minute," A slick male voice slithered from behind the curtain. "I think I want to talk to her."

The woman hissed like a tractor tire going flat, "For god's sake, Brian! You'll roll over for any two bit bimbo!"

She crashed through the curtain, pushing aside the male who was leering out at Cassandra.

"I take it you're Brian Fowler?" Cassandra spoke in the direction of the grungy strips of plastic.

He brushed them open again. "And who may I take it are you?"

" A private investigator," She considered how much else to say. "We are doing an investigation in which your name came up, and I'd like to ask you a few questions, then I'll be on my way."

"Who hired you?"

"Does it matter?"

"That's a dumb question," Brian studied Cassandra's face. "Your ex father-in-law."

Brian greased a smile, "That's better, now I understand what direction this conversation may take."

"What direction do you think it might take?"

"What's the investigation?"

"The murder of your former sister-in-law."

"Shit, that was well over a year ago, and I didn't have anything to do with it," Brian relaxed, lounging on a chair in front of her.

"Then maybe you can clear up some fuzzy details for me," Cassandra felt his eyes sleazing over her body. She immediately regretted giving him the 'fuzzy detail' opening.

"I'm real good at handling fuzzy details," Brian said slowly.

His smile was painful to watch. She guessed he was socially deficient, but not stupid.

"Do you have any idea who would have wanted Marcia killed?" She asked.

"Don't know," He paused to consider what he was saying. "Marcia hung out with a bunch of really tough characters, she always did. Then there was her father, he could kill anyone."

"What makes you say that?"

"You met him already?"

"Well, yes I have, only once," She knew the next question he would ask.

"After meeting him, can you doubt he might kill someone."

"No," Cassandra felt very uncomfortable speaking to this lecherous creep. "What were the names of some of the tough characters she hung around with right before her death?"

"Hell, I don't know." He paused dramatically. "I had a brief affair with her after Nancy threw me out, but I never knew that much about the rest of her private life, or any of her business life; that woman kept everything she did a secret."

"What kind of business did she have?"

"She worked for the immigration service when she died."

"We know she had at least one shady deal going on the side which netted her large sums of money, do you have any clue as to what it was?"

"None," Brian shook his hand in front of his face as if he were pulling a reluctant thought from his mind. "Wait a minute,

I remember the name of one of her close associates, if you can call an ex-con an associate."

"What was his name?"

"I don't remember a last name, but his first name was Hank. He's one hell of a bruiser, I mean that guy was six foot six, by six foot six."

"But, what did they do?"

"I haven't a clue. I think they screwed a lot, but beyond that you'll have to ask Hank," Brian shrugged his shoulders. "You know Marcia was rich enough so that she never had to work or pull shady deals."

"Is that so," Cassandra was growing tired of his evasiveness. "Look, I'm not digging up dirt on you, I don't care at all about you. All I want is some real answers about what Marcia was up to."

"Why should I tell you anything?" Brian half smiled.

"You've already told me a lot, why not the rest of it?"

"That's not an answer," Brian's sounded cross.

"You should tell me because what you say won't hurt you."

"Come again?" Brian looked confused.

"I'm not a cop, and I don't need to tell the cops what you tell me. But, you know Zeb Satterwhite. I work for him, and I'll find out who killed his daughter and I'll collect a large sum of money for doing it," Cassandra paused for a breath.

"What's that got to do with me?" Brian leaned back in his chair.

"If you don't cooperate, you still don't have to worry about the cops. I will, however, tell Zeb that you didn't cooperate with me."

"I get the picture," Brian cleared his throat.

"Okay," Cassandra stared at Brian. "What was Marcia up to, and who, besides you, was she up to it with?"

Brian thought a few more seconds, "All right, his name was Hank Cummings. Marcia, Paul Peterson, Hank, me and some front man named Irving Lopez cooked up a scheme to import foreign babies for adoption; I flew them in, and Marcia

134

did the rest. She paid off some government personnel bozo to get a job with immigration to do whatever she did. We made some money which was mostly legal. Zeb knew about it, but I'm not surprised he didn't tell you."

"How long did the baby scam go on?"

"Not long, maybe a year or two, then she went on to something more profitable," Brian became agitated.

"I've got to ask," Cassandra tossed her notebook in her purse. "Why did you give up being a professor for this? I mean it had to take you a lot of years to get your PhD, why waste it?"

Brian laughed, "Zeb wanted me dead because Nancy threw me out. I swear she told her father to kill me, so I had to hide out. Plus, I own this air charter service now and we fly the more difficult runs for a higher fee. Hell, I make more in a month here than I'd make in a year at Berkeley."

Cassandra stepped back, "Thanks for the talk."

"Don't go now. I was nice to you, now you have to return the favor."

"I don't think so," She pressed her left arm against her ribs to assure herself that her pistol was still in its holster.

"I just want to take you to a late lunch," Brian cocked his head to one side.

"I'm not hungry, thanks."

"It's my restaurant, I'm the owner; here's my card," He thrust a business card at her.

"Okay, I have a flight to catch now, but I'll keep this for the next time I'm in town."

"Call me first, you'll get better service," He sleazed one last smile at her as she left.

20

Checking it twice

Richard Snively had opened a private OB-GYN practice as soon as he moved to Miami. The fact that he had few clients, but seemed to make a lot of money, had Captain Osborne doing a lot of searching, but never succeeding, in finding the source of Snively's money. A physician teaching at a medical school didn't bank enough money for Snively's extravagant Miami lifestyle and he had been fired for several years before he moved to Miami.

The police ruled out drugs, illegal operations, prescription drug pushing and a long list of other less than honest activities as possible sources of income. All that Carl Osborne had left for a murder motive was possible blackmail over Snively's sex life. Captain Osborne was never happy with that resolution, but since I had not heard from him since it was announced, I assumed that Carl was happy enough with it.

I found out in the five or six calls from captain Osborne that the medical school fired Richard Snively from his teaching position for irregularities in his research, and for improper use of university facilities, although Osborne never did tell me what those improper uses were.

I scheduled a flight to get into Miami at nine o'clock in the morning so I could begin working as soon as I arrived, which meant that I was leaving Los Angeles well before dawn. The good thing was that I could see the sun rise somewhere over the mid-west.

At night the lights from cities and towns shine, but not all that bright at the early pre-dawn time I was flying. At 35,000 feet I can still see individual cars on the highways, their headlights look like cones pointing to the front of the cars. At that height, there aren't any clouds between you and the sun and the blue of the sky is much softer.

As the morning sun streamed into the airplane cabin, I began to assess my fellow passengers, most of them asleep or nearly so. My mind began to play the guessing game: who are you, why are you here. Middle management flying to a meeting, executives sleeping in first-class, a retired couple returning from a visit to their married kid and grandchildren; many other labels suggested themselves. That younger woman looked too haggard to be traveling for fun, I bet she is someone's daughter flying to visit a sick parent; those worry lines on her face didn't belong on a calm thirty year old. I wondered if anyone of them guessed I was in search of a murderer.

After claiming my baggage and renting a car, the first stop for me was the office of captain Carl Osborne. It was a slack time at this station, only a few hookers and a small assortment of drunks were waiting around to be booked. I heard a familiar voice behind me.

"What brings you back here?" Carl walked around to my chair. "You can throw your suitcases in the corner over there."

"The same thing that brought me here before, Richard Snively."

"Wait, let's go into one of these interrogation rooms." Carl walked to an open room to my right. "What is it now, any new information?"

I waited until we both were in the room, and the door closed before I said a word, "I might have the person who shot Snively, but neither you nor I could prove it yet. Help me, and I'll guarantee his name and motive delivered to your doorstep if he's guilty."

I looked straight into Carl's eyes as I set my suitcases down.

"I think you would, who is he?"

"Since I don't have any real evidence yet, I'd rather not say right now. Trust me for a week, and I'll tell you and the cops in Los Angeles everything."

"You're asking a lot, you know. Legally you're withholding information on a murder case, so why should I go along with you?"

"First of all it's not a fact, just a hunch, and besides I've always given you all the information you've asked for. I think you owe me at least a week plus some help for it,after all, I flew here just to talk to you in person so that three hundred extra I paid for the flight should count for something."

"Okay, what do you want to know? Not that I care how much money you spend, but this Snively case has had a lot of us bothered. I don't think anyone'll mind waiting a week longer if you think you can scare up a real suspect."

Carl leaned forward on his desk.

"Why was he fired by the medical school?"

"They said it was because he was doing experiments on human fertility without following any guidelines. But when we looked into that aspect here, none of the hospitals said he did anything like that. A few of them said he did infertility counseling, but every hospital said he did nothing but routine gynecological procedures," Carl replied.

"Did he do that with a lot of women?" I began to ponder the possibilities.

"Two of the hospitals said he had a large number of upper class woman as clients," Osborne thought for a second, remembering the details. "I guess Snively might have had hundreds of women patients."

"What did he do, exactly?"

"I'm not a doctor, but the hospital staff told me he did only routine exams and procedures."

"What about in his office?" I asked.

"There wasn't enough equipment in his office to do anything but exams."

"All right, I think that Snively, Marcia Satterwhite, and her sister's ex-husband were into some sort of scam. Snively, and Marcia are dead, and Fowler has been missing for the whole time, or at least that's what I've been told. There's your connection, but what I need to find out is, just what that connection was all about, and who else was involved in it."

Carl Osborne leaned back in his chair and folded his arms across his chest.

"What about the mother, Florence Satterwhite?"

"She's still missing," Osborne replied.

"Has any of her family filed a missing person's report?" I asked.

"Not a one of them," Carl answered. "The Naples police opened the case because of the connection to our murder case."

"I'd be willing to bet she's dead, and her murderer is mixed up in this scheme somehow."

"I think so too," Carl agreed. "The Naples boys are on the verge of changing the case from a missing person to a murder investigation."

"Why?" I asked.

"All her money and property is in just her name, but she lets her banker pay the bills," He answered. "From the time she disappeared to now, not a dime has been spent, other than normal bills."

"Just another piece to a bigger puzzle," I muttered.

"You've got one week before I pull in the reins, all I can speak for is myself. Have you told the LA cops about any of this?"

"Some, they know I'm back on the case, but only you know what I've just told you."

"Make it good, Katz, make it stick."

. . . .

Telling the staff at the medical school that I already knew Snively had been working on some sort of human fertility project, would put them at ease. Telling them that I had come directly from the Miami police with this information might shake loose further clues.

My energy had begun to wear thin because of all the traveling in one day, but I managed a smile and sufficient social amenities for the departmental secretary.

139

"May I tell him the reason you're here?" she asked.

"I've just come from the Miami police, and I'd like to talk to Dr. Billings about a former employee, Dr. Richard Snively."

"I never met the man, but he sure is popular around here." The secretary shook her head.

I threw her a questioning look.

"As you know, the Miami police department has been asking about him as long as I've been here, and so has some detective named Lepus from up north somewhere," she said. "Let me tell Dr. Billings you're here."

A few moments later I was in his office. "I'm glad to meet you in person, Dr. Billings. I was on my way to Washington to try to find a sleaze ball detective, Fred Lepus. I thought I'd stop by and introduce myself, and ask you a few more questions about Dr. Snively," I said, picking up on what the secretary had just told me.

"We've advised that man Lepus that we would turn him over to the police if he continued to call us. Could you insist he stop bothering my secretary if you find him?" Dr. Billings asked.

"I sure will. Could you tell me again exactly what Snively was working on? Captain Osborne said that he was involved in human fertility, but what aspect was he working on?" I asked.

"He was working on fertilization outside of the womb, it's known as invitro fertilization, but Dr. Snively had been working on it for over a decade, before it was common knowledge. He was using women's eggs without their permission, and sperm from cryogenic storage without our permission," Billings shook his head.

"Was he successful? From your reaction, something else was going on."

"No, I'm just remembering what I found in the lab when one of his assistants tipped me off as to what he was doing," Dr. Billings said.

"What did you find?"

140

"He had been growing the fertilized eggs in solution. Some of them had lived for quite some time, and the sight of them was. . . ." Dr.   Billings grimaced. "The first thing I thought of was how much trouble the whole university would be in if the news of this got out.   I reported it that night, and fired him the next day, thank god it never reached the newspapers."

I never did find out how the hell the good doctor managed that; he must be a master at managing the press.

"Did he have any helpers, those who kept quiet?" I asked.

"Only one that we've discovered. That was Paul Peterson." Dr.   Billings leaned back in his chair.

"Paul Peterson? Where is he now?"

"He's dead, he disappeared right before we fired Dr. Snively.   His airplane crashed in a very remote spot in Arkansas; the authorities only recently discovered his body," Billings answered.

"Where in Arkansas?"

"I really don't remember, but it was in the local paper a while ago," The doctor answered.

"Is there anyone here who was around when Snively was here doing his work?"

"No, not in this department. We've had a tremendous turn over in the past few years. There have been many retirements, and about a third of the faculty in this department has moved to other universities. I'm the only one left in this department who was here, and I'm going to retire this year."

As I began to walk to the hall, I turned to Dr.   Billings and asked, "What was the name of the assistant who turned Snively in?"

"Oh, that was Dr.   Aaronson, he started a private practice in Washington, D. C. ; Melissa can give you his address," Dr.   Billings turned to his secretary. "Can you give this policeman the address of Dr.   Aaronson."

21

Down the hole

Becky looked through the small peep hole in the front door. The face looked distorted, and agitated.

"Open up, we don't have much time."

"Oh, it's you, Mr. Lepus."

"Yeah, kid, it's me, now open up."

"Did Dad send you for me?" Becky opened the door.

"Sort of."

"What do you mean, sort of?" Becky sat back down on the sofa and tilted her head in confusion.

"We just have to get out of here fast, like we did from Maywood," Lepus exclaimed.

He checked behind his back and ducked in, shutting the door behind him.

"The bad guys are back at it again, and you'll be safer with me for a while."

"Not again," Becky lowered her head. "Did Phil send you."

"Yeah, he wants me to keep you on ice for a while again."

"Do you want to hear a secret, Mr. Lepus?"

"If the secret's about six million bucks, it ain't no secret, kid."

"My mama gave her money to me, all of it," Becky didn't change her expression. "I didn't know she had so much of it, where did she get it all?"

"Nancy and your grandfather have a pile more cash than your mother did, the whole family's rich as hell," Fred flashed an intent look at Becky. "How'd you find out about the money?"

"I listened in on a phone call Phil made to Los Angeles just before he left."

"Hey," Fred beamed. "You did learn a few tricks from me."

"You have to help me."

"Hey, kid, I'm in enough trouble as it is without trying to cross Phil too."

"You've got to help me, no one else will; no one else even likes me anymore."

"Come on, kid, you've got to hold up better than that. I've always liked you and Cathy likes you a lot too, I'll see what I can do."

Fred sat down next to Becky on the sofa.

Becky smiled at Fred, "Then you'll help me?"

"Not so fast," Fred held up both his hands. "I said I'd think about it, and that's all I'll do for now."

"When do I have to leave?"

"Yesterday; don't get anything except your toothbrush and one change of clothes."

"You seem awful nervous, is there someone after me now? Is there someone who wants me dead because my mama gave me all that money?"

"Don't flatter yourself, they're after me. I'm the one who knows too much about very dangerous people, you don't know a thing that'll hurt you," Fred paused. "Least ways I don't think so."

A smile came and went across Becky's face, "What trouble did you get into this time?"

"Stop flappin' your jaw, and get ready now. We ain't got much lead on the creeps who're after me."

In five minutes, Becky and Fred Lepus were riding in Fred's rental car towards downtown Chicago.

"I gotta get some stuff from a safe deposit box downtown."

Fred noticed that Becky was silently watching the scenery flying past the passenger window as he drove the car south on Interstate Ninety Four. The two of them were silent for the rest of the drive downtown.

"Do you see that black Caddy behind us?" Fred strained to look into his rear view mirror.

Becky checked the side mirror just outside her window.

"I see it, I think it was there from the time you picked me up."

"I don't think so," Fred cleared his throat. "I would have noticed it before; it's taken every turn we have for the past ten blocks," Fred's voice had begun to turn gravelly with annoyance and fear. "We should try to lose them."

"How?" Becky asked.

"I'll park the car and we can blend in with the crowd for awhile."

"I don't think that's a good idea, maybe we could go to a police department, they would stop following us for sure," Becky said.

She knew Fred's weak points after the time she spent with him.

"That would not be my choice," Fred cleared his throat. "Not my choice at all."

"Well, then, there's a parking place on this side of the street one block up."

Becky pointed through the front windshield.

Fred plowed his large car into the space, leaving it quite askew in the spot. He rushed to the meter and stuffed a large amount of change into it as Becky joined him on the sidewalk. Three steps down the sidewalk, Fred grabbed Becky's arm and pulled her towards a bus; she yelped, then stifled herself.

"Those three goons behind us are the ones who picked up my trail in the airport, I recognize them," Fred hissed.

He pulled Becky on the bus and threw the coins into the receptacle.

"I thought I lost them back at the airport. Just act cool, and pretend that Uncle Fred is showing you the sights, just stay with the crowds and we'll be safe."

Three large men followed them onto the bus before it began to move. Fred ignored their presence and pretended to show Becky all the important landmarks of downtown Chicago.

His gross errors in naming buildings and streets caused several nearby passengers to correct him. They pointed the correct landmarks out to Becky, who tried to laugh at the whole scene. She managed some nervous giggles.

After what seemed like forever to Fred, the bus lumbered to the stop where he knew he must get off in order to get to the bank and his safe deposit box.

He saw a glint of a stainless steel blade sticking out less than one inch from one of the men's coat sleeves. They would have to walk by the three men to get to the door, and he knew what this gauntlet meant.

"Look, kid," Fred whispered in Becky's ear. "Trust me, one of them's got a knife, and we've got to get by. Just stand up with me and when we get near him, scream as loud as you can for him to get his hand off your ass."

"Mr. Lepus!" Becky said in a loud whisper. "Please don't ask me to do something like that, it's too embarrassing."

"Getting stabbed in the gut's a whole lot more embarrassing, especially for me," Fred spoke in a firm whisper. "Please do it, then run like hell to your right when we break out the door. We'll just try to make it back to the car, unless they towed it; I'll have to come back to the bank later."

"Towed it?" Becky's voice faded to almost nothing.

"Don't worry, it always works out for me somehow," Fred patted her shoulder. "Ready?"

Becky nodded, dazed, and stood up with Fred.

The two of then trudged down the isle with one other passenger, a two hundred pound woman in her late fifties. Becky was second in line, and Fred followed, wiping sweat off his forehead with a dingy white handkerchief.

As Becky passed the man with the knife, Fred poked her in her back with his finger and Becky, almost involuntarily, screamed in a shrill voice, "Get your hand out of my ass!"

"I said off of, not out of," Fred whispered.

"I'm nervous, Mr. Lepus," Becky squeaked.

The heavy woman in front of her turned and looked directly in Becky's face. She swung her handbag sideways over Becky's head and aimed it at Fred.

The leather bag made a loud slapping sound as it glanced off Fred's balding head.

"Not him," Becky pointed at the shocked man with the knife half drawn from his sleeve, "Him!"

The woman mumbled an apology to Fred as he rose from the floor of the bus, then she leaned towards the man with the knife as the thug's two friends rose to help him. Fred managed to punch one of them in the stomach, then Fred shoved Becky forward. She was able to squeeze past the woman, but Fred was stuck in the aisle, wedged between a seat and the woman who was now clubbing the man with the knife.

"He's got a knife!" someone shouted.

The bus driver radioed for the police, and stayed in his seat.

The man Fred had stomach punched recovered and grabbed Fred's coat. Fred turned and slammed his fist directly into the man's face, knocking him unconscious. The third thug drew a pistol from under his coat and started to aim it at Fred.

"He's got a gun! Hit the floor!" Several passengers shouted.

The large woman fell to the floor, pinning the man with the knife under her, minus the knife.

Jostled by several passengers trying to get out of their seats, the second man dropped his gun . It went off as it hit the floor; the roar was deafening inside the bus.

Fred clambered over top of the woman and the thug under her and stumbled out of the bus to Becky who was waiting for him outside. The two of them ran to Fred's car and raced to the airport.

22

Splitting hares

I have met Fred Lepus only once before and once should have been enough. He's the type of private investigator who has seen too many detective movies; Lepus behaves as though he must act the part of the investigator who has it 'all under control'. Only partly due to poverty, he works out of a rundown office with a secretary who dresses like a twenty dollar hooker, no, make that a ten dollar hooker. He lives out of the bedroom in the back of his office.

Fred Lepus is average build, average height, average looks, and less than average intelligence. Washington DC is the perfect place for him to center his activities because his investigative technique lives up to the phrase 'good enough for government work'.

From National Airport, I called the Lepus Agency, and got a recording. I then phoned Lepus' home number, and heard yet another recording. Having been propositioned by Fred Lepus' secretary the first and only time I met her, I still had her phone number, so I called her home. I keep every number and name anybody gives me because sometimes it works out for the good, although most of the time it just takes up space in my address book. This phone call left me speaking to a live human being.

"Hello, is this Cathy?" I asked in an eager voice.

"Why, yes, who is this?"

The voice on the other end of the phone was quiet and television-commercial sexy.

"This is Benjamin Katz, do you remember me?"

"Why, yes, oh, yes I remember you, are you here in town?"

"Why, yes, I'm here in Washington. I came here to see your boss about a case, but I'd like to see you too."

"You can see me tonight, if you like," Cathy said with a purr.

"Does that mean I can't see your boss."

"Sure, but he's hiding out and I'm not," Cathy replied.

"I need to talk to him about a case. He and I could share a huge fee if he can solve a few problems I'm having," I asked in a pleading tone.

"How much money?"

"Ten thousand."

"Total, or his share?" Cathy asked in a flat voice.

I paused; it's all a lie anyway, so, "His share."

"Do you know where I live?" Cathy asked.

"I have your address, when should I be there?"

"Whenever, maybe we can have that date afterward?" Cathy asked.

"Maybe, see you both soon, tell him not to leave."

"How did you know he was here? He's not back here yet!"

"I hear music playing, don't tell me, I'll guess what it is; it's a little game I play whenever I get the chance."

I do like to play it at the most inopportune times, though.

"I hope that's not the only little game you play," Cathy said softly.

"The sound track recording from South Pacific by Rogers and Hammerstein."

"How did you guess?"

"Where else would you wash that man right out of your hair?" I laughed.

"Oh, yes, I'll turn it down if you like."

"No, that's all right, bye."

I hung up the phone, laughing out loud.

She lived just off Jeff Davis Highway in Arlington, so it wasn't far from the airport. The taxi dropped me off at Cathy Rumson's house at ten minutes after midnight. Dumping my overnight case and suitcase behind a large bush to the left of the front door, I rang the doorbell. It was hard to see much of the house and neighborhood in the dark but I could tell there were a

148

lot of trees and shrubs around her house. Cathy came to the door almost as soon as I rang.

"It sure takes you a long time to come; that's a fine habit in men like you," Cathy said.

She pulled me inside and slammed the door behind me.

"Well, I'm glad to see you too."

I turned around to look Cathy in the face. The cheap perfume was deadly thick.

Before I said another word, I felt the barrel of a pistol in my back.

"Hello, Fred, you should greet my face, not my back."

I raised both my arms slowly. Fred felt around under my coat for a revolver, finding none.

"Just keep your hands up, and you can turn around slowly and say hello to me," He poked my back again with the barrel of his pistol, "I didn't mean nothing bad for you, but I'm in a heap of trouble now, and I can't take chances."

Turning around to face him, I spoke, "You certainly do have a flair for the dramatic. Do you have the kid, Becky?"

The front door led directly into the living room. I could see back into the dining room and kitchen from where I stood and I assumed the bedrooms were off to my right, down a narrow hallway. The living room was wall papered in a hideous floral pattern which looked like it could be worn by a clown in a small county circus.

"I thought you'd been sent here by that crazy family. Well, I'm only going to talk to the court appointed attorney!" Fred sputtered.

His hands shook as he put the gun back in a waistband holster.

"Calm down, I wasn't sent here to get the kid; they did hire me, but only to find out who killed Marcia Satterwhite," I insisted.

"Who killed Marcia? I don't know, but I wish I did," Lepus said.

"Why?"

"Because whoever did it might be the one after me now; someone's been trying to kill me for the past week," Fred said in a shaky voice.

"Are you sure it's connected to this case?" I asked with a smile.

"Cut the crap! The dead woman, Marcia, and a queer doctor, and who knows who else, were involved in a scheme to import babies from Mexico. This group had a multi-million dollar adoption racket going, as well as a bunch of other seedy stuff, and it may still be going strong for all I know."

"What does that have to do with you now?" I asked.

"All I wanted to do was make a few bucks looking after a little kid, but when I located her, I also found out what her Mommy had been up to. All of a sudden a lot of people want me to forget this assignment, along with everything else, permanently!"

Cathy interrupted, "Yeah, he's been here, and in every flop house in town for the past week; he's been shot at three times."

Against my better judgment, I began to feel sorry for this guy.

"Fred, what have you uncovered, who else was in this deal?"

"I don't know, I said I didn't know!" Fred's voice was rising as he pulled his revolver back out of his holster and pointed it at my knees.

"Look, you're not bright enough to get into the middle of this mess all on your own. Who hired you, and to do what? How did you find out enough dirt on somebody to get killed over?" I asked.

"What?" Fred answered.

"Who hired you in this case?" I grabbed the pistol out of Fred's hand.

"I ain't gonna tell you. Where's the money you said you'd pay me? You wanna tell me who's hired you?" Fred retorted.

Ignoring his questions, I said, "I already know Marcia and Snively were in some sort of a scheme, but I don't know who else was in it. Whoever else was in it, and is still alive, might have killed Marcia, and now be trying to kill you. It might be the person who hired you, did you ever think of that?"

"Yeah, I thought of that, why do you think I'm so scared. I'm scared as shit about it."

"Do you think you were working for the mob?" I asked.

"Yeah, maybe," Fred muttered, not happy with the idea.

"Get serious, Fred, what do they want with a penny ante deal like adoption? There's not enough money in it to bother killing you for."

This character was delaying me, adding to the danger, not only for me but the kid, and he was too dense to figure out the danger. The more I thought about this aspect, the more pissed I became. Meanwhile, he was still talking.

"There's more money in it than you think, but I don't care who you think is behind it, or what they want. Whoever they are, they want me dead."

I grabbed Fred by the collar and slammed him against the wall. Even though I didn't want to hurt the idiot, some show of force might make him tell me what I needed to know, besides, by this time it made me feel good.

I pointed the pistol at Fred's face and asked, pausing between words, "Who hired you?"

"I won't tell you."

Twisting Fred's collar tighter, I asked again, "Who hired you? Don't push your luck."

Fred swallowed hard, then blurted out, "Irving Lopez."

His white speckled eyebrows twitched. Surprise made me relax my grip.

"Do you know who the hell he is?" I demanded, as Fred backed away from me, rubbing his neck.

"He runs an agency in New York, it's a front for a syndicate that deals in just about everything."

Runs an agency? This bozo called one of the top mobsters in the country an agent?

"Why would he want Becky?" I asked.

151

"He told me he wanted her for leverage over some lawyer in Chicago."

"Phil Peterson," I said under my breath.

"The kid's in Chicago, this Peterson guy's been raising her for the past six months or so," Fred continued.

"Is she still in Chicago?" I asked.

"No, she's here in D. C."

"Did you kidnap her?"

"Well, not exactly."

"You dip shit! Do you know how much trouble you're in?"

"More than I care to be in alone," Fred shifted on his feet as he rubbed a hand over his face.

"You think you've pulled me into this, so I'll have to help you?" I sighed. "I should have left you alone to explain that dead body to the police when I first met you."

"Yes, as a matter of fact I think you will help me; I'll tell them you know it all now, and that you're much more dangerous to them than me."

"Where is she?" I asked.

Cathy started to say something, but Fred immediately interrupted her, "Shut up!"

I began to turn around towards Cathy to see if she might say something when I caught sight of a raised vase lowering towards my head. But it was too late to move, away from the sudden pain of hard ceramic shattering over my all too often pummeled skull.

My hand lost its grip on Fred Lepus' collar, and I collapsed to my left side. Everything seemed to happen in slow motion as I completed the turn to face Cathy. Cathy stepped back one pace, slapped both hands over her mouth, staring wide eyed at me as I plummeted leisurely to the floor.

Although I couldn't do anything but fall into a boneless lump in front of Fred, I could still hear and see what was going on in the room. It all seemed like a half dream, but I was aware of everything; I was all too aware of my bashed head.

"Thanks for helping, but what in the hell are you doing trying to tell him everything!"   Fred demanded.

"I didn't tell him anything, is he dead?"   Cathy asked, anxiety making her voice uneven.

"No, look, he hasn't even shut his eyes."

"Let's just get outta here. You're in enough trouble as it is, don't piss him off too, he's kind of big," Cathy nodded her head to emphasize what she had just said.

"But I oughtta kick him around a bit, he deserves it for messing with me."

"If you kick him around now, what's he going to do to you when he wakes up and catches up with us?"

"Yeah, I guess so."

"What do ya want to do with the girl?"   Cathy asked.

"I guess we should take her to LA   soon," Fred answered. "Like we're supposed to, only give her to the cops instead; Peterson's a snake, and I sure ain't going to give her to Lopez."

"Better make your mind up in the next few seconds, look, you forgot to take the gun away from him and he's getting up!"

Cathy stepped back several more steps and pointed to my aching form, bit by bit rising from the floor.

"Oh shit, let's get the hell outta here!" Fred shouted as he ran for the front door, with Cathy following. I heard him mutter, "Katz' an all right guy when he's needed; he'll take care of the kid for me."

I shook my head and rubbed the spot where the vase had landed.   When I tried to rise all the way to my feet, I began to stumble and fell again to one knee, grabbing the edge of the nearby couch. Collapsing into the couch, I gingerly massaged the lump on the back of my head.

"This time I have enough reason to kill the bastard," I mumbled to myself. "The next time I'm going to shoot him first, then talk to him."

A full five minutes passed before I attempted to climb from the couch and this time I was able to rise without falling. I walked on rubbery legs towards the bedrooms down a small hallway to the right of the living room. Ahead of me down the hall were four closed doors with a light radiating from under the door at the end of the hall. How about if I pick what's behind door number three, the one with the light on. Okay, Don Pardo, what's there?

I stood on the right side of the door, with my back to the wall and the revolver pointed to the ceiling. Slowly turning the unlocked door knob, I shoved the door all the way open and hesitated outside it.

"Is that you Mr. Lepus? I fell asleep, what's happening?" A young female voice said from within the room; she sounded exhausted.

"Are you alone?" I asked in a composed voice.

"Yes, who are you, where's Mr. Lepus?"

I pivoted, pointing the revolver in front of me, and walked through the door. In front of me, huddled on a pink canapé bed, a young girl lay in the fetal position.

That bedroom had to be Cathy's because it was one of the worst decorated bedrooms I've ever been in, and that covers a lot of territory. Everything was some shade of pink, making it look like the inside of a pig's stomach with lots of frills and bows. And, the source for that nauseating smell must be that cheap overwhelming perfume. The girl on the bed didn't shift as my eyes focused on her. She was big enough for an early teenager, but still possessed the face of a very young girl. She dressed in designer jeans and a long sleeved pullover blouse with 'Paris in the Spring' printed on it.

"Are you Becky Peterson?" I inquired as I lowered my pistol.

"Yes, I'm Becky Peterson," The girl said in a weak voice. "Did you kill Mr. Lepus while I was asleep, are you going to kill me too?"

"My name is Benjamin Katz, I'm a private investigator and I didn't kill Mr. Lepus, yet; he almost killed me, though," I put the snub nosed thirty eight under my belt. "I'll take you to whatever relative you want, right now."

"I want to go to Daddy now," She answered.

"You mean, Phil Peterson?"

"Yes, please."

"He's in Los Angeles, for the reading of your mother's will; I'll take you there tonight."

"Mr. Lepus, is he gone?" Becky asked.

There was dignity to this kid, she sat up on the bed, and looked at me like she was my equal, but non-threatening. She also radiated a kindness that immediately overtook me.

"Mr. Lepus is long gone, and I'm here to help you; all I want to do is take you to Los Angles. Your step-father and all your mother's relatives are there. Your aunt Nancy, and your grandfather Zeb, are there."

"Everybody? Will I be all right?" Becky straightened herself out and began to sit up in the bed.

"Is someone after you?" I asked.

"Yes, Mr. Lepus was almost killed in Chicago," she answered. "Can you tell me about the will? Mama's will?"

"You mean money grubbing Fred didn't tell you you're worth over six million if you get to Los Angles in the next few days?" I asked.

"What?" Becky answered in a stronger voice, clearing her throat. "Mr. Lepus isn't all that bad, he's really been nice to me for a long time; he's been my friend since I was about thirteen years old."

"Do you want to come back to Los Angeles with me tonight? Your father is there, as well as the court appointed lawyer handling your mother's estate."

This girl had a charisma to her that none of her relatives showed a hint of so far, even Nancy.

"I want you to take me there, now," she answered.

I called the airline and arranged for two tickets that night to Los Angeles. After calling a cab to pick us up, I then called the Los Angeles police while Becky listened on an extension phone in the living room.

As I left Cathy's house, I dissembled Fred's pistol and tossed the pieces into the toilet tank, then I collected my suitcases from behind the bush in front of the house. Becky didn't say a

155

word the whole trip to the airport, nor while I paid for the tickets for the trip back to Los Angeles. I noticed her color and energy slowly come back and she seemed to grow gradually more sure of herself, standing taller as the time for departure came closer. When we sat down in the waiting room at our concourse, Becky finally relaxed, sinking down into the plastic chair.

"Do you know your mother was murdered?" I asked, knowing that I would have just this one opportunity to talk to Becky before she arrived in Los Angeles.

"Yes, Daddy told me she was murdered. He said she was mixed up in something very bad, and that the men she was working with killed her for it," Becky stared blankly forward.

"Do you feel like talking about it?" I asked.

"Not now," she answered.

I felt the words shove themselves out of my mouth, "My mother was also shot, years ago."

"I don't believe you," Becky said, quickly.

"I didn't believe it either, but it happened. When I was six years old, my father, brother and I came home to find my mother dead on the kitchen floor."

"Phil told me my Mama 's body was on the kitchen floor," Becky looked suspiciously at me. "You're lying."

"I know where your mother's body was found, I found it about the same time the cops did; it looked just like my Mom's body laying there," I stopped talking and turned around.

Why was I telling the kid all this? She doesn't believe me and besides, she's not even a shrink.

"You found my mama 's body?" Becky broke the silence. "Why?"

"I was working for her to find you; she hired me to find you right after Lepus picked you up for Phil Peterson."

Becky broke the silence again, "Was your mother really shot?"

"Yes, the police never solved it, just like your mother's death. My mom was a farmer's wife, and the cops could never find a reason for her murder; nothing was missing from the house, no mess, nothing," My voice trailed off in the memory of it.

"Just like my Mama 's murder, almost," Becky continued. "Why did you come looking for me now?"

"I didn't, your grandfather hired me to find out who exactly did kill your mother."

"You'd like to solve your mom's murder, too," Becky said. "Like me."

I couldn't help showing surprise, "Well, I gave up looking for you over a year ago."

I didn't know what else to say.

"You found me anyway, didn't you?" Becky asked.

"I've got to go check on the flight, maybe we can talk later."

My mind didn't want to be in this conversation anymore, it kept drifting. It was hard to concentrate.

Murdered. Murdered and never solved. No one ever saw a thing, no one ever knew a thing. Three years later, a neighbor from the closest house, an affable single lady and Mama's best friend in the whole wide world moved away, leaving no other adult but my father to talk to. He was a silent man. The loneliness grew. No one to hug, no one to care about me. My brother coped. My brother used my grief as a crutch. The mystery has remained for so long, I even tried to find the killer myself. Who could kill my mother? She was loved by everybody. It had to be a traveling maniac, a serial killer, someone who drives through a town and kills, changes the lives of everyone, then moves on. Moves on to change more lives, to end more lives. As a teenager I wanted to kill, I wanted to die. That's why I left home as soon as I could and joined the Marines to fight in a war, any war.

23

Lost and found

As the airplane took off, Becky Peterson, born Becky Satterwhite, leaned back into her seat and shut her eyes.

She had dark blonde hair, standing a little under five foot three, she was quite beautiful, and only had a faint resemblance to her dead mother, Marcia Satterwhite. She looked more like her aunt Nancy, except that her nose and cheek bones were slightly softer than Nancy's.

As I stared at her, she spoke quietly, not opening her eyes.

"Why are you staring at me?" Becky turned towards me and opened her eyes.

"I'm wondering a lot of things about you, Becky," I answered.

"I'll scream as loud as I can if you even try to touch me," Her eyes did not stray from mine; her voice was calm, certain.

"Not every adult male thinks that way," I paused. "I'm wondering why Phil Peterson took you away from your mother, and why has your location been a secret for so long?"

"Daddy took me away from her because I asked him to. I don't know why no one ever looked for me, because I've been in Chicago for the past ten months."

"It seems unusual for a thirteen year old girl to ask to be taken away from her own mother."

In the silence that followed, I watched her come to a decision. Maybe it's easier to talk to a total stranger about one's very dysfunctional family.

"My mother was losing her mind," Becky said. "Even now, I can remember her leaving me alone in that house for days at a time, sometimes more than a week. She would bring strangers to our house all the time, men, women, little babies. She would cry and scream before they came and after they left."

"What would she cry about?"

"I don't know, but it got worse. Then when my daddy visited for a week I asked him to take me away from there."

"Do you know what all those strange people were doing there?"

"No, mama would always tell me to go to my room, and stay out of her way," Becky looked down at the floor. "I just read a lot of books."

"Do you remember what the strange people said?"

"No," Becky sighed, but her voice had gone flat. "Mama beat me real bad a few days before Daddy sent Mr. Lepus to take me; it was right after Daddy went back home. My nose took a long time to stop bleeding; mama was drunk. The next afternoon she didn't remember what had happened to my nose."

Becky faced front and slid down in her seat.

"Did you know your mother was rich?" I was mostly curious about when she figured that one out. Was she calculating, or just damaged by being brought up in the worst family ever, or both?

I knew that Marcia was worth millions, but she sure didn't live like a millionaire. Why would someone worth six million take a mid level government job and live in a working class house?

"No," A quick look of confusion crossed Becky's face, replaced by sadness again. "I didn't know she had a lot of money until now. Back when she was alive, we lived all right, but Mom never bought me a lot of stuff. She always had a nice car; she always said that was the one thing she wouldn't skimp on; no fancy vacations and no fancy clothes, and no fancy toys."

"That seems strange," I commented. "A woman worth millions working at a low paying job and living in a working class neighborhood."

"One thing I'll never forget is that she was cheap," Becky nodded. "She would always talk about how she would never be poor, and she would do anything to make sure she wasn't."

159

"Kind of like saving until she had enough?" I paid attention to the pronoun Becky had used; her mother was selfish in addition to everything else.

"Yeah," Becky wrinkled her brow. "Only, it seemed there never could be enough."

"Did she ever take you to Malibu?" I wondered. "Did you ever visit anyone with a beach house?"

"No," Becky looked puzzled. "I wish she had known someone at the beach, I loved the beach."

"Do you remember your Aunt Nancy?" I asked, changing the subject.

"Yeah, a little; she's okay. How's she doing, does she still have that maid? Paula always took me to neat places and bought me treats," Becky's eyes focused directly on me. Her body language said that she actually liked the maid, perhaps a lot more than her blood relatives.

"I don't know if Paula's still with your aunt, but I've met her and she seems like a good person," I looked at Becky in what I hoped was an encouraging manner. "The last time I spoke to her she asked about you."

"Aunt Nancy was always good to me, mama acted differently around her."

"How do you mean?"

"She was quiet, she never hit me, and she was always nice to everybody."

"What did you think of your grandmother?" I asked.

"I only met her once, after Mr. Lepus got me," Becky paused. "She's the meanest grown up I've ever met."

"Did you ever meet your grandfather?" I asked.

"Yeah, once when I was nine years old, and then right after Mr. Lepus took me away from mama. All I remember is him calling me a bastard and telling me to get away from him, both times."

"Well, he hasn't changed much."

"How's your life been in Chicago?"

"Fine, daddy's been okay. He says that he tries to be father and a mother also. He does as best he can, I guess," Becky looked down again at her seat.

He struck me as a mother all right, and Becky's lack luster, response led me to think her answer wasn't quite the truth.

"He never married again?"

"He and Mom never married, they just lived together; he told me that last year. She wanted him to sign an agreement about money before she would marry him, and he refused to, so they just lived together."

"Did he ever legally adopt you?" I asked.

"Yeah, we went to court and everything a while ago and I'm legally his daughter."

The girl smiled; it was forced, she wanted me to think that everything was all right.

I turned, looking at Becky eye to eye, "I'm going to find out who killed your mother, not so much for the money your grandfather is paying, but more for my own peace of mind. I'd like to tell you some names, and have you tell me if you know them, and what you know about them."

"OK. I wish I knew better what to do, but I'll tell you if I know them," Becky answered.

"Richard Snively?"

"Never heard of him."

"Cassandra Pales?"

"Never heard of her."

"William Aaronson?"

"Nope."

"Irving Lopez?"

"Who?"

"Irving Lopez?"

"No way, I'd remember a name like that if I'd ever heard it before."

"Paul Peterson?"

"That's Daddy's brother, he died a long time ago in an airplane crash. They found his body six months ago, and I went with him when he picked up the remains," She hesitated, then continued. "Any more names?"

"Not now, maybe later," I turned around in my seat and faced forward. "Do you remember any of your mother's friends in Los Angeles?"

"Yeah, there was the lady two doors down, Ms. Alvarez. Then, there was that man she was always seeing."

"Was he her boyfriend?"

"No, I don't think so, I don't think she liked him very much," She said.

"What was his name?"

"All I remember is Hank, I never knew his last name," Becky answered.

"What did he look like, was he tall? What color hair did he have, stuff like that?" I hoped for a possible clue.

"He seemed tall, and had a lot of muscles. He had blonde hair, real blonde hair. He spoke with a southern drawl, like the people on the Beverly Hillbillies," Becky made a sour expression. "And he was always grumpy."

"Do you know where your mother met him, was it in Los Angeles, or in Atlanta, or in Chicago?"

"I don't know," she answered.

The two of us sat, drinking and eating snacks, without talking, for thirty minutes. I finally broke the silence, "Where did Paul Peterson crash?"

"What?"

"Your father's brother, Paul Peterson, you said he crashed in a plane. I assumed it was a small plane, and I was wondering where it crashed?" I asked.

"Oh, it crashed in Arkansas. They didn't know why he headed in that direction, because he was supposed to fly from Atlanta to Pittsburgh."

"Was he alone?"

"Yeah."

The seat belt sign flashed and I knew we would be in Los Angeles soon. Becky told me the name of the small town in

Arkansas where she and Phil Peterson had stayed while he arranged the transport of his brother's remains to Chicago.

"The police will be waiting for you in the airport, if they aren't, I'll take you to them. They'll give you, and your father, a hard time for not coming forward sooner," I said.

"Daddy's never wanted me to have anything to do with any of my mother's family," Becky blurted out, as if to defend her father.

"Did he ever say why?" I asked.

"He said they're all dangerous; none of them have any morals, and I believe him."

Becky turned away from me and stared straight ahead.

"I can believe that of your grandfather, but Nancy seems pleasant," I tried to defuse her hard feelings.

"I guess she's nice, but I liked her maid better," Becky still stared ahead.

"Yeah, she's okay," I agreed, not wanting to continue the conversation.

As we walked off the airplane, I handed Becky one of my business cards and told her that she could call me anytime she felt she needed a friend.

"I'd like to think I'm working for you, not your grandfather," I said, smiling in what I hoped was a reassuring manner.

The police knew which flight I had booked from Washington, and they were waiting for Becky; Phil Peterson was standing near them.

Becky walked slowly to her father and looked at him, then at the ground. The police led both of them to the front of the airport, and to waiting police cars. I was curious about the reason Becky didn't rush up to Phil and hug him as a lost daughter should.

Lieutenant Hatton greeted me as I arrived at the police station, "Thank you for calling us, it makes it much easier when you cooperate."

"Do I detect some sarcasm, Mark?"

"Not at all, I'm hoping you'll cooperate some more and tell me what you know about Marcia's Satterwhite's murder."

"I don't know any more than I did right after she was murdered.   More points to her father as the killer than anyone else, but it could have been Brian Fowler too," I said.

"Why would you say that?   He had no real connection to her, other than relationship by marriage."

"Marcia, Brian, that doctor in Miami, and a Paul Peterson were partners in an illegal adoption scam eight years ago."

"What?"

"Don't tell me you haven't heard that before," I replied.

"I have now," Mark said with a surprised look on his face. His shoulders sank down into his loose suit.   "I'll have to check into that. What type of scam?"

"I'm not sure, I think they imported babies from somewhere outside the United States. I also think they were bankrolled by Irving Lopez; you do recognize that name, don't you?" I asked.

"Most certainly," Mark leaned back on his heels.   "Is there more?"

"Not yet. If there is I'll be sure to tell you first," I paused. "Can I go home now?   I'm tired."

"Sure, you've been a good citizen, Benjamin."

"I'm your friend; if you were any other shit kicking cop, you would've gotten none of this," I was tired, and maybe a bit too blunt.

"In that case, thanks," Mark was silent for a second while he collected his thoughts.   "No, I really mean it, Benjamin, I do appreciate your help."

24

Only the lonely

The cab ride from the airport to Cassandra's apartment in the early morning hours was refreshing. She lived in Santa Monica, about five blocks walking distance from the pier, in a lot better neighborhood than I do; a top floor apartment in a three story flat roof building. It was very light, with lots of sunshine in most of the rooms, and quite fifties retro.

When an over muscled giant answered Cassandra's doorbell, without his shirt on, I knew she hadn't been alone for the evening.

When the large individual took a swing at me as he asked for some time alone with Cassandra, I guessed that Cassandra would most likely be occupied for a while longer.

As I shoved the large, clumsy man's head into the door jamb, I surmised that Cassandra might soon be free after all to talk to me about the case since the large man was now asleep.

I stepped over the unconscious hulk, still in the doorway, and came face to face with Cassandra, rushing from the back room with her automatic pistol in hand.

"Wait a minute! I'm sorry I ruined your romantic interlude with Atlas over there, but don't shoot," I pointed at him; he looked even larger on the floor. "Atlas lunged, I shrugged."

"Oh, it's you," She lowered her pistol. She was talking between gulps of air. "This jerk followed me home, and insisted on insisting."

"I warned you about those kinds of bars, Cassandra."

"Oh, go jump in a lake! I was trying to find someone named Hank, not Hulk," She snorted.

"I would say something rude, but I know who you're talking about. Hank was a friend of Marcia, wasn't he?"

"Yeah, but how'd you know?" She sat down, a bit winded.

"Becky told me, I found her in D. C. Lepus was holding her, and I brought her here; I just left her loving reunion with the cops and her father, Phil Peterson."

"You have been busy, haven't you?" .

"So have you," I looked at the large man in her doorway. "I take it he's not wanted in here."

"I kicked him where it should have hurt, but he took that as a come on. I was going to try shooting him, figuring he'd have to take that as a rejection. Please shove him out the door before he comes to, I've already reported him to the police."

She waved in the general direction of the door, then she looked tangentially from it.

"Let's lock him and his shirt out, then go back to the office. I need to make some plane reservations for both of us," I pushed the large man out into the hall with my foot. "The cops will take care of him when they get here."

"Shouldn't we wait for them?" she asked.

"I guess you could leave a note on him if you want," I looked down at the large man. "But, I think they'll get the idea when they show up here."

"Very funny."

"Maybe not," I shrugged my shoulders. "But, we do have to get going."

"Where do I get to go, some place exciting, like Ventura, right?"

Cassandra dumped the shirt on the large man in her hallway as we walked past him to the stairway.

"I'm sure there's some very exciting places in Ventura," I grinned.

"Sometimes I wonder why I'm doing this," Cassandra retorted.

"What do you mean, are you talking about this case?" I asked.

"No, this line of work. I could have gone to grad school full-time, and be teaching somewhere safe now," She sighed.

"Please take note of what you'd be missing."

I pointed back towards the large man in a pile in her hallway.

"Yeah," Cassandra replied, shaking her head. "Look what I'd be missing."

"You'd be missing me."

There, I was direct this time; I finally said what I was thinking unlike all the other times this discussion came up.

"Excuse me?"

Cassandra stopped right outside her apartment building and looked me straight in the face.

"If you dropped out of the detective agency, you'd be missing me," I repeated. "I love you, and I love working with you, and I love seeing your beautiful face in front of me almost every day in the office, and I love having you in my life and more than you missing me, I would miss you."

"That was a mouthful," Cassandra leaned towards me. "I love you too, sweetheart."

She kissed me longer than usual.

. . . .

On the ride to our office, I told her what had happened in Miami and Washington. It took the whole ride to go into the details of everything, and what I thought of Becky.

"Something's different about that kid, she doesn't act like a normal fifteen year old should," I said. Not that I had been involved with teenage girls all that much since high school. But something kept nagging at me, just out of reach.

"What do you mean?" Cassandra asked.

"I don't know," I thought for a moment, "She acts more like an adult than she should, and she seems to have her act together more than most adults do."

"Like how?" Cassandra asked. "What did she do, or say to make you think something was unusual?"

"She isn't afraid like I thought she'd be and for a kid who supposedly loves her father, she acted pretty cool towards him when she saw him at the airport this morning."

167

"Don't you think that poor girl has been through hell?" Cassandra asked. "She's probably been at least mentally abused by Peterson; maybe she's numbed out, that alone would make her actions now seem a little unusual."

"I guess so," I sighed.

As she opened the door to our office, I asked. "How did you find out about Marcia's friend, Hank? I take it that wasn't Hank back at your apartment."

"No, that wasn't Hank, but he had to be a friend of his. I got Hank's name from Brian Fowler," Cassandra replied.

"You found Fowler, where?" I asked.

"In San Francisco, he wasn't that hard to locate. He had changed his name and social security number, he now owns a small air charter business."

"A fly by night outfit?"

"Cute," Cassandra remarked, and put her right hand on her hip. "Do you want me to continue?"

"Okay."

"His name is now Brian Satterwhite, clever right?" Cassandra smiled.

"No."

"To continue, Brian said that he and his partners were in an adoption scam. They provided the babies to willing couples for a high price, with no questions asked. Richard Snively, Paul Peterson, Irving Lopez, Hank Cummings, Marcia Satterwhite, and he were partners," Cassandra said.

"Why is he so cooperative all of a sudden, are they still in business?"

"He says they aren't. He also says that they stopped doing it years ago, and that it might have been shady, but not completely illegal," She answered.

"I find that hard to believe."

"Me too; I asked him why he changed his name, and went into hiding," Cassandra said.

"And, why did he?" I asked.

"He claims it was to escape his ex father-in-law, Zeb; it seems that Zeb threatened to kill him."

"So, he hides by taking the name of the man who wants to kill him; not likely. Does he think that Zeb killed Marcia?"

"I asked Brian the very same question," Cassandra answered. "He said Zeb was capable of killing her."

"You said Paul Peterson was a partner, he's dead, so is Richard Snively, and Marcia Satterwhite. I think the connection is there, although there has to be more to it." I said.

"One of the partners killed the others for the exclusive territory, or was there competition moving in on their scam?"

"Or even both. So, do we talk to the living members of the gang, or look into the dead members of the gang?"

"I'm going to Arkansas," I said, "to find out what I can about the death of Paul Peterson. I want to know what he had in his plane when it crashed; he was a thousand miles off the course he had filed. Maybe I can find something, even after all these years."

"So where do I go, oh great white hunter?"

"You can go to Ventura if you like, or you can go to Chicago and look into Phil Peterson, and Becky. We need to know more what the relationship is between those two."

"Better Chicago than Ventura," She grinned. "How much money do we have left?"

"I don't know, but don't lose any receipts," I said. "I think we have a thousand or so left. Before you leave, send the old fart a bill for another thousand; tell him we're hot on the trail of Marcia's killer, and that he himself is the prime suspect."

"Great, you have a way with our paying customers."

"Okay, leave the last part out, then."

"Good idea," Cassandra paused, then smiled at me. "And, I would miss you a whole lot if we didn't work together."

25

Somewhere to run, nowhere to hide

"Fred?" Cathy Rumson looked at her boss.

"Yeah," Fred crumpled his eyebrows together into a mass of hair in the middle of his forehead. "Where can we go now?"

Cathy had parked her car on the shoulder of Crest Lane which parallels Washington Memorial Parkway, only a few blocks away from CIA headquarters. The thin woods lining the side street showed some slight budding in response to the warmth of Spring.

"Well," Cathy sighed and leaned onto the door of the old Buick. "We can't stay in my car forever."

"I know," Fred said, irritated. "What do you suggest?"

"Who owes you a favor?" A glint of hope spread across Cathy's broad face.

Fred twitched his nose and relaxed his face; one eyebrow raised slightly, "You do."

Cathy shook her head with emphasis, whipping her blonde curls from cheek to cheek.

"No way, not here, besides you were just run out of your last hideout by Lopez' friends; I'm sure they know what this car looks like."

"So, where then? Montana? Hagerstown?"

"Too cold, and too close," Cathy closed her eyes to think. "I know!"

"I wish I did."

"That Congressman you tailed, you remember?"

"Yeah, but I worked for his wife," Fred argued. "She wanted to get something on him for a divorce."

"But where did you find him?" Cathy grinned broadly.

"Oh," Fred nodded. "In bed with a Senate page, but I haven't given the photos to the wife yet."

"Right," Cathy's head nodded in unison with Fred's.

"Show him the pictures," Fred stopped nodding his head. "But, that's blackmail, and, besides, what do I tell the wife? After all, she hired me."

"All you want to do is stay in the congressman's place for a while. The wife can find out in a week, and the congressman will have the heads up; they both will come out winners," Cathy thought for a second; she guessed that made sense. "Both the Senate and House are on a recess now, and I could make a discreet phone call for you, I do it all the time."

"I know," Fred shot a seductive grin at her. "And I love you for it, each and every time."

"Great, now, take your hand off my boob, and drive me to a phone."

26

What goes up, must come down

It was nearly five o'clock in the evening when I arrived in the small town of eleven hundred, nestled in the shadow of Fourche Mountain. I had flown into Little Rock, rented a car then drove the somewhat long, but beautiful route to the small town in the Ozarks. Rolling hills covered with evergreens looked like a large rumpled green bedspread piled at the foot of a giant's bed. The sun was bright, the sky a piercing blue with small puffy white clouds darting from west to east with the wind. High humidity was mediated by a mild temperature, so I turned off the air conditioner and opened the side window. The air was fresh and clean, something I miss all too much where I live.

As the city limit sign passed by, I began to keep an eye out for a place to spend the night since I had decided to wait until the next morning before I contacted the local sheriff. There was a choice of only two decent motels in what passed for a downtown in this Ozark community; the place looked like it would attract only the overflow, a few tourists, from more popular areas. Lots of empty rooms and parking lots. I settled in the better looking motel.

Some builder had meant to create the impression of a rustic Ozark inn, the motel was covered by a half-log exterior veneer; the lobby interior paneled in fake knotty pine. A big fireplace stood on the wall opposite the desk. All the rooms stretched out in two directions from the central lobby, like a lot of old motor lodges. The rooms, however, were built to resemble individual log cabins, even though they were all connected. My room was fitted with the same fake knotty pine paneling, as well as the requisite kitsch magic-fingers bed massage.

I asked the clerk for recommendations about a restaurant, and received only a grunt and a nod in the direction of a cafe a block from the motel.

The food was hot and home cooked, but the cuisine was not very appetizing; the smell of overcooked beef permeated the whole diner. The only redeeming smell in the establishment came from the outstanding scent of home cooked apple pie. The scent of cinnamon, crust and sugar made me wolf down the meatloaf special in anticipation of dessert. While I was finishing my apple pie, a policeman walked up to my table and sat down next to me, the leather of his holster loudly creaked as he sat.

"I accept this kind welcome to your delightful town with the sincerity with which it's offered," I said, careful to stay friendly.

I knew that I was probably in trouble, even though I didn't know why.

The policeman never changed his set expression, "Are you Benjamin Katz?"

He had a gravely voice that echoed from his flat face. He stood about five foot seven and had to weigh at least two hundred thirty pounds. Although his gut spilled over the wide belt carrying his pistol, baton, handcuffs and extra ammo, he seemed tough enough to kick my ass if he wanted to. His nose was small and pocked with irregularities and he looked as if he had never smiled in his life.

Oh great. I was back traveling in the wonderful world of shit, and I had let my AAA membership expire again.

"I am indeed Benjamin Katz, why do you ask?" I tried to keep my smile in place.

"A lieutenant Mark Hatton from Los Angeles called me this afternoon and said I should be seeing you sometime today," The policeman still stared at me, expressionless.

173

Mark, you son of a bitch, don't you know what these small town cops are like. I could be stuck with sheriff Taylor for the next ten years. If I were lucky, Aunt Bea would cook a mean grits soufflé for me and if things got bad, Barney could use his single bullet on me.

"Well, I'm here, may I answer any questions you might have?" I lost my faint smile.

"Sure, what the hell're you doing in my town? If a cop from Los Angeles calls me all the way out here to warn me that you're coming, you must be trouble," The policeman said.

"Either I'm trouble, or he's in trouble and I promise you I'm not any trouble."

"What the hell're you doing here?" The policeman repeated.

"I came here to ask you about the plane wreck of Paul Peterson," I answered.

"And what else?" The policeman asked.

"Nothing else."

"The cop friend of yours said you're looking into a murder case of his, and he didn't seem too pleased about it," The policeman said, speaking more slowly with every word. "There ain't been no murder out here yet, so keep it simple and keep it quick, and you'll have no trouble from me."

"All I want to do is look at the crash site, plus anything that you brought out of the site."

"That'll be quick, there ain't much," he said.

I told the policeman a brief version of the murders and the missing child, and my part in the plot.

"Can I get you something to eat?" I asked, trying to ease the atmosphere.

"Naw, meet me at my office at eight o'clock in the morning, I'll show you what we got from the wreck."

The policeman rose and walked out of the café, without me in handcuffs behind him. Thank you God; small, but consistent, miracles will keep me faithful.

The plump, middle aged waitress, who had been hanging back while the sheriff was talking to me, spoke up, "My brother

174

found that plane, he said there weren't nothin' but bones left of the pilot, bones everywhere."

"Is your brother around? I'd like to talk to him," I said.

"Sure, he's at his house, I can call him, if ya want?" She asked.

"Tell him I'll pay twenty dollars for his story. I guess you heard why I'm here?"

"Yeah, I'll call him, wait here."

She rushed to the phone behind the counter.

Within ten minutes, I was talking to John Caldwell, one of the hunters who had happened on the crash site of Paul Peterson. He was a ruddy complexioned man who appeared eager to tell his story. I began by laying a twenty dollar bill on the table, which John folded into his plaid shirt pocket. Had he washed that shirt this decade? Had he washed himself this week? What a pungent odor. I hadn't smelled that ripe a human since my last trip to France.

"It happened a bit under two years ago, on the third day of gun season. It was real weird, I never seen nothin' like it. There weren't nothin' left but bones, little pieces of bones, and they was all over the place. His head was twenty feet from the rest of his bones; there was this big steel pot next to it," John spread his hands, as he relived the moment.

"What kind of steel pot?"

"It was still shinny, and the lid was bent real bad, but it was still on. Looked like the pot hit the back of his head, and knocked it clean off his body."

"What was in the pot?"

"Don't know. The sheriff took it back to his office, along with a bunch of other junk," John answered.

"What do you think caused the crash?"

"I bet on the weather. I bet he was flyin' too low when a storm and the mountain caught him," John replied.

"Were there any drugs around?" I asked, paying careful attention to his reaction.

"We didn't find none. My huntin' partner's a deputy sheriff and he looked plenty hard for it. That's his guess for who was flyin' the plane, a drug runner," John said, not changing his expression.

"I got me an eight pointer that mornin,' " he added. "We was trackin' it."

"It must not have dropped quickly," I said, to keep him talking.

"Naw," He paused.

I got a mental picture of the deer running. "Dropped to one knee, then bolted away. I got him good in the boilermaker with my 45/70, though. He bled out and dropped right where the plane wreckage started."

"Did they tell you who the pilot was?"

What the hell was a boilermaker and would the sheriff want to shoot me there too?

"Yeah, the sheriff said he was some professor from Atlanta goin' on a business trip, but I don't see it," John said. "Hell, he crashed way back in sixty seven. His bones was up there on the mountain for a long time a'fore we found 'em."

"Why do you think he wasn't going on a business trip?" I asked.

"The sheriff said he wasn't supposed to be out here; he was supposed to be goin' to Pittsburgh in Pennsylvania. What the hell would a fancy guy like that be doin' way off course way out here unless he was doin' somethin' illegal?" John asked.

"What do you think he was doing way out here?"

"I think he was goin' to Mexico," John leaned towards me. "He might 'a had somethin' illegal in that big metal pot. It might'a leaked out, or someone might'a stole it, I don't know."

"What other stuff did you see around the crash?" I asked.

"Like what, what kind a stuff?"

"You expect to find pieces of airplane, clothes, and electronic gear around a crash site, but things like the steel pot you don't expect. I'm asking about anything else like the steel pot."

"I didn't see much else. After so many years, I guess there wouldn't be that much anyway."

"I guess not. You say the sheriff has most of what remained still in his office?"

"I guess he still does."

"I'm going to talk to him tomorrow morning, what's his name?"

"Oh, he's Billy Hasbroke."

"Is he all right, I mean, will he throw me in jail if I ask the wrong thing?"

This was perhaps the most important question I asked that night.

"Naw, he acts mean, but he thinks he's got to 'cause he's sheriff. He's an all right ol' boy. You treat him square, 'n he'll treat you square," John answered.

. . . .

The next morning I awoke in a panic. I was supposed to meet the sheriff at eight o'clock, and it was now ten minutes to nine. I dressed as quickly as I could, not taking time to shave.

I rushed out the main door of the small motel at five minutes after nine, not realizing that I didn't know where the sheriff's office was. Slowly walking back into the motel, I tried to keep calm as I asked a plaid shirted old man behind the desk where the sheriff's office was located.

Behind the counter, he cocked his balding head to one side, "Take a left, go two blocks, then take a right, can't miss it."

Following the old man's directions brought me to a small brick building standing by itself at the end of the block. I walked slowly through the door and observed the sheriff looking at me as I walked across the small room and sat next to the desk.

"You must be in good shape to run all the way here and not be huffin' and puffin'."

"The old man at the motel called you, right?"

"Yeah, old Cyrus's a good fella. Well, what do ya want to know about the plane crash?" The sheriff asked.

"First, I want to know why you're going to help me, especially after you thought the Lieutenant was trying to get you not to?"

177

"He sounded like he has a problem with a murder back in LA , sounds like he's got too much of his ego wrapped up in it," Billy said. "His murder's his problem, I've got enough of my own to bother worrin' about his too."

"Well, You're right, he does have a lot of ego wrapped up in it. But that still doesn't answer my question." I began to like this fellow.

"Paul Peterson died in my county, and I want to know why," Billy answered. "It ain't a big burnin' issue in my life, I just want to know why."

"His plane crashed, that's why."

"I meant why he was here; he was up to somethin'. I know it, but never have found out what it was," Billy said.

"Why be so concerned with a plane crash?" I wondered out loud.

"Not much happens up here, 'n when somethin' does, I wanna know why. It may seem like nothin' to a big city cop like your lieutenant Hatton, but I just don't like any loose ends in my county."

"Do you still have all the things you found at the site?"

"Sure do, and you're welcome to look at them,"

"Why did you keep them? Didn't the family want any of it back?"

"No one ever answered any of my questions, so, to me, the case's still open. Peterson's brother came down here to claim the remains, but he didn't ask for nothin' but the bones and the cash," Billy answered.

"Was there a teenage girl with the brother?"

"I didn't see one, but that's not to say she wasn't at the resort."

"Resort?" I asked slowly.

"Yeah, if you go on past town for about ten miles, there's a first class resort with private cabins, Peterson rented one while he was here."

The sheriff shook his head and smiled as if I were a dumb ass city slicker. Well, maybe I was.

178

Resort? Expense account and resort go together like a 45/70 and a boilermaker; I should have kept driving last night.

"But, when he came here to claim the body?" I managed to ask.

"He was alone," Billy answered. "He seemed strange for kinfolk. He acted like it was the biggest bother in the world coming here to look after his own flesh and blood."

"Why? Did he talk much about his brother?"

"Naw, he didn't say two words, he was only here for a little more than an hour."

The sheriff stood up and walked towards a back store room.

"The weirdest thing is this pot."

Billy pointed at a fair sized stainless steel pot with a bent lid.

"There was a lot of broken glass inside it. There also seemed to be some crud in the bottom of it, so I sent some of it to the state crime lab to look for drugs. They said there wasn't no drugs in that stuff."

"What was it?"

"They said it was some kind of organic material. They said it was human tissue, but they didn't know exactly what kind," Billy answered.

"Did anyone check out this stuff besides you?"

"A friend of mine who works for the state patrol looked at this stuff, but he couldn't make any sense out of it; you got any ideas?" Billy asked.

"That pot looks like a shipping container I've seen before, it looks like something used to ship frozen samples in; a shipment of frozen tissue samples, frozen in liquid nitrogen, I saw shipped in a container like that once."

"What was he carrying?" The sheriff asked himself, or the room at large.

"I'm not sure, but I have an idea. Can I take a sample of the stuff in the bottom and take it to a lab?" I asked.

"Yeah," The sheriff answered. "Only if you call me back and tell me what it was, and why he was headed to, or from, Mexico with it."

"You think he tried to fly to Mexico too?" I asked.

"Take a map, and draw a line, where does it lead?" Billy asked.

"It depends on where the line starts, but Mexico isn't that far from here by air, I guess. He took one unplanned turn, he might have taken another," I observed.

"Too many crooks fly across here, both ways, for me to believe otherwise. The sky over Florida and California are too crowded with cops if he wanted to really sneak there and back. He was up to something illegal, I want to find out what, I'll even use a detective like you to help me," Billy said with a grin.

"If there are charges against Peterson, they'll be filed in Atlanta, not here. A plane crashed in your county, that's all," I replied.

"But he died here, and I need to settle it here, if only for me," The sheriff said. "We don't get much crime here, 'n when there is, I have to solve it. A matter of pride, nothin' else."

"Can I look over some more of these things."

"Yeah, but if you think of something, tell me about it," Billy sat back down in his chair.

As I sifted through the items I saw that most of the metal had rusted. I was amazed at the extent of things the sheriff had recovered, items ranging from the stainless steel container, to Paul Peterson's wallet.

"Did Peterson ask for anything of his brother's?" I shouted from the closet.

"He just asked for anything he had been carrying in his pockets and any cash, nothin' else," Billy answered.

"I see you didn't give anything to him."

"Only the cash, he seemed happy enough with that. I told him as soon as I found out what his brother was doing here, and why he crashed in my county, I'd give him everythin'," Billy answered.

"How much cash?" I asked.

"A little over six thousand, mostly in hundreds," The sheriff answered.

"I take it you checked the serial numbers," I casually asked.

"I ain't dumb," he snorted.

"Sorry," I quickly replied.

"The money was clean," Billy said.

"That's a lot of cash for a nerd to be carrying around," I chuckled.

"And, that's why I said, drugs," Billy answered.

"Did the FAA ever do an investigation?" .

"Yeah, they said a down draft caught him in a big thunder storm, but they didn't know why he was that far off course. They said they would look into the reason later, but they never did, least ways they never told me why."

Meanwhile I carefully flipped open the weathered wallet I had found in a box of decayed detritus. In the card section of the wallet was a still usable Diners Club Charge card, although the expiration date was nine years ago. In the picture section were several membership cards for professional organizations, all of which were normal for a person in his position. The driver's license included a horrible picture of Paul Peterson.

There were only three other pictures of people in the wallet. One picture had a group shot of Paul, his brother Phil, and an older woman, most likely their mother because they all looked alike. The second picture was of Marcia Satterwhite as a young woman, and the third was of a small twin engine airplane. That last photograph seemed familiar, it was most likely the airplane Paul had been flying when he crashed, but I thought I had seen the photograph before, somewhere else. I wrote down the numbers that appeared on the airplane's wings, body and tail.

In one of the back compartments of the wallet was a long, almost decayed piece of paper with a series of phone numbers below the names of various cities.

"This list of telephone numbers, the one in his wallet, did you call any of them?" I shouted in a booming voice from the store room.

181

"Yeah, but they mostly were just people's home phones, some were disconnected. It was a long time from the crash to when we fished all this crap off the mountain," The sheriff answered.

"Was there any connection between the valid numbers?"

"Can't say they were still valid, people move a lot in that many years. All kinds answered the phone; some were old retired folks, some young couples, some single men and women, and a few awful queer sounding men."

"Oh," I continued sifting through the junk.

I noticed a half decayed small black spiral notebook and picked it up carefully. The ink had faded so much that the pages almost appeared blank.

There seemed to be only names, at least I thought that's what they were because I could not read too many of them, no addresses followed any of the names.

Looking at several pages, I noticed two things: the names were in alphabetical order, and all the names that I could make out seemed to be female Spanish first names.

All the clothes, and one suitcase, lay in the back corner of the room. Finding one business suit, and one casual suit, I searched through all the pockets, or what was left of them; I found nothing. The last item appeared to have been a surgical gown of some sort. There were no pockets on it, nor any markings which could be made out.

The suitcase was torn in many places, and all the contents were gone. I rummaged around in a box near the torn suitcase and saw a hair brush and a broken tooth brush.

"You emptied out the suitcase?" I asked in a loud voice.

"Yup, the stuff's all near it, in the boxes," Billy answered from his chair.

Picking up the suitcase, I noticed several airline baggage tickets, still readable, attached to the handle. I could make out the names of the Atlanta, Chicago, and New York airports. There were two others which I could not make out.

"Find anything?" The sheriff asked.

"Not much, there's a list of Spanish women's names. Did you check any of them out?" I asked.

"Can't, we couldn't figure out where to start looking. There's a lot of places down South where they speak Spanish," Billy answered. "But that's one reason I guessed he was goin' to Mexico, or somewhere like that."

"Did you know there was a picture of the woman, murdered in Los Angeles, in his wallet," I asked.

"Yeah, kinda interesting," Billy said. "He was married to her too."

"He was, I didn't know that," I said in a surprised voice.

"Yeah, they were only married for a year or so before he bought the farm; I understand that his brother took over after he died," Billy said.

"Yes, he did. I wonder if he took over more than Marcia?"

"When you find out, call me, collect if you like," Billy said.

"Did he have a gun?" I asked.

"Yeah."

"Don't tell me, it was a nine millimeter," I asked.

"You guessed it, that's what killed his wife, wasn't it?" Billy asked.

"You did check the gun out, didn't you?" I asked.

"Like I said before, I ain't dumb. I sent it to the FBI and they sent it back. This gun wasn't used in any crime they knew about, including the Los Angeles murder of Marcia Satterwhite."

Billy pulled a nine millimeter semi automatic pistol out of his center drawer. It was in remarkably good condition to spite its long repose in the woods and weather. It still had half of its original bluing and I would bet it would still shoot and not blow up.

"Who owned the pistol?" I asked.

"The only record of this gun was the transfer from the manufacturer to the dealer," Billy said with a smile.

"Okay, who was the dealer?" I asked.

"This Colt was purchased by Zeb Satterwhite," Billy answered.

"Curiouser and curiouser. Let me take a sample of the stuff in the container and I'll be in touch by tomorrow morning some time," I said.

"Be my guest," Billy handed me a knife and a small bottle. "I figured that if I left this problem alone for a while I'd get a new slant on it; I had no idea that I'd be getting free help."

27

Turn over a rock and you have a rolling stone

The flight east was uneventful, Cassandra always drew uneventful flights, which is not a bad thing. Her thoughts circled around the case. What had Phil been up to all this time? What was Becky's life like for the past two years? How did these two connect to Marcia's murder?

Chicago, a hell of a town, something about slaughtering cows, and broad shoulders, definitely a macho sort of a city. Not much of a place for a little girl to grow up all alone, especially one who lost her mother and was raised, kind of, by a two bit mobster.

Cassandra picked the closest car rental booth, instead of the cheapest this time. Actually, they're all about the same, or so she told herself as she handed over the company credit card to pay for the mid sized Chevrolet with power everything and air conditioning.

"I guess It's easier to take I-294 up to I-94 and go over to 41 and up. Or is it better to go I-94 up to Deerfield Road and then straight East?" Cassandra looked up from the crude map the clerk gave her.

"I think the interstate will be quicker."

"Yes, but they both seem to be Interstate roads to a certain point."

"I see," The clerk looked at the map in front of them. "I really don't know which one will be best."

"I guess not," Cassandra sighed. "I'll decide when I get to I-94."

The drive up was boring, at least by herself it was boring. She loved Katz, but didn't admit it to herself all the time, although she was becoming more likely to admit she loved him as time went on. Investing several years with one man must mean something, especially if she kept thinking about investing even more time with him. It wasn't a bad life, but she wished she could spend more time with Katz instead of traipsing off on separate trips. Out here everything felt different, but she was alone, the sole person watching it. She'd like to hear what her best friend thought of this park, or whatever this was that she was driving through now. She'd like to tell him about the camping trips her folks took when she was kid. Why wouldn't Katz take her to Europe when he had a case there? She stopped her thoughts, and quickly turned on the radio. Her best friend and lover was hiding something. Katz had told her a lot about his childhood, and the pain he was still having coping with the death of his mother; she knew there had to be more.

Highland Park was easy to find, it was a big place, although Phil Peterson's condo was quite another matter. Cassandra spent three hours and endless conversations with gas station attendants and non-English speaking convenience store clerks locating Peterson's neighborhood before she found the right building. He lived in a housing development which appeared to have a gate as an entrance, but the gate had never been finished. The buildings were three and two story brick construction and seemed to be clustered in fours, each having its own cul-de-sac with spacious common grounds. The whole development looked no more than five or so years old, by the growth of all the planted trees. It appeared as if the developer leveled the entire site before building.

. . . .

"Did you see much of Mr. Peterson?" Cassandra asked the seventy something man, big and burly, standing part way out his front door.

The good thing about condominiums, she thought, is that everybody has lots of close neighbors, lots of people to talk to.

"Not much at all," His eyes looked carefully beyond Cassandra. "They was real quiet types."

"When was the last time you saw Mr. Peterson?"

"Why are you askin' all these questions?"

Cassandra gave him the company smile, "I'm conducting a background investigation of Mr. Peterson for a financial institution."

That was almost true. Zeb Satterwhite had almost as much money as a small bank, although he belonged in an institution more than he resembled one.

"He gonna sell his place?" The elderly man changed his focus to Cassandra's face. "You wanna come in here and keep warm?"

"Sure."

Cassandra followed the man inside. It wasn't that cold outside, maybe a bit cool, but not enough to justify the tropical temperatures inside the living room.

"Is he gonna sell it?" The man repeated.

"I don't think so," Cassandra spoke cautiously.

"He gonna start a business there?"

"No."

"What does he want with all that money," The old man looked even more curious. "I mean they don't send a real cutie like you out just for a master card. He's gotta want some serious jack, I just wanna make sure he don't start some business in his house next door, you know."

Cassandra smiled extra wide for him, "No, he just wants a large increase in his line of credit with us, and all I need to do is ask you a few very simple questions."

"Okay, shoot."

"Well, First of all, what kind of neighbor is he?"

187

"He's hardly ever there, I guess you couldn't ask for a better neighbor. No noise, no trash, and he keeps to himself when he's here."

"Doesn't he have a daughter?"

"Yeah," The old man nodded his head. "Becky's a great little kid, she plays with my youngest granddaughter when she comes to visit me. You know my daughter's the only one who visits me now. I got two sons, one in Muncie, and the other in Calumet City; they both got family, but none of them come see me more than once every three years or so. You know, when my wife was still alive they come more often, but I once had words with the oldest boy, and now him and his brother don't visit much, don't remember what it was," The old man's voice trailed off, long enough for Cassandra to speak.

"If Mr. Peterson's away so often, who takes care of his daughter?"

"Is that a money question, or are you just curious?"

"I'm just curious," Cassandra nodded.

"Yeah," The man nodded in agreement. "Me too."

"Do you take care of her?"

The man smiled for the first time, "When I can; she runs errands for me, we eat a meal or two together, you know. She's a real grown up little kid, real polite too."

"Back to Mr. Peterson, was there ever a Mrs. Peterson living here?"

"No."

"Does he ever have any wild parties, or anything strange going on in his house?"

"Not that I've seen. He does have a few business suit types come over every once and a while, no loud stuff or nothin' though."

"Does his daughter have any loud parties?"

"No, not that sweet thing," The old man shook his head. "She's real quiet and stays to herself, she likes to read a lot. I don't hear much out of her."

"Thank you very much for your time," Cassandra paused on her way out the door. "Can you tell me the name of Mr. Peterson's other next door neighbor?"

"That would be Mrs. Benson, Sally Benson. She and her little girl live there. Her husband left her two years ago, up and moved to Virginia with his secretary," The old man chuckled. "It's just like Ann Landers around this place!"

. . . .

"Mrs. Benson?" Cassandra smiled at the pleasant woman peering through the storm door. "My name is Cassandra Pales, and I have been hired to investigate your neighbor, Mr. Peterson, for a financial institution."

"Has he done anything wrong?" The woman furrowed her brow.

"Not at all, I just need to get some background information for a financial decision on Mr. Peterson."

"Oh," The woman looked about. "Are you alone?"

"Yes, just me."

This was the second neighbor with a security concern, it might just be the area. No, this was a fairly classy condo development so it might just be Peterson.

The woman stood there silently, biting her lower lip,"Please come in and sit down. I don't know much about my neighbor, except that he's hardly ever there."

"So his other next door neighbor said," Cassandra studied Sally Benson.

"Did he tell you about Becky?" Sally acted anxious. Tell us how she acted anxious

"He mentioned that she was alone a lot, and was well behaved and quiet."

Cassandra waited, consciously relaxing her shoulders, letting herself breathe slowly.

"You have to understand I didn't like doing it, but I just felt so heartbroken for that girl."

Cassandra knew she hit pay dirt, "What did you do?"

189

"I called the child welfare people," Mrs. Benson's anxiousness turned to sadness. "Becky is such a special child, she baby-sits for me all the time. My daughter just started kindergarten and goes to the school just down the street from Becky's school. Well, the high school is right next to the grammar school and middle school. I work part-time and Becky keeps Julia for me," Sally began to cry. "I just wanted to help her."

"I understand," Cassandra sat on the sofa next to Sally and put her hand on her shoulder. "Do you know where either one of them are right now?"

"I never know where Phil is. No, I don't know where Becky is, and that worries me so much."

Cassandra wondered if she should say more, but decided to wait.

Sally stared at her, "Who are you, you don't act like you work for a bank."

What the hell, she decided she would tell the woman.

Cassandra sighed, "I don't, I'm a private investigator from Los Angeles. Phil and Becky are party to a large inheritance, and a murder investigation. My partner and I are investigating the murder side of the whole thing."

Sally's face showed shock, "Who was murdered?"

Reluctantly, Cassandra answered, "Less than two years ago Becky's mother was murdered."

"She never mentioned a mother, I always wondered about that," The tears spread down Sally's cheeks. "I didn't know what to do."

"Tell me about Becky."

"I wish she were mine. Between Mr. Fishbine on the other side, and me, she has a family, sort of. Phil is a worm, lower than a worm; he leaves her money, and takes off for months, I think he's a mobster."

"Why?"

"Some of the people who visit, they look like mobsters. I've seen guns hanging from inside their coats. Some of them come in chauffeured limos. Who in the hell in this neighborhood knows people like that?"

Cassandra nodded, "What does Becky say about all this?"

"Nothing," Sally wiped her face and sighed. "We just don't talk about it because it upsets her. I. ," Sally paused.

"What?"

"I've been afraid for a long time she would run away, and that would be a disaster. You read about kids, especially girls, on the streets, runaways; I did everything to keep her here until she was old enough."

"Does anyone else know about her situation? You mentioned the child welfare people."

"They came only once," Sally's face brightened. "Becky's teacher knows, she also called the child welfare office. I talk with Becky's teacher, I go to parents' day for her and everything," Sally began to cry again. "You know, that child needs a mom; she hugs me like she wants to devour me when she leaves to go home next door."

Cassandra waited until school was out, then spoke to Becky's teacher; she got the same story Mrs. Benson gave. Becky came in to the school this September, and had to test to get into her grade since she was missing a year from her transcripts. Phil was looming large as a first class swine.

28

Now, where was I?

"Good afternoon, Dr. Billings is expecting you," The secretary greeted me.

"Good to see you again," I paused, looking for something else to say. "I talked to that man Lepus in Washington, he hasn't called you again, has he?"

"No, he hasn't. Go right on in to Dr. Billings' office, he's expecting you," she answered.

"What's so urgent that couldn't wait until tomorrow?" Dr. Billings got up from behind his desk and started to walk towards me.

"To make a long story short," I replied, "I visited the place where Paul Peterson crashed. He had a stainless steel container in his plane; it was the kind in which you ship frozen samples, stuff frozen in liquid nitrogen. I have a sample right here," I pulled the bottle from my coat pocket. "What I'd like is for you to look at this and tell me what he was transporting. The tissue is rather old, but maybe you can do something with it."

"Sure, I don't see why not. I'll call someone up here and have them look at it. You are spending the night here, I hope? It will be the late morning before they can complete all the tests."

"Yes I was planning on doing some work downtown tomorrow. What time should I come back here?" I asked.

"About eleven, that should be enough time to do any testing. My guess is that this was some sort of organic tissue," Dr. Billings studied the sample in the glass bottle.

192

"That's my guess too, but I need to make sure it's the type of tissue I think it is before I can go on in my investigation."

The hotel I chose to stay in had seen better days. In fact it appeared to have survived, barely, the Civil War. It was close to the court house, or I wouldn't have chosen it. The clerk seemed to have been one of the original Confederate guards, still confused over the disappearance of his comrades. He was, however, quite willing to wait for their return, and collect money from Yankees while he waited.

Almost as soon as I checked into the hotel, and dropped my suitcase and clothes on the floor, I fell into the bed and asleep.

The beep from my alarm woke me up at eight the next morning.

....

I knew I'd seen that picture of the twin engine airplane before. The picture in Paul Peterson's wallet was the same picture I saw years before in Brian Fowler's den, on the shelf of the curio cabinet. I remembered it in conjunction with the shooting trophies.

I bet more than one person owned that airplane. If two of those people were Brian Fowler, and Paul Peterson, the tax records should list all the owners.

Finding the old tax records office was easy. When I asked the clerk for help, and for what I was searching, she stopped and stared at me; I was taken off guard by her expression.

"All I want is to find the tax records for this airplane. It crashed in nineteen sixty seven, so there should be a record for that year. I've written the name of two of its owners and the number of the plane."

"Are you a police officer?" The clerk asked.

"No, I'm a private investigator, why did you ask?" I inquired.

"Some Los Angeles cop called us about this same airplane yesterday," She stared at me. "These folks must sure be popular."

"So you know where this record is?" I asked.

"The copy's right on my desk. And let me tell you, it was no easy job findin' it," She leaned over to a folder on her desk and handed it to me.

"The Lieutenant, probably named Hatton, wants a copy, right?" I asked, taking the folder.

"Yeah, you two know each other?" She asked.

"We do," I opened the folder and looked at a copy from microfilm of the old tax form.

The tax form had all the information about the airplane, and how much it cost, and how much tax was paid, and when it was paid. The form also had a list of names of all the owners: Richard Snively, Marcia Peterson, Brian Fowler, and Paul Peterson; all four had Atlanta addresses.

I closed the folder. "Do you think you could find the owner of record for this address for the past ten years?" I asked, writing Nancy Satterwhite's Atlanta address down on a piece of paper.

The woman led me to the clerk of court's records vault, then pointed to the grantor-grantee index.

"You'll find the property deeds by looking the names up in those books. These are the indexes for all real estate transactions in a county. You look up the name you want, and it will tell you which book to go to in order to find the deed for that property. Just leave the books on the table, the folks who work here will put them back."

I spent the next hour looking up not only the owner of Nancy and Brian Fowler's property, but all the other property belonging to Nancy, Marcia, and Zeb Satterwhite. They purchased each property without a mortgage. Nancy had owned the house she was in free and clear from the beginning and Brian Fowler's name never appeared on any deeds. Nancy Satterwhite held even more property in Fulton county than her father did. All of them owned office buildings and rental houses, lots of

194

rental houses. I took my notes and strolled out of the court house.

. . . .

As I walked into Dr. Billings' private office, I saw him seated behind his desk, and another man leaning on the edge of his desk.

"This is Dr. Matthews, he did the tests on the sample you brought in, and he'd like to tell you what he found," Dr. Billings said.

"Yes," The man extended his hand to me. "I found something very disturbing in those samples, did you have any idea what they were?" William asked.

"I think they're human embryonic tissue," I answered.

"How did you know that?" Dr. Billings looked stunned.

"The work Richard Snively was doing, remember? Paul Peterson worked with him, and I bet they were taking a bunch of samples of their work somewhere in South America for some reason. Do either of you know what they might have planned in South America, maybe Mexico?" I asked.

The two men at the desk looked at each other, then back at me.

"I was stunned that this could have happened in the first place," Dr. Billings sounded distraught. "Those were human embryos in that container, not simple tissue samples, there were many different embryos in that container. Now you're telling me that those two were conducting some sort of Frankenstein experiments in Mexico? "

"Good God, it does make sense, remembering Snively. That plane crash took place years before I uncovered Snively's experiments, and this means he had been at it for a long time," Dr. Billings shook his head sadly. "But Peterson didn't seem the type at all. Damn, this means another report!"

"I wouldn't worry about it, they're all dead now," I said.

"That doesn't matter, I'll have to report this anyway."

195

"Do either of you know of anyone in Mexico who was interested in this type of thing that long ago? Interested enough to pay large sums of money for human embryos?" I asked.

"There are a lot of fly by night operations in South America, but I don't know of any labs back then that could ever do anything like that, especially in South America," Dr. Matthews replied.

"I'm more concerned with how those two got all those human eggs," Dr. Matthews puzzled aloud. "I mean, getting sperm is a piece of cake, but those eggs had to be harvested, and that's not an easy thing to do."

"Not something you'd find in a supermarket," I looked at the doctor.

"Not hardly," He chuckled. "Humans don't produce more than one or two eggs a month at best."

"Can a female be chemically forced to produce more?" I asked.

"Yes," Dr. Matthews replied.

"What would they do with the embryos?" I was thinking out loud. "Maybe they just implanted them in women for normal births?"

"That's possible, I don't know. I guess they could use them for drug testing, for tissue, or hormone production, I just don't know," Dr.   Billings speculated.

"Maybe they thought they could grow them in laboratories and have a source of human tissue. Some scientists now seem to think stem cells show a lot of promise for a multitude of diseases," Dr.   Matthews added.   "No, that's a little far fetched given the time frame of all this."

"That all sounds a bit implausible, especially for the likes of Snively. Correct me if I'm wrong, but he didn't seem that far sighted," I asked.

"He may have had no morals, and have been the worst person on the face of the earth, but he was a genius, he was working decades ahead of his contemporaries," Dr.   Billings said.

196

"So, he could have been up to almost anything?" I asked.

"Could, and probably was, up to almost anything."

Dr. Billings nodded his head in agreement with his colleague.

"I thank both of you for your help, but I need to catch a plane to Washington soon."

I called Billy Hasbroke, collect, from a pay phone and told the Arkansas sheriff what had been in the stainless steel container. The sheriff seemed thankful, but not very surprised.

The plane trip was rough from Atlanta to Washington. A storm front was moving in from the West, and had decided to arrive on the East coast at the same time my plane passed over North Carolina.

I wondered if these were the same conditions Paul Peterson had seen before he crashed in his small plane; it must have felt lonely. It must have been terrifying those last few minutes. I wonder what Paul Peterson felt before he crashed? No one deserves to be lost to everyone for so long. I continued to look out my window and stare at the gray skies and the fast moving low clouds periodically lit by lightning.

29

Good night, sweet prince

M y airplane dove out of a black cloud, lit by blue green
lightning, onto a runway at National Airport across the Potomac
from the heart of Washington. The storm was waning and,
although the weather looked spectacular, the plane landed
without a hitch.

Just before ten o'clock at night, I walked to the front desk
at the Marriott in Crystal City near the Pentagon. I asked the
closest clerk if there were any rooms available; the clerk shook his
head. My next question was an inquiry about Cassandra Pales.

"Ms. Pales is registered with us, sir, but we cannot give
out room numbers. Is she expecting you?" The clerk asked.

"She was expecting me yesterday, you had better ring her
room before I get into more trouble for being late. Oh, by the
way, is she in a single, or a double?" I asked.

The clerk stared at me for a second before he rang
Cassandra's room. While the phone was ringing, the he told me
it was a double.

"Could you ask her to meet me in the lobby, please?" I
asked. The clerk didn't answer, because he began to speak to
Cassandra over the phone. "Ma'am There's a gentleman, a. ,"
The clerk paused and looked at me. "Whom shall I say is
expecting her?"

"Benjamin Katz," I said.

"Yes ma'am that's who it is, could you come to the lobby
to meet him? Thank you, ma'am," The clerk turned to me. "She
seemed to be expecting you, sir, please wait in our lobby for her."

This place seemed to be a bit formal about who is in what
room, maybe they were having a security problem, whatever. I
moved to the lobby and sank down into a deep, comfortable

chair, which felt so good that I almost fell asleep. As I began to close my eyelids, I heard a familiar voice.

"You're usually not this late," Cassandra stood next to my chair.

Looking up at her, I said, "There's no rooms available tonight, how about sharing yours with me?"

"You always were lacking in the social graces," She answered.

All I could do was shrug.

"All right, I guess I can put up with you for at least one night," Her voice sounded resigned.

"You tell the clerk, I don't think he'll believe me."

"Does this improve the macho image, or something?" Cassandra teased.

"No, it gets me a place to sleep tonight."

Cassandra couldn't help noticing the very broad grin on the clerk's face when she changed her room from one to two persons, but I was too tired to tease her about it on the elevator. When we got to her room and we moved through the door, I almost fell on the nearest bed.

"I hope this one wasn't yours, I just don't have the energy to move from it," I said.

She shook her head.

"I'm glad you haven't changed your brand of perfume," I added. "I always loved it."

"You never quit, even when you're half asleep."

"I never started, I just said I liked your perfume, and I do. What did you find out in Chicago?"

"Why do I always go first?" Cassandra asked sharply.

"Because you're the prettiest," I sat up and grinned at her like I did when we were more intimate.

"Oink, oink."

"I'm not a chauvinist pig!" I insisted.

"Chicago was interesting, I stopped by county records before I drove back to the airport," Cassandra said. "Peterson did adopt Becky, but he did so only two months ago."

"Where was she for the year and a half, then?" I asked.

199

"She was with Phil Peterson for the last ten months more or less; Becky came to him of her own free will it seems. I was able to trace the exact day she showed up at Peterson's house from the school records. Peterson finally did marry Marcia less than a year before she died. He had to sign a paper, filed in the court house, giving up his rights to any of her money if they ever got divorced, or if she died of natural causes or was murdered."

"Murdered? That's strange language for a prenuptial agreement."

"That's what I thought too."

"Were they ever divorced?" I asked.

"As far as I could figure out, they were. The papers were finalized less than one week before Marcia was murdered and less than four months after they got married; that fact was very difficult to find out," She walked into the bathroom.

"Well, don't stop now, it's just getting interesting."

"Keep your shirt on, I was just getting my hair brush. It's late and I've had a hard day," Cassandra walked back into the room, brushing her hair.

"Well, how long was it between Marcia's death and Becky's appearance in Chicago?" I asked.

"About seven months, how did you guess she didn't go there right away?"

"Just a lucky guess," I paused. "I think she must have passed through several hands before she went to Chicago. Peterson knew Marcia would be looking for Becky, and the kid needed to be hidden for a while."

"But, why was the kid so important?" Cassandra mused. "None of her relatives seemed anxious about her. That stinks."

"I don't know," I mused. "Maybe the goons just wanted to hurt Marcia by kidnapping her daughter."

"Then, why all the secrecy after Marcia was dead?" Cassandra asked. "Besides, I got the impression Marcia didn't even like her own daughter."

"Maybe Becky knows something?" I guessed. "What about the kid's life in Chicago?"

"Becky's High School English teacher said the child was about the most confused girl she had ever seen. She isn't rebellious, just at a loss as to who her friends are, or which adults to trust," Cassandra said. "The teacher tried to reach out to her, but doesn't think she was able to. Becky's neighbor is such a kind woman, she tried to be a mother to the girl, and that affection might just have kept her going this past year, but I have the feeling Becky is walking right on the edge now."

"Abuse?"

"Several of her teachers thought so," Cassandra sighed. "No proof, no complaints, yet."

"Did the school people check into her family situation?" I asked.

"Yes, they did, it was when the school and his neighbor began to have the children services people look into her home life that Peterson legally adopted her." Cassandra said as she took her dress off.

"Don't steam up the bathroom," I commented. I began to feel slightly steamed myself.

"I'll be out in a minute."

She picked up her night clothes and walked into the bathroom. I moved a chair near the bathroom door, which was open a crack, while she was in the shower; I went over everything I had discovered in Arkansas and Atlanta.

"Shut the damn door, I'm cold," Cassandra stepped out of the shower.

I admired her naked body briefly before I slowly shut the door and returned to my bed.

"Where do you think Becky was for the missing year? And, do you think Phil Peterson has anything to do with Marcia's death?" I asked.

"I don't know, she could have been with her aunt, Nancy Satterwhite, or she could have been with her grandfather, even though he claims to disown her, or even her grandmother." She answered.

"I really think the grandmother has been dead the whole time," I added.

"So, you think she was killed and didn't go underground with the granddaughter?"

"If she were still alive and cared that much about Becky, she would be in our face now," I replied.

Cassandra walked out of the bathroom, dressed in a long flannel nightgown.

"My, how lovely."

"I'm not the entertainment, you twerp!"

"Sorry, what about Peterson's mother or father, could they have had the girl with them?" I asked.

"I checked into that. The Peterson mother died in an automobile accident five years before Marcia's death, and their father died several years before from illness," she said. "Phil and Paul were the only children; there are other relatives, but none close enough to consider checking out."

"Becky had to be somewhere, but where?" I asked as I went to take a shower and get ready for bed.

"Beats me, I do have an idea who might help, and I know where to find him."

Cassandra stretched out in her bed and pulled the covers over her.

"Fred Lepus, right?" I closed the bathroom door.

30

The Katz' Pajamas

Sunlight filtering through the half open Venetian blinds woke me up. Wiping the sleep from my eyes, I noticed that Cassandra was sitting down on the edge of her bed, facing away from me, fastening her bra. Her back was smooth and lightly tanned, with only a faint bathing suit strap line across it. My eyes followed the soft shape of her shoulder blades down to the sensuous curves of her hips. I felt my physical awareness of her beauty grow.

"What time is it?" I asked, refocusing my gaze to the closed window.

"Eight thirty."

"You said you knew where Lepus was," I rose from bed and stretched.

"I wish you'd wear something to bed," She retorted.

"Sorry, I forgot," I pulled on my shorts.

"Sure you did," Cassandra said from the bathroom. "Glad you still find me attractive, though."

"After what we've been through together, why be insulted?" I asked, continuing to dress. "Besides, you know I don't use pajamas, I wear the emperor's new clothes to bed every night. You know, the Katz' pajamas."

"That tired old joke of yours has a double meaning; not just your body, but you bare yourself, more than you think, while you try to hide the real you all the time."

"All right, back to Lepus, where is the little worm?"

I always have been unnerved a bit by her assessment of me.

"After seeing you naked again, I'll leave that line alone," She muffled a small laugh. "Lepus is earning money by house

203

sitting for a Congressman; he's in a Georgetown condo, laying low."

I headed to the bathroom.

"You know," She paused. "I think you and I do need to talk about us as a couple."

"What?" I answered from the bathroom.

Where was this headed? Somewhere good I hope.

"I just get the feeling that you're hiding something from me," She walked to the bathroom door. "That 'Katz' Pajama' phrase, it brings up the whole unspoken side of your life."

"What do you mean?"

I was worried. What did she know, what did she suspect?

"Maybe it has to do with your childhood," She said, caution in her voice. She didn't want to hurt me, I could tell that. "Your mother was murdered, and your father was cold and distant after that, it has to have had a devastating effect. Maybe we should talk about it more, maybe we could go talk about it with a professional."

"How about waiting until we finish this case?"

So it was just my troubled psyche she was on about, I was relieved. Maybe I could let her help me deal with that.

"In spite of our on again, off again love affair, I do love you," She assured me.

"You know I want it on again," I turned and smiled at her.

"I know."

To change the subject, I began to recount what Dr. Billings had told me about Charles Aaronson and how I suspected him of being involved in Snively's baby manufacturing experiments in Atlanta.

"So, now we divide and conquer?" Cassandra asked, as she put on her shoes.

"I'd like some company this time out, what do you say?" I shrugged on a jacket.

"Only if you buy me breakfast," She said.

"Okay, only if I can use our company credit card."

"This one's on Zeb," Cassandra replied. "But if I remember correctly, we can only charge about one more meal on that card."

"You're no fun at all."

As we finished our coffee, Cassandra looked at me over her half empty cup and told me again that she couldn't pin down exactly who killed Marcia.

"I can't prove anything, but I'm beginning to see what might have happened," I grinned a bit. "The patterns are beginning to jell."

Or it could be no particular pattern, just my wild and sometimes correct guesses. Sometimes in real life it isn't the obvious choice either.

"And I suppose you're going to keep it to yourself, " Cassandra sighed. "As usual. Until it's obvious to all but the mentally deficient."

"Well, I'm not sure yet; I have a name and a motive," I said. "But it's too simple."

"When we find out who did it, you'll claim you guessed that person all along," Cassandra said in a mocking voice. "I don't think it can be all that straightforward."

"I'm better than that, I'll write the name on this napkin, and put it in my pocket then I'll let you pull it out and read it as the police haul the person off," I said in a cocky tone.

"In your pocket, do you think I'm crazy? Give it to me."

"You'll look at it," I said.

"I promise I won't; put it in the center section of my purse, the one with the zipper. All I keep there is my gun permit, and an extra hundred dollar bill."

"Deal. So what's the bet?" I pretended to write something on the unused paper napkin next to me as I slipped the hundred dollar bill over the napkin.

"The hundred dollars next to the name," Cassandra looked away from me, to avoid seeing what name I had written.

"Deal," I stuffed the folded napkin back into her purse. I also slipped her C-note into my pocket. "Now, let's go see Lepus."

"I rented a car yesterday, but not a compact. I figured since we're on an expense account, from a client who's a millionaire, why not go full blast," She proudly said.

"What did you rent?" I asked as I signed the charge ticket.

"A Caddy."

"What happens if the old man is the killer, and he goes to jail, and he doesn't pay us a cent for expenses," I asked, as we walked out of the restaurant.

"You didn't read the contract he signed, did you? I'm talking about all the fine print in the standard contract," Cassandra asked.

"He pays even if he's dead?"

"You get the prize for being the first caller with the correct answer," She pulled out the car keys from her purse. "You picked a very good lawyer to draw up your contracts, you should read them better, though."

Actually, she picked out the lawyer and I thought I did read the fine print; what other fine print has she put in my life? I looked over the vehicle after we got in.

"At least you got the small Cadillac. Do you know where this place is?"

"I was there yesterday, I saw him leave and come back." She started the car and drove out of the parking garage.

"How long did you stake out his place?" I asked.

"Three hours."

"Did he see you at all?"

Cassandra shook her head, "He doesn't seem to pay attention to all that much going on around him."

"He hasn't changed that much since the first time I followed him," I chuckled.

"How does he manage to stay alive?" Cassandra asked.

"Who came and went?"

"One of the most bizarrely dressed woman I've seen in awhile," Cassandra answered.

"That's his secretary, Cathy Rumson; she's a fine woman, if you're into bimbos," I shrugged.

206

"And I'm sure you are." Cassandra's eyes narrowed. They pierced my expression for a moment, before she relaxed.

"Did Billings say anything to make you suspect him?" She asked.

"That's kind of off the wall, isn't it?" I looked at her thoughtfully.

"Not really," She glanced at me, again. "He worked in the same place as Snively, he might have been part of whatever was going on."

"I don't think so. When he talked about what he found in Snively's lab, his expression was horrified, even after all these years. I don't think he was party to it."

"That's the condo," She pointed to a two story brick townhouse on P Street.

After locating a parking spot, Cassandra and I walked the short distance to the condominium containing Fred Lepus.

"How do you want to do this?" Cassandra asked.

"The last time I walked into the same house with Lepus," I told her, "he stuck a gun in my back and his hired bimbo knocked me over the head with a vase."

"Why don't I go to the door and start to talk to him. I'll put myself inside the door, and you can come bounding up the stairs to shove your way in past him." Cassandra liked planning these things .

We had both halted, two houses away from our destination.

"I don't bound," I replied.

"Well, you come up with something."

"I guess we're bound to use your idea anyway," I reluctantly agreed.

Cassandra climbed the stairs and rang the doorbell. She rang it several times before Fred Lepus answered the door, dressed in a bathrobe.

"Good morning, sir, I represent the Welcome Wagon for this neighborhood and some of the local merchants would like to offer you a few gifts, welcoming you," She stepped halfway into the doorway.

"I don't know who sent you here this early in the morning, lady, but unless you've got some hot coffee to offer, I wish you'd beat it," Lepus started to close the door.

Cassandra stepped inside and blocked him.

While they struggled, I reached the stair landing. When he recognized me, he tried harder to shove her out the front door.

Cassandra pushed her knee into Lepus' groin and held fast to her position in the doorway. The bump on my head still hurt from our last encounter, but I walked up to him calmly, then I grabbed him by the collar and threw him into the living room. Cassandra straightened herself up and closed the door carefully, after she looked both ways to make sure that no one had seen us.

Meanwhile, I stood over Lepus with my Smith and Wesson pointed at his face.

"You were supposed to bound up the stairs," She glanced at me.

"I said I don't bound," I turned my attention to Fred. "And now, Lepus, we have some questions you're bound to answer for us."

"Stick 'em where the sun don't shine! I've got a lot worse shits after me than you two!" Fred Lepus still held on to his crotch.

"You see that my partner can be as fierce as anybody. Tell us more about Becky Satterwhite, or we'll tackle you again," I smiled at Cassandra, who glared at me.

"You got the kid, and you can have her! She's better off with you anyway."

Lepus tried to stand up, but let out a small groan and sank back down to the floor.

"We don't have her anymore, she's with the police, and her father," Cassandra said.

"Father! That dumb ass doesn't deserve to be a father to a dog, let alone a kid. Besides, he never did pay all his bill," Lepus groaned.

He struggled to his feet and slowly walked, half bent over, to a couch.

"You did some work for Phil Peterson?" Cassandra asked.

"No comment!" Fred replied, leaning backwards and falling onto the sofa. "This is a hell of a way to be woke up, kicked in the nuts!"

"Why did Peterson hire you?" Cassandra demanded.

"Which Peterson?" Fred answered.

"Marcia Satterwhite's ex-husband."

"Which ex husband?" Lepus asked again.

"The living Peterson ex-husband," I said. "Gees, Fred, since when have you gotten so picky? You know damned well who I'm talking about, why did he hire you?"

"It's no secret, he hired me to get the girl a year and a half ago, right after you and I had our first run-in," Fred answered.

"Did you shoot Marcia Satterwhite before you took the girl?" Cassandra asked.

"Why would I shoot a dame with that much money? Don't be stupid."

"Money's a good reason by itself, besides, how did you know how much money she had?" I asked.

"Her ex told me, I knew her old man, and I knew her before then, that's how," Fred stammered.

"Did Peterson hire you to kill her and take the girl?" I asked.

"No one, I repeat, no one, could hire me to kill anybody," Fred shook his head, hunching his shoulders "You know that from the first time I met you; I can't kill anyone, and you know it."

"No I don't," I snapped. "I just found out you didn't kill that particular man."

"Who did kill Marcia?" Cassandra interrupted.

"Hell if I know, or care, for that matter," Lepus said. "All I care about are the people who want to kill me now."

"Who does want to kill you?" Cassandra asked.

"A man from a very famous New York family who doesn't like me exposing his operations, or anything else," Fred replied.

209

"Are you talking about an adoption business?" Cassandra asked.

"Are you talking about what Snively, Peterson, and Brian Fowler started?" I asked.

"Yes and yes."

"Is Fowler still in it?" I asked.

"I don't know who's still in anything, except for Phil Peterson, and he's the one who wants me dead," Lepus said.

"What about Lopez in New York?" Cassandra asked.

"He's a hell of a lot tougher than Peterson, and he wants me dead too," Fred answered. "Just who the hell do you think's after me with so many hired guns, anyway!"

"But which one is after you Fred, Peterson, or Lopez?" Cassandra objected.

"Do you have any idea what experiments the dead Peterson, and Richard Snively were doing?" I didn't give Fred a chance to answer the other question.

"I have no idea what those intellectual scum bags were up to, none what so ever," Fred replied. "That was a long time ago they got into that mess, at least that was my impression."

"Let's get back to your kidnapping the child, Becky," Cassandra said.

"Hey, wait just a minute, that was no kidnapping!" Lepus insisted. "That kid would have done anything to get away from that excuse for a mother, I was glad to do it."

"The day before yesterday in Chicago, I found out that Becky took about seven months to show up after her mother was murdered," Cassandra said. "Where was she for that period of time?"

"Peterson told me to keep her in hiding for a while, he didn't say why," Fred shrugged his shoulders. "He just kept stalling me, telling me not to bring the kid to him yet."

"Where was she?" I asked.

"Here with me, that kid was at my office almost every day, she stuck to me like glue the whole time. She was okay, but a little girl just doesn't fit into the life of a hard hitting detective

210

like me," Fred paused. "She's a good kid, though, she's better than any of her relatives."

"You'd make the perfect father," Cassandra's expression transparently mirrored her sarcastic comment. "Where did she stay, not with you, I hope?"

"No way, she lived with my secretary, but she'd hang around my office all the time," Fred relaxed a little. "Me and Cathy were real used to the kid, we like her a lot."

"Didn't she wonder where her father was?" Cassandra asked.

"She asked me, I told her that her father was trying to get the heat off her before she could go to Chicago. After awhile she stopped asking," Lepus replied.

"What kind of heat, the cops?" I quizzed.

"I don't know, I guess so," Fred sounded irritated. "Probably heat from that whacko family, at least."

"Phil was afraid of Marcia, wasn't he?" I asked.

"Hell, everybody was."

"So what kind of relationship does Peterson have with Becky?" Cassandra asked.

"What do you mean?" Fred asked.

"Does he treat her all right?"

"He treats her like shit, but she doesn't have anyone else. Peterson wants her money, but I think Becky's just waiting to get hold of some of it to get away from Peterson and be on her own," Lepus said. "I don't blame her, I was glad to take her away from that weird family of hers the second time too."

"Why did you take her to Washington this time?" Cassandra asked.

"Peterson paid me. Well, actually he paid me to lose her; he wanted her out of the way until the time was right, but Becky didn't want to wait for him, she wanted to get away on her own this time," Fred answered.

"And when was the time right according to Peterson?" I asked.

"Just by coincidence, it was about the time you picked her up," Lepus grinned.

211

"You mean he played into Peterson's plan?" Cassandra pointed to me.

"Sort of; Peterson wanted one thing, but I was going to work for Becky, and against him. Now Peterson and Lopez want to get rid of me because of what I know about them," Lepus's voice escalated into a whine.

"Besides whatever business they're in, what else do you know about them?" Cassandra asked.

"Oh, hell, the baby business is long gone, what they're in now is drugs. I found out a whole bunch of details about it last month by accident and, let me tell you, they're not too happy about it," He answered.

"Do these details have anything to do with Marcia Satterwhite's murder?" Cassandra asked.

"No," Fred said. "I don't think so."

"Then, that's your problem, Fred," I stared at him. So, that's why this dweeb is spilling all this information, to throw us at the mob to take some heat off him.

"If I remember right from the dead body two years ago, right here in DC, you must have some pull here, since neither you nor I had any bad press from it," Lepus said.

"So."

I thought quickly. All of a sudden this conversation was taking a bad turn, I didn't want Cassandra to know this.

"All that means is that my fingerprints were nowhere to be found, and that no one saw us there."

"Besides, you know all the details of the big drug deals, and we don't care about them," Cassandra turned to me, and continued talking. "Let's go."

"Okay," I agreed.

"If you don't move, we won't tell anyone where you are," Cassandra opened the front door. "You're not as bad as Benjamin makes you out to be, as a matter of a fact I kind of like you."

"Just get the hell out of my life, now!" Lepus shouted as he slammed the door behind us. "Kick Katz in the nuts first thing in the morning, will you!"

212

"What a grouch, we weren't that bad, were we?" Cassandra asked.

"At least I didn't kick him in the nuts," I said.

"What about that murder he was talking about?" She asked me as we walked back to the car.

"I told you about it."

"No, I mean what he said about neither one of you having anything to do with the police investigation."

Damn, she wasn't going to let this go.

"Like I told him, there was no trace of us at the scene, nobody could put us there and since neither one of us did it, what's the harm?"

"But, that's not how we do things," Cassandra seemed confused. "If we find a body, we tell the cops immediately."

"I did," I looked away from her, briefly.

Not a good move, that's a sure sign what your about to say is a lie. Hell, it was, but I just couldn't tell her the truth, I was beginning to hate this arrangement.

"Then, why didn't the cops keep you for questioning?" She kept on asking.

"After I called the cops and gave them the address, I called the bank," I thought quickly. "They told me the FBI was calling them about the case and that it might involve a foreign spy or something like that."

"A spy?" She seemed even more confused.

"That's what I thought," I shot her my evasive grin. "It was starting to sound like a whole bunch of trouble to me."

"What did they say?" Cassandra still looked confused. "I mean, what did the bank guy tell you?"

"He said to just drop it and get the hell away from it."

"Why?" Cassandra asked. "Since when do you pay attention to what a corporation tells you, especially if you disagree with them for moral reasons?"

"I stuck around town long enough to uncover enough facts to make me get on a plane and fly home quickly," I continued to regret telling this made-up story to her.

"What did you find out?" She asked

213

"This time I had to agree with them since it involved a Chinese spy."

"Say, what?"

"Sometimes we peons have to let some things go."

"Sometime you'll have to tell me the whole story," Cassandra looked at me thoughtfully. "Better yet, why didn't you tell me back then?"

"I didn't know you as well as I do now, and I didn't want you to know something that could get you into trouble later," I replied.

At least that was the truth.

"I guess so."

I could tell my tale wasn't going over that well with her.

"Let's go see the doctor now," I said, trying desperately to change the subject.

I ignored the questions hanging in the air and unlocked the rental car. As soon as I could, I'd contact my government handler; he and I needed to have a long discussion about all this. I hadn't known how much I wanted to trust Cassandra, until now, when I had to directly lie to her, I didn't like doing that at all.

After a few minutes of silence, Cassandra snorted but didn't make any comment.

"We do need to concentrate on this case," I ventured.

She acquiesced and began discussing her impression of our encounter with Lepus. We both agreed that he told us a lot, but not the whole story. I wonder if Lepus will ever tell the whole, unvarnished, truth.

"I feel sorry for Becky, no adult around who gave a damn about her," Cassandra made a turn through an intersection.

"You're right, she needs to open up to somebody soon, or she may turn out like her mother."

"Meaning Marcia was that badly treated as a child?" Cassandra asked.

"You've met her father, Zeb, so what do you think?" I asked.

"Becky was alone, and lost," Cassandra said. "She was reaching out for the only person who was there, unfortunately Fred Lepus was there. He's well meaning in his own way, but not quite enough of a family for Becky."

God, she looked sexy right at that moment, even though she was drumming her fingernails on the car door handle. It just kept me thinking about misleading her; I didn't like that feeling.

She broke the silence. "You know, that moron back there and his clueless secretary probably gave Becky enough of a breather in her life to give her a chance to be normal,"

"That moron is normal?" I replied, amazed at this assessment of Fred Lupus.

"What about Becky's future?" Cassandra looked sad and a bit too serious.

"You can't be the keeper of all lost waifs in the world," I smiled at her.

"Why," She paused. "I took you in, didn't I?"

"Turn here, on Wilson Boulevard, the doctor's office is three blocks up that way," I interrupted, pointing to my right.

She was right, she took me in, she accepted me, why didn't I accept her?

"What is this guy's specialty?" Cassandra parked the car.

"Gynecological surgery."

The expensive office Cassandra and I walked into was as well decorated as many small museums. At the far end of the expansive waiting room a glass window stood half open to reveal an crowded inner office. In the waiting room itself, twelve women sat in expensive chairs, with worried looks on their faces. I wondered if the worried expressions were from their fear of diseases, or their fear of the fees this doctor must charge to support the waiting room.

Cassandra walked towards the far wall, motioning me to follow her. A plump middle aged woman in a white uniform met us at the open glass window.

"Do you have an appointment?" she asked.

"No, we need to talk to Dr. Aaronson about a dead woman in Los Angeles; we're investigators from there. Tell him

215

that a colleague of his, a Dr.   Billings from Atlanta, suggested that we speak to him," I said in a soft but forceful voice.

The woman straightened in her chair, stared through the glass window at me, then at Cassandra, back to me for fifteen seconds, before she did anything. She pointed to the expensive chairs in the waiting room, telling us to wait there, she then disappeared into one of the inner offices.

"You were very subtle, Benjamin," Cassandra sat down near the window.

"He'll see us though, you'll see," I replied.

"Either that, or he'll call the cops." She glanced over at the empty receptionist's window.

"I told the woman we were detectives, he'll think we are the cops."

"We'll see," Cassandra slowly shook her head.   "Do you really think he has something to do with any of this?"

"Not recently, not in a long time, but I think he'll tell us what he does know to keep his name out of the papers," I answered.   "Look at this waiting room, look at all he stands to lose."

The woman reappeared at the window and called to me, "Sir, Dr.   Aaronson has been called to the hospital on an emergency; if you can come back later this afternoon, he'll be able to work you in."

I stood up quickly, than ran to the door of the waiting room, and then outside the building.

Cassandra followed me, shouting, "Hey, wait for me!"

As all the waiting patients' eyes followed Cassandra and me out of the room, the worry lines on their faces deepened.

"You go that way, and don't let him get by you!"   I shouted, pointing to my left.

"What if he isn't even here?"   Cassandra shouted as she looked over her shoulder at me.

Rushing to the left side of the building, Cassandra ran into a middle aged balding man who was bolting from the opposite direction.   Both of them let out a shout as they bounced off each other and fell to the ground. Cassandra stood up first, reached for her holster and pulled out a three eighty automatic pistol.

"I presume you're Dr. Aaronson?" She dusted herself off with her free hand.

"Don't shoot! Don't shoot!" He sat up and shoved his hands into the air.

Meanwhile I arrived from around from the rear of the building.

"Is this the Doctor, or are we about to be sued?"

"He needs to tell us," She nodded towards the man sitting on the ground.

"I'm Aaronson," The man spoke, starting to stand up. "Am I under arrest?"

"No, do you think you should be?" I asked.

"I knew you'd get to me soon," Charles said.

"Who, who would get to you soon?" Cassandra asked.

"The police, the Los Angeles police," Aaronson nervously answered.

"What makes you think we're with the Los Angeles police?"

"Aren't you someone from Lieutenant Hatton? He said he'd send someone out here to talk to me." Charles stepped away from me.

"Don't go too far," Cassandra moved in behind the doctor. "We just have a few questions; we'll ask them, then be out of your way in no time."

"What was Dr. Richard Snively doing right before he was fired?" I asked quickly.

"I gave a complete statement to the federal authorities years ago; illegal experiments involving human embryonic tissue. As soon as I realized what he was doing, I gave all the information to Dr. Billings," Charles spoke rapid fire, as if he wanted get all words about this out of his mouth and away from him.

"We know that, but what was he doing with them?" Cassandra asked.

217

"He was trying to grow human beings outside of a uterus, it was the most disgusting thing I've ever seen."

Cassandra gave him a skeptical glance, "If you knew nothing else about it, why are you so afraid of being arrested?"

"Taxes," Charles blurted.

"Bullshit," I said, just as quickly. "It has to do with Snively, and perhaps Brian Fowler."

"Who?" Charles looked down at the ground.

"You know who, the one who helped you two in your experiments," I declared.

"They weren't mine!" He insisted.

"Look, we aren't the police, " Cassandra said. "Someone hired us to find out who killed Marcia Satterwhite, that's all. It's obvious that you didn't kill her, so we'll be out of your life forever as soon as you tell the truth."

"Marcia who?" Aaronson asked.

"Marcia Satterwhite was Brian Fowler's sister-in-law, she was murdered two years ago."

"Why contact me, am I in danger?" Charles asked nervously.

"Funny you should ask, probably not, but you'll be in a world of trouble with us if you don't answer my question in a hurry," I glowered at him.

"Snively and Fowler wanted to mass produce embryos and freeze them. They had a plan to implant these embryos in women so they could grow to birth," Charles said slowly as he leaned against the wall. "They were producing so many of them, I couldn't see that operation going on undetected."

"Why did they have such a big operation gong on?" Cassandra asked.

"They wanted to mass produce babies for high priced adoptions," Charles answered.

"Why not just pay the women to have babies the normal way?" I asked.

"The babies produced were all blonde, blue eyed, and very intelligent, all the traits of an ideal, adoptable baby were held in the genes of these embryos. It's much easier to deal with known eggs and known sperm and not let mother nature screw it all up. The adoptions cost the couples tens of thousands of dollars more than usual and the deal was done outside of the law, but the product was guaranteed," Charles sighed, he looked, after all these years, almost happy to tell someone this dark secret.

"Were the women used to grow the babies in Mexico?" I asked.

"Yes, there were thousands of them lined up. I found out about it from Phil Peterson, he wanted me to come in on it and I might have, but I got scared and turned them all in," Charles stared blankly ahead. "You know the Mexican women were coming out of the woodwork to sign up. Snively fed them better than they ever thought of, and there was lots of supplements and medical care so the babies would be healthy; some women signed up for more than one baby, you know."

"You turned them in after you took part in some of the dirty business, didn't you?" Cassandra asked.

"Yes," He said in a muted voice. "It seems so long ago, and I have felt so bad since."

"One more thing before we go," I said. "What were the names of all the people connected with this thing."

"Snively, Peterson, and Fowler. There was a contact with some gangsters in New York who put up the front money, but I never knew their names. I'm sure Snively was the mastermind, he bragged about working on the details for almost a decade," Charles looked straight at me. "You know, after awhile, even the mob thought it was wrong; they took back all their money and told Richard to stop, he didn't listen to them, and now he's dead."

"You never did tell the Feds what the scheme actually was, did you?"

"I told them everything," He insisted.

"Like hell you did," I moved closer.

"I told the authorities Richard was working with embryos, that's when he got fired and moved to Miami. I don't know if they kept up operations after he moved, or what."

219

"But, you didn't tell anyone about mixing up custom babies in test tubes or about the mob backing the whole thing."

"Well," Charles paused. "No."

"How many babies were born in Mexico?" Cassandra asked.

"Don't really know, it didn't work nearly as well as they had hoped it would. Maybe a few hundred that I knew of, some more before I turned them in. The Federal authorities never knew exactly what Snively was up to, so I suppose he could have continued for a while but they could have been doing it for a long time before I found out about it," Charles said.

"Heard from Brian Fowler recently?" I asked.

"Yes, he called about a week ago."

"What did he want?"

"He wanted my silence." There followed an awkward, silent pause. We didn't help him any by talking.

Finally Aaronson, said, speaking louder, "He's still in some sort of a shady business, and he didn't want anyone to know where he is, or what he did in the past."

"What else did he say?" I asked.

"Nothing."

"Are you sure he didn't mention another name, like Hank, or Lopez?" I asked.

"No, no he didn't," But Charles was speaking a little too fast.

"You're lying. You know Hank, the contact in California who helped get the babies into the U. S. Didn't Fowler say that he was sending Hank out here to take care of your big mouth. Didn't he say that his own name kept coming up in the wrong conversations, and that he suspected you as the source?"

"All right, he did say that Hank Cummings was coming out here. I've never met the son of a bitch, and I thought you were him," Charles retorted. "Fowler's been blackmailing me for years, I thought he was finally going to end it all, everything's happening so fast, everybody knows what went on, I'm ruined!"

"Calm down, Dr. Aaronson, you might have a heart attack," Cassandra said. "Did Fowler say who he was working for this time?"

"The same gangsters he was working with before. He didn't exactly say, but he sure indicated that if Hank didn't get me, his friends back East would," Charles said. "Can I go now? I'm scared as shit and I need to settle as much here as I can before I try to disappear."

"Sure, have a nice day," Cassandra chuckled.

Charles Aaronson raced into a back entrance to his building and slammed the door shut.

"Did you guess what they had been up to?" Cassandra asked me.

"Yes, just the basic scheme, which was simple to guess."

"Is that why Marcia was killed, what did she have to do with the deal?"

"Marcia worked for U. S. Immigration. Although she didn't need to work. With that job she made those babies look like genuine United States citizens. They not only would be perfect for rich, blonde Anglo Saxons to adopt, but also be easy to adopt."

Cassandra sounded doubtful, "Maybe, I think it may have had something to do with her murder, but there has to be more to it. Do you think we ought to keep an eye on Aaronson for a while?"

"In order to catch Hank Cummings?" I asked.

"Right."

"Why wait, isn't he over six feet tall very large, light brown hair, blue eyes, and had a big scar on the right side of his face?"

"Yes, that's the police description," Cassandra answered.

"Doesn't that look like him across the street? He just walked up from the end of the block."

"Yes."

"Feel like taking your life in your hands today?" I asked.

Cassandra nodded, a grin took over her face.

221

"You aren't cheap, but you sure are easy; let's split up. Walk up behind him after I start to talk to him but don't wait too long," I said.

All on its own, my brain was hatching one of my world famous plans.

She walked behind the building and crossed a parking lot to get to the next block without being seen. I walked directly across the street and up to the guy, who had just taken up a position on the corner across from Aaronson's office. We were still within sight of the garage for the building.

"Good morning, sir," I happily said.

All the while, another inner conversation told me that I knew this creep, but from where? In what context?

"Get lost, bum," He had a low, powerful voice.

"I'm from the national health monitoring service, sir, I'm conducting an on the street interview about the nation's health care."

"Who gives a shit," He turned away from me.

"I couldn't help but notice that you're looking at the office of Dr. Charles Aaronson, one of this city's best surgeons," I continued.

"Is that what he is?" The man said, still not facing me.

"Yes, sir, that's what he is. What I would like to ask is, do you know the reputation of any doctors in this city, like the man across the street?" I asked.

"No, I don't know nobody in this goddamn town, so beat it," The man turned to glare at me.

"What's the matter, Hank, you forget Aaronson? The guy who squealed on your partners?" I stepped back one pace and reached into my coat.

Hank Cummings stood stunned for a second; he didn't move, nor did he turn around. So he didn't see Cassandra step out between two buildings, stride up behind him, pistol drawn. Stepping back another pace, I opened my coat, my hand on the butt of my Smith and Wesson.

"I suggest you walk with us to our car, the Caddy over there," I motioned to Cassandra's car with my head.

"Us who?" Hank answered in a belligerent tone as he inched his hand towards his coat.

"Us, us," Cassandra declared, jabbing his ribs with her pistol.

"Okay," Hank lifted up his hands, walking slowly to the car.

Finally it hit me. "I know where I saw you before!"

"What are you talking about?" Cassandra said, surprised by my obscure revelation.

"I know where I saw this son of a bitch the last time," I shoved Hank a bit harder towards the rental car. "He was the one who took a pot shot at me with a shotgun the night I took on Marcia Satterwhite as a client."

"Him?" Cassandra cocked her head. "How curious, if he worked for Marcia, why did he try to kill you when you were working for her too?"

"Will you two quiz kids shit or get off the pot," Hank growled. "What the hell do you want with me?"

By this time, a small crowd had gathered in several of the store windows facing the three of us. I motioned to one of the closest windows but no one was willing to come out of the storeSeveral people ran out of my range of vision.

"Keep your gun in his ribs for a second," Jogging over to the closest building, I leaned in the front door and shouted. "Call the police, that man is a wanted felon, and we are detectives."

"They're on their way already, buddy," An older man shouted back to me.

That was not exactly the timing I had in mind.

I ran to Cassandra and Hank, quickly shouting, "Get him to the car, we don't have long to talk to him alone."

We shoved Hank all the way to our car, pushing him into the back seat. Cassandra slid into the front seat and pointed her pistol at Hank's head. I tossed the 45 automatic I had extracted from him into the front seat, away from his hands.

"We only have one question, who killed your partner, Marcia Satterwhite?" Cassandra asked.

"What?" Hank asked.

223

"You're Hank Cummings, Marcia Satterwhite's old partner in the babies for bucks scam several years ago; Marcia was murdered and all we care about is who killed her," I almost shouted in his face.

"You're all nuts!" Hank shouted back at me. "First you accuse me of shooting at you, then you babble about this Marcia bitch, you're all nuts!"

"You're wanted in California; we'll pin more on you than you could ever get out of when the cops get here, unless you tell us who killed Marcia Satterwhite," I said. "You came at me with a sawed off twelve gauge, and Snively was killed with one. You were supposed to be working for Marcia, but you in fact worked for Lopez."

"I checked on you before we left Los Angeles," Cassandra added. "You're out on bail for an attempted murder charge; I don't think you are supposed to travel this far from home, are you?"

Hank thought for a second, then spoke, "All right, I'm Hank, but I don't know who the hell killed that bitch."

"So who wanted her dead?" She asked.

"Who didn't, her ex-husband, her father, her mother, maybe her boyfriend, even me."

The police sirens could be heard in the distance, getting louder.

"Who was her boyfriend?" I asked quickly.

"Brian Fowler, one of the big shot brains who was makin' the babies, he was sniffin' after the bitch like she was in heat or something," Hank said as three police cars pulled next to Cassandra's rental car.

"Who wanted me dead?" I had to ask.

"Me," Cummings threw me a menacing grin.

"Who else?"

Before he could answer, a score of policemen flew out of the patrol cars. No less than twelve blue uniformed cops spilled from half as many cars, taking a tactical stance behind their open doors; at least a dozen revolvers and shotguns pointed at Cassandra's rental car.

224

Hank shouted out of the open window, "Arrest them! They're kidnapping me! Help!"

I stepped out of the car and held my hands up.

Cassandra handed her pistol out the open window to the nearest policeman and shouted, "Don't shoot, the car's a rental!"

I told the police that Hank Cummings was a known felon and had skipped bail in California. Both Cassandra and I showed them our bounty hunter credentials and I gave the D. C. police Lieutenant Hatton's name and phone number to check on our identity and to confirm the wanted status of Cummings.

Hank Cummings insisted that he had been kidnapped, demanding to see a lawyer in order to get bail and squawking about pressing charges against Cassandra and me. The police let him talk to a public defender long enough to confirm that he had outstanding warrants in California, then they then held him without bond.

I later gave his name to my friend at the Miami police department as the killer of Snively. He killed the Miami doctor on a contract, I guessed at the time that Zeb had paid him. The Miami police uncovered enough evidence later to charge Zeb Satterwhite with paying Hank Cummings for the job.

The police let Cassandra and me go, with the promise that we would catch the next available flight out of Washington. We were also given a hard time about our weapons by the police. But when Cassandra told them about the previous doings of Charles Aaronson, the police were interested enough in that to let both of us go with a minimum of grief. Several painful hours later, Cassandra drove the car back to the hotel, with her sullen partner next to her. Neither one of us said a word until she pulled into the hotel parking lot.

. . . .

"You were right about that bounty hunter stuff," She slowly shook her head. "I thought that was the strangest thing you ever did at the time."

"It's a legal thing in this country, like I told you, a bounty hunter in pursuit of a bail skipper has more leeway than a police officer; it's the same in every state," I nodded. "We get ten percent of the bond he skipped too; what works, works well."

"It did make today go a lot smoother than it could have," Cassandra sighed.

"I know, but I'm still pissed off."

"What're you so mad about?" Her eyebrows rose.

"I'm not mad at you, I'm mad at not having that Cummings bum longer. Hatton will have that son of a bitch for as long as he likes, but he'll never be able to do anything with the information," I said.

"Hatton's not that stupid, besides, maybe he'll share some of it with you," She offered.

"We need to get back to Los Angeles," I said abruptly.

"No, we need to go to New York, remember Lopez, the mob connection? He's in New York, and New York's a lot closer to where we are than Los Angeles."

"But I keep getting the feeling that Becky Satterwhite's in trouble," I said.

"Becky?" Cassandra asked in a surprised, annoyed voice. "You need to fill me in more on this angle, partner."

"She's in the middle of this more than I thought and she's in danger because of it. But, as long as she's with the cops out in Los Angeles I guess she'll be all right," I was trying to make myself feel better.

"If all that's true, she's been in danger since you last saw her and before, not that much will change over the next few days." Cassandra looked worried, then shrugged her shoulders. "We can't get to Los Angeles immediately, anyway, so we should to go to New York for a short visit. Let's take an early night flight to New York and see our friend early tomorrow, then we can fly back home."

31

No rest for the weary

I had just nodded off to sleep when the wheels of the aircraft touched down on a runway at Newark Airport. The slight jerk made me open my eyes and turn to Cassandra, who was still asleep. What a crappy airport, but the cheap flights all seem to land there;. The darkened buildings seemed to match my mood. We both were able to doze off on the cab ride to Manhattan.

I was somewhat awake as we pulled up in front of our hotel. I had to try several times to wake her up enough so that she could move on her own out of the cab.

As we checked into a upper crust, mid-town hotel, again sharing the same double room, Cassandra was the first to break the silence.

"We need to step back and look at this thing, Benjamin."

"If you mean sharing the same room, remember, we're running out of money. If you mean the Satterwhite family, you're right, we do." I opened the door to our room.

"Will you stop giving flip answers all the time. Most of the time I don't mind it, it's even funny, but I'm tired as hell. I need some serious discussion from you now."

She sat down, heavily, in a chair.

"All right, sometimes I can't help it. I go on automatic and wise crack through life. A lot of the time, it helps me to relate to people."

"You've said that before, but I never understood it. If you act like that most of the time, how can anyone get to know you?" Cassandra asked.

"Some people I don't want to know, or have them get to know me, so it works fine; they're put at ease and think I'm their friend. I can relate better with them that way, and they with me," I sighed. "Besides, in our line of work it's a good skill to get information out of perfect strangers."

"What about people you want to be real friends with? Like Mark, or me?"

"I don't always joke around with you, or Mark, or my other friends, you know that. Sometimes I feel uncomfortable about some of my inadequacies, and I fall back on my alter ego to compensate, but don't we all?"

I lay down on the bed.

"Like what? What do you feel inadequate about?"

"What is this, Psych 101?"

"Don't get defensive; I enjoy talking to you like this, we don't do it enough," She said.

This was a good sign, she was still interested in me even after that obvious snow job I'd just given her back in Washington.

"I guess not, one thing is the fact that I've never been to college, and most of my friends have, including you; hell, you're going to be a doctor in less than a year."

"So what, you're smarter than most of your friends, not just in common sense, but you've read more, and can carry on an intelligent conversation in almost any field," Cassandra observed.

"You can, maybe not Mark, but you can. You graduated Phi Beta Kappa, number four in your class and you were two years younger than the rest of your class. You were on your way to a PhD before you started working with me. Haven't you almost finished your course work? Why don't you finish? What made you decide to keep working for me instead?" I asked.

I'd slipped, I truly didn't want to chance an honest answer from her; maybe I did, but I was surprised by my own question.

"That's the first time you've ever asked me that, straight out."

"I've been afraid to, up until now, the question just sort of sneaked out," I sighed.

"I thought long and hard after you offered me a job at your agency," she said. "It was for the Summer; we'd only known each other for three weeks, and I was already falling in love with you."

"Was I the reason you sort of gave up academia?" I asked. Whoa, she just said she was in love with me right after we met, this has to be a good thing.

"Who said I gave up academia?" She looked at me as if I had said something bad.

"Well, to rephrase it, why are you only taking one or two courses a quarter," I smiled, trying to correct any mistake. "Is it because of the detective work, or me?"

"Only a very small part of the reason. I saw myself ten years from then, with a PhD, teaching political science to a bunch of college freshmen. Like you, I want more out of life than a safe and quiet job, I'm only twenty five years old; there's enough time for me to go back to school and teach college freshmen. I'm here because I want to have something exciting to look back on when I'm settled into teaching,"

Cassandra slid further down into her chair.

"Are you tired? I'm beginning to feel very sleepy," She commented.

"Not really," I was tired, but this conversation needed to continue. "Do you want to talk some more?"

She kept looking anywhere but straight at me. "Tell me about your mother."

"Why?"

"You never really told me the whole story. You started to several times, then you would always fall silent."

"What's to tell?" I said in a low voice. "She died from a gunshot wound while my Dad, brother and I were out in the fields planting. Dad used to like to take us out with him, we were too young to do anything but ride the tractor with him, or sit on

229

the truck bed and watch. He just wanted us to love the land like he did."

"She was murdered, right?" Cassandra's sadness mirrored my own.

"No one saw anything, they never caught anyone, and Dad never wanted to talk about it."

"Your father died this year, didn't he?"

"Yeah," I nodded. "He passed away about four months ago."

"And, he didn't say anything?"

"No," I fell silent and lay back on the bed. "Not really anything."

Bullshit! He had told me exactly who killed my mother, damn it! That son of a bitch had to tell me just before he died, so I'd have to live with it now just like he had to for so long.

"I can't imagine what it would be like to grow up without a mother and with a father who was cold and distant all the time," Cassandra didn't want to quit. "I bet he was depressed the whole time."

"I suppose."

I really didn't want to talk about that.

"How did you cope with the loss?" She asked.

Actually, I was glad she cared enough to ask.

"I was pissed off a lot," I let her in a little. "I got in a lot of fights, and argued a lot with my teachers."

"Did you get into fights with your teachers?" She looked surprised.

"No," I shook my head as I remembered some of the incidents. "I just got into verbal arguments with them about the topics we covered in classes like history and English."

"Really?" She chuckled. "I bet you were their favorite."

"In fact, my history teacher senior year almost had me convinced to plan on law school."

"Why didn't you?" She snuggled next to me on the bed.

"Like I said, I was just pissed off and didn't want to waste time in college."

"So, you joined the Marines? She stroked my arm.

"Yeah," I sighed. "I joined the Marines."

"What was it that drew you to enlist?"

"It was something which I thought would focus my anger," I said, reluctant to continue this train of thought. "At least that's how I interpret it now. I was only seventeen when I joined and didn't think that clearly then."

"I assume it changed you," She held my hand. "You aren't pissed all the time now."

"It did change me," I squeezed her hand. "But, I really don't want to talk about that now, please."

"You know something?" She took my cue to change the subject.

"No, what?"

"You don't always wear your Katz Pajamas just to bed."

"Very funny."

"And, you don't look too bad in them either," She smiled an inviting smile at me.

"I'm tired."

But not that tired, not after that comment.

I sighed. All this business with the baby manufacturing was probably going on when I was investigating Brian Fowler. If I had looked deeper then, I might have unearthed it sooner. Becky had been right, the crime was too much like my own mother's death. In some ways, that girl is like me when I was her age, the same expression of life exhaustion, repressed anger. Some things have to be finished; some things, however, are never finished.

"I just don't want you to get too involved in this potential mess, it might be too close to your own tragedy," Cassandra said. "Sometimes two events happen close together, synchronicity, do you know what I mean?"

"I'll be all right."

I knew what she meant.

"Do you think Zeb did it?" I asked as she got up and headed to the bathroom.

231

"Is that the name you wrote down on the napkin?" She turned on the shower.

"I won't tell, and don't look," I exclaimed as I lay back down on my bed.

I stared at the ceiling as Cassandra showered and got ready to go to sleep.

"Why do you think Zeb killed his daughter?" I asked when she came out of the bathroom, dressed for bed.

"Well, he's mean enough, why do you think he did it?" Cassandra asked.

"I don't; there's not enough motive, unless there's something else going on that we don't know about," I replied.

I came out of the shower and lay in my bed; the lights were out and I could hear her soft breathing in the next bed. Life felt good to me, right at that moment in that quiet room. A few minutes later, I heard Cassandra get out of bed, I thought she was headed to the bathroom, but she stood over me, silently. My eyes had adjusted enough to the dark to make out her naked body. She pulled back the covers and lay to my side, partially draped over me, life was much better then.

"In spite of our problems, I do love you, Benjamin," She whispered in my ear.

"It feels like I have loved you forever," I enveloped her in my arms.

32

Watch your mouth

Waking before her, I went to the restaurant to have breakfast alone. As I was finishing my second cup of coffee, Cassandra joined me. She had packed our things, and checked out for us.

"I already told the waitress to bring coffee, and one egg, over easy, as soon as a beautiful woman sits down at my table," I grinned at her.

"You didn't."

"Why don't you ask her for yourself, she's coming over now," I pointed to the waitress walking to our table with a cup and a pot of steaming coffee.

"I guess we have to see Lopez today?" Cassandra asked, sipping her coffee.

"I already called his office, his secretary said we could see him at nine thirty," I replied.

"We won't make it."

"We will if you eat your egg fast."

The same waitress was carrying a plate to our table.

Cassandra smiled at me, "I love you."

"I love you too," I answered. "Not to change the subject too abruptly, but I called my uncle this morning."

"The one you're named after?"

"Yeah, the cop."

"Isn't he a deputy chief here?" She was wolfing down breakfast.

"Yes, he is; we had a marvelous long talk, lots of information you might want to hear," I offered.

"I don't feel right talking to, or about, someone that high up in a police department. After the run in with the DC police, I'm just weary of talking to more cops about this case. Just call me superstitious if you like," Cassandra said.

She finished the coffee and put down her cup.

"Okay, but don't say I didn't try."

. . . .

As a businessman specializing in whatever made the most money, Irving Lopez housed himself in his own private office building. It was a forty story edifice no more than five years old. Both Cassandra and I, as well as every police department in every major American city, knew that Irving Lopez was the major player in a New York based mob family. He was almost as powerful as a mob boss himself; he could arrange any shady deal and make it look as American as apple pie.

We posed as Mr. and Mrs. John Adams. I told Lopez' secretary to announce us as friends of Brian Fowler, which got us in to see Lopez exactly at nine thirty.

A medium height fat man, about fifty years old with dark, slicked back hair strode into the waiting room to greet Cassandra and me. He extended his hand, and smiled as he introduced himself. He looked like a South American Santa Claus with something up his sleeve, more like what I had pictured Aaronson to be.

"Come on into my office, make yourselves at home. I have a few short calls to make, and I'll be right back in," He said through a large smile.

"If you want to call Brian, you might have a little trouble, my guess is that he's flown out of the country for a while," I said, not smiling back at Irving.

Lopez lost his smile faster that he had grown it as he pointed back to his office and groused, "Get in here, and talk!"

His private domain was decorated with leftovers from the set of a depression era musical. As soon as he got behind a very large oak desk, with a white marble insert in the middle of it, he demanded crossly, "OK, get to the point, who the hell are you two?"

"We're just simple private investigators from California, hired to find the killer of Marcia Satterwhite," Cassandra answered.

"Before you say you don't know who she is," I interrupted, "we've talked to several people who name you as the financial backer of the plan to manufacture tailor-made babies for expensive adoptions."

Cassandra added, "All we want from you is some information about the old group of baby makers, Fowler, Snively, Cummings, Peterson, and Marcia."

But before she had finished speaking, Lopez bellowed, "I don't know who the hell you think you are, but you'd better get out of my face now, or I'll have your fuckin' legs broke!"

I drew my revolver as Lopez rose from his chair and moved around to the front of his desk. A door opened in the back of the office and two large men entered. They were both in cheap suits which didn't fit all that well; their oversized guts were straining to be free.

"If you don't send your elephant patrol back where they came from, I'll splatter your fat belly all over this ridiculous office," I declared.

I pointed my forty one magnum at Lopez' stomach.

"Who the fuck let this ass hole in here with a piece?" Lopez shouted.

"What do ya want us to do, boss?" One of the large men asked in a heavy voice.

"I want you to blow both their brains out, what d'ya think?"

"But he'll shoot you, and maybe us, the broad's got a gun too," The larger man said.

235

"Shit, let'em talk, then get'em the hell outa here," Lopez said in an annoyed voice.

"Thank you, now, was there anyone else in on the deal?" I asked.

"No!" Lopez shouted.

"How many babies were made and sold?" Cassandra asked.

"I don't remember, five or seven hundred I guess, maybe a couple thousand," Lopez sat back down in his chair. "That was a long time ago when we set those smart ass shit heads up; nineteen sixty eight, I think. They'd been playing around with it for a few years, and I set them up for a bigger operation."

"Get your fat ass back up, I don't want you reaching into a drawer for a mistake," I pointed my revolver at Lopez' head. "So, you did put up the front money for the adoption scam and how much of the profits did you keep?"

"What the hell do I look like, a charity?" Lopez huffed. "Of course I kept half the income."

"And, now you just sell drugs and run the numbers?" I stared at him. "Back to the basics."

"That's right, you prick," Lopez sound more and more enraged. "I go where the best deals are, and the most bucks. Can I do anything else for you, turd-head?"

"Yes, you could clean up your language a little," Cassandra said, mock reproach in her voice.

"Am I hurting the little bitch's virgin ears?" Lopez said in a sarcastic voice.

"Are you after Fowler for some reason?" I asked.

"He's another shit ass, all he wants to do is set himself up in business, my business," Lopez began to shout again.

"Calm down, or you'll have a stroke," Cassandra said. "What business, illegal kids?"

"Or illegal drugs?" I interrupted.

"What is this, the sixty four thousand dollar question? Of course drugs, there ain't no money in kids no more. Fowler used to be our west coast supplier, until he became an independent," he yelled.

Then, amazingly, Lopez seemed to run out of steam, and said in a lower voice, "Any more dumb questions?"

"Only one, who killed Marcia Satterwhite?" I asked.

"That I don't know; I wish I knew who did it, I liked her. She had money and class, which is more than I can say for the dip shit brothers she married," Lopez sighed. "And, she went for that wimp, Fowler too, I never could see why."

"Who do you think could have killed her?" Cassandra asked.

"Not me, maybe her crazy old man, maybe her money grubbing ex-husband, maybe her bitch ass mother; it could have been any of 'em, I don't know," Lopez answered. "OK, shit head, is that all?"

She nodded in my direction as she spoke to Lopez, "That's Benjamin Katz, did you hire Hank Cummings to kill him two years ago?"

"That's Katz?" Lopez sputtered.

"Gee, thanks for the introduction."

He glared at the two goons in the back of his office, "A thousand extra right now for the one who splatters him."

"He who splatters me, splatters the boss also," I smiled towards the back of the room.

"Well then," Lopez smashed his face into a smile. "Is there anything else that you might want of me?"

"Yes," I answered. "Just one more thing."

"What?" Lopez shouted angrily.

"You come with us to the front door; after that, your goons can try to kill us if they want," I said.

"You've made my morning. Break every bone in their fuckin' bodies, first," Lopez shouted over his shoulders to his body guards.

Cassandra gave me a puzzled look as she moved to the office door. I motioned with my revolver for Irving to walk through the door first.

As I walked close to her, she muttered, "I hope you know what you're doing."

"I do, why did you tell him my name?" I whispered back.

The three of us moved silently out of Lopez' private office, through the outer office, and to the elevator with the two bodyguards following closely. As soon as the elevator arrived, I stuck my Smith and Wesson tightly into Irving's back, shoved him into the elevator.

"Tell your friends to meet us at the front door, they can't ride down with us," I insisted.

The bodyguards stepped back as the doors to the elevator began to shut. There were other passengers on the elevator, but when they saw the two drawn pistols, they ran off the elevator and down the hall.

When the elevator doors opened on the ground floor, all three of us could see the flashing lights of many police cars in front of the building.

"I don't believe you've met my uncle Benjamin," I smiled at Cassandra.

"Uncle Benjamin! ?" she shouted at me. "You son of a bitch, why didn't you tell me?"

"You didn't seem to be interested to hear about him this morning, so I just shut up."

As my uncle walked towards us, Lopez raised his hands. I reached into my coat pocket and handed my uncle a medium sized radio transmitter with my free hand.

"I think this belongs to you," I stuck my revolver into my holster and hugged my uncle.

"You have a good radio voice," Uncle Benjamin grinned at me.

"So you set up Lopez, with all those questions, right?" Cassandra asked.

"He admitted to a lot of illegal stuff of his own free will," I put my arm around her waist and smiled. "All I did was ask questions."

"Won't his lawyers be able to throw what Lopez said out since we had our guns pointed at him?" she asked.

"He had his goons pointing guns at us too, and I didn't turn it on until right after they entered the room."

Maybe it would work, maybe not, I guessed the police had more than our tape to arrest him, anyway.

"Enough already with talking shop," My uncle put his arm around both Cassandra and me. "Can't you two stay for a few days?"

"I wish we could, Uncle Benjamin," I answered. "But I think we had better get back to Los Angeles right away to finish this case up, there's a ten thousand dollar bonus at the end of all this."

"We could come back for a visit after we're through," Cassandra looked at me, then at my uncle.

"Sure," I nodded. "Maybe later this summer?"

"Call me with a time," Uncle Benjamin patted my back. "Your Aunt will be mad as hell you didn't stay now, but we would both love to have you here for a week or so, anytime."

....

The New York police and the FBI had been building a case against Irving Lopez for two years. They had had almost enough evidence to arrest him when I had called my uncle earlier that morning. The information I gave them, along with the recording, gave the police more than enough evidence to convict Irving Lopez of several crimes, but not the crime I was looking into.

My uncle gave Cassandra and me a ride to the airport since we had already booked a flight which would put us in Los Angeles early the next morning.

"I really like him," she said, as we both sat in airport terminal, waiting for our flight.

"I do too," I began to remember my childhood. "He's my mother's brother, and he was a big help to me when my mom died."

"I knew there had to be someone there for you when you were growing up," Cassandra smiled at me. "Has he always been a cop?"

"Yeah," I sighed. "I stayed a bunch of summer vacations with him and my aunt. They have a real neat old house in Brooklyn, the house belonged to his father. It's four stories high with lots of room to play in. They had three kids, the middle son was my age and we used to raise hell sometimes."

"What's his name?"

"That would be my cousin Bernie," I grinned, remembering some good times. "He's an intern at Mount Sinai; I think he wants to be a cardiologist."

"Cousin Bernie?" Cassandra cocked her head to the left. "Your mom was Jewish?"

"Yes, she was."

I had never told her, and she had never asked.

"I didn't know that," Cassandra said.

She looked at me like she actually did love me. I liked that a lot.

"I enjoy hearing about your life," she added.

"Well, I like telling you about it too, right now, anyway."

Unusual for me. I don't talk about my childhood with anybody, it was too painful. But, this finally seemed right.

"When we get back home, settled into our regular routine, I want to know all about your growing up."

Cassandra continued to smile at me, her smile felt so good.

I nodded, "I think we both should try to talk to Becky, alone, if possible."

"Do you think Lieutenant Hatton will demand information when we get back?"

"You've got a point, if he thinks we know more than he does, he won't let us alone."

"We've always known more than he does, he should realize that by now," Cassandra grinned.

"I'll let you tell him that, you could get away with it," I teased. "He's not all that bad, you know, we could have to deal with worse."

"Are you going to talk to any of the rest of the Satterwhite family?"

"Like who?"

"Nancy, maybe?" Cassandra purred. "She has what you need."

"Actually, she might have what I need," I said in a serious tone. "I think I'll call her when we get back."

33

Who comes around, goes around

By the time we got to LA, I felt like a broken record, in fact, I felt like a smashed record. I dragged myself to the baggage claim area where we both searched for our bags with Cassandra beside me, her eyes also half open. My suitcase came around the carousel first and I slowly grabbed it then set it down beside me. Cassandra moved closer to the conveyer belt full of luggage as she saw her bags emerge from behind the rubber flaps. As I picked my bag up again, I slowly walked closer to join her.

Someone tapped my shoulder. I turned quickly around, prepared to punch whoever was behind me, but I let my fist fall slowly to my side as my eyes focused on Lieutenant Hatton.

The Lieutenant was dressed in a rumpled suit which looked as if he had purchased it in a hurry at a Salvation Army thrift store. Mark Hatton always kept a rejected expression on his face, even when he was happy. His mustache was cut so that it drooped over his lips in a depressed manner. Mark was tall and thin, and his shoulders were in a permanent droop. Just before Mark would make a strong point in a conversation, he would stand up straight and rise to his height of six feet. After he made his point, he would stoop over to his five feet eleven inch norm.

"You're looking quite dapper this morning, Mark."

"Do you still carry that cannon in your suitcase everywhere you go?" he demanded.

"I do have a permit for it, you know that."

"For here, yes, but not for everywhere; I have heard about your escapades from coast to coast," Mark continued.

"You always catch us at a bad time," Cassandra gave Mark a placating smile. But, bless her, she couldn't make it quite convincing.

"You two look a bit ragged."

"Boy is that an understatement," She waited; I waited.

Mark cleared his throat, "It seems as if you did a good turn for the police in New York, so I was wondering if you could repeat the effort at home."

"What's wrong?" I asked.

The semi-permanent sad expression spread to Mark's eyes, "Becky Satterwhite is missing."

"What?" Cassandra, like me, suddenly woke up.

"As you probably have found out for yourselves, Phil Peterson isn't the best possible guardian for Becky, so I had her stay with her aunt, Nancy Satterwhite," Mark's glance traveled between me and Cassandra.

"You what?" I interrupted.

"We all thought it seemed like the best thing, besides you two have nothing to do with this, it's an active police case now," Mark said in a defensive voice.

"So, why are you here? " I asked.

"What I want out of you two is all the information you found on all your trips. Also I want to know the minute you hear anything about the location of Becky Satterwhite," He concluded, in firm control.

"All we found out is that you already knew everything we spent a lot of time and money finding out for ourselves," Cassandra's exhaustion was blurring into annoyance; I shot her a warning glance.

"We'll tell you if we find Becky, don't worry, Mark," I said.

"Thank you, and good morning."

243

He turned to walk away. Mark didn't like acting official with us, but he was too good a cop not to.

"Wait," I said. "Have they done anything about the will yet?"

"No, the court has delayed the whole thing another week," Mark turned around. "Why?"

"It seems funny that Becky wasn't found before; she was in Chicago, easy to locate, so why didn't they? The police, that is?" I asked.

"Not one member of her family ever asked us. A missing persons report was never filed; I know what the family says, but they're lying. There was never a missing persons report filed for Becky Satterwhite in any state jurisdiction that I've contacted. Even after Becky was named in her mother's will, no one ever filed a missing persons report on her, until the court finally asked us to locate her. The judge assumed that the family had already done so, and asked us for the file; that's when they filed their own missing person's report," Mark replied.

Cassandra and I looked at each other for a second in silence, as Mark trudged away.

"Where to now?"

"I gave Becky my business card, maybe she left a message for me," I guessed. "Do you feel up to it, or do you want to get some sleep?"

"I need to get a shower and check my mail, but I'll be ready in a few hours for almost anything," Cassandra answered, all grim determination. "We need to find that girl before she gets into more trouble than she deserves."

"I agree, we need to get to work now, and sleep later."

I walked to the nearest phone and called our answering service. No messages from Becky Satterwhite, but there were several messages from Zeb and Nancy Satterwhite, as well as messages from George Sterling, Dr. Billings and Fred Lepus.

Cassandra joined me at the telephone. "Anything interesting?"

"Yeah, just about all the usual suspects called us. I think I ought to take Nancy Satterwhite up on the offer she gave me a few days ago, I'll call her and set up a meeting for this morning."

"Are you sure you're up to her this morning? She acts so seductive around you, you know you're not very quick to react unless you've had eight hours sleep."

"Cut the bull, I'm only going to be there for a short while."

"I'll wait for you," Cassandra teased. "Take as long as you need."

"Where do you want me to pick you up?" I sighed. "Or, do you want to meet me at my apartment?"

"I've never been to your apartment, remember?" Cassandra replied.

"Okay, I'll pick you up at your apartment in two hours."

"Oh, take your time," She continued to smile.

"Could you take my suitcase with you? I can pick it up at your apartment," I asked.

"Sure," She threw me a last wicked grin. "Take as long as you need with Nancy."

I shook my head with slow emphasis. "I'll meet you in two or three hours, depending on traffic. Do you want me to take pictures?"

"Sure, make my day."

. . . .

As I called the hotel and arranged to meet Nancy Satterwhite in forty five minutes, I wondered if Cassandra was right; Nancy was beautiful, but dangerous. What information would she want to trade, or just steal as she seduced me?

She was staying in a large, expensive hotel in West Hollywood near Beverly Hills. These modern, glass monoliths are as impersonal as most of the people who prefer to stay in them. Carpeted in expensive astro-turf surrounded by expensive tile, the foyer also looked as if it were decorated by a leading

245

plastics manufacturer. The music which softly wafted through the building was pre-programmed not to be noticed by humans.

No one observed me as I went through the lobby to the elevators and directly to Nancy's room; I knocked twice on her door.

"Is that you, Benjamin?" Her voice called from inside the room.

"Yes."

"Just a minute, let me get decent."

"Cassandra was wrong," I thought. "She's going to be all business."

Nancy stayed slightly behind the door as she opened it and I stepped into the hotel room. As the door shut and I turned around to face her I held my breath; Nancy was wearing a sheer nightgown, it was light green and didn't have a single ruffle or piece of lace to hide any part of her body beneath it. I just stared for a second, not knowing what to say.

The room was large and finely decorated with two double sized beds, both artfully made up. The blinds on the two windows which faced the street were closed, a small tape recorder softly played music. The only light in the room came from the small reading lamp on the wall over one of the beds. Her perfume brought back memories of my first encounter with her. In no other place or time had I ever encountered the combination of that scent, and her beauty, until now.

"You are as stunning as you've always seemed," I stumbled. "But I thought you were slipping into something decent?"

"Aren't I decent?" Nancy purred.

"That's not what I had in mind when you said decent," I said, stalling to regain composure.

Her body looked great to me, damned decent, but business was business, Cassandra was Cassandra and I had to regain my composure.

"Well, I might as well be comfortable if you already don't think I'm decent."

Nancy put her thumbs under the two straps holding her nightgown up, and flipped it off, letting it fall to the carpet around her feet.   I took in another deep breath and walked to a chair by the television set and sat down.

"If you want to talk to me in the nude, that'll be fine, I just want to know where Becky is."

My daydream to see what she looked like without clothes on was fulfilled, with one jarring added note; this woman scared me.

"All in good time."

Nancy walked to me and sat sideways in my lap, putting one arm around my shoulders and starting to unbutton my shirt with the other.

"Now I recognize that music, it's Barry Manilow. Oh my God! You've been digested by this building," I smiled, trying to deflect her obvious intentions.

Nancy stopped unbuttoning my shirt and cocked her head to one side and leaned it slowly against my cheek.

"What ARE you talking about?"   She whispered in my ear.

I stood up slowly, giving her just enough time to rise before falling to the floor.

"Talk is all I want from you, answers. Where is Becky?" I asked as I sat in the only other chair in the room.

Oh God, why were you testing me, why?   Give me water to walk on, not naked women.

Nancy strolled up to me, sat on my lap again, facing me, pressing her breast against my face.

"Talk is not what I want to give you, silly boy."

She moved her nipple close to my lips.

My head was angled slightly towards the ground as I lifted my face up, still pressed against Nancy's bare breast.

Nancy shouted, "Ouch! You son of a bitch!"   She pulled her body back from me. "You haven't shaved, and that hurt!"

"I guess I'm trying to tell you that your intentions, no matter how desirable, are a bust. Conversation's all you're going to get, even though, God knows, I'm rising to this occasion. Call it professionalism, but I don't screw people I'm investigating, at least not like this. If you want information from me, you'll have to pay me for it, not in cash or sex, but by telling me what I want to know."

Nancy stood up, feet apart and hands on her hips.

"What if I've always liked you, and wanted to sleep with you from the start, nothing more?"

"Believe me, I'm very flattered," I looked at her whole body and grinned.

"Well," Nancy sat down on the edge of the bed and crossed her legs. "So you tell me, who killed my sister?"

"I don't know yet, but there's a lot of possible candidates," I answered. "Where's Becky?"

"I don't know, I don't think anyone took her, I think she ran away by herself; she always was so difficult to handle."

"I thought she was a reasonable girl," I insisted. "She seems very grown up."

"Whatever," Nancy replied in an annoyed voice. "What did you find out?"

"I found out about your ex-husband's baby scheme, and that Marcia was up to her eyeballs in it."

"Yeah, I didn't know about it until the divorce was almost over. My sleazy ex-husband had been working on that for over to ten years before I found out about it. That little shit could have warned me before the New York hoods started arriving on my doorstep, looking for him; they arrived right before the FBI."

"Why did he do it?"

"I'm worth millions, and so was my sister. Daddy wants the money to pass down through family blood lines only, so any man we married had to sign an agreement which knocked him out of the big money. If there was an heir produced, the father would get a little, but not enough for the greedy men Marcia and I married."

"Why isn't your father happy about Becky? She seems too respectable a granddaughter to ignore," I asked, glancing at my watch.

248

"I never did guess why he hates Becky so much, Becky is the only likely blood heir he'll have since I've always been sterile."

"I've got to go," I stood up, still staring at Nancy. "I can't say it hasn't been interesting, and I can't say I don't want to stay, but. . ."

Nancy lay back on the bed, slightly spreading her legs and spoke softly, "Come back when you're ready to be friends."

34

Home sweet home

The short drive towards the Pacific calmed me down. I drove to Cassandra's apartment with the top off my car; I needed to. The day appeared brighter than it had in quite some time, the smog seemed to have taken a short holiday and the air rushing over my head helped to get the memory of Nancy off my lower brain. As I merged onto Interstate Ten, the brown hills and the contrasting green trees stood out in sharp focus.

I parked my Porsche and walked through the front door of Cassandra's apartment building. Arranging a smile on my face, I knocked on her door.

"Well stud, how did it go?" She swung the front door open.

"It went as you expected," I grinned.

"No," Cassandra's smirk disappeared as she motioned for me to come in.

"Well, not exactly as you expected, all we did was talk; she was naked, but all we did was talk."

"I've only seen her once before from a distance," Cassandra paused. "Is she as well preserved as she looks with her clothes on?"

"How catlike; I always thought you were much better looking than she is."

250

I just had to add that. I knew what to say, besides, it was true. "Although she's built better than average women dream, I wouldn't touch it with a ten foot pole."

Cassandra stopped, looked at me and smiled, "It's not THAT long."

"Very funny, let's go to my house now; Becky might've left a message on my answering machine, since my home number was on the card I gave her."

"I'll bet Lieutenant Hatton got our answering service to give him all our messages, and that's why he arranged to visit us this morning."

She motioned that she needed to go back in and get something inside her apartment.

"Should we tell him if Becky did try to contact us?" I followed Cassandra back into her apartment.

"Eventually, I suppose," She answered, opening a drawer, taking out her automatic pistol.

"Don't forget extra clips," I reminded her. I looked around her apartment and noticed several pieces of pottery on her shelves, next to the stereo.

"Are they new?"

"What?" She looked at me, and then at the shelf. "Yes, I'm proud of those, I got them at the dig I went on last summer, remember, that's when you were in Paris. I got credit for that dig, which was a good thing because it left me only two more five hour courses to take which I have just about finished; it was sort of related to my major, and it was a whole lot of fun."

"Yeah, I remember, you went somewhere in Greece for almost two months; it sounded like a great trip." I answered as I looked at the vases. "These are in pretty good condition, how did you get them out of the country?"

"The director let me have them, I gave up my salary for the three weeks in order to take something back with me. I paid the program and the Greek government a lot for this stuff; it just came in a package from Greece two weeks ago."

Cassandra grabbed her jacket and tugged at my sleeve. "You ought to go with me next year, I've lined up a trip to Morocco."

"How does a dig in Morocco relate to political science?" I had to ask. Maybe I should have kept my mouth shut, but she was trying to drag me along.

"Hey, I'm just taking a summer off from my required courses to have a change of pace and do something different and fun; it's an Arab country, and that's my dissertation topic so it's related anyway," Cassandra voice tightened up a bit. "Besides, since when do you have a problem with having fun?"

"I don't," I smiled a little as I shook my head. "But, digging in the hot sun isn't my idea of having fun."

"I know you like archeology, and you're no dummy either, so you'd fit in. See, I invite you to go along with me on overseas trips."

She got in that dig, I knew she was still pissed about not joining me on my last case in Europe.

"You've been to Morocco before and to Jordan," I feigned a sigh. "You didn't invite me for those."

"I didn't know you the first time I went to Morocco, and if you'll remember it right, I did invite you to go with me to Jordan."

"Right." I had forgotten; that was the first year we knew each other.

"So, do you want to come with me this summer?" She asked again.

"I'll think about it."

I walked out of her apartment behind her, and closed the door.

. . . .

I had lived in the same apartment for over five years, it was in a semi-rundown part of town, but close to lots of shopping and museums. It's in the central part of Los Angeles, near Little Tokyo. I lived on the fourth floor of the building which was next to a movie theater that showed movies twenty four hours a day. None of the titles they show would ever make it to television, but none of their clients own a television set anyway.

An old black man was sitting on the steps to my building. Over his tattered jeans he was wearing a dark blue oversized shirt with 'JAZZ MAN' screen printed on it. Over the shirt, he wore an open in the front, light brown rain coat with many rips and stains. In his late fifties, he had a broad pleasant face with a noncommittal expression.

"How's it going, Reverend?" I waved.

"Awl right, brother," The man drawled back in a smooth voice as Cassandra and I walked into the building. "See me when you leave, I've got somethin' for ya."

I nodded my head and walked into the building.

"Who the hell was that?" Cassandra asked as we walked into the building.

"He's the Reverend, he used to be a preacher and a singer, but now he guards this building," I answered. "He's also sort of the maintenance guy too."

"Guards this building? He looks like a drunk, sleeping it off," Cassandra observed as she stepped into the elevator.

"Just try to come into this building if you don't belong here, he'll blow your head off," I said.

"You mean that bum out there's armed?" Cassandra asked in disbelief.

"He's got a forty four automag hidden under his old coat, the tenants pay him well for sitting out in front,it keeps the dope heads out of our place," I opened my front door. "Besides, he does it because he wants to."

She was investigating the shelves near the front window, "How much did that stereo cost you?"

"You know how much music means to me, I can't relax without it."

"Yeah, but that set up costs more than some houses," Cassandra stared at it.

253

"It's not that much, put something on if you like." I pointed to shelves of records and tapes next to the stereo.

"I won't embarrass myself trying to figure out how to turn it on," She sounded skeptical.

"I'll put something on, keep the volume low so we can pay attention to the messages, how about an opera, Marriage of Figaro?"

"You know I hate that type of singing."

"I know, but it's just music."

I put a tape in the player and turned on the music, keeping it quiet.

"What is that?" She pointed to a picture frame leaning on the top shelf of my tallest bookshelf.

"That's something from the Marines."

I hadn't thought about them for ages, I didn't really want her to look at it, but saying so would be a sure way to make her want to look at it.

"Are they medals?" She stood on her tiptoes to pull it down.

"I suppose they are," I replied in a flat voice.

"I recognize the purple heart, but what are the others?"

"Expeditionary Medal, National Defense Service Medal, RVN Service Medal, Navy Marine Corps Medal and a Silver Star. Those little things on the purple heart indicate how many times I got wounded in action," I sighed. "My captain had them framed before I left active service, and I kind of keep it as a memento; can we change the subject, please."

"You really have to tell me more about yourself before we become closer, you know," Cassandra was serious. "Your time in the military is something you have never talked about."

"There are some things I'm not ready to tell you yet, and it isn't all that sinister, in fact you know most of the bad things about my past already," I sighed louder. "Can we change the subject already?"

"Okay," she acknowledged. "What kind of neighbors do you have? This is the first time you've brought me to your place."

"Oh, they aren't so bad, there's a lawyer next door, he's an assistant D. A. Across the hall's an agent for the IRS, I think the guy on the bottom floor is with the CIA, then there's three cops on the second floor." I rapped out the details. Why was I telling her this much?

"You're serious?" Cassandra asked.

"Sure, why not? The rent's only one twenty a month, and we're close to everything. All the folks here are single, most of us are in some kind of law enforcement work and we're all well armed," I rewound the tape on my answering machine. "The gangs leave us alone, and we don't shoot at them so it's a good arrangement, don't you think?"

"I guess so, I see why you wanted to live at my place when we were," Cassandra paused. "Going together."

"Going together? That sounds too high-schoolish."

I didn't have to think long for the rest of the sentence. "I'd like us to, though."

"Just play the tape," She sounded exasperated.

We listened to the calls; the first three callers didn't leave any messages.

"This is Brian Fowler," The fourth caller on the tape machine said. "Your adorable partner didn't leave me her number, so I'll call you. Thanks for dumping Lopez for me, I'll return the favor if you meet me in 'Frisco, day after tomorrow, the beautiful partner knows where."

There were two more 'no message' callers, then a soft female voice purred, "Big Ben, I miss you, please come and fix my broken heart."

"Give me a break," Cassandra sounded very annoyed.

"That was Lepus' bimbo secretary."

No, it wasn't but no way I'd tell Cassandra that was a request for me to call my government handler.

"Sure it was," Cassandra's sarcasm was in fine form.

As Cassandra finished talking, Becky's voice said something; I rewound the tape a little to hear the whole message.

"This is Becky," A weak, broken voice said. "You said to call you if I needed a friend, I need you," The voice stopped

255

for a second, then began again. "I'll call you back," The voice said, then hung up.

There was one more 'no message' caller, then Becky called again.

"I just can't stay with Aunt Nancy, I'll come to your place, I've got nowhere else," Becky said, then hung up.

There were no more calls on my answering machine.

"Where is she, that was yesterday, where is she now?" Cassandra asked.

"Oh my God, the Reverend," I said, running out the front door.

I didn't look back to see, but I heard Cassandra following me. We rushed into the hall, I pushed the button to summon the elevator back up. The old, slow elevator clanked up to the fourth floor and stopped. The inside door slid to one side, then the iron grill work rattled to the same side, the two of us rushed in and pushed the button for the first floor.

"If he's got her, where is she?"

"Most likely his apartment," I answered.

"I hope his apartment isn't as sloppy looking as he is," Cassandra mumbled as the elevator door opened on the first floor.

"Reverend, I think I'd like to meet the package you're holding for me," I said to the old man, still sitting on the front steps.

"In my place." He did not turn around to face me. "You knock three times, real quick, then two times real slow, she'll open up."

"How long have the cops been out front?" I asked, nodding towards a late model brown Crown Vic parked one block up from the building.

"They been here since yesterday. The kid hot?" The old man asked.

"Not too hot, just scared," I answered.

"You got that right," The old man turned around and looked at me.

256

"If those cops come here, could you let me know? Make some noise or something," I requested.

"Where does he live?" Cassandra looked around.

"There's a double apartment in the basement, it used to be the old maintenance man's, but he moved out. He said it was too dangerous to live in this neighborhood. The Reverend fixed it up a lot in the last year or so."

I opened the stairwell door and walked down the one flight to the basement.

"It looks a whole lot better since he put the pool table in," I added.

"Pool table, just what is this place?" Cassandra's confusion became more obvious.

"Just look for yourself when you get there," I answered.

The stairwell to the basement was musty smelling, looking as if it hadn't been painted since the building's construction. The cement stairs had various colored paint spills all over them and below, the dimly lit landing led to a small hallway. Two doors stood off the hallway, one on each side. The one to our right led to storage rooms, furnace, and hot water heater, the door to our left led to the guardian's apartment.

I knocked three times, quick, on the door, waited a second or two, then knocked two times slowly.

A soft voice of someone standing right behind the door spoke, "Is that you, Clarence?"

"It's me, Benjamin Katz, only my partner is with me."

We heard the sound of several locks being unlocked, then the door opened, slow motion. Becky's face peered out from behind. She looked as if she hadn't slept in a week, her face pale and drawn; her face seemed ten years older than she had appeared just a few days ago.

"May we come in?" Cassandra asked.

Becky opened the door all the way and stared at Cassandra for several seconds with her mouth wide open. The apartment was many times larger than mine. The door opened onto a large living room, which had an oak parquet wood floor, several oriental rugs lay on the oak floor. The furniture was all in

257

an Arts and Crafts style, most of it original.   Several reproductions of works by Matisse and John Wyeth hung on the walls; just off center in the living room was a Yamaha baby grand, leaning against it was an old Gibson twelve string guitar. The ceiling's light panels helped make the entire living room seem very light and airy. Two massive speakers rested next to the back wall.   The sound of blues music floated from them at a low volume.

"Wow," Cassandra glanced around with a bewildered look on her face. "Life is throwing me a lot of surprises today."

"Later, let's talk about Becky's problems first."

I looked at Becky, who had walked to a chair by the back wall, and sat down.

"Why are the police searching for you all of a sudden?" Cassandra sat nearby.

Becky didn't answer, she just stared at the floor as I sat down in the other nearby chair.

"I want to help you; I've been looking into your family's past and I think you could use some help," I said.

I wanted to gain her trust, she needed more friends, and I wanted to be one. Cassandra got up, walked to the stereo and studied it for a second.   Finding the on-off switch, she turned the music off.   Becky kept her expression blank.

Cassandra looked back at her.   "We can hear you better with the stereo off."

"Clarence is a nice man, he's got a real neat place here, have you seen his night club?" Becky's expression lightened.

"Yes, I've seen it, I helped him build it; but what about your problem?" I asked.

"Night club?" Cassandra whispered to me as her eyes opened wider.

I ignored the question and continued.   "Becky, tell me what's going on?"

"I'm going to be rich, I'll be able to go home again, alone," Becky looked at one of the pictures on the wall instead of acknowledging what we had said. "I like being home by myself, I have good friends who live next door, I like being alone."

"Why did you call me?" I asked.

"You seemed nice; you didn't ask for something from me," Becky glanced at the floor, then back at me.

"Can you tell us what's been happening?" Cassandra asked, sitting down near Becky and me.

"Starting from where?" Becky asked.

"How about from the time Fred Lepus took you from your mother's house almost two years ago?"

Several tears began to form in Becky's eyes, then slid down her cheeks. Cassandra got up from her chair and stooped down beside Becky, taking Becky's trembling hand between hers.

"I could always tell when something bad was going to happen," Becky began. "Mama used to beat me when she was in trouble, all I'd have to do is come out of my room, and Mama would slap me so hard."

Becky withdrew her hand from Cassandra's soft grip and stood up. She was speaking somewhat slowly, but she never paused, as if afraid to stop.

"I asked Phil to take me away from Mama, he had to be better than she was. He didn't beat me, but he treated me like I wasn't there at first, he was just like Mama, he would leave me alone for weeks or more. He gave me money for food, and just left me alone; later, he tried to sleep with me, but I was too big and could fight him off. It was only when he was drunk, and anybody could beat him up then."

More tears ran down her cheeks as she sat back down in the chair. After taking a handkerchief out of her pocket, she blew her nose and continued talking.

"I wish someone like Clarence could be my Daddy, he's so nice, he cares about how I feel, and he treats me like I'm somebody special. I wish he could meet Sally next door, they would get along all right. All Phil cares about is my money, he knew all along that Mama left me all her money. He adopted me and set up a trust where all my money would go until I was twenty five years old. He'll be in charge of the trust, and I'll be surprised if there'll be any money in it by then."

259

"The whole money thing has me a bit confused," I said. "The court has identified several millions invested in banks, stocks and real estate, but people like your mother like to hide money from people and the government."

Becky turned to me with a quizzical look.

"How did you know?" she asked.

"I've been a detective long enough to know about people like your mother," I replied.

"You mean crooks like my mother?"

"Not to sound too cruel, but, yes."

"She hid cash, gold and jewelry in safe deposit boxes," Becky said, opening her own clenched hands on her lap. "She always told me her father taught her to do that. Never trust bankers or brokers, hide as much as you can."

"Did she tell you which banks the safety deposit boxes were in?" Cassandra asked.

"No, she just gave me the keys."

"The keys?" Both Cassandra and I said in unison.

"Where are the keys?" I quickly added.

"In my jewelry box, on a gold chain," Becky answered. "Mama insisted I carry that key necklace with me everywhere I went. I should never let it out of my sight, ever."

"Where is it now?" Cassandra asked.

"In my back pack," She replied. I'm sure that's what Phil was after, and maybe Aunt Nancy as well."

"Who would know what banks to look in?" I asked.

"I don't know," Becky replied. "Maybe the information died with my mother."

"Not to change the subject, but what did you do when Fred Lepus took you out of Los Angeles?" I wondered.

"It was real strange, I was real happy, I thought it would be a great adventure to follow this strange detective Phil had hired to take me away from my Mama, but nothing happened like I expected," Becky said.

"Where did you go first?"

I knew the trail would be significant.

"Mr. Lepus took me first to New York. I think he got in trouble there, because we rushed off real quickly to a camp in the woods somewhere, but we only stayed there for a few hours, it was my grandpa's place, but he didn't want anything to do with me. Next we went to visit my grandmother in Naples, but she was even meaner than my grandpa. Then we went to Mr. Lepus' place and I stayed there for a long time, I lived with a woman named Cathy, you met her, she's Mr. Lepus' secretary," Becky answered. "I liked Mr. Lepus, he pretended not to like me, but he would always take me out to the movies, and out to eat, we had a lot of fun, he was real friendly to me, he let me be myself. His friend Cathy enjoyed taking me shopping and girl stuff, you know. They both treated me like a real person, a kid," Becky took a deep breath. "I wanted to go to school that year, but they said it would be too dangerous, so I missed school that year."

"Yes, I've met both Lepus and his secretary, several times. What was Phil Peterson doing all this time, do you know?" I asked.

"No, but I think he was negotiating with the rest of my Mother's family to leave me alone," Becky answered.

"Why do you think that?" Cassandra asked.

"Because after I went to live in Chicago, no one ever bothered me, it was like I was all alone, the only one I ever saw from time to time, besides our neighbors, was Mr. Lepus," Becky said.

"What did he do, why did he come to visit?" I asked.

"I don't know, he would come to talk to Phil at his office, then stop by for dinner, or lunch, then go away again," Becky said.

"What did he talk about when he was at your house?" Cassandra asked.

"Nothing much, he'd talk a little bit about my grandfather, then about my aunt, then he'd talk about dumb stuff," Becky said.

"What kind of dumb stuff," I asked.

261

"Well, he'd talk about how he had to be somewhere real soon, it always seemed like he was in a hurry to leave, like he had a party to go to, that he was late to. He seemed to talk like he was a lot busier than he was while I was with him all day when he first came and got me."

"Yeah, the only thing busy about Fred is his mouth. Did he ever say where he had to go?" I asked.

I began to wonder about this Lepus creep, the first person who liked Lepus had turned out to be a respectable kid.

"No, but he always seemed anxious when he got to my place," Becky got up and walked to the piano. "I think he just wanted to see if I was all right, maybe he was paid by someone like my grandfather to check on me, or maybe he did it on his own."

Becky wiped her face with her hand, and sat on the piano bench. She faced the piano and began to softly hit keys at random.

"Do you play the piano?" Cassandra asked.

Becky didn't answer, she began to play a classical piece. Part of the way through the piece, she stopped, got up from the piano and sat back down in her chair.

"That was very beautiful, Becky, how long have you been studying the piano?" Cassandra asked.

"Since before my mother was killed, I love music, it makes me feel good," Becky said. "Cathy had a small upright her mother gave her, she taught me too, although all she likes are show tunes."

"Don't tell me, I know that piece you just played," I raised my right hand. "It's Valse in C sharp, by Chopin."

"Yeah," Becky brightened. "Do you play the piano?"

"No, I took lessons, but all I can do without embarrassing myself is listen to music," I answered.

" Benjamin," Cassandra said in a reproachful tone. "Stop playing games, for now, and pay attention to Becky."

"That's okay, I like him, he's funny," Becky remarked.

"All right," I turned back to Becky. "Why are the police after you?"

262

"Phil wants his meal ticket back," Becky said flatly. "As long as I was under his thumb, everything was fine. As long as he knew he stood a chance of getting the money, everything was fine. But I'm gone, and he doesn't know where, now he calls in the cops and plays like a poor childless father."

"Didn't Phil find the safe deposit keys?" I asked.

"As soon as I moved into his house, I hid them. I kept moving the hiding place and he never found them."

"Did Lepus find them?"

"If he did, he never said anything, and he never took them," She answered.

"When did Phil adopt you?"

"Two months ago, I figured he was the only thing I had for a parent, so I finally went along with him," Becky answered.

"What was going on when I got you out of Lepus' house a few days ago?" I asked.

"Phil told me that I had to disappear for a few days, for my good health to continue. I didn't want to go because I listened in when he was talking on the phone to the Los Angeles lawyer about my mother's estate. I heard that I inherited everything, I didn't know it was that much money. I wanted it, I didn't want Phil to get his hands on it, and steal it from me. I didn't want to disappear at all; he paid Mr. Lepus to take me away, but Mr. Lepus wanted to help me more than he wanted to help Phil, then you came and helped me too," Becky's voice became louder before she paused. "You know something?"

"What?" I asked.

"I lied to you back in Washington."

"I know, you did know that your mother had given you all her money. That's all right, I knew anyway."

"I'm sorry, but I didn't know you at all then, and I felt I had to cover up and everything," Becky grinned sheepishly at me.

"Where can she stay, Benjamin?" Cassandra asked.

"I'll ask the Reverend if she can stay here, it looks like she got in here without anyone knowing," I said.

"Oh, I'd really like to stay here, please tell Clarence to let me stay here," Becky pleaded.

"I'll ask, but you can't stay here long," I remarked.

"The police will soon come here looking for you, but I don't think you should go back to Phil Peterson, ever," Cassandra said.

"Yeah," I nodded. "We have to go now."

"Where to now?" Cassandra asked.

"Away," I answered.

"Before we leave, you have to tell me about this Reverend named Clarence," Cassandra insisted.

"Go into the room to the left off the hall back there, I'll follow you, and tell you what you're seeing," I pointed to one of the back rooms.

All three of us walked to a room, decorated as a nightclub. There was a small stage with a stool and a microphone on it behind two small round tables, surrounded by three chairs each. In the back of the room was a double bed, with a medium sized spotlight, hanging from the ceiling over the bed, pointing to the small stage.

"What's this?" Cassandra asked.

"It's Clarence's stage, just like the one he sings at," Becky blurted out.

"Clarence writes and sings jazz and blues songs, he's been doing that, and preaching, for a long, long time; he still sings occasionally, but only when he wants to. Look at the labels on that pile of records in the living room, his name's listed as the composer for most of them; he's also an ordained Baptist minister. Clarence preaches every other Sunday at the mission down the street. He made a fortune with his music, but he kept the fortune he made in music for himself, which separates him from all his poverty stricken fellow singers, he even owns this building," I added.

"If he's so darn rich, why does he sit out there like a bum?" Cassandra asked.

"Because he wants to, and we like him, so we pay him to do what he wants in addition to paying him rent," I said. "He says that this is what he was like when he was young, and if he plays the rich man he'll lose touch with the people and the feelings that got him to where he is now."

"I like him ," Becky said. "When I finally get the money, I'll pay him to do what he wants, too."

"I'm out numbered; he has to be a great guy," Cassandra raised her hands, Becky smiled for the first time.

"Becky, we have to go run a few errands, but we'll be back. You stay here, and don't let anyone in except the Reverend, or us, all right?" I asked.

"Okay," Becky answered as she walked back out into the living room, and plopped down in her chair.

Before I walked out of the apartment, I called to Becky, "Lock the door after we leave, and don't open it unless it's one of us, or the Reverend."

"I've got to erase the tape on my machine, before the cops listen to it," I said.

"Good idea," Cassandra replied.

I stopped on the ground floor and stepped outside to speak to the Reverend.

"That kid already loves you," I said.

The Reverend turned around and spoke in a serious voice, "She needs to love someone, and somebody needs to love that child back."

"Can you keep her for a while?" I asked. "She's worth a lot of money, and I think someone's going to try to kill her for it."

"You bet I'll keep her, as long as it takes," he answered.

"Your bodyguard amazes me," Cassandra said.

"Everybody in this building would do anything for him, he likes to look at the world go by from his vantage point; in this neighborhood, the world is never dull."

I finished erasing the tape on my answering machine.

"Are you sure you should erase that?" Cassandra asked.

"Why not?" I asked. "The cops will find out eventually where she is, but I think Becky will be safer here until we find out what's really going on."

"Speaking of Becky, where do you think the list of banks is?" Cassandra asked.

"I don't know yet," I paused. "It makes sense to keep the keys with Marcia's kid, then hide the list of banks somewhere else; only Marcia or someone she trusted could combine the two to get ready cash when needed it."

"Do you think all the banks were out here?"

"I don't know," Again, I paused. "Probably not. Moving all that stuff around might attract attention. It would make better sense to set up the safe deposit boxes, then just keep them forever."

"If that's so, where are they?"

"It depends on where she was living at the time she set them all up," I guessed.

"So back to the case, do we see Zeb now?"

"You took the words right out of my mouth, we go see the world's nastiest old man." I walked to my door and motioned for her to leave first.

35

He was a dark and stormy knight

"I got your phone call, and I think I can be of some service," Fred almost stood at attention with a broad grin across his whiskery face.

The grin on his face didn't distract anyone from noticing his hands, which periodically would make twitching movements; he would stop them, and in a few moments the movements would start again.

"You came because you got the thousand dollars I wired you," Zeb growled.

"Whatever, Daddy," Nancy sighed. "Let's get on with it."

Zeb walked toward the open window of his hotel room.

"Becky has run away again, you wouldn't know anything about that, would you?"

"Not this time," Fred relaxed. "Katz took the kid away from me at gun point, and I have no idea where he took her."

"The hell you don't," Nancy stared at Fred, who couldn't seem to stop twitching. "You know damn well he took her out here to LA , and gave her to that weasel, Peterson."

"Don't get all huffy with me," Fred let out the remainder of his nervous breath, then dragged another one in. "You lost her this time; just how did you do that?"

"The little bitch went to the bathroom at the restaurant downstairs, and didn't come back," Nancy glared at Fred.

267

"So," Fred returned Nancy's gaze. "What do you want me to do besides talk to you?"

"Don't start acting like an ass," Zeb took one giant step closer to Fred. "It could be very dangerous."

"I know it could, everybody I've met in the last month or so wants to impress on me how dangerous they are."

"But, I am dangerous," Zeb's voice fell into a heavy monotone.

"I know, you're all dangerous, and all I want to do is stay alive, but, I repeat, what do you want me to do?"

"Find Becky," Nancy answered as she sat in a chair near the door to the hotel room.

"How?" Fred shrugged his shoulders. "I don't know this town; I don't know many people out here either."

"You know Katz, and I think he has her stashed somewhere." Nancy looked coldly at Fred. "We're pretty sure she isn't at his apartment, nor is she with that bitch partner he has, just find her."

"I don't care how you do it, or how long it takes," Zeb sat back down in the chair near the window. "Nancy wants her niece back, so that's fine with me, I just don't care."

"If you don't care, why should I do it?" The words popped out before Fred could stop them.

"Because I'm paying you," Nancy said. "Not my father."

"Yeah," Lepus screwed up his courage a notch. "I know he truly loves his granddaughter, we've already had a long discussion about that a few years ago."

"What's your problem?" Nancy rose and leveled her eyes on Fred.

"It's not so much my problem as it is Becky's," Fred stammered, somewhat more steady this time. "It's obvious you don't give a shit about her well being. So why do you want her?"

He stepped towards Nancy and lost most of the fear in his expression. "That kid has been jerked around by this family too damned much, I'll find her if I can, but I'll be honest with you, I'm going to do what's best for her, not you."

"And, you expect me to pay you for that?" Nancy asked indignantly.

"Well, yes," Fred looked flustered, as he realized that he had again said more than he planned. "Will you people for once be honest and tell me why you want her?"

Zeb stood again and walked over, grabbing Fred's collar and slowly tightening the grip.

"You will find the little bastard, and you will bring her here to me, she is my daughter's child, and that is her aunt," Zeb's voice was even and calm, dripping with violence. "We always have paid you well to do our bidding, we pay all our servants well to do our shit work, but don't you ever talk back to us like that or you will be very dead, sooner than even you expect."

Fred blinked his eyes three times quickly and wrinkled his brow, "Yes, sir."

"Yes you will," Zeb let go of Fred's collar. "Let Nancy know where the little snipe is, and soon."

36

Who's that knocking at my door?

The ride to the glass palace hotel where Zeb Satterwhite stayed was not as painful as I had expected, traffic was lighter than I anticipated. It took no time to drive over to the Harbor Freeway. As we moved from the central city towards West Hollywood and the Santa Monica Boulevard turn off, the buildings got lower, the neighborhoods more prosperous, and less trash littered the roadsides. Cassandra almost fell asleep three times while I drove, deep in thought.

It had been a cool Spring day last year, on my father's last day on this earth. I had moved him from his apartment in Harrisburg Pennsylvania to a nursing home in Glendale only four weeks before. Dad now hated the place he had once loved and my brother could no longer make any headway with him so I agreed to move him out here for his health, mostly for the warm climate and so I could keep an eye on him as his health failed.

After my mother had died, he lost all his desire to improve the farm. For awhile he still worked a small portion of it and rented out the remainder until my brother was able to take over. After his health declined, my brother and I moved him to a pleasant private home for terminal patients in California. The an old man talking seemed like a stranger to me; on that beautiful Spring day, he was finally unburdening himself of decades of guilt.

According to Dad, there was no murder, my mother took her own life. She shot herself in the head with the twenty two rifle Dad kept in the hall closet, the old rifle he kept loaded to shoot the local dogs which would come after our chickens. That rifle had been in our closet for years, and that's what my mother shot herself with. At the time, even though I wanted to scream out in pain, I felt nothing and I still feel nothing.

His story sounded like a bad television script; this old man I no longer recognized told me how he had come back to the house to get a five gallon can of diesel fuel which he left on the back porch for the tractor when he noticed something in the kitchen. It was my mother's body, blood still flowing from her head. He also had noticed the faint scent of gunpowder in the kitchen.

My father moved the kitchen chair his wife had placed the rifle on, then he threw out the string tied to the trigger and cleaned and put away the rifle. He took some cash from the bedroom dresser, then threw some stuff on the floor in the bedroom, family room and kitchen to make it look as if someone had been there. He tore up the suicide note and hid it in the hen house, under a nest. He burned the note the next day with the rest of the paper trash, then he tore up his memories and hid them as well.

He left her body for someone else to discover, that someone else was me, I was the first one running through the kitchen door to see my mother. Why did he do that, how could a man do that to his son? I was only six years old, damn it.

"What do we say?" Cassandra interrupted my thoughts. "Do we say what we want, or do we lie?"

"I'm sorry," I looked at her. "I wasn't listening, what did you say?"

"I asked, what should we say to old Zeb when we get there?"

"I've been thinking about that on the way over here," I replied.

"Well?"

"We just ask him for more money, and tell him we'll have the suspect by the end of the week," I answered.

"That's two days from now," Cassandra's voice held surprise. "Do you want me just to give him the piece of paper in my purse with the name on it?"

"I don't think he'd take it too well, besides, I can't make it stick yet. Let's just talk to him for a while, and try to get some more money."

"But we don't have any expense reports ready."

At the hotel, I let the attendant park my car for me; I never did get used to valet parking, especially when I cared so much about the car I drove.

"I've got all my receipts in my pocket, where are yours?" I asked.

"Most of them right here, in my purse."

"Well, he can just pay us for those, I want to know what he actually thinks about his granddaughter," I said.

"He already said what he thought," Cassandra replied. "'She's a bastard' were his exact words, but I don't believe him; Becky's the only child in his family to carry on, at least the only one we know about."

"You caught my line of thinking; Zeb seems so impressed with himself, that it's unlikely he would disown the only existing hope of carrying on his genes. Nancy has to be close to forty by now, and says she's sterile, so Becky will most likely be his only chance." I remarked.

"Sterile, how do you know that?" Cassandra demanded, stopping me with her hand outstretched.

"I told you, she said she is," I replied.

"That sounds like a line if I ever heard one," My partner retorted. "I won't get pregnant, I'm sterile; sure!"

"I think she is," I said. "As concerned with progeny as he is, do you think Zeb would allow her to hide a kid?"

"I guess not, not if HE knew about one," Cassandra let go of my arm.

. . . .

A sour look quickly appeared on the hotel clerk's face when we asked for Zeb Satterwhite's room number, "He's in room eleven seventy six, it's one of our luxury suites"

"Looks like he treats everybody like shit, not just his friends," I said to Cassandra.

"You said it sir, not me," The clerk remarked.

"He is something, isn't he?" Cassandra smiled at the clerk and shook her head.

"Something isn't the word, Ma'am," The clerk responded.

272

"Does anybody go up to see him, I mean besides us?" I asked.

"You, the cops, and his daughter are the only ones so far who're willing to go up there, at least while I've been on duty."

"How long have you been here at the desk?" Cassandra asked.

"Six years now," The clerk sighed.

"That's not what I meant," Cassandra looked at me as if to keep from laughing at the poor man. "How long have you been on duty today?"

"Oh, two hours."

"Is the other clerk, the one who was on duty before you, still here?" I asked.

"Sammy didn't make it in today, the manager stood in for him," The clerk leaned toward us. "I think he's about to be fired."

"Is the manager here?" Cassandra asked.

"That's him."

The clerk pointed to a short thin, balding man in a dark suit who was listening to our conversation from the far end of the counter.

"Did Zeb Satterwhite have any visitors before us?" Cassandra asked the manager.

"Not that I should tell you anything unless you're cops, but he had one visitor," The manager walked towards us. "An average height man in a rumpled suit, with a receding hairline with small tufts of white hair sticking up, went there about two hours ago, and came down in less than thirty minutes."

"Thanks," we both said at the same time.

As we stepped back from the desk, the same phrase came out of each of us, again at the same time, "It's Lepus!"

. . . .

"This is what an elevator is supposed to look like, not that thing that's in your building," Cassandra teased me on the ride up to the eleventh floor.

273

"Yeah, but it's got no character, and no adventure to it; in this one you know you'll make it to your destination,"   I said. "His daughter Nancy's two doors down from him."

"Did you see this old man the last time you were here?" She asked.

"No, and I didn't feel like staying around long enough to look him up then, either."

We walked down the hall until we saw room eleven seventy six. I knocked on the door, while standing to one side of it while Cassandra waited on the other side of the door frame. The door opened a crack, I could see Nancy Satterwhite's face peer out of the crack.

"Oh, it's you two, come in, my father wants to talk to you anyway, and so do I," She opened the door all the way.

I walked in first, then Cassandra walked in behind me. Zeb was sitting in a chair by the window, with an open file folder in his lap. Standing up, Zeb closed the file folder and threw it on the bed; several typed pages slipped out of the folder. Cassandra moved closer to the bed in order to look at them, but before she could, Nancy moved quickly to the bed, stuffed the pages back into the folder, and picked it up.

"I'm sick and tired of dumb ass private dicks who don't give me information and do what they're paid for, so what the hell have you been doing with my money?" Zeb demanded.

"Spending it to find out what a son of a bitch you are," Cassandra replied. "We have also been putting names on a long list of suspects who had some motive to kill your daughter."

"Well, who are they?" Nancy asked.

"Everybody she met," I answered.

"Don't hand me that bullshit, I didn't want her dead, neither did her sister; there were a lot of people who loved her," Zeb sat back down in his chair. "There was her daughter, the kid loved her mother very much."

"Where is Becky?" Nancy asked. "The police said you might be able to find her."

"We're paid to find the murderer of Marcia Satterwhite, and that's all," Cassandra answered.

274

"Hell, I'll pay you another ten thousand to find her," Zeb said in a quiet voice.

"I thought she was a bastard, I thought you disowned her?" Cassandra asked.

"She's all I have, she's all mine," Zeb muttered.

He looked out the window, then turned around to face Cassandra and shouted, "What the hell difference should it make to you anyway, I pay, and you get!"

"Speaking of paying, we have some bills to give you, and you have some money to give us," Cassandra stepped back a few paces.

Zeb stood and faced Cassandra and me, his face became flushed as he raised one fist in the air, opened his mouth wide and shouted, "You faggots, I want the name I'm paying you for, I know you've got it, I know you've got my little girl stashed somewhere, and I want them both, now!"

I walked up to Zeb as close as I could get. As Zeb drew his raised fist back as if he was going to strike me, I slammed my foot down on the arch of his foot. He yelled an obscenity and fell back onto the bed, holding his smashed foot. I lifted him by the collar of his bathrobe off the bed and spoke into his face.

"If we come up with the name of her murderer, and the proof to convict him, or her, we'll give it all to the police first, and you'll pay us. If we come up with your granddaughter, we'll give her to the police, none of your family can be trusted with her well being, and you'll pay us for finding her, too."

"Big friggen deal, you can rough up an old man. I pay you for what I get, not what the cops get; you get jack shit if you don't give it all to me!" Zeb shouted back at me.

"We know who killed your daughter, and we're not going to tell you, yet. We could find Becky in an hour or so, but we would never give her to any of you. What you want will get done, and you'll pay for it, starting now," I threw Zeb back down on the bed.

Nancy had been moving closer and closer to a nearby end table while Zeb and I had been roughly conversing. Cassandra had been looking at Zeb and me, and didn't notice Nancy pull a small twenty five caliber automatic colt pistol out of her purse.

"I think you two should stop your discussion, Benjamin, slowly pull your gun out of its holster and drop it on the bed," Nancy said in a loud voice.

Both Cassandra and I turned to Nancy and looked at her for a second.

"Shoot the sons of bitches, now!" Zeb shouted as he reached for my holster.

I grabbed Zeb's arm and twisted it behind his back.

"Don't break his arm!" Nancy shouted.

"Drop your pistol," Cassandra bellowed back at Nancy.

The four of us stood silent for a second, staring at each other.

Nancy pointed the barrel of her pistol at Cassandra's head, "I'll shoot the bitch if you don't let him go and give me your gun."

"Look, this isn't a movie, if you shoot, the cops will be here in a second, didn't you see them outside? They've got you and us under surveillance," Cassandra said in a calm voice. "They're probably in an adjoining room listening to us right now."

"You put your gun back in your purse, and I'll let him loose," I added.

"All right." Nancy agreed.

Nancy shoved her pistol back into her purse and threw it on the dresser. I pushed Zeb back down on the bed.

"Pay us now for these expenses and we'll be gone," I insisted.

"What the hell are we paying for?" Nancy asked in an annoyed tone.

"Take a look if you want," Cassandra pulled a fist full of receipts out of her purse and handed them to me.

I pulled receipts out of my coat pocket and walked to Cassandra and took hers.

"I'll ask again, what are we paying for?"

"I'll say it again, we'll give the name and the proof of Marcia's murderer to the police by the end of the week," I quickly added up the total of all the receipts in my hand.

"I don't like it, I want the son of a bitch delivered to me," Zeb muttered.

"Pay them, we'll get what we want anyway," Nancy said to her father.

"Four thousand and fifty nine dollars, thank you, that includes our daily rate up to today," I said.

"We don't take credit cards; a check will do," Cassandra added

Zeb stood and reached for a dresser drawer.

I pulled out my Smith and Wesson and pointed it at Zeb, Cassandra pointed her already drawn pistol at Nancy.

"Keep your panties on, I'm getting my money."

Zeb pulled out a large leather money pouch from the top drawer of the dresser next to him.

"What the hell is that oversized thing, anyway, a forty four?" Zeb asked.

"A forty one to be precise, but just as bad." I stared at him.

"Too much gun," Zeb grumbled as he pulled out five one thousand dollar bills and threw them at me.

"It's better than the pimp gun your daughter carries."

"It's my purse gun for shooting dickless wonders like you," Nancy almost spit out the words.

"I hope you brought more than that," I cast a quick glance at Nancy. "Even you can't hit a barn over twenty feet away with that thing."

"Don't worry, big boy, I brought my two favorite nine millimeters with me just for you." Nancy scowled back.

"How the hell do you make it through an airport with all that hardware?" Cassandra sounded incredulous.

"When you're worth a few hundred million, you might buy a private jet too, you dumb shit broad," Zeb shook his head slowly as he stared at Cassandra.

"Do you own it or lease it?" I can't help myself when it comes to gathering information. "What kind of plane is it? I have a fascination with aircraft."

"It's an 1124 Westwind, I just traded in my old 1123 for it." Zeb sounded confused. "I own it, and I lease the pilots."

"That's a corporate jet," I replied with as much of a smile as I could. "Made by the Israelis, right?

"Yeah, but," Zeb paused in more confusion.

"What the hell is your problem," Nancy interrupted. "You were supposed to leave now."

"I just need some more seemingly trivial information before I do leave," I answered.

Cassandra was beyond confused by my odd behavior.

"Most wealthy people like you have a favorite place to hide money," I paused as I looked from Nancy to Zeb, "where do you tend to hide yours?"

"What the hell!" Zeb exploded.

"Look," I made a calming motion with my hands, "Marcia may have hidden a lot of her wealth the same way you both do, and that might have been a factor in who killed her, and why she was killed."

There was a few seconds of total silence in the room.

"You're not that stupid after all," Zeb paused. "Swiss bank accounts, Some in Caribbean banks, and at least twenty percent in jewels, gold and cash in safe deposit boxes."

"Daddy!" Nancy loudly protested. "Why the fuck did you tell him that!"

"Who knew exactly where?" I asked Zeb.

"Only Marcia knew, she learned that from me."

"Is there a master list of accounts and safe deposit boxes?" I quickly asked.

"Mine's up here," Zeb tapped his temple. "If I die, the map goes with me."

"Thanks," I smiled. "That's all I need for now."

"Daddy!" Nancy couldn't contain herself any more. "If you don't kill these bastards, I will, the first chance I get!"

"Well," I interrupted. "Thanks again for the prompt payment."

I scooped up the five bills and holstered my revolver. Cassandra and I walked out the door to Zeb's room and shut it firmly behind us before Nancy could restart her rant against us. I stood to the left side of the door and leaned towards it, listening for a conversation.

"How common," Cassandra whispered to me.

I held up my finger to my lips for quiet, as I listened intently to a conversation behind the door we had just exited.

I quickly motioned for her to run down the hall, and into a side hallway, then I hurriedly ran in front of her. Nancy stormed out of the door, just as Cassandra ducked into the hallway behind me. Nancy walked two doors down from her father's room, unlocked it, walked in, and slammed the door shut.

"What did they say?" Cassandra asked as we walked to the elevator.

"The old man's paid off someone in the Los Angeles Police department, he wants us dead too."

. . . .

After having the high school dropout retrieve my car, I drove away slowly, looking back to the unmarked police car which had pulled into the slot two cars behind us.

"Why are you going straight to your apartment, why don't you try to lose the tail?"

"You'll see when we get there, besides, we absolutely have to see Becky before we go to San Francisco," I replied.

"Just what the hell was all that stuff about hidden money back there with those Satterwhite people?" Cassandra was bursting with that question.

"It's all about motive," I replied. "As soon as Zeb said something about a map to all those millions and safe deposit boxes, I remembered something that Marcia told me when I first met her."

"What?"

"She said her daughter had a birth mark on her butt."

"So?"

279

"It could be a map."

"Why?" Cassandra paused to process the information. "No, she had a daughter that she at least professed to care about."

"If she were to die, Becky would never know about the hidden stuff, so she had to leave a map to the safe deposit boxes for her to follow," I added.

"She gave Becky all the keys, and printed a map on her butt that she doesn't now know about so eventually she'd be able to find them," Cassandra exclaimed.

"I'll bet the bank account numbers are in one of those boxes, too."

"So, why do we want to talk to Fowler?" Cassandra asked.

"You talked to Fowler, what do you think he wants to tell us?"

"He claims to know nothing about the family since he left Nancy, but I don't believe him," Cassandra said. "He has to know a lot, maybe even who killed Marcia, and why."

"The why is what we're still trying to nail down," I nodded my head.

Cassandra said, "What are we going to do about Becky?"

I looked at her with a concerned expression, "I honestly don't know, that's got me worried, she needs a lot of care and attention, but there's no one left for her; all her family's unfit, and most of them will be in jail soon."

"There's our guardian angel," Cassandra pointed to the policeman, sitting in a brown Ford one block from my apartment building. "Mark must think we're important because he's got one tailing us, another watching your apartment, do you think he knows Becky's in there?"

"No, if he thought that, he'd have a search warrant and be in there in a second, looking for her," I answered. "Besides, she technically isn't in my apartment."

I pulled my car in behind the brown Crown Vic, walked around to the other side of the car and opened the door for my partner. After I locked the doors, the two of us walked up to the policeman in the car, who was pretending to read the morning paper.

I knocked on the closed passenger window; the policeman grinned sheepishly, leaned over and rolled down the window.

"I've seen you in homicide, aren't you Sean?" I asked.

The policeman just grinned, and said nothing.

"Tell Mark Hatton that my partner and I were very tired, so we went up to my apartment and caught up on our sleep for a few hours. Could you make sure that we're not disturbed, because we're going to make love first, don't tell Mark that, he'll be jealous," I said with a smile.

The policeman looked at Cassandra, then back at me, "I'm jealous too."

He rolled up the passenger window of his car and opened back up the morning paper.

She grabbed my attention as we walked to the front steps of my building, "Very funny, but no chance in hell."

The Reverend was still sitting on the front steps of the apartment building, he appeared to be asleep as we walked up the stairs.

"Anybody come in the building this morning?" I asked.

"Nope, just Aaron," He didn't move from his position.

"Who's Aaron?" Cassandra asked, as they walked into the building.

"He's the FBI guy who lives here," I answered.

"Oh, couldn't this Aaron guy be a problem?" She asked.

"Not without a warrant," I answered.

I knocked three times quickly, then two times slowly on the door.

"It's Benjamin and Cassandra."

Becky cautiously opened the door, checking who it was, she undid the security chain, and let us into the apartment.

"I have a question you may not want to hear, but I have to ask it," I said.

"Go ahead," Becky said, she sounded listless again.

"Who is your father, your real father?" I asked, looking worriedly towards Becky.

"I don't know, Mom was artificially inseminated, she told me that thousands of times, like it was my fault or something, I don't know," Becky sat down and stared at the piano. "But. . ."

"But, what?" Cassandra asked, sitting on the piano bench.

"But, I think some people knew, I got that impression because of the way they would always stare at me when my mother's name was brought up," Becky said.

"Who are 'they'?" I asked.

"Phil, Mr. Lepus, and Aunt Nancy."

"Did they always know who your real father was?" I asked.

"No," She paused. "Yes, I don't know, I think they found out after my mother was killed," Becky continued, looking at the floor. "But, no one ever told me anything, the rest of the family just stopped talking when my mother's name was mentioned by someone. They never brought her name up on their own, only Phil would bring up Mama's name, and then only to tell me what a bitch she was."

"What do you know about Brian Fowler?" Cassandra asked.

"He was Aunt Nancy's husband, I don't know where he is now, and I don't care."

"Why?" Cassandra asked.

"He always acted sneaky, I never believed anything he said and he always pinched my rear end too," Becky sighed.

"I hate to bring this up," I began, "But, your mother told me that you have a birthmark on your rear end."

"Well," Becky answered cautiously, "I do."

"Have you always had it?" I asked.

"What?" She sounded puzzled. "I suppose so."

"Do you remember any time when you were younger when your mother had a doctor, or some one else look at the birth mark, or do any medical procedures back there?" Cassandra asked.

I'm glad Cassandra took over, this was fast getting into embarrassing territory for me.

"I vaguely remember Mom taking me to a doctor to do something back there, I was about five and she said they were going to remove a growth or something like that."

"Exactly what do you remember?" Cassandra asked.

"Not much at all, they put me to sleep, and I woke up with a big bandage over the spot."

"Can I look at it?" Cassandra asked very politely.

"Why?"

"We think you mother tattooed a map on your rear," I quickly answered.

"A map?" Becky sounded queasy.

"Why were you so blunt?" Cassandra questioned me.

"Honesty is always best," I replied to both women. "Becky deserves to hear the truth from us."

"Thank you," Becky looked at me for a second. "I'll go into the bathroom with Cassandra and she can look at my birthmark, or whatever it is."

"Take a pen and paper with you and make an accurate drawing of it," I added as they walked towards the bathroom.
. . . .

"Her mother said it looked like a butterfly," I squinted at the drawing along with Cassandra and Becky.

"It definitely is a road map, with dots, probably indicating banks," Cassandra added.

"But, where?" Becky asked.

"Where were you living when she tattooed you?" I asked.

"We were still in Atlanta," Becky smiled as she looked up at me. "All I have to do is get a map of Atlanta and match it to the tattoo on my butt!"

"I think you might want to stay put until we figure out who killed your mother," I said quietly, "That person may kill you for this information."

"Is that why my mother was killed?" Becky asked.

283

"Maybe," I paused. "She was also into many illegal schemes; she could have been murdered because of any one of them."

"I want to stay here with Clarence," Becky insisted. "I'm safe here."

"You can stay here for another night, I think you'll be safe here," I agreed.

"I'd like to stay here for the rest of my life," Becky stood up.

"At least for one more day," Cassandra said.

"You'll be safe, just stay here," I added.

There were three loud, quick knocks, then two long, slow knocks on the front door. I pulled my revolver out and jumped to the side of the front door, holding my forty one magnum up in the air. Cassandra motioned for Becky to go to the back room, as she walked to the front door. Cassandra slowly opened the front door, and saw the reverend standing alone in the hallway.

"Tell that crazy man to put his cannon away," The Reverend walked into the room.

I stuffed my revolver back into its holster and stepped out from behind the front door.

"What's happening, Reverend?" I closed the front door and locked it.

"You tell me, there's been a black Lincoln circling the block ever since you came in here," Clarence said.

"I told you the girl's a little hot, can you keep her?" I asked.

"That makes it a little harder, but she needs it, okay," The Reverend answered. "You want some lunch, darlin'," he said to Becky.

"I'll make it, you wait in there and talk to your friends," Becky insisted. "Are they staying for lunch?"

"Thank you, but we have to go," Cassandra answered.

"Where?" Becky asked.

"San Francisco, to see Brian Fowler," I replied.

"He's a nasty man." Becky shook her head as she walked back to the kitchen.

"I can't keep that little girl too long, she's sweet as she can be, but this ain't no place for her," Clarence said, sotto voce, to me.

"I know; we were talking about it earlier, I need to come up with a place for her, she needs someone who cares," I whispered back . "But I think I know a place for her."

"I'm gonna keep my eye on what you do, that girl's been shown the specter of evil by the Devil, 'n told it's her own reflection. So far, she looks right through what the 'ol devil's shown her, 'n sees hope, don't you show that child more pain," The reverend pointed his finger at me.

"Stop preaching to me, we agree; you've taken on another case, haven't you, Clarence?" I smiled at him.

"Just you don't forget it. Now, I'm gonna have some lunch, so 'scuse me," Clarence unlocked the front door, ushering us out.

Cassandra and I walked up the stairs and into the elevator, not speaking on the ride to the fourth floor. I unlocked the door to my apartment, and began to take off my jacket, then my holster, and shirt; Cassandra just stood and looked at me with curiosity.

After stripping to my waist, I walked to the open window, facing the street and looked out the window at the brown Ford. Waving my hand, I closed the blind on that window, and then the blinds on the other three windows; I turned around and noticed that she was now smiling.

"Bragging, weren't you?" She began to laugh.

"It's an illusion, all done with smoke and mirrors; Hatton will love it," I said, with a broad smile. "Mirrors, now that's an idea."

"I think you're getting the wrong idea," Cassandra smiled back at me. "At least right now."

Spring hopes eternal, at least it put a spring in my step. I put back on my clothes, sat down next to my telephone and began dialing the police department.

"Lieutenant Hatton, please," I began, "Thank you," I held my hand over the receiver. "Look at these thousand dollar bills and see if you can tell if they're real."

"I know I worked in a bank once, but I haven't seen too many of these. She took the bills from my hand. "These bills haven't been printed in a long, long time, you know."

"Yes," I took my hand from the receiver. "Mark Hatton, as I live and breathe," I paused, listening to Mark's side of the conversation for a while, then I resumed talking. "Yes, the girl did try to contact us, I think we can figure out where she is, but we won't," I paused. "Why? Because I think she's probably safe enough where she is, and you have a crooked cop in your department." I paused again. " Calm down, Mark, I know that Zeb Satterwhite's bought a cop, and the kid won't be safe if I tell you where I think she is. Just find the dirty cop, then I'll tell you where I think she is."

"Are you going to tell Mark about the map?" Cassandra whispered.

I shook my head.

"One more thing, Mark" I continued my conversation with the lieutenant. "Zeb Satterwhite owns his own jet, an 1124 Westwind. He used to own an 1123 Westwind when Marcia was killed. I'm fairly sure his daughters and ex wife may have also used the family jet, and it might be interesting to find out who used it to go where around the time of Marcia's murder. And, please don't call me for a while, I'm going to catch up on some long overdue sleep, even heroes need to rest." I hung up the phone.

"Now how do we get out of here?" Cassandra asked.

"Just follow me, quickly," I replied.

I led her back into the elevator, and back to the stairwell on the first floor, leading to the Reverend's apartment.

"Why are we going back down here?" Cassandra asked.

"Trust me." I opened the door on the other side of the hall from Clarence's apartment.

I turned on a dim light, revealing a basement storeroom and furnace room; Cassandra took a step into the room and looked around. To the left were a row of caged off storage areas, crammed full of junk, to the right was a long bench with a row of florescent lights over it. Several loads of equipment covered the bench. Large containers stood beside it, a fire extinguisher was hanging on the wall near by. Along the back wall was a large water heater, and a dehumidifier as well as a door to the small garage for the building.

"That must be why it doesn't smell musty in here," she observed.

"Yeah, the powder has to be kept cool and dry," I answered, pointing to the three large boxes at the end of the bench.

"You must do your reloading here?" Cassandra asked.

"We all do, those presses and dies belong to all of us," I pointed to the bench. "I reload for the reverend because his ammunition is real hard to buy, you have to make that pistol round by trimming down rifle brass."

"Isn't reloading dangerous, why don't you just buy it at a store?" Cassandra puzzled.

"If you shot as much as we all do, you would better understand how cheap it is to load your own. Besides, I don't like the ballistics of most factory stuff for my forty one, I may start using my forty four because of that,. I noticed her impatience with these technical details.

"I practice a lot at shooting now, you saw me at the range, but I always did hate this aspect of the job," she said. "Most of what I've done so far hasn't required anything more than a few hostile words."

"I know, but this case is different," I paused for a moment.

"You're used to all this violence, it's such a testosterone kind of thing," She shook her head.

"You haven't been shot at yet, but it could happen and you had better know what you're doing, or you'll be dead."

"What a morbid conversation."

"It's going to happen, we're stepping on some very nasty feet, and shots will be fired before this is over with." I put on my

287

best wry smile. "Take it from one of the best targets in Los Angeles."

"I know, I know," Cassandra said in a resigned voice. "But if I don't think about it too much, maybe I'll react quicker when I need to."

"Whatever works, but pay attention to this aspect of the job, your life may depend on it real soon."

"Okay, okay, stop lecturing me." Apprehension joined irritation in her glance.

Next, I led her to the back wall of the store room. I stopped and began counting bricks, starting in the corner, next to the hot water heater and working my way to the right.

She looked a question at me.

"I have to count to fifty five," I remarked as I reached for a brick to my left.

I pulled the brick away from the wall, revealing a crude handle made of wood. I pulled the handle, and a door became apparent in the seemingly solid brick wall. Cassandra stared at it, then at me, but didn't hesitate to follow me into a very dark passageway that started on the other side of the brick door.

"Okay, this building holds too many surprises for my peace of mind, now what?"

"In a minute," I felt around in the dim light for something.

The tunnel had a strong musty odor to it. The dirt on the sides still showed shovel marks, but the floor of the tunnel was well packed dirt, almost as hard as pavement. It was wide enough for two people to walk side by side, and it appeared to be sturdy enough to last for a very long time, at least until the next large earthquake.

I held up a dirty flashlight and turned it on, the light was weak, but enough to see the passageway which was tall enough for her to stand, though I had to stoop over a bit. I closed the brick door, after replacing the brick over the wooden handle.

I told her the story about this famous building being a bank about forty years ago, right before the war. A group of stupid would be bank robbers built this tunnel to rob the bank, but they were caught.

"Don't tell me, they tunneled to the vault, and the tunnel remains as a reminder of the futility in a life of crime," Cassandra said.

"Something like that, there isn't a bank next door anymore, it's now a used car lot run by my friend, Dennis," I said.

"He'll sell us a fine used car, and we'll live happily ever after," she replied, nervously.

"No, he'll rent us a car which will barely make it to San Francisco, and charge us a fortune for it but the cops and the strangers in the black Lincoln won't find out we're gone for a while."

"What about your car?" " Cassandra asked. "You love that thing too much to leave it out in this neighborhood."

"Clarence will park it in the garage for me before sunset."

"You let him have a key to it and not me?"

"He can afford to buy another one for me if he breaks it," I turned and smiled at her.

"Sometimes, you can be such a pest," Cassandra snorted.

She pushed me to keep walking.   I stopped at the end of the tunnel, looked up a short shaft to the underside of a dirty piece of plywood.

"Where does this thing lead?"

"Under the trailer Dennis uses as an office, there's only about three feet of headroom under that trailer. That's the problem, no matter how I try, I can't help getting dirty when I sneak out using this tunnel."

I reached for a short wooden ladder.

"Wonderful, you go first, and I'll watch from back here."

She crouched down and moved back into the tunnel a few steps.

I carefully stood on the ladder and slid the plywood to one side. A moderate amount of dirt fell on me as the plywood slid out of the way then a small amount of sunlight streamed into the hole we were in, through the cracks in the metal skirt around the trailer.

I pulled myself out of the hole, then I helped her out after me; she peered out from underneath the trailer while I shoved the plywood back over the hole.

"I don't see anyone out there."

She lay flat in the dry, dusty dirt under the trailer.

"Let's go."

I removed a small panel in the back of the trailer's skirt and wriggled out into the sunlight, Cassandra followed me up the front stairs and into the trailer.

Dennis Isaacs was alone, eating a tuna fish sandwich.

"Benjamin, been digging up dirt again?" he asked.

"We need a car, how much?" I asked.

"We have to stop meeting this way," Dennis swallowed a bite of his sandwich. "How much car do you want, how much can you afford?"

"This time, I'll pay when I get back; that way I'll be sure the car will make it back," I gave Dennis a wink.

"I don't think you've met my partner, Cassandra," I motioned towards her.

"No, I think I'd remember someone that good looking," He smiled at her. "Does he drag you through the dirt all the time?"

"Metaphorically, yes," Cassandra nodded at Dennis. "But, this is the first time he actually has."

"So, how about a set of keys," I interrupted. "We're in a hurry here."

"You're too rough on my cars," Dennis said. "Take this one, it's right outside, first one to the left of the trailer as you walk out."

He threw a set of keys to me. We dusted ourselves off as best we could, but the front of her dress had several dark spots. I drove the nineteen sixty nine Dodge out of the lot with Cassandra laying in the back seat, continuing to brush off as much dirt as she could.

37

Reach out and slap someone

"Cathy," Fred spoke loudly into the pay phone receiver. "Wire me some money real quick."

"Why?" Cathy answered. "Are you in jail or something?"

"No, I might be in a mortuary soon if I don't get out of this place quick."

"Oh, who's after you now?"

"Zeb Satterwhite."

"Oh, the old guy who kills people."

"And, it looks like I'm on his 'must do' list now."

"I thought he sent you a thousand bucks," Cathy asked.

"He did, but I ain't gonna do what he wants me to."

"What's that?"

"Find Becky and give her to him."

"Oh," Cathy paused. "I thought that's why you wanted to fly out there."

"Yeah, but I ain't gonna give her to Zeb, I'm going to fly her back to Washington and hide her out there."

"Why?"

"Didn't you like the kid?" Fred asked.

"Yeah, sure, but why hide her here again?"

"Because this crazy family wants to kill the kid; I asked around, and I don't like what I found out, one of this fruitcake bunch wants to kill the kid."

"That ain't nice!"

"You said it, just wire me about five hundred more so I can get the kid out of here fast."

"Do you know where she is?"

"She ran away from Satterwhite and his daughter, and I guess she went to hide out with Katz somewhere."

"But, can you find her?"

"I thank you from the bottom of my heart for your vote of confidence."

"Oh, you're welcome."

"Geez, just send me the money, I'll call you back after I have a chance to snoop around Katz' building a while."

38

Will you have fries with that?

I maneuvered the old car onto Interstate five and forced it, under much protest, backfiring, and clouds of blue smoke, to go fifty five miles per hour. Twenty minutes after leaving my neighborhood, I wondered why Cassandra had not crawled up to the front seat, or at least sat up in the rear seat. I looked around at her, and saw that she had fallen asleep.

I knew I was in real trouble when she looked absolutely gorgeous to me even when she was dirty and crumpled up on that disgusting back seat.

The needle on the gas gauge was even with the short red line marked with an 'E' so I pulled off at the next exit and went into the nearest gas station. As I pulled up to the pump, I reached back and shook her.

"Wake up, I don't want them to think I'm transporting dead females out of state."

"What?"

That was all that she could muster as she slowly arose from the back seat.

"Wake up, we're at a gas station; do you have to refresh yourself, or something?" I teased as I got out of the car and began pumping gas.

Cassandra slowly pulled herself out of the car, stretched, and straightened up her dirty and wrinkled clothes. I raised the hood of the old car after I filled up the tank, looking around the raised hood at her.

"I don't think this thing will make it very far; there's hardly any oil in it, the air cleaner is missing, and the radiator is held on with a coat hanger," I complained.

293

"Buy some oil, don't go on dirt roads, and don't go too fast," She climbed back into the front seat of the car. "Hurry up, let's get going."

"Yes, Ma'am," I obliged.

The grimy engine drank three quarts before it was satisfied. I put the five extra quarts of oil in the back seat, and got into the old car, started the motor, and pulled back onto the Interstate.

"This is Interstate Five," Cassandra noticed the Interstate sign on the side of the on ramp.

"Yes," I replied.

"Are we going to San Francisco on the interstate in this car?"

"I don't think so, I don't want to drive for nine hours, especially in this car, so we're going to Bakersfield and catch a plane to San Francisco," I replied. "The cops won't be looking for us in Bakersfield, so we can catch a plane from there," I paused. "No one would look for us in Bakersfield; no one would look for anyone in Bakersfield."

"Oh," She seemed disgusted at something. "I'm sorry, without sleep, I get crabby and, those Bakersfield jokes are a bit old, sweetheart."

"Yeah, well, we all can't be in top form all the time. It'll be over in a day, then we can both take a long vacation," I said. "Maybe I'll even take you to Europe."

"You think it'll be over in one day, I don't think so; you have no idea who did it, and I don't think you'll come up with the name of the murderer that fast."

"I already know who did it, I wrote it down on that napkin for you, remember, the one in your purse?" I said.

"Did you actually think I wouldn't look at that?" Cassandra asked.

"Well, no, I guess not," I replied.

"That was very funny too," She said in dry voice. "Writing an IOU for one hundred dollars and stealing my hundred dollar bill was a downright scream."

"You weren't supposed to look, anyway," I smiled, handing her a one hundred dollar bill from my coat pocket. "Do you still have those thousand dollar bills?"

"Yes, but don't think I'm going to give them to you," She was awake enough now to banter.

"I want you to check them out at the Federal Reserve Bank in San Francisco, I still don't trust Zeb. But, if they're real, let's sell them to a coin dealer for more than face value," I grinned, briefly. "You're right, those bills haven't been printed for some time, and I understand they're worth a bit more than face value."

"Sounds good to me," She muffled a yawn. "I did look at them, and they seemed all right to me."

"Have you seen them before?" I asked.

"The Fed stopped using them in 1969, but the bank still made us memorize what they looked like," She paused. "Grover Cleveland on the front, nothing but the denomination on the back, green like all the other paper money. The bills Zeb gave us were the 1934 issue; I suppose the 1928 issue might be worth a bit more, but 1934 is all we have. And, just to let you know that I'm on the ball, I've written down the serial numbers of the five bills."

"I'm impressed," She sure knew a lot more about the thousand dollar bill than I ever did.

"I do have sort of a photographic memory," she admitted to me.

"Like an elephant, you never forget."

"Never use an elephant when referring to a woman," She scolded. "Ever."

"Right."

"What's the plan?" Cassandra asked.

"Where does Fowler want us to meet him? He said you'd know where."

"Yes, he did, but the only places I know of are the airport where he works, or a restaurant he owns part of, on the water somewhere. He asked me out for a date at least a dozen times while I was talking to him," Cassandra said.

"Why didn't you take him up on it; you know those drug runners make big bucks, he could've shown you an expensive time."

"I've got his card with the address of his restaurant on it somewhere in my purse, I hope he's there when we arrive," she replied.

"He said in the message he left us on my answering machine that he'd meet us the day after tomorrow; that would be tomorrow since the message came in yesterday," I said.

"Don't talk like that to me when I'm half asleep, it's not fair." She shook her head slowly.

"We need to buy you and me at least one change of clothes, and in the rush of things, I forgot something," I said.

"What?"

"I only have the five rounds in my pistol, plus six in one speed loader. I need to get a box of cartridges."

"I thought you hated the factory stuff?"

"They're better than running out while you're being shot at." I nodded for emphasis.

"Are you expecting trouble?"

"Yes, we've pissed off a lot of people so far, and we've been very lucky, our luck has to change soon," I replied.

"You're right, Lopez's people aren't very happy with us, neither are Zeb and his friends"

"And, I don't trust Fowler and his friends since they know that we're on to their drug running operation by now," I added.

"I've got four extra clips for my pistol," Cassandra paused, then grinned at me. "That should be more than enough for me, besides if I carry any more than that in my pockets, it just ruins my look."

"We'll get what we need in Bakersfield. Keep an eye out for a sporting goods store, and a decent department store for our clothes," I said.

"All right, but I won't shop just anywhere," she teased.

She leaned towards the broken window on her side and tried to go back to sleep while I continued coaxing the old car towards Bakersfield as fast as it would go.

Just past Wheeler Ridge, I pulled onto the shoulder of the Interstate and checked the oil level which was down a little more than a quart. Burning oil smoke rose slowly in front of my face as I fed more petroleum products to the greasy car.

Damn that Dennis, I hope he has to spend ten thousand years in purgatory driving a car just like this in search of salvation.

"I hope the State Patrol doesn't stop us for driving a rolling wreck, I don't want to think how many pollution violations alone we could rack up," Cassandra said out her broken window to me as I poured the oil into the engine.

"Just go back to sleep," I replied in a very annoyed voice.

She grinned and closed her eyes again.

I slammed the hood, climbed back into the car, and pulled back onto the interstate in a small cloud of blue smoke.

Cassandra opened her eyes and saw a shopping mall ahead. "Stop here!"

"I was going to, there's a gun shop over there." I pointed to a store just beyond the entrance to the shopping mall. "Let's do this fast."

"Just make sure you hurry up," Cassandra retorted.

She opened her door as I set what was left of the parking brake on the old Dodge.

"Just meet me here in thirty minutes," I added.

I locked my revolver and holster, wrapped in my old coat, in the trunk of the car before we entered the mall together.

It was two forty five when I came back to the car and I was five minutes early but Cassandra was already sitting in the front seat of the old car, wearing a new dress. Two new small suitcases were stashed in the back seat.

"I see you found a cheap men's shop; don't get me wrong, I like Polyester on you," she said.

"Very funny," I sneered, getting into the car. "What's in the suitcases?"

"My old clothes, you don't think I'm going to carry around my clothes in a common sack. Besides, I needed something to carry around our tooth brush, hair brush, and other essentials that we left behind as we rushed away in such a hurry, and that I bought for both of us," she replied in one long breath. "Besides, we both need a suitcase to haul our guns in anyway."

I threw my common sack of old clothes into the back seat and drove to the gun shop down the street from the shopping mall. I bought one box of cartridges for my Smith and Wesson and several additional speed loaders. I opened the trunk, brought out my revolver, and climbed back into the front seat of the car, opening the small suitcase and stuffing the revolver into it.

"Nothing like being subtle, you did notice that this parking lot is full of people, didn't you? And, didn't you notice them all staring at you while you threw your gun around?"

"Don't worry, people expect this sort of thing in the parking lot of a gun shop, that's what America's all about." I shoved cartridges into the speed loaders, and also stuffed them into the suitcase. "This is the land of John Wayne and Ronnie Reagan, and you know what they say, when in Rome. . ."

"Just get going, I want to make it to San Francisco before midnight." Cassandra settled back against the seat, closing her eyes.

. . . .

We were able to get a late afternoon flight with little problem. Soon after we landed and collected our suitcases, we found a nice hotel on Fulton Street. After cleaning up a bit, we took a taxi to Brian Fowler's restaurant. We had difficulty locating the correct establishment, but with the help of the taxi driver, and a large tip, we were able to find it, not that far from Interstate 280. The driver didn't seem to mind me strapping on a large sidearm as I sat in the back of his cab, as a matter of a fact he seemed to enjoy watching me do it. I did point this out to

298

Cassandra, who said he was probably bored out of his skull and would have enjoyed seeing me pick my nose.

Cassandra led the way into a small seafood restaurant in an old building in need of many repairs. The smell of thousands of different seafood dishes, cooked over the last fifty years, permeated the air. Old crusted fried seafood smells worse than almost any other food, at least to me it does. A young woman, about twenty years old, dressed in a very low cut striped pirate's shirt, and an extremely short black skirt, walked up to us.

"How many are in your party?" she asked.

"Two." I was enjoying her low cut pirate's shirt.

"This way, sir." She motioned us to follow her past the bar which was directly to the left of the entrance.

"We were supposed to meet Brian Satterwhite here," Cassandra cast a bothered glance towards me.

"Oh, I think Mr. Satterwhite's been waiting for you, come this way." She led us to a booth all the way in the back of the small restaurant.

Seated at the booth was Brian Fowler, alone. Cassandra slid into the seat across from Brian, I slid in next to him.

"Brian, your friends are here," the waitress said.

"I can see that, but they're late," Brian sounded annoyed.

"We were delayed, but we're here," I replied.

"I'm glad she came with you." Brian smiled at Cassandra.

"Just tell us the tale of babies for sale," she said.

"Don't mess with her; when she starts rhyming, she's likely to shoot you. Just tell us about yourself, Snively, Peterson, and anybody else you can think of," I put an unusual harshness to my voice.

"What do you want to know?" Brian forced a crooked smile.

"Who was involved?" Cassandra asked.

"First of all," Brian looked at the table, unfocused, for a second, then back at Cassandra, "I want to let you know that I'm telling you all this because I feel the need to dump all this on somebody other than my business associates; it has always bothered me and I just want to tell someone about it."

299

"This isn't a confessional," I chuckled. "Besides, you don't strike me as a penitent soul."

"Oh," Brian grinned. "Don't get me wrong, I don't mind dealing drugs and killing people, but Snively's baby scheme bothered me."

"Just get on with telling us who your partners were," Cassandra was losing patience.

"You know the names of all the people involved; me, Marcia, Cummings, Peterson, Snively, Lopez, and sometimes Aaronson," Brian answered.

"Which Peterson?" I asked.

"Paul, Phil's just a money grubbing lawyer who's too chicken to do anything dangerous to get rich," Brian answered.

"How long did the operation go on?" Cassandra asked.

"Actually quite a long time, Richard started by himself about nineteen sixty four, and Paul joined a few months later. Those two were decades ahead of the curve in that procedure, only no fellow scientist will ever know. I joined in about four years later because they needed a pilot to shuffle the embryos after Paul crashed. We couldn't do much volume until the New York mob threw big bucks at us in sixty eight; I think the total since the mob got involved was about twelve hundred and fifty five babies. And at ten to twenty thousand a crack, that ain't bad," Brian said with a wicked grin. "And that's my gift for you; I kept the book with all the adopted names, with their addresses, of all the kids we custom made in Mexico."

"Nineteen sixty eight." My mind wandered a bit.

"Yeah, that's when the business really took off," Brian said.

"I was only seventeen then." I don't know why I said that.

"A pimply faced high schooler." Brian laughed. "A punk."

"Actually, I had skipped a grade, and had graduated from high school by then." Why was I prattling on? "I joined the marines in July, and after basic I went to advanced combat training. In September, I was in Viet Nam and in October I got

300

my first purple heart, the following February I got a silver star for saving three of my buddies and killing seventy enemy soldiers."

"Big fuckin' deal, soldier boy," Brian's contemptuous look also contained puzzlement.

"What were you doing at seventeen, punk," I calmly asked.

I did not consciously know why was I doing this; maybe I needed to tell Cassandra some of this, but why was my brain doing it then and there?

"I was pimping cheerleaders back then, what do you think," Brian's confused look grew more pronounced.

"What did you people do to manufacture those babies?" I switched back to the main subject.

"How do you mean that?" Brian asked.

"I mean, did you just pick the egg and sperm, then implant the embryo, or did you do more?"

"All we did was pick the right egg and sperm; lots of them; Snively had a private practice so he had access to smart, rich pretty women. He would tell them they had something wrong and couldn't get pregnant on their own. He would inject them with hormones so they would produce lots of eggs, then he'd harvest their eggs, keeping many of them without them knowing. Aaronson also helped harvest eggs later on, but that was never enough, so Snively started with his experiments."

"What experiments?"

I sensed this might lead to something I didn't want to hear, but I couldn't quell a morbid need to know.

"He harvested stem cells, grew the viable lines in great abundance, then began producing Petri dish eggs from them by drenching them with his own mixture of proteins," Brian answered flatly. "There were only three of us who knew about this, and two of us are dead."

"He did what?" Cassandra sounded incredulous.

"He was able to grow eggs from ten women's stem cells," He sighed. "Even I thought that was going a bit far, but you have to admit his science was at least thirty years ahead of its time."

"Just how did that work?" Cassandra asked.

"Differentiated stem cells are what a human uses to grow specific organs, like a kidney or a heart." Brian paused as if collecting himself. "Undifferentiated stem cells, like those in umbilical cord blood, must be coaxed into forming specific cells, like heart muscle cells."

"So, he took cells from women's ovaries?" I asked.

"No," Brian answered, apparently preferring to talk about anything technical. "Richard was able to culture the ovarian stem cells and to produce large numbers of them from human skin stem cells, then he could coax an individual cell into growing into a human egg. He then was able to fertilize about ten percent of those eggs."

"How many was that?" Cassandra asked.

"Considering he could come up with a few hundred thousand human eggs in a month, ten percent of that is still a lot of fertilized eggs," Brian answered her.

"Even though I don't really understand it, I will admit it sounds impressive." I nodded. "But, what was the next step?"

"We froze the fertilized eggs and shipped them to Mexico for implantation. Later on, we just froze the eggs and sperm instead, and did the fertilization in Mexico; the yield was a lot better doing it that way." He paused as if to refocus on past events. "As it was, Richard had a big lab built up in his home in Atlanta, but he still used the university facility for too much production work and that's how he got caught. Our success rate was only one viable baby for every forty implantations," He paused again, this time I could see a wave of pride wash over his expression. "You know, if we were able to publish our work in the sixties, we'd be rich and famous now, maybe even get the Nobel Prize."

"I don't think what you did was so great," Cassandra interrupted. "It's actually kind of disgusting. Harvesting a woman's eggs without her knowledge is a form of rape, and growing more of them and using them like that is even worse."

"Don't be so prudish." Brian looked insulted.

"So, when did the baby scheme stop?" I interrupted.

302

"It died with Marcia," Brian answered. "She was going to quit anyway since she hated it, and found that drugs were a lot more profitable, especially using her new immigration job."

"I thought she was selling drugs when she died," Cassandra said. "That's what the cops thought too."

"Doesn't matter now, all I wanted to do is give you the book with all the kids' names, and the people who bought them."

As I took the small black book Brian handed me, I asked him, "Who is Becky's father?"

Brian leaned back in the booth and began to laugh. He stopped laughing in a few seconds and turned to look at me.

"Ha! You're smarter than I thought, or you just know how to ask good questions."

"She's Zeb's daughter, as well as his granddaughter, isn't she?" I asked.

"How the hell did you figure that one out?" Brian asked.

"I listen to what people tell me, it's not that difficult."

"Yeah, that nasty trick was Snively's doing," Brian half smiled.

"The why, I don't know, so tell me." I was more in the dark about this than he thought.

But by this time, Brian seemed to be on a roll. Maybe he had not dared to ever talk about this subject to anyone else. We needed concrete details, and weren't really challenging him for his role in the affair, maybe he let himself think we were a safe audience. Or maybe he was this clueless most of the time. He told us that all took place when Snively and Paul Peterson started their baby scam way back when. Paul Peterson had married Marcia only a year before he started into the baby production with Snively. Paul Peterson and Richard Snively were homosexual lovers for several years before Paul got married; Paul broke the affair off, and Snively thought it was because of Paul's wife, Marcia Satterwhite. Only seven months into his marriage with Marcia, Paul was disgusted with her. Paul was bi-sexual, but decided to stay straight for some woman he met in Mexico but Richard never knew that. However, Richard did know that

303

Paul wanted to have a child to carry on his name, he assumed Paul wanted to have the child with Marcia.

Snively didn't have the guts to kill anyone, so he played a joke on Marcia since he thought she was permanently taking Paul away from him, even though she wasn't. Zeb Satterwhite had been donating his sperm for years to a sperm bank run by a neo-nazi fringe group who wanted to save the pure white race for generations to come. Snively was Marcia's gynecologist when she wanted to be artificially inseminated; Paul was the infertile partner with a low sperm count so it was difficult for him to get a woman pregnant; Snively played his joke on Marcia for the benefit of Paul.

"Who knew about the disgusting practical joke?" Cassandra asked.

"Paul did, after all the sick joke was for his benefit. I don't know if anyone else did, but Marcia sure found out right before she died, she was real pissed off about it, let me tell you," Brian said. "Paul died when Becky was less than a year old, and he never told Marcia."

"Did Marcia tell her father?" Cassandra asked.

"No," Brian paused to think. "I'd bet that she didn't, given his opinion about her daughter all this time."

"Zeb killed Snively, didn't he?" I abruptly interrupted. "Marcia found out who was the real father of her baby so she wanted Snively dead, and the good doctor found out. He tried to hire someone to kill Marcia before she had him killed, but the assassin was a friend of Zeb, so he killed Snively. Zeb is too rich, and too squeamish to do anything like that himself, my guess is that he always hires out killings."

"Not quite, you're not as sharp as you think."

Brian slipped me a knowing grin, or was it a wise ass grin. "Marcia told Zeb that Snively raped her and Snively was the father of her baby. You're right about one thing, though, Marcia wound up finding out who the real father of her baby was and did want Snively dead. Snively tried to hire a business partner of Marcia's to kill her to save his own ass, but Zeb found out. Because he thought Snively had raped his daughter, and because

Snively tried to hire someone to kill Marcia, Zeb had Snively killed."

"So," I nodded my head. "That's why Zeb had Snively killed."

"I couldn't prove it, but I'd bet my airplane on it," Brian said. "He sent that goon, Hank to Miami the same day Richard died; I think there's more than just a chance Hank did something other than get a tan in Miami, don't you?"

"Could be, did Zeb kill his own daughter, too?" Cassandra asked.

"I don't know," Brian answered.

"What do you think?" Cassandra asked.

"What do you think?" Brian quickly answered.

I looked at both of them, "Did your ex-wife participate in any of this?"

"I think she knew what was going on towards the end, but she didn't take part in any of the baby stuff," Brian said. "All I wanted to give you was the little book with the names of the babies in it, nothing else."

"But that's not all we want; we need to find out who killed Marcia Satterwhite," Cassandra said.

"I told you I don't know who did it, she was such a bitch, it could've been anybody," Brian insisted.

"If she was such a bitch, why were you interested in screwing her?" Cassandra surprised me with the intensity of her question.

"She had a great body, though not as outstanding as yours," Brian leered at Cassandra. "But, she did have a few million bucks more than you do."

"Did you hope to get your hands on some of her millions?" I asked.

"That would be nice, but I'd have to butt heads with Zeb and Nancy to do that, and I value my life more than that," Brian replied.

"You knew about the real father of Marcia's baby, but did Nancy?" I interjected.

"Maybe, Paul, Cummings, and Lopez knew about it, the idea was to make Marcia out to be an incestuous slut in Paul's eyes. That was the idea, to humiliate Paul, ruin Marcia in his eyes, and ruin Paul's idea of having a child by Marcia to carry on after him. Snively wanted Paul back as his lover." Brian paused. "But, all it did was to get Snively killed, and Paul died right after the kid was born."

"You married into the Satterwhite family, what are they like?" I asked.

"They're a pit of vipers, each and every one of them tries to attack each other as much as they can, or in Marcia's case, could," Brian answered.

"What about Nancy, is she as bad as her sister?" I wondered aloud.

"Not as bad, but almost. Marcia had a partner before Hank Cummings, he tried to squeeze more money out of her so she killed him and dumped his body into the Pacific Ocean, all by herself. She boasted about it to me once while she was drunk, I believed her then and I still believe she did it," Brain said.

"What type of pistol did she carry?" I asked.

"Always the details you want," Brian said with a knowing smirk. "She carried a nine millimeter, just like the one she was shot with; nine millimeter is all Zeb would allow in the house, and that's what the girls grew up shooting."

"Where did Satterwhite get his money?" Cassandra asked.

"He claims to have made it in real estate. He did, but he got the money to buy the real estate from a whole lot of shady deals. Who do you think I work for now?" Brian asked.

"Lopez thought you wanted to go into business for yourself," Cassandra said.

"I don't have the cash to deal in this volume, Zeb does, and has for years," Brian seemed to enjoy telling me that.

"Why are you telling us this?" Cassandra asked. "I don't buy that moral crap you handed us before."

"Because Zeb paid Brian to kill us," I said, while I stared directly at him. "But be careful, I said my partner is mad; she's had her gun pointed at your nuts for the past ten minutes at least."

"At least," Cassandra tapped the underside of the table with her automatic pistol.

I reached into Brian's coat and pulled out his semi-automatic pistol; he was carrying a full sized 45 automatic. I pulled the clip out of the Colt, and ejected the round which was already in the chamber. I then dumped the ammunition onto the floor and began to disassemble the pistol.

"What the hell are you doing!" he protested .

"Making sure you won't shoot us with this thing," I dropped the different parts into a water glass.

"I wasn't going to kill you, they are," Brian said in an annoyed voice, pointing to his left, where the kitchen entrance was.

Two men, one of average height, and one very tall and stocky lumbered through the swinging doors.

"Didn't Zeb want you to find out who killed his daughter?" Cassandra asked.

"Yeah, but I don't give a shit who did it, besides, I want you dead more than he wants his daughter's killer." Brian started to stand up. "You have to know there's still a hit out on you from some New York mobster. For some reason, not many people want to go after you, but I will."

"Move one more inch, and I'll drop you where you are," Cassandra insisted.

"Don't be stupid, there are two of them over there, and you don't stand a chance," Brian said.

I had slipped my Smith and Wesson out of its holster by this time and stuck it sharply into Brian's ribs.

"You go first, then." I pulled back the hammer of my revolver.

"All right, let's move outside and discuss this, don't ruin dinner for my paying customers," Brian said.

"Just showing up here at this place ruins their dinner." Cassandra stood up, still pointing her pistol at Brian. "The smell in here is about to make me puke."

307

Brian's henchmen men drew their pistols, and what few customers who were in the restaurant tried to escape as quickly as possible from the impending battle.

All five of us, never losing sight of each other, walked to the front door while I kept Brian Fowler ahead of Cassandra and me.

As we all walked slowly by the bar near the front door, a hand with short stubby fingers rose from behind the bar and slammed a snub barreled thirty eight revolver on the top of the scarred redwood counter. Before I could reach the gun, Brian grabbed the revolver while the two other men jumped apart.

Cassandra fell to the floor, firing her pistol at the man on her right who had already opened fire on her. She pushed a table over and jumped behind it as she continued to fire at him.

Meanwhile, I fell backwards, sitting on the floor near the bar as I shot Fowler. As he grabbed the thirty eight and turned to shoot me, the loud roar of my magnum was amplified by the room we were in. One shot through his forehead, and he was dead, a dime sized red hole on entry, and a gaping canyon across the rear of his skull.

The two men ahead of me both fired at Cassandra who rolled from one piece of furniture to another, trying to stay alive. Bullets ripped holes in the table she toppled for cover, luckily missing her as they exited the wood. She emptied one clip of ammunition, then stuffed another into her 380. When they heard my revolver , both of the other men turned to me and began to fire.

I shot at, and hit, the man on my right with one round, which landed in the center of his chest. The man jerked backwards in an instinctual reaction to being shot, then fell over a table, dying before he hit the food encrusted floor.

The other man, to my left, stopped to look at his friend, falling dead not ten feet away from him. Cassandra fired two bullets through his chest before he had a chance to turn back towards her. Cassandra fired three more rounds into his chest as he lunged towards her, discharging his pistol one last time into the floor.

"Are you all right?" I shouted towards Cassandra who lay on the floor.

"Yeah, what about you?" She answered, almost out of breath.

Before I could answer, I heard a noise behind the bar. I fired a shot into the floor and shouted, "Get the hell out of there before I start blasting holes in the bar!"

A fat man, with a full head of curly black hair, wearing a bar apron rose from behind the bar with his hands raised.

"Don't shoot!" he pleaded. "I'm not armed!"

"Yeah, you gave your gun to that dead man, so he could shoot me, right?"

I hit him across the head with the butt of my revolver; the bartender fell unconscious to the floor behind the bar.

"I'm glad we talked to Fowler before we killed him, but I don't look forward to talking to the police," I said.

As we heard the sirens roaring in the distance, I opened up my revolver, emptied the cylinder into my left hand and dumped the empty brass into my coat pocket. I then took out a speed loader, stuck six new rounds into the Smith and Wesson and pushed the cylinder back up.

"Should we leave?" Cassandra asked, standing up.

"No, we should stay; it's a pain in the ass, but we want to keep our business going, don't we?"

I slowly put my revolver back into its holster and walked out the front door of the restaurant.

"What are we going to tell them, everything?" Cassandra asked, following me outside.

"Not everything, we're investigating the death of Marcia Satterwhite, we found out in our investigation that Fowler was running drugs in his airplane for someone from our investigation. He found out that we knew he was a drug runner so he tried to kill us. It's the truth, not all of it, but that's all we tell the cops right now," I walked to the edge of the sidewalk. "Don't tell them about Zeb or Lopez, don't say anything about them."

"What about the babies, the book he gave us? You know what I would do."

309

I yanked the black book out of my pocket and split it in half, then proceeded to tear the halves into yet smaller pieces. I flung all the torn paper into an open sewer grate and glanced at Cassandra.

"That's what I would have done," she said softly.

The police cars came tearing around the corner, sirens screaming.

"We're on now, partner, this is one of the toughest things you'll ever have to go through. Killing is the worst, talking to the cops afterwards is next." I paused to take in a slow breath. "Remember, don't say anything until they let us get back together, or until I call a lawyer for us, okay?"

She nodded as we walked to the police, who were crouching behind the open doors of their patrol cars with their weapons drawn. Both of us raised our hands and kept walking towards them.

A uniformed captain approached both of us and held out his hand, "Let's have the artillery!"

I very slowly opened my coat and, using my thumb and index finger, handed my revolver to the captain. Cassandra followed my lead, and also gave her pistol to the policeman.

We were handcuffed and stuffed into separate cars, then the plainclothes policemen in each car read us our rights and explained the charges.

I worried the most about Cassandra; her expression as they led her away from me and into a separate police car was one of shock and sadness. I had seen that expression pass across her face only once or twice before; both times she cried for hours afterward.

Meanwhile, my captors informed me again that I was going to be charged with at least manslaughter, and several weapons charges.

"Why give us such a hard time, do you guys have any idea what that creep Satterwhite, also known as Fowler, was up to?"

The detective in the passenger seat turned and gave me a business like smile.

310

"Yes, we know, we've known for a long time, and we've been trying to find out who he gets his stuff from, but now we'll never know, will we?"

I knew who Brian got his cash from, and who set up the drug deals, I knew two names Brian worked for; I had something to bargain with, unless Cassandra gave Zeb and Lopez to the police for free.

"I take it a lieutenant Hatton called you guys and told you where you could find us?" I asked.

"Something like that," He paused. "Just what did you want with Fowler?"

I gave the police a brief summary of the past events, emphasizing the past fifteen minutes.

"All we wanted to do was to ask Fowler a few pointed questions about his sister-in-law's death."

"They must have been very pointed," The detective who was driving observed.

"We just asked him a few questions about his ex-wife's family, then he got all mad and told us he was going to have us killed. Two of his trained apes tried to kill us, but we didn't want to die more than they wanted to kill us, so they're dead and we're not."

"I think there's more to it than that. I think you might have some information we could use," the first detective said.

"I think we need to have a serious discussion about your license to be a private investigator in this state," the driver added.

"When the crime scene guys are finished, you'll see that those three men shot at us first." I paused. "They shot at us a lot, so, what are we supposed to do, go out in body bags?"

"It'll take a while to get the report back about who shot at who." The detective shook his head. "Let's not try go get ahead of ourselves."

"Self defense is self defense, you know," I insisted.

"You and your friend killed three men back there, and that's a crime, buddy," The detective insisted back at me.

"I think I need to see my lawyer, boys, before I open my mouth any more," I insisted.

311

The rest of the trip to the police station was silent. After squishing my fingers through that horrible black goop for a set of fingerprints and the ritual of taking a disgusting photograph, they brought me into an interrogation room and left me alone for five minutes. The captain who had met us at the scene of the shooting walked into the room with another man.

"Hello, my name is Captain Minisk, and this is chief deputy District Attorney Roger Atkinson, we want to lay out the facts for you."

"I want to call my lawyer, now," I stared at them.

"All in good time, first we want to talk."

"Formally charge me, and let me call my lawyer, or let me and my partner loose," I continued to stare at them.

"Look, all we want is a little conversation, and maybe some cooperation, it might be refreshing." The captain spoke in a stern voice.

"I'll talk only when my lawyer's here with me."

"He's got a one track mind, sounds to me like he's got something to hide," Roger said to the captain.

I wrote a name and phone number on a piece of paper and shoved it towards the captain.

"That's my lawyer's name and number, let me call him, or you call him for me, then we'll talk; not until."

I pay a yearly retainer for the best lawyer in every major city in which I do business; San Francisco was one of those towns. These legal expenses pay off at times like this.

Roger picked up the paper and studied it.

"I know this lawyer."

He gave the paper to the captain.

"Don't you?"

"Damn right I do, this all of a sudden is getting very serious," the captain replied.

"It's always been serious to me, I take getting shot at by three criminals seriously, and I take the cops jerking me around for defending myself very seriously. Yeah, I've got some information for you, and I'll give it to you, but I don't trust any of you as far as I could throw you, so I want my lawyer here to keep you guys honest."

In these kinds of pissing contests, the stakes are too high not to call in the high priced lawyers.

The captain raised his hands. "All right, we'll call your lawyer, then we'll talk, but don't expect me to be as friendly after your lawyer comes in as I might be now."

"I don't see a lot of love and kindness right now anyway, so call the number I gave you."

My lawyer arrived in fifteen minutes and joined the captain, the D. A. and me in a long discussion about Zeb Satterwhite, Irving Lopez, Hank Cummings, Marcia Satterwhite, and the two thugs who tried to kill Cassandra and me.

"We had Lopez tied into Fowler's operation, but Fowler disappeared from the drug operation a month or so ago when all those ties seemed to vanish. Thanks for Zeb Satterwhite's name, but what proof do you have?" The D. A. asked.

"None, if you want records, pictures, marked money, I don't have any of it. Zeb's such a bastard that somebody in his organization has to have a big enough grudge against him to hold some evidence on the old fart." I was thinking out loud again, but this time for the audience's benefit.

"That's a long shot, all you have is a name, and nothing else," the captain said.

"No," the lawyer said. "He gave you the tie in between the two. Fowler admitted that Zeb Satterwhite paid him to kill my two clients, and he also admitted that Zeb was his financial backer."

"You know that won't stand up in court," the D. A. said.

"But you have more to go on than you did before. My client delivered his side of the deal, now what are you going to do, back out on yours?"

"No, we'll let both of them go, for now. No formal charges will be brought until we have a chance to look into what he just told us. We also have to wait for the report from the crime scene," the captain said. "But he and his partner had better stay and enjoy San Francisco for a while."

"Like hell," I interjected. "I need to get back to Los Angeles as soon as possible; if you want a smoking gun before you go after Zeb, I might be able to get it for you, but I need to travel in order to do that."

"We can't agree to that," the captain glanced at the Assistant District Attorney, then back at me.

"I'm a good risk," I insisted.

I kind of wished I was on a government job because getting out of jail is so much easier.

"If my client is not under arrest, you cannot force him to stay in San Francisco," my lawyer added, finally.

The captain looked at the D. A. and then at me, "All right, go; two days, and I'm yanking you both back here, got it!"

"What about my stuff?"

In spite of my complaints, I still left the interrogation room without my weapon and without the thousand dollar bills. The cops didn't seem too happy when I informed them I had a list of the bill's serial numbers, not that I didn't trust them. All I got was a signed receipt from them for the bills and my pistol.

"What about my partner?" I asked.

"She goes too, do something with her, she's a wreck; she's got no business being a private investigator if she starts to lose it that easily."

Cassandra met me on the front steps of the police station three minutes after I left the interrogation room and spoke briefly to my lawyer.

"How are you doing?" I asked cautiously.

"Did you know I was strip searched? Some bull dyke cop poked and prodded all my private parts looking for a thrill, I've never been more humiliated in my life!"

"You sound mad, not hysterical, but mad as hell." I explored Cassandra's eyes.

"I was already upset, almost in tears," She looked at the steps beneath her. "I killed a man; I saw him die, and I killed him, I don't think I'll ever forget it, but those insensitive shits in

314

there pushed and shoved, and stripped me, and humiliated me, trying to get me to tell them everything, but I wouldn't."

"Don't let them get to you," I put my finger under her chin and gently lifted her head. "They were just trying to rattle you so they could get all the information for free, but, we made them deal with us, didn't we?" I softly pressed my lips against hers.

She encircled me with her arms, pressed her lips hard against mine and began to cry.

39

By any other name

As the small commuter airplane landed in Bakersfield, both Cassandra and I awoke. We trudged slowly to the old Dodge, which was still in the long term parking lot waiting for us with a crooked smile on its face.

"I hope it'll start." Cassandra climbed into the front seat.

"Starting doesn't seem to be its problem, everything else is." I turned over the smoking motor.

"How much money do you have left?" Cassandra asked.

"I don't know, look in my wallet." I handed her my wallet.

"You've only got thirty four dollars after paying for parking, I've got two hundred and some left." She handed me back my wallet.

"Along with our pistols, the cops kept the five thousand dollars; they said it might be stolen, and we couldn't take it until they checked it out." I sighed. "Why do you care how much we have?"

"The way our luck has been running, we'll get stopped by the cops, for driving this wreck." Cassandra declared.

"Don't be so pessimistic."

"What do you think they'll do to us in San Francisco? We killed three men back there," she said in a sad voice.

"We killed three gangsters; don't forget that fact. What we'll do is get today's <u>Examiner</u>, then we'll read how the press is reacting to the shootings," I said in a firm voice. "Our lawyer and I made a deal with the District Attorney, but I want to read today's paper to make sure they stick to the deal."

"I still have a bad feeling about this." Cassandra still sounded sad.

I tried to give some perspective. "This job does have some down times, and this is one of them. What you did, you had to do, and you did it well, you saved my life, and I saved yours; we're a team, and we acted as one."

"You were in a war."

She looked out the window, I could tell the events of the past evening were still occupying most of her thoughts. "You're used to killing, I'm not."

"Don't ever think I'm used to killing." I turned somber in a flash. "I can still see the faces of most of the men I've killed, it never goes away; if it did, I couldn't live with myself."

"Then, how can I live with myself?"

She turned to face me, I could see some tears on her cheek.

"This is what we do, for whatever reason." I wiped her cheek with my fingers. "If you did nothing last night, we would both be dead."

"I know that." Her voice trailed off; I could barely hear her. "That's what I'm kicking myself about."

"What?"

"If I finish my degree and teach political science, the worst thing I'll do is flunk some hapless freshman." She looked back out the side window. "How bad can that be."

"Since you've worked with me these past few years, you now know how harmless that would be." I took in a deep breath. "You've been after me to come clean about my childhood; why did I join the Marines and go off to war to kill so many people, why did I take this job with all its inherent danger?"

"Yes."

"I think I'm asking you the same question," I stroked her arm. "Why are you doing this?"

"Damned good question." She sniffed. "When I figure it out, I'll tell you."

"I think you have the same need to do something less conventional, something dangerous." I observed.

"Why?"

"I guess I do this to forget my mother's death, at least, that's why I started doing this job. I guess I still do this job because I like the excitement of not knowing what's around the

317

next bend.   I guess I need to have a lot more stimulation in life than the ordinary guy."

"Maybe I do too." She picked up my free hand and held it between hers.   "Maybe I do this because I love you."

"I've seen you in fights before, and I've seen you in all types of stressful situations." I pulled her hands to my lips and kissed them.   "You never show fear, I know you have it, but you don't show it, you act cool and collected in everything."

"But, killing someone?" She slowly moved her hands back to her lap.

"It's not like you just shot Bambi, or old Yeller."

I hoped she was beginning to come out of her depression.

"Those were very bad men who wanted both of us dead, it's called self-preservation," I added.

"Intellectually, I know all that." She shifted a little.   "It's just the gut reaction of seeing all that blood."

"I do want to get a copy of the San Francisco paper as soon as we can." I changed the subject.

"What'll the newspaper have to do with anything?" she asked.

"If the press thinks it was a good idea to shoot the gangsters, then we get our lawyer to press the prosecutor."

"Press him for what?"

"Press him not to prosecute us for anything since he knows he has to go before a jury. If public sentiment is against him and for us, he knows he doesn't stand a chance if he goes for any conviction," I answered.

"So he won't prosecute?" Cassandra asked.

"I hope not, we did make a deal with them, besides, even if he does, it'll be for some minor charge, and we'll get out of it," I said. "I'm not too worried."

"Well, I am, I'm damned worried!" Her voice quavered again.   "One felony and I'll never teach at a university, ever."

We drove the smoking car as fast as the other mass of commuters were traveling early that morning, neither one of us said anything for twenty miles.

She broke the silence, "How did you guess that Zeb was Becky's biological father?"

"I had a hunch that Becky's natural father had to have something to do with all this. Why else, besides the money she stood to inherit, was she so important to everybody. The whole Satterwhite family always knew exactly where Becky was, that's why they never called the cops."

"Who said what to give you the final idea?" Cassandra asked.

"It was more a general feeling I've gotten over the last week, everything fell into place, and the black humor of the whole thing made me wince."

"You mean the whole thing about Becky being Zeb's daughter and granddaughter?" She shuddered. "It's all so, Chinatown."

"What made you so queasy?" I was curious. "The slack toothed hillbilly factor?"

"I guess so," She sighed. "The whole idea is a bit repugnant; I know it doesn't reflect on the child, but it just doesn't seem right."

"I think that was the whole idea," I thought for a minute. "Besides, with sperm banks bursting at the seams now, it may well be a problem for the future."

"What are you talking about?"

She looked at me like I had abruptly changed the subject.

"Just say a college student with a good medical and IQ profile donates his DNA for dollars over a five year period," I took in another breath. "Also assume that only upper middle class and higher can afford this method of getting pregnant if they have fertility problems."

"And, your point?" Cassandra seemed more tired than ever.

"My point is that the offspring of that one college student within one geographical region and the same social and economic class will in twenty years start marrying each other, then you have half brothers and sisters having kids."

"So, you're saying it could already be happening, and that the taboo is no longer justified?" She looked back out the front window. "Oh well, I guess we'll find out over the next few generations."

"What I'm saying is that I don't have any idea what the effect will be on Becky, and I don't want to judge her based on it," I paused. "Getting Marcia pregnant by her father was the joke Snively played on his lover's wife; that joke lived to haunt Marcia's sister, and now her father."

"I see your point," Cassandra agreed. "That joke, as you just called it, is a real live person, a person who seems better than the whole lot of her relatives."

"You're right, she is, and that's the ultimate joke played on this family; she'll get all the money and property to be had, and not even have to visit any of them in jail, not even on Christmas." I turned towards Cassandra. "Think back to the last time we spoke to Zeb, did anything he say sound a little funny to you?"

She thought for a second, "When Zeb was talking to us in his hotel room, he was admitting that Becky actually did mean something to him. Most people would say that she's all I have, but he said that she's all his, she's my little girl."

"Yeah, his wording struck me, too," I paused. "That's why I guessed Zeb's sperm might have been used to conceive Becky."

"Where to now, great white hunter?" she asked

We were approaching the city of Los Angeles with a trail of smoke following us.

"To my apartment to rearm myself, and get my car; you'd rather ride in my Porsche, than this limo, wouldn't you?" I asked.

"I guess so, but then where? Zeb, Mark Hatton?"

"Where would YOU go?" I asked.

"I've been curious why George Sterling hates Zeb so much, and why he wouldn't tell you about it."

"That's where we shall go."

. . . .

320

As we walked back towards the used car lot office where we had picked up the smoking junker, I opened my wallet and pulled out a one dollar bill.   Walking up the steps of Dennis' office, I opened the door and threw the dollar and the keys on the desk.

Dennis, sipping his morning coffee, looked at the dollar bill and said, "Is that all?"

"No, I want my change," I stared at him.

Dennis reached into his pocket, pulled out three quarters and tossed them on the top of the desk.

"You owe me for the gas, and oil; lots of oil." I turned around and winked at Cassandra.

As we walked to my apartment building, both of us saw the Reverend, still sitting on the same front step he had been on the day before.

"How goes it, Reverend?"   I walked up the steps beside Cassandra.

"It goes fine, your friends in the big black car disappeared shortly after you did, but I figure they'll be back now," Clarence said.   "You find a place for her yet?"

"I think I have, I'll tell you later today or tomorrow, all right?"

I stopped on the top step and turned to him.

"Okay," he replied.

"Hi, Mr. Katz,"   Becky greeted us.   How is Brian?

"Dead," I replied flatly.   "I shot him last night as he was trying to shoot me."

"Really?"   Becky sounded apprehensive.

"Really," Cassandra confirmed.

"I can't say I feel bad." Becky considered.   "Maybe a bit sad."

"Did you look at maps of Atlanta?"   I asked, mostly to change the subject.

"Yes, I did,"   Becky perked up.   "This line," she pointed to a portion of the drawing of her tattoo, "corresponds to Peachtree Street, downtown Atlanta. I think these three dots are banks."

"As bad as your mother was, she did take care of you in the long run," Cassandra commented.

"Or, she just used me as a human map to her ill-gotten gains," Becky glumly replied.

"It doesn't matter, you still get to keep everything the DA can't prove came from illegal activities," I assured her. "In the end, in terms of money anyway, Marcia did take care of you."

"When can I go look in these banks?" Becky asked.

"In a few days," I smiled at her. "I'll take you myself, if they'll let me."

At my apartment, I checked for calls on my answering machine. The first person hung up and didn't leave any message. The second caller was a woman with a soft, sexy voice.

"Benny, more than my heart is broken now, my whole body squeaks from lack of use, please come and fix it, now," the soft voice pleaded.

Damn, I hadn't called my CIA contact yet; it looked like I'd have to work it in sometime soon.

Cassandra threw an exasperated glance at me.

"This time, I have no idea who she is, I promise," I crossed my heart solemnly.

The next voice was unmistakable, it was the gruff tones of Zeb Satterwhite.

"Give me my girl back by noon tomorrow, or I'll make sure you're dead meat myself."

"He sure is agreeable," Cassandra observed.

"Katz, you either sleep without waking, or you screw without stopping," a new voice said. "Believing neither, I want you two to come downtown tomorrow and see me, I do not want you to go any further in this case alone. See me soon, this is Mark Hatton, and it's nine o'clock at night."

"He must not have heard about the shooting yet," I said, but Mark's voice interrupted me again.

"Naughty, naughty you two, you can't go around shooting everybody, you could lose your license that way. Now you'll have to see me tomorrow, if they let you out of jail that is."

I turned off the machine since there were no more messages.

Cassandra had opened the blinds on my front windows and looked out, the same brown police car sat parked on the next block.

"Good, let's say good bye to the cops out front as we drive over to George's office," I said. "What size pistol do you want?"

"A big one; after last night, I want a cannon like you carry."

"I've got another forty one magnum," I considered the best choice for her. "It's got just about all the stopping power of a forty four, but not as much kick and muzzle blast

"No," she said calmly. "I want the kick, I want the blast, I want all that noise, I want to make damn sure I live through the next gun battle I get into."

She was coming around to my point of view, if only for the moment. I pulled out a Colt 45, officer's model, two clips and a box of ammunition for it. She was used to a semi-automatic and this should work for her. I handed her a shoulder holster for the 45. It was a lot bulkier than the one she was used to, but, given her present state of mind, it had to be.

I picked out a replacement for me, a Smith and Wesson model 29, which was a bit more potent than the one the San Francisco police took from me the night before. I stuffed rounds into three speed loaders, putting them into one of my pockets, then I placed the rest of the ammunition back into the closet.

Cassandra held up the large pistol in her hand, weighing it.

"Even if I don't shoot this thing, I could still kill someone by braining them with it."

"I gave you lighter loads," I said as she stuffed cartridges into the clips.

"I don't want them, give me the big ones."

323

"Trust me, you don't want them; this kicks a bit more than your 380, besides these are big enough to stop anything on two feet."

"I'll have to think about this." Cassandra held up the holster I had given her. "This is going to take some thinking to dress for."

"Just wear it in a hip holster." I shrugged. "I've got one of those too."

"No," She paused. "That will take even more thought, and maybe some pants suites with baggy coats."

"Then, what?" This talk was taking up too much time.

"For now, I'll stuff it in my purse."

"That wouldn't be my choice, but what do I know."

I shrugged again; I just wanted to get going.

Cassandra and I walked up to the side of the brown Ford and rapped on the window, the policeman rolled it down and looked at us.

"We're done now, we're going to see Lieutenant Hatton, good bye, and have a nice day," I said.

The policeman smiled as we walked to the garage to get my car.

....

Janet, George Sterling's trim white haired grandmotherly type receptionist who always seemed to genuinely like whoever she spoke to, was the same woman who had worked there when I had started my detective career at George's agency. She was in her late fifties.

"Benjamin, good morning, how have you been? I haven't seen you in months," Janet greeted me with a smile.

"I'm tired, but alive so far; you remember my partner?" I asked.

"Yes, of course I do, good morning, Cassandra, how is your mother doing these days?"

Janet smiled as she appraised the daughter of one of her best friends.

Cassandra smiled back at Janet. "My parents are in Europe, my dad's business sent them there, they're supposed to be back for a visit in six months."

"I helped your mom pack, remember? I wish I could visit them there." Janet paused. "What can we do for you, Benjamin?"

"We'd like to see George, if he's in," I answered.

"He told me he's been here since seven o'clock this morning, you two can go right on in, I'm sure he's alone now." Janet pressed a button on her intercom and announced us.

I opened the door and looked at George, sitting at his desk reading a newspaper. He was a heavy set balding man in his late forties. George had a large office, it had to be twenty by thirty feet, with his desk near the large window at the back of his office. To the right of the desk was a door to a private bathroom. All the perks. George liked to decorate his office walls with signed photographs of his more famous clients. His furniture, including one small sofa, four chairs and a low glass topped table, were from a Swedish design shop in West Hollywood. Many exotic looking indoor plants and pale blue walls completed the effect.

George put down the newspaper and greeted us, "Welcome back, I was just reading about your vacation in San Francisco."

"How did you get the paper so quickly, I want to read about it, can I take the paper with me?" The questions shot from my mouth much faster than I had intended.

"Slow down, old boy, you'll have to buy your own, what can I do for you so early?" George asked.

"Tell me about Zeb Satterwhite," I demanded.

"All right, but be specific."

"Did he kill his daughter, Marcia?" Cassandra asked.

"Now, that's specific," George answered.

"Well?" I asked.

"No," George paused. "Well, I'm not sure, but I doubt it."

"Be specific," I was running out of patience.

325

"I don't know," He answered, with a nervous laugh.

"Why do you want to kill Zeb?" Cassandra asked.

"I lost almost all the men in my unit in Korea because of Zeb Satterwhite's stupid orders in the one and only battle he commanded. Even the top brass saw that he was crazy, but they noticed it too late to save the lives of several hundred men." George was getting flushed in the face. "He was in the reserves, and thought he was God's gift to combat even though he had never seen any action, he didn't care who got killed except himself. He was quite a coward in the actual face of battle, you know; he loved the killing though, and I think he still does."

"He hired you, what for?" I asked.

"He hired me to find Richard Snively, then he offered me money to kill him," George answered, looking at me.

"Did you?" Cassandra asked.

"If I did, do you think I'd tell you?" George looked back at her.

"I guess not." She shrugged her shoulders.

"Zeb had Snively killed, and you've been trying to prove it, right?" I asked.

"Without much success," George answered. "What have you two found out?"

"We can't help in pinning Snively's murder on Zeb, but we can pin a whole bunch of drug deals on him. The Washington D. C. police have Cummings, the New York police have Lopez and the San Francisco police have the rest of Fowler's helpers, all those people have to be able to come up with enough information to put Zeb Satterwhite away for a few years." I studied George's face.

"You have to be involved in this thing too," Cassandra said.

I turned and gave her a surprised look, but when I looked back at George, I noticed that my old boss had not changed his expression.

"George?" I was sort of caught off guard.

"Yes, George," she said. "I've been watching your face; you had an affair with one of the women, didn't you?"

326

"Nancy, but that was long before any of this mess started. Her father put up the money for me to start this agency, he's still a partner and he won't let me buy him out." George looked down at his desk.

"Don't open any drawers, I'm a little edgy still." Cassandra reached toward her purse.

"What does Zeb get in return for his investment?" I asked.

"Not what he asked for; he wants me to kill you," George looked up at me. "I've dug up dirt for him in the past, but I've always kept the dirt I've dug up on him for myself. I'm going to give it all to the FBI today, Benjamin. It's taken a long time to decide to do it. I'm still in love with Nancy Satterwhite."

"You're pathetic." Cassandra sounded angry. "You let that crazy old man get away with murder for money and because you love his equally crazy daughter!"

George stood up and opened his left desk drawer. I reached into my coat and pulled out my revolver.

"Take it easy," George shouted as he handed me a file folder. "I am pathetic; you take this to the cops, take the paper too, enjoy reading about how San Francisco likes your killing a wanted murderer and his two low life friends."

I holstered my revolver and took the folder and the newspaper off George's desk.

. . . .

Uncharacteristically, I had been able to get street parking almost in front of George Sterling's building, just before our unsettling meeting with him. Cassandra and I trundled hastily back into my Porsche and buckled up.

As I started up my car, she shouted, "Benjamin!"

We both heard a loud thump; a body landed, then bounced off the top of the brown unmarked police car and onto the hood. From the hood it took a slower, short bounce to the pavement behind us.

"Shit, George!" I shouted as I started the engine. "None of them was worth it, none of them."

327

I pulled my Porsche into traffic as if I were starting a race; soon I had my car speeding down the crowded street.

"Calm down, Benjamin, where are you going?" She took the folder from my lap.

"To see Zeb Satterwhite."

"Do you think that's a good idea?"

"A damn good idea, read that folder and tell me the good parts."

She opened the folder, reading silently.

"He knew about the babies," She turned some pages. "And about the drugs, and some arms shipments to several countries in Africa, arms shipments for God's sake!" She turned more pages. "He dug up lots of dirt for Zeb to use against Lopez, and it looks like George was a major informant for the FBI against Lopez, he also has plenty of proof that Brian was running drugs for Zeb."

"What else, there has to be more."

"The last page in the folder simply says, "I killed Marcia Satterwhite," and it's signed by George Sterling," Cassandra said softly.

"Why?" I asked.

"It doesn't say why, it just says that he did it," She closed the folder, staring ahead thoughtfully.

"I'm still going to Zeb's hotel."

"So is that black Lincoln following us?" Cassandra asked.

"I guess it is." I sped up and quickly turned into an alley.

I stopped my car, jumped out and drew my revolver; she opened her car door, and crouched down behind it, with her pistol also drawn.

The big black car roared into the alley and screeched to a halt, just short of crashing into my Porsche. I grabbed the door handle to the driver's side of the large car, opened it quickly, and stuck the barrel of my pistol into the driver's side.

"Get the hell out of there, now!" I shouted.

Cassandra stood up, pointing her pistol at the black car. I pulled out the driver as the three other men followed him out of the car, all four of them raised their hands up as the driver, the smallest of the four men, began to speak.

"What is the meaning of this, who are you!" he demanded.

"Why the hell have you been following me for two days; I've run out of patience, and I just might blow all your heads off right now!" I pulled back the hammer on my magnum and stuck the barrel against his nose.

"We work for Irving Lopez; he wants that we should kill you and Zeb Satterwhite." He raised his hands higher and smiled, "But we don't have to."

"Throw all your guns into your car, be careful, and do it slowly." I said, watching all of them carefully.

Each of the men, one at a time, tossed a revolver into the open door of the black car. Several bystanders moved quickly into nearby stores, no doubt to call the police. I then demanded that all four men take off their clothes.

I locked their car with their clothes and guns in it, I then took the keys, leaving the four men, naked, in the alley.

The police arrived, seconds after I had sped out of the other end of the alley. I had scrawled a note explaining who they were, and had left it propped up against the inside of the windshield, angled so it was easy to see, before I threw the keys in and closed all the locked doors. I hoped that the police would see the note at least by the time they broke open a window to get the bad guys' clothes back and if all went well, they'd arrest the four men.

"Are we still going to Zeb's?" Cassandra asked as we sped through traffic.

"Damn straight, I want my money from that son of a bitch, before the cops get him and freeze all his assets," I said. "Come to think of it, I might just freeze his assets myself, permanently!"

"At least you're being logical; dramatic, but logical," she observed. "But, I don't recognize where you're going, where are we going?"

329

"We're going to Mark Hatton's house, his wife's home during the day so I'm leaving this folder with her; that way he'll get it, and not us along with it."

I turned into an apartment development in Culver City, just off La Cienega Boulevard. I left the motor running while I raced to Mark's home. Mark's wife, Mary, a nurse who worked the second shift at her hospital, was quite asleep when I rang the doorbell ten times. Although she seemed still asleep and not too sure why I was there at that time of the morning, she finally took the folder.

"Is there something else, Benjamin?" Mary asked.

"No," I was pondering what might be a clue. "Does Mark still use that cologne you've been giving him since you two met?"

"What?" She seemed startled. "Why, yes he does, but why do you ask?"

"Something familiar about it."

I rushed back to the car. It was one thirty in the afternoon as I drove my car as fast as I could towards Zeb Satterwhite's hotel, where I knew the sour old man would be waiting for us.

40

I can see clearly now

While I negotiated traffic at much greater than legal speeds, Cassandra read the San Francisco newspaper we had taken from George Sterling's office.

"I can't read a thing if you keep throwing this car around corners at seventy miles per hour."

"Don't complain, just read it out loud," I responded.

"Keep your shirt on, I can read to myself a lot faster."

"I'm not in the mood right now to get undressed anyway."

"Do you remember the big guy you shot?" She put the newspaper down.

"Not really, we didn't have that long to get to know each other," I kept my eyes glued to the road in front of me.

"This article says that he was wanted for murder in San Diego, what I mean is that he was convicted of murder there, and escaped from prison a year ago. The man I killed had twenty two arrest warrants outstanding on him, most of them for major crimes," Cassandra said with an amazed look on her face.

"What does it say about Brian Fowler?"

"All it says about him is that he was suspected of working for the mob, running dope for them."

"What does it say about us?"

Most of my concentration was still out the front windshield of my Porsche.

"It just said that we were two private investigators on a job which involved interviewing Brian Fowler, we uncovered his illegal activities and he tried to kill us, but we killed them first; all this is a quote from that lawyer you hired," she said.

"That's great, he's doing his job well, so they'll never prosecute us." I smiled.

"That's not all, there was a small editorial about us," She said.

"And, what did it say?"

331

"It said that although we shouldn't be allowed to run around their city shooting people, the D. A. 's office shouldn't prosecute us for defending our selves from known criminals." Cassandra fell silent for a second. "They do give us hell for blasting away without giving the local cops any warning of what we were doing."

"I think we can get them to drop all charges against us," I said in a relieved tone.

I parked near Zeb Satterwhite's hotel in a small pay lot a few blocks away.

"I'll bet the cops are all over here," Cassandra remarked as she got out of the car and locked her door.

"That's why we'll go in the back way, through the kitchen entrance on the first floor, near the restaurant."

I motioned for her to follow me across the street and down an alley. The alley we took dead ended into a service entrance for the hotel, where a service access ran behind the two buildings beside the hotel, then stopped at the loading dock for the restaurants and gift shops in the hotel. Three men were unloading a truck full of produce when we jumped up on the loading dock, using the steps on the left side of the dock.

"We need to talk to the restaurant manager," I said to one of the hotel workers unloading a large shipment of oranges.

"Who?" The man asked.

"The restaurant manager, could you point the way to his office?"

The man shrugged his shoulders. "Just who are you, and why are you here?"

Cassandra unbuttoned the first two buttons of her blouse, leaned over slightly and looked sweetly at the hotel worker.

"Sir, we are late, we are sundry salesmen and we were to go through this entrance to meet the manager, please help us to his office."

The man stood nonplussed for a second as his eyes fixed on Cassandra's exposed cleavage, he pointed to his left.

"Thank you, you're very helpful," she said softly.

"Sundry salesmen?"

"He didn't pay attention to that; as soon as he fixed on my boobs, I knew he'd let us go into the hotel without a hassle." Cassandra buttoned up her blouse.

"Don't get too cocky," I said.

"Yeah, that's your job."

She looked at me for a second, then gave me a grin. We were now in the kitchen with a dozen restaurant employees quickly walking around, picking up, or preparing food. Ignoring their stares, we walked out into the restaurant. Several policemen in the lobby were watching the front door and the elevators, so we decided to walk up several flights of the stairs before taking an elevator to Zeb's floor.

After she stopped at the second floor landing in the stairwell, Cassandra asked, "There has to be cops on Zeb's floor, so what do we do then?"

"We look first, if they aren't in the hallway, then we go directly to his room. If they are in the hallway, then we rethink our options."

I opened the door to the stairwell and checked both ways. Seeing no one in the hallway, Cassandra and I walked into the elevator, then pressed the button for Zeb's floor; I also pushed the button for the next floor up. If the police were in the hallway, I wanted another way out.

The elevator door opened on Zeb's floor, and I stuck my head out of the elevator.

"I don't see anybody, let's take a chance," I whispered.

The two of us rushed to Zeb's room and stopped by his door. Both of us took out our pistols and stood on either side of the door as I slowly reached for the door knob; the door was slightly ajar so I very slowly pushed the door open. We both took a step back from the edge of the door and waited a second. I crouched down and jumped in front of the door, pointing my revolver ahead of me.

Zeb Satterwhite sat in the chair by the window with its curtain fully open, sunlight filled the hotel room, and now spilled into the hallway. The beds were made, with two packed suitcases sitting on them, nothing but a mechanical silence filled the room.

"I thought you two were the bellhop, I'm expecting him." Zeb looked at us with contempt. "How did you get past the cops?"

"That's not too hard since they're waiting for you, not us." Cassandra walked into the room and scanned all around it.

I stepped aside to let Cassandra around me, then I followed her and looked through the bathroom door which was open.

"I'm alone, except for you two, now, what the hell do you want?" Zeb asked, in a louder voice.

"We want our ten thousand dollars," she stated.

"Who did it?" Zeb asked.

"George Sterling," Cassandra said.

"I don't believe it," Zeb quickly replied, turning to face Cassandra.

"He wrote and signed a confession, admitting to it," Cassandra answered.

"He also saved a file of all your transgressions, we gave that to the police about an hour ago," I added.

"I never knew the son of a bitch!" Zeb stood up.

"Like hell you didn't," Cassandra retorted. "Write us a check for ten thousand dollars; we lived up to our side of the bargain, now you live up to yours."

Zeb paced several steps in front of his chair by the window, then looked at me.

"Do you believe your friend killed my daughter?" Zeb asked.

"George did sign a confession, and the police have it," I answered.

"But do you believe him?" Zeb insisted.

"I don't want to, but what choice do I have? That confession was the last thing he wrote." I returned Zeb's glare.

"Last thing?" Zeb asked.

"He jumped out of his window and landed on a police car in the street." My voice trailed off.

334

"On a cop car?" Zeb said to himself, shaking his head. "He gave information on me to the cops?"

"Enough for a long jail term," Cassandra answered.

"That's why they're out there." Zeb turned to look out the window. "Well, screw 'em!"

"Where's your daughter?" I asked.

"She went to see the lawyer early this morning, once she sees the cops, she'll get the hell out of here," Zeb answered.

Cassandra repeated the request for our money.

"What makes you think I'll pay you anything?" Zeb stared at me.

"Hey, dip shit, answer me!" Cassandra said in a loud voice.

Zeb turned and stared at Cassandra, not saying anything.

"I don't know if you've heard the news today," I said, "but we killed Brian Fowler and two of his friends last night in San Francisco. Fowler admitted that you hired him to kill us, and I think that's why my partner's a little pissed off at you."

"Write the damn check and make it perfectly legal." Cassandra pointed her pistol at Zeb.

"She's changed from a three eighty to a forty five; that gun makes a very big hole, so I wouldn't make her too mad," I remarked.

Zeb walked to the bed and began to open one of the suitcases on it; I raised my gun and stuck it into his side.

"Be very careful, and very slow when you take your hand out of that suitcase," I said.

He slowly pulled a large money sack out of the suitcase.

"I don't have a fuckin' checking account."

Zeb pulled a stack of thousand dollar bills out of the sack; he counted out ten of the bills and handed them to me.

"I'll bet she's mean in bed too." Zeb leered at me.

I silently took the bills and stuffed them into my coat pocket.

"Why did George kill my daughter?" Zeb asked.

"I truly don't know," Cassandra said. "Maybe it was to get back at you?"

335

"Bull shit, if he wanted to get back at me, he would've shot me." Zeb sat back down in his chair.

"Well, why do you think he shot her?" she asked.

"I still don't think he did." Zeb looked out the window.

"Who do you think did kill her?" I asked.

"I always thought Fowler did, I was half expecting you to kill that son of a bitch, so I guess I didn't waste the money I just gave you." Zeb still looked out the window. "I never did trust him as a son-in-law, all he wanted was my money. That's the reason I told Nancy, in front of him, that I was going to cut her out of my will and take all my money away from her; he dumped her right after that."

"Who were you going to give all your money to?" Cassandra asked.

"Who else, Marcia," Zeb replied.

"How much money do you have?" I asked.

"Four or five hundred million. They can take me and shoot me, but they'll never get my money, they'll never find a trace of most of it," Zeb bragged.

"Who told you that Becky was your daughter?" I asked.

"George did; he sent me a report on the insemination right after I talked to that little white haired shit from Washington yesterday. I didn't know, I just didn't kno," Zeb turned and looked out the window again. "I thought all this time she was just a stranger, is she safe?"

"She's safe, and will remain so, but not because of you." Cassandra answered.

That white haired shit from Washington remark had me thinking.

"Oh, no, Lepus," I said to Cassandra under my breath.

"You have Becky?" Zeb asked again.

"We have her," I answered.

Zeb took another stack of thousand dollar bills from the bag he still clutched in his hand and handed it to me.

"Nancy promised you that for finding Becky, I'll pay her debt, now get the hell out of here." He spit the words out.

I asked Cassandra, "Should we tell him?"

Not knowing what the hell I was about to say, Cassandra shrugged her shoulders.

"Tell me what?" Zeb asked in a normal voice.

"He did pay us, and I would love to torment him with the right answer." I whispered to Cassandra.

"Tell me what?" Zeb stepped towards me.

"That Nancy actually killed Marcia," I stared blankly at Zeb.

"You lie." Zeb stepped closer to me. "You're lying!"

"He usually doesn't," Cassandra turned her pistol towards Zeb.

"And the police will arrest you along with your only remaining daughter for at least one hundred different charges," I said. "But for now, we will leave you alone."

Cassandra and I walked out of the still open door and into the hall. I had just stuffed the second wad of thousand dollar bills into my coat pocket when I looked up and saw Mark Hatton coming out of Nancy Satterwhite's hotel room just down the hall. He stopped after a few steps and stared at us, halting two blue uniformed cops followed him from Nancy's room. I could hear several more cops in her hotel room shuffling through her remaining belongings.

"This is all so confusing, first I tell you to stay out of it, and you don't, then I tell you to see me immediately, and you don't, then I tell you to give me all the information you have on this case, and you don't." He headed towards us.

Mark motioned for two uniformed policemen to go into the room and arrest Zeb Satterwhite.

"Well, hello to you too, Lieutenant Hatton," I said. "Did you find your wayward policeman?"

"I don't know what you're talking about," Mark said sharply.

"This person you don't know about wouldn't have had access to the fact that Becky Satterwhite is in my apartment building, would he?" I asked.

"I just told you I don't know what you're talking about," Mark repeated.

337

"If that non-person did know where Becky is, and if that non-person told Zeb or Nancy, then Becky may be in big trouble." I walked up to Mark and spoke right into his face.

"Maybe there is someone who might fit that description." Mark blinked several times.

"What did that person say?" I asked, not moving.

"What did Zeb say?" Mark asked.

"I don't think he knows anything, he didn't know that we killed Fowler last night, and he didn't know that George Sterling jumped out of his window this morning," I answered.

"George didn't jump." Mark stepped back a pace.

"What!" I said in a very loud, surprised voice.

"If you'd stayed there a few minutes longer, you would have found out that George was shot twice, the bullets went through him and broke the window; he fell onto the car below. It's hard to jump anywhere when you're already dead," Mark said.

"Who did it?" Cassandra asked.

"We don't know, they must have used a silencer, because the secretary didn't hear anything after you two left, until the window broke. She ran downstairs when she found out her boss was on the street, everybody ran downstairs, no one saw who came out of George's office," Mark said. "I could pin it on you two, you were the last ones in there."

"Get serious, what caliber gun was it, nine millimeter?" Cassandra asked.

"Looks like it, isn't that strange." Mark shook his head.

"Can't be us, Cassandra's carrying a cannon, just like me, besides, you can't use a silencer on a revolver," I said. "If you have no further use for us, I would like to go to my apartment and rescue Becky. We'll turn her over to your people; I'm sure they're still there waiting," Anxiety put an edge to my voice.

"That information on Satterwhite's private jet was interesting," Mark added.

"What?" I had to leave, yet I had to know this clue.

"Nancy flew here the day Marcia was murdered," Mark said. "She flew back that afternoon to Atlanta, then flew to Naples, Florida that evening. She was at the Naples airport

338

when her mother's flight arrived; her mother was flying in from Los Angeles."

"And, her mother was never seen again," I paused.   "I really have to go back to my apartment, right now."

"What's the hurry? Isn't everything solved? Zeb was behind Fowler's drug deals, and he hired Cummings to kill that man in Miami, and George Sterling killed Marcia," Mark straightened up and looked at me.

"Wrong, George didn't kill anybody, maybe the same person killed both Marcia and George, and now she wants to kill Becky.   If you don't let me get back to my apartment, and if you don't send a lot of cops there right now, she might be dead in a very short time." By now, my voice was loud.

"What are you talking about?" Mark asked.

"Just take a good whiff of yourself, and that'll be a good enough clue," I answered.

"You have gone off the deep end a bit, haven't you?" Mark asked.

"Not really, now, will you let me go back to my apartment?"

"I guess it would be better if you two met the girl, she seems to trust you for some reason, but my people will be with you the whole way, so don't stray off, we have a lot to discuss." Mark waved us away with his hand.

41

Are we there yet?

I took Cassandra's arm and pulled her quickly towards the elevator.

"Don't squeeze so tight! We'll get there in plenty of time, and besides Clarence and the cops are there," Cassandra assured me.

She brushed my hand from her arm. The two of us rushed into the elevator, out the front door of the lobby, to the parking lot and sped off in the direction of my apartment building.

"Do you really think Nancy did it?" She asked.

"I had a hunch early on, but it was nothing more than that; I kept coming back to Nancy as the murderer."

"When did you guess who did it?" .

"Did you spend that hundred dollar bill I gave back to you?" I asked.

"No, not yet."

"Take it out of your purse and look at the back side of it, I wrote the name of the person I suspected on the top left hand margin of the bill; it's real small, but look closely and you'll see it." I took a turn so fast that the car slid almost sideways. "I know it's a cheap trick, but you started this whole thing by accusing me of cheap tricks."

"Careful!" Cassandra pulled the hundred dollar bill from its storage space. "You're wrong, you wrote Hank's name here!"

"Look harder."

She squinted and looked closer at the bill "Wait a minute, you wrote something else." She looked up at me, "You wrote that Nancy hired Hank to kill Marcia, that's not quite right, and I don't owe you a cent."

"I did write her name down, though, didn't I?"

340

"Yeah, but you wrote Hank's name down as the trigger man."

"Well, I'm not perfect, just good." I paused. "But, with that flight information Mark just told us, I could be completely wrong."

"Hell, I thought Zeb had his daughter killed, maybe using Hank as the hit man, but I have to admit, I never thought of Nancy," Cassandra paused. "Why do you think that answer is wrong?"

"Both Nancy and her mother were in LA on the same day Marcia was murdered, it could have been either one of them," I paused. "I still think it was Nancy."

"A mother couldn't kill her own daughter." Cassandra shook her head. "Even in a crazy family like them, the mother couldn't do such a thing."

"That family cares about money, and that's all; there's no love between any of them. Zeb had most of the money, and Nancy would get it all if Marcia and Becky were out of the way. Besides, there's that whole Zeb being Becky's father and grandfather thing," I said. "Who knows how that would play with Zeb's ex-wife, or Nancy."

"Not to sound crude, but that's one fucked up family." Cassandra shook her head.

"Nancy's ex-husband was making a play for her sister, and Marcia also had the old man's attention. Remember, Zeb threatened to cut Nancy out. She didn't know that all he wanted to do was scare Brian off so she was terrified she would literally be cut off from the millions. Jealousy is a powerful motive."

"So is greed," Cassandra added. "If Zeb gets killed or sent to jail, Nancy will get her old man's money."

"And," I chimed in "If Nancy knows about the map on Becky's butt, she can get all her sister's private cash."

"But what was that stuff about the bad smell?" Cassandra asked.

"I hate to admit it, but it's a clue to Nancy being the killer, didn't you smell Hatton's cologne?"

"It was bad, but not all that awful."

341

"He smelled like that only once before, when he was at Marcia's house two years ago, at the murder scene. His cologne doesn't smell like that, it only smells like that when it mixes with something else, Nancy Satterwhite's custom made perfume; when hers and Mark's scents combine, they make that weird smell."

"So, Nancy had to have been in Marcia's house close to the time she was murdered."

"Good assumption, but circumstantial. If she's the murderer, we have to catch her with the gun that killed Marcia and George."

"If Nancy only wants the map to Marcia's stash, she doesn't have to kill Becky," Cassandra said.

"Ah. But if she wants to be the last Satterwhite left standing to claim all the family money, she does have to kill the kid," I pointed out.

"How can she hope to get away with this?" Cassandra asked. "Doesn't she know that the whole thing is crashing down around her head right now?"

"She's not thinking right now." I sighed. "She's just reacting."

"I hope we're not too late," Cassandra looked out the front windshield. "Nancy must know she won't get anything from the old man; Zeb will rot in jail, and he won't give a dime of his money up."

"Like I said, Nancy is just plain desperate, she isn't thinking anymore," I said.

"Killing Becky doesn't make any sense."

"Well, Nancy's off the deep end now."

"Jealousy and greed are strong human motivations, and in sick people they're dangerous ones," Cassandra said, quietly.

"I should have taken Nancy out of action sooner." Morbid anxiety was finally catching up to me, followed by guilt. Too much adrenaline for too many days.

"When should you have done that, how soon could you have known?" Cassandra asked.

"When I went to her house two years ago," I said.

"Why?"

"She was just back from a long trip; I bet it was an airplane trip from Los Angeles. Her maid almost told me as much, but I didn't pay attention to her. I had already noticed that she was a marksman, so she had motive, opportunity, and the skill to carry it out, I knew all that two years ago." I rounded the corner and pulled up in front of my apartment building.

"Nancy killed George Sterling, didn't she?" Cassandra got out of the car. "She saw him early this morning and forced him to sign that confession. After we left, she shot him, and pushed him out the window."

"That's my guess, she was probably hiding in George's office restroom while we were talking to him," I locked the car doors. "Jealousy." I stared blankly.

"What?" Cassandra asked.

"Jealousy, humiliation, and hurt," I said, quietly.

"Just what are you talking about?"

"You've been after me to talk about my mother's death."

I know this was a strange time to bring this up, but when the light bulb goes off, I just open my mouth and talk. It's a guy thing, well, at least it was my thing, I saw the connection between this case and my mother's death for the first time.

"She died from jealousy, humiliation and hurt."

"Not now." Cassandra looked concerned.

"She committed suicide because she found her husband and her best friend in bed together; she saw them the day before she took her own life."

Cassandra put her right hand on my shoulder and spoke softly, "Later, lover, later, we'll talk."

The Reverend was not in front of the building and the policemen who had been in the brown Ford were not in the immediate vicinity.

Jumping out of my car, I drew my revolver while Cassandra sprinted after me to the front steps of the building. As we cautiously walked into the front door, a light blue Ford swung around the corner, with a magnetic red light flashing over the driver's side, but no siren blaring, screeching to a stop in front of the apartment building on the other side of the street.

343

Two policemen were in the car, but neither one of them got out and one of them was shouting at the microphone of his radio.

I slowly walked into the entrance way, and motioned to Cassandra to follow me; we silently moved to the basement doorway.

As I cautiously opened the door to the stairway, two shots roared from the area of Clarence's apartment; one shot from a pistol echoed a split second before a much louder retort.

Both of us barged into the stairwell and looked down to the basement landing. Seeing no one there, we rushed to the first landing, then the second landing, which was filled with the strong scent of burning smokeless gunpowder.

The door to the Reverend's apartment was half open and we heard the sound of Becky screaming; we ran to the front door, and pointed our pistols into the apartment.

Behind the front door, partially blocking it from opening all the way, the body of Nancy Satterwhite lay in a pool of red blood.

Becky was in the arms of the Reverend, who was still holding his pistol towards Nancy's body.

Seated on a chair against the back wall was Fred Lepus, with his hands and legs bound, and with a rag stuffed in his mouth.

"That woman's evil, hard evil! She even died hard. Why would anyone want to kill their own flesh 'n blood?" Clarence asked as the two policemen, who had been waiting out front in the blue Ford, came rushing in. They pointed their guns in his direction.

"Put those things away!" Cassandra said to them, as she and I lowered our weapons.

"What the hell's going on here!" One of the policemen retorted, looking at the dead woman near the front door.

"First, you can't keep up with his Porsche, then a woman gets killed." The other policeman said as his partner shook his head.

"Hatton's going to be pissed off."

"Lieutenant Hatton'll be very happy, his murder case is solved, and he won't even be confused about it, the guilty one is dead." I pointed to the body of Nancy Satterwhite. "All he'll have to do is fill out a pile of paperwork and figure out what the hell that creep is doing in the middle of all this," I pointed to Fred Lepus.

"Untie Mr. Lepus," Becky asked. "Please?"

Cassandra yanked the rag out of Fred's mouth.

"All I was trying to do was get the girl out of here, I guessed that either Zeb or Nancy killed Marcia Satterwhite, and that they would also try to kill the kid," Fred paused to take a breath. "All I wanted to do was to get her out of here, after all, I've invested a lot of time with this kid."

"Aunt Nancy didn't kill my mom," Becky blurted out.

"What?" I was surprised.

"My grandma killed my mother, Aunt Nancy wouldn't say why, but she did say she killed my grandma for doing it," Becky said.

"I didn't see that coming," I muttered. "The grandma really did it?"

"Really." Cassandra smiled at me.

"Well, you didn't guess that outcome either," I whispered to her.

"Aunt Nancy made me tie Mr. Lepus up, I think she was going to kill both of us." Becky's look pleaded with 6e. "Mr. Lepus is a nice man, he did try to help me."

I looked in turn at the policemen, "You take care of him, I couldn't live with myself if I cut him loose."

"That was one crazy bitch," Fred stammered as soon as the gag was out of his mouth. "She was demanding keys and a map from the kid, like Becky has anything valuable anyway."

345

42

All's well that just ends

All twenty five of the thousand dollar bills were real; they were all 1934 issue, and we got more for them than I would have thought over face value from a coin dealer in Los Angeles. That was the highest paying case Cheshire Katz Agency had to date, although my San Francisco attorney took about half of it to get us off the hook with the local police.

Marcia Satterwhite's inheritance was contested; Phil Peterson claimed he should get the money, but I hired a lawyer to fight for Becky, a battle which turned into the final resting place for the remainder of our fee, plus some of my savings.

Cassandra insisted we go ahead and spend the money to help Becky since no lawyer would go on a contingency, with the Federal Government threatening to take all the money since it was probably from illegal activity. The government bulldog accountants were able to uncover just under four hundred million dollars from all three of the Satterwhites, most of it came from the grumpy old Zeb. I don't think anyone could find the rest of it, if it ever really existed at all, Zeb could well have been lying about all the hundreds of millions more he claimed to have.

Marcia Satterwhite's safety deposit boxes held many surprises, besides the three million in cash, gold and jewels. Marcia had accumulated evidence against her father, mother, sister and brother-in-law. Cassandra and I agreed with the cops

346

that this was probably the reason Nancy desperately sought out Becky. Nancy's last words to her niece were a confession to murdering her mother and dumping the body a mile off the Naples shore tied to an anchor.

Snively sent Becky's grandmother a note disclosing that Zeb was her biological father, along with the lab work to prove it. The grandmother was a religious zealot, Snively's aim was to throw as much trouble at Marcia as he could as a distraction until he could find someone to kill her before she killed him. That plan didn't work for him, but the grandmother was so unstable that her response was to eliminate the 'abominations'. Nancy found Marcia's body. Clutched in Marcia's hand was the note to the grandmother about Becky's real father. Nancy was fed up with her mother's odd behavior and ended it forever.

The Federal government and the lawyers wound up with most of the cash but Becky did receive about eight million, four hundred thousand dollars after legal fees. As part of her inheritance, she took possession of about a dozen properties in California, North Carolina and Atlanta.

The lawyers we hired set up a trust fund for her, which she would control when she reached twenty five. Becky did, however, retain the ability to spend a slowly increasing amount of the income from the trust before then, if she wanted to. Becky agreed to the trust, and even wanted to extend the payout to her thirtieth birthday.

Zeb Satterwhite got out on a two million dollar bond after being charged with fifty seven separate charges, ranging from murder to tax evasion but he died of a massive stroke only three weeks before his first trial date.

Phil Peterson lost all his appeals, and was sentenced to fifteen years in a Federal penitentiary for his dealings with Irving Lopez. Lopez' fate was four life terms for his crimes.

Fred Lepus became a star witness in the trials of Phil Peterson, and Irving Lopez. After this notoriety, Fred returned to doing what he loved best, being a second rate detective in Washington, DC.

Dr. Aaronson lost both his freedom and his license to practice medicine for his part in the adoption scheme.

The majority of George Sterling's clients took their business to the Cheshire Katz Agency, a change which encouraged Cassandra to pick out a new building in downtown Los Angeles for larger office space. Because of the six new investigators we took on, we started a search for a manager to take care of all day to day operations.

George's old secretary, Janet Cobb, accepted a job with our firm as an office manager. But after a month with us, she decided to retire since her husband had already retired, and she wanted to be with him more; besides, she had grandchildren to play with.

Becky, after a long discussion with her attorney, set up a two hundred and fifty thousand dollar trust for the daughter of her old Chicago neighbor, Sally. She also paid Lepus ten thousand dollars for services over the past two years, even though I tried to tell her he wasn't worth ten dollars. She wanted to pay Cassandra and me a large fee, or at least pay us back for fronting the legal money. Although still somewhat greedy, even I couldn't accept money from her. Then, before all the real estate was sold, Becky deeded a building in Atlanta to Cassandra and me in payment for the money we fronted her to fight for her portion of the Satterwhite millions. I, of course, wanted to sell it immediately and plow the cash back into the business, but Cassandra asked me to consider another plan.

She insisted that I sit in the most comfortable chair in her living room, as she served me a nice Napa white wine to soften me up.

"I'm from Pennsylvania," I said.

She had just mentioned that we were both from the East coast, I was confused.

"I thought you were from California?" I asked.

"I've lived here in California since I started high school." assandra shook her head. "I guess you never asked, and I never thought to tell you."

"But your folks?"

I knew they were from here, I had heard her mother talk about the San Diego of her childhood.

"My mom's from California, but my dad was born in Chicago, and I was born in Washington, DC."

"Oh, God, the land of Lepus."

"Calm down, Benjamin." Her voice turned briefly sour. "All I mean is that we're both from the East coast and I think we should consider setting up an office there."

"Do you mean using the Atlanta building Becky gave us?"

"Yes," Cassandra answered, caution in her voice.

"What about our office here?" I was confused.

"Do you like Los Angeles?" She asked.

"I like the people here."

"Do you like the area in general?"

"Hell no." I had to be honest. "But, I do like some people here a whole lot."

"I do too," She shook her head. "If I think of staying here long term, though, I go crazy; this area is bad for our health in more ways than smog."

"I can't argue, but I don't want to leave."

"I'll go with you." Cassandra sat on the arm of my chair. "Besides, if we open an office in Atlanta, we'll have both coasts covered, think of the market."

"Yeah, well."

I thought about it; she was a better businessman than me but there were more considerations. I couldn't tell her, but, maybe living on the East coast wouldn't be so bad.

"What if one office goes broke?" I asked.

"If we only had one office, it could go broke by itself."

"I guess."

Cassandra smiled and settled next to me on one of the chair arms.

"I like the East coast better, I know I'm prejudiced. Atlanta is a big city, with a pretty good market, but it avoids some of the bad qualities of Los Angeles or New York. Plus, it's close enough to all the East coast markets, also we own the building free and clear," She ran out of breath and took a sip from her glass.

"What about your school?"

I knew she shouldn't give up on that, since she had put so much time and effort into it.

"After the end of this quarter, I'm through with the classes." She brightened. "All I have to do is finish writing my dissertation and there are several university libraries in Atlanta I can use, besides I can use inter library loan to get anything I can't find there."

"If it doesn't work in six months, we sell and run?"

I was ready to leave this place anyway, too many bad memories. It was like visiting my brother, in my mother's house; Cassandra knew all this anyway, she knows me too well.

She slipped from the arm of my chair into my lap, "We'll be happy there, if you don't like it in six months, we'll beat it back here."

"But Atlanta has such a terrible baseball team," I moaned.

43
I do?

Before the move to Atlanta, Cassandra and I decided to take a trip to my family farm, in order to visit Becky and to show Cassandra where I grew up, and for her to meet my family. Although we still received letters from Becky about once or twice a month, we wanted to see her in person. My brother and sister-in-law had sent glowing reports of her mental state, and her ability to integrate all the stories about who she was. Eventually, she tested into sophomore year of High School, which was where she belonged. Although Becky hadn't made too many friends her own age in the first fifteen years of her life, she was socializing well in her new school. Two of my brother's adopted children were in the same grade with her, so that had to help. With her negotiated allowance from her trust, Becky was able to dress like her peers at last.

Right after Zeb Satterwhite was arrested, I moved into Cassandra's California apartment and it felt like we were moving to a new level in our relationship. I was happier than I had been in a long time; she was still my best friend, and my lover.

. . . .

As the seat belt sign went out, and the airplane leveled off at cruising altitude, she slipped her hand into mine.

"What are we going to do?" she asked.

"About what?" I felt a little startled. "Sometimes, what you say comes out completely out of context."

"I know, you'll just have to get used to it." Cassandra paused. "What I mean is, what are we going to do about our relationship?"

351

"What do you want to do about it? I think it's going stronger than it ever has before." I smiled and winked at her.

"Okay, the sex is great, but what else?"

"Explain, please."

She was starting to worry me.

"This is the second time we've lived together; the first time it ended when we just couldn't seem to combine work together and living together."

"This time I have a commitment, this time I've thought it through." I looked into her eyes. "When we move to Atlanta I want us to continue to live together."

"And?"

"Will you marry me?"

"Will I. . ." Cassandra leaned against my chest and put her hand on my cheek. "You have called me everything from a living goddess to a dose of Castor Oil. You've asked me go get the hell out of your life forever, and now you ask me to marry you, for the first time ever, you ask me to marry you."

"It must mean that I'm serious, then; will you marry me?" I asked, picking her hand from my cheek and softly kissing it.

"Are you ready to quit the business?" she asked.

"What?" I gulped. "You talked me into expanding the business to the other coast; I stick myself out on a shaky limb, and now you want me to quit the business?"

"Are you ready to quit the detective business?"

"No, how are we supposed to make a living?"

I felt torn, I couldn't get out of the detective business, it was a front for my work with the CIA, just how the hell was I supposed to tell her that?

"I'm in love with you, I'll always be in love with you, but as long as we work in this business, our life together won't be ours, there's too much stress on us, and our relationship."

"Is that a no?" I asked meekly.

"Not to you, just to marriage."

Cassandra kissed my cheek and held my hand tightly.

"At least for awhile," she added.

"I guess we'll assess our life together when we get to Atlanta."

I didn't like this wrinkle, not at all.

Cassandra paused as a small tear formed in the corner of her right eye. "I do love you."

"Me too." I replied, "Maybe that's all it takes to be happy."

I leaned back in my seat, still holding tightly to Cassandra's hand as I put on my earphones and twisted the selection dial until I found the music I wanted.

"Maybe you're right." She kissed my cheek again.

"I know that one," I said softly. "It's Bach, Fugue in E."

The Author

Bob Henneberger has been writing for the past decade, working mostly in Science Fiction and Mystery, He has also written short stories, plays, television scripts and articles for professional journals. He lives in Vermont, close to Lake Champlain with his wife and several cats; not that that's an indication of anything unusual.